Sins of the Son

Sins of the Son

Based on the true experiences of Tony Tancredi

Tony Tancredi and Cindy L. O'Hara

Library of Congress Control Number:		2009902748
ISBN:	Hardcover	978-1-4415-2190-3
	Softcover	978-1-4415-2189-7

Graphic artist acknowledgement:
Jacket design and illustration by Michael Spillane.

This is a work of fiction. Names, characters, places and incidents either are the product of the author's imagination or are used fictitiously, and any resemblance to any actual persons, living or dead, events, or locales is entirely coincidental.

This book was printed in the United States of America.

To order additional copies of this book, contact:
Xlibris Corporation
1-888-795-4274
www.Xlibris.com
Orders@Xlibris.com
58204

Tony Tancredi dedicates this book to his parents,
Anthony and Mary Tancredi

Cindy O'Hara dedicates this book to her late
mother, Crystal Anne Dalrymple.

ACKNOWLEDGEMENT

Tony Tancredi would like to thank numerous people for their help in getting this book published. If not for them, "Sins of the Son" would still be a vague idea instead of the (completed) work that it is today. Due to my inexperience in writing and publishing, there were many setbacks and discouraging moments. Without the input of several of my colleagues, this book may never have come to fruition. I would like to especially thank Ronnie Bell, Marge Carty, Dave Covyeau, Craig Fabre, James Garecht, Dave Halterman, Bill Intihar, Ed Lyons, Frank Mulvihill, Carl Johanson, Arthur Nelson, Kim Nicoll, Mike Perretti, John Siddons, Rich Spino, Patty Westbrook, Bill Wheeler, Alexis White, and Paul Whitt. I am forever grateful for the invaluable assistance and encouragement I received from the Federal Security Director and my friend Bob Cohen. Your encouraging words after you read the manuscript meant the world to me. With your father's background in boxing, your opinion gave the book the credibility it needed. I would also like to thank Assistant Federal Screening Director Rhonda Vickery, who after reading the manuscript offered her complete and total cooperation with anything I needed concerning the book. I am deeply indebted to Linda Snyder for her constant support and belief in me and my dreams. You have been everything a friend should be and more. Most importantly, I would like to thank my parents, Anthony and Mary, for providing the basis on which this story was based. You created the most loving home a person could ask for. Last, but certainly not least, I would like to thank my uncle Al Tancredi, who supported me throughout this process and urged me (often and repeatedly) to tell this story.

Cindy O'Hara would like to express her heartfelt appreciation to Tony Tancredi for giving me an opportunity to be a part of something special and fulfill a lifelong dream of writing and publishing a novel. Despite our daily tug-of-wars on minor things like characters, locales, names, dialog, and other inane details that go into creating a novel, we somehow found a way to compromise and come up with the work that we can both be proud of. I am deeply indebted to my husband, Terrance O'Hara who always pushed me to write and lent an ear when I needed to work out details (or vent about my co-author, whichever came first). I thank my daughter Devon, who was patient beyond belief about my need and desire to get this book done before we collaborated on our own children's book. (The next one we do, Devon, is ours, I promise—one, two three, rigarole). And to Caelan who was also tolerant of my working sessions with "Mr. Tony." Additionally, I would like to thank my grandmother, Mary Dalrymple, who always inquired about how the book was coming along and showered me with a lifetime of love and support and to my father, Jack Dalrymple, for blessing me with his ability to write in the first place. To my sister-in-law Dot, thank you for being one of the first people in the family to read my baby, and give it a rave review. I would also like to thank Sondra Allison and Nicole Reynolds for acknowledging the amount of work and dedication that went into producing this novel and encouraging me throughout the process. Just when I thought I couldn't get up one more day at 4 a.m., they told me I could and applauded me always. You both fortify my creative soul and I wouldn't have been able to complete this project without you. My very sincere gratitude goes out to Paul Thayer, editor extraordinaire, who showed me that the art of writing and telling a tale is nothing without editing and revision. And although tedious, can take a mediocre story and turn it into a page turner. On that note, I would like to thank Robert Barton, my first editor, who gave me my first job as a reporter in Washington D.C. and throughout the years has been a standing (if not sometimes silent and missing) force and mentor in my life. Lastly, I would like to especially thank Michael Spillane, our cover designer, who seemed to never tire of the constant sleeve-tugging and changes that accompany two co-authors who have very divergent views and opinions on everything from art to writing. He did this with aplomb and rarely pushed back.

ONE

Philadelphia, Pennsylvania
Early February, 1972

A S HE SAT on the training table swinging his legs, someone outside the locker room yelled, *"It's time!"* Watching his legs reminded him of being a kid again.

The boxer continued to stare, mesmerized by the flexing muscles and taut skin. He watched them swing in time to the hands of the small clock on the wall, ticking away the minutes to the fight.

He hopped off the table, ambled over to the sink, turned on the scratched metal fixtures, and waited for the loud *thrum* that preceded the rush of water.

He smiled grimly, wrinkling his nose at the distinct rotten-egg-like smell as he splashed his face.

He knew this was the time when boxers were supposed to be psyching themselves up for the fight. For some reason, his brain would not allow it, or maybe this was just another way of doing it.

His thoughts turned to his childhood and all the things he had to overcome. All the sacrifices his parents made for him. How they did it without ever complaining or a harsh word to him. The stories he heard of about his birth, the doctors telling his parents that he most likely would not live through the night. Of his father praying around the clock, hoping that God would spare them this child, since he had taken their first one with a miscarriage.

Then when Tony was a six-year-old they—were told that their son had a disease in his left leg and that he would probably never walk again. If he did, it would be with a brace. Sports and other physical activities would be out of the question. They kept him at home against the doctor's advice, insisting they could give him better care than if he was in a hospital. Over the next ten years, they proved to be right. With all their love and care, he beat that damn disease. But at times it was hard for him, the verbal abuse still echoing in his ears:

Hey, brace leg!
Yo crip, You can't play with us! You're too slow!

After all these years, Tony could still feel the blacktop and concrete ripping into his ass, his thighs, and his knees, his palms cut all to hell from instinctively breaking his fall as the kids laughed and took turns pushing him to the ground.

No matter what, though, he'd always get up and fight back. He never let them win or gave them an inkling of how badly he hurt.

So lost was he in the past that he never even heard his trainer, Jake, calling his name. Whatever awaited him in the ring, he was now ready.

"What the hell you doin', kid? Get yer head outta yer ass! They're calling for 'ya, and you're not even warmed up yet."

Tony snapped back, the water still running. He turned it off and gazed at his reflection in the mirror. Thankfully, all trace of the boy he had been was gone. Or was he? Tony wondered.

His trainer yelled again for him to get his ass moving, his three-pack-a-day voice grating, as it always did, on Tony's nerves. He knew the harsh tone wasn't personal. It was just Jake's way, and in his way, the words were practically terms of endearment from the old man.

"I'm ready, Jake!" Tony yelled back, lacing his voice with just enough annoyance to make a point and get away with it. "I'm ready," he echoed softly.

Tony entered the aisle leading up to the ring. His stomach gave a small burp of protest at the noxious mixture of grease, smoke, and sweat; that, along with the loud cheers and voices, combined to greet him like a slap in the face.

As he was trotting past the throng, hands reached out and patted him on the back and touched his shoulder, but these small acts of encouragement barely registered, other than to irritate him. Rather, they did the opposite—distracted him from concentrating on the man who was waiting for him in the ring.

Tony allowed himself one brief luxury, which was to look for his father and his uncle. He glanced at the seats reserved for family and spied his dad. His father's eyebrows were knitted together, his mouth turned into a frown.

Give 'em hell, his father mouthed.

This small act of support soothed Tony and helped him focus.

Beside his dad, his Uncle Mike stood on a chair, waving his arms wildly and urging the crowd into more of a frenzy by cheering, yelling, and screaming to "Start the damn fight!" For a moment, Tony saw the chair wobble under his uncle's considerable bulk, but he didn't have time to worry about whether or not Mike would end up ass over teakettle, as his father had always said. He had to focus. Still, it was difficult for Tony to clear his mind completely of his uncle.

After all, Mike had a lot riding on this night, not the least of which was that he had been the one who had talked Tony's father into letting him have this one fight.

"This kid, he's like a hunk of granite. If he ever got in the ring, no one would touch him!" his Uncle Mike had said.

He hoped his uncle's prediction would prove true and provide some small consolation to his father now.

When Tony entered the ring, the announcer had already begun the introductions.

Jake quickly removed Tony's robe and rubbed his arms. While Jake continued to warm his muscles, Tony heard the whistles and catcalls from some of the girls in the crowd.

He had forgotten that it was Valentine's Day.

His opponent was a big brute of a man, bald, heavily muscled, with the tattoo of a hairy skull on his right shoulder. His pale face was almost albino-like in its whiteness, his face twisted into a sneer of confidence.

The bell rang to start the first round. Tony stared back at the man across the ring. All noise ceased to exist.

Then the man charged.

Tony took a lengthy two-and-a-half seconds to size up the fighter who was hurtling straight at him, throwing haymakers as he came and trying to knock him out.

Backing into the ropes, Tony felt his opponent's punching power as the blows rained down on his arms. He smelled the man's sweat as it flew off in droplets, covering Tony in a dewy mist. After about fifteen seconds, Tony had seen enough. He moved the man to the center of the ring by bobbing and weaving his way there, avoiding each blow as it came. Tony sensed the man's growing self-assurance because he had not yet thrown a punch.

Once in the middle, the fighter lunged at Tony. Tony responded by snapping a hard left jab that caught the man square in the nose. The albino rocked back two or three steps, swiping at his nose with his glove. His opponent looked down and saw that the white laces were now crimson, wet and sticky with blood.

Tony faked a second left, and then slammed the man with a hard right to the jaw. His opponent flew across the ring, his mouth open in a silent scream. When he came to rest against the ropes, his knees buckled; he fell face-first, a pool of blood seeping out of his mangled nose.

The referee ran to the downed fighter, disbelief and horror clearly etched on his face.

The referee hesitated briefly, and for the life of him, Tony didn't know why. He assumed the ref didn't know whether to call for the doctor or declare the winner, but the decision was taken out of the official's hands when the doctor came under the ropes and began working the downed fighter.

The crowd, once unruly and excited, became still and silent. The doctor looked at the referee and shook his head, indicating that the fight was over. Instantly, the ref grabbed Tony's hand and raised it in victory. At this, the crowd erupted in jubilant screams, a euphoric rapture of bloodlust and appreciation that lasted longer than the fight itself.

Tony bumped through the crowd on his way to the dressing room. He gritted his teeth in an attempt to keep from brushing off the hands that groped his back and shoulders. Tony knew it was just the crowd's way of trying to inherit some of Tony's skill, courage, or simply his winning aura, and that they hoped it would rub off on them and change their lives. Still, it annoyed him.

He heard voices shouting to him. "Great fight, man," and "way to go," but Tony could only focus on finding his father.

When he finally spotted his father in the crowd, there was a look on his dad's face that Tony recognized but hadn't seen in what felt like a thousand years—pride and respect were what looked back at him. And hadn't he been waiting his whole damn life for that look?

TONY TANCREDI AND CINDY L. O'HARA

TWO

Levittown, Pennsylvania
One decade later

THE HILL IN Levittown had, like its Boston counterpart, been dubbed Little Heartbreak Hill because of its steep grade and its ability to break even the most dedicated and fit runner.

On this day, Tony took the hill at top speed, determined to make it to the top without walking, even if it killed him. *Which*, he thought, *it just might*. His legs—strong and well-defined from countless hours spent fighting and sparring in Philly gyms a lifetime ago—pumped rhythmically, in harmony with each other and the rest of his body. He barely noticed the sweat pouring off of him and did nothing to keep it from draining into his eyes. Although it burned, he welcomed the sensation because it meant he was alive, and the pain diverted his attention from everything else running through his head.

As Tony trudged along, every step making his calves burn, an inquisitive breeze blew back his dark hair, hair that was just now starting to show signs of gray. The sun beat down on his back, infusing his muscles with warmth and heat. But he took no joy in the beautiful afternoon.

Instead, Tony thought of the boy he had been years ago—the one who had his leg encased in an iron vise for two years, the one who had endured verbal taunts and jabs that bordered on abuse by kids both younger and older than himself, the one who was never supposed to walk again, let alone run. Yet here he was—sweating his way, drop by frigging drop, through his workout. Despite the intensity and hard work, no matter the task, he had promised himself that he would always be thankful. And he was. So what the hell was his problem?

Topping the crest, proud of himself for beating the godforsaken hill that until today had always broken him, he paused and allowed himself a smile. He gave his lungs a break by taking a minute to get his breathing under control and reflected on what was bothering him. He paced in small circles, hands on his hips, while taking deep gulps of air. When his breathing calmed to a mere whisper instead of the wracking swallows that always preceded oxygen depletion, his mind returned to what he had been thinking about during his run, which was, *What the hell was wrong with him?* What was he so unbelievably dissatisfied with? After all, he had a good life—no, *great* life, he corrected himself—with Laura and his stepsons. Even his job was okay—not great, by any means, but working construction paid okay and kept him in good physical condition. And while he would've rather been sweating it out at Mahoney's—a hole-in-the-wall gym in Philly that sat atop a beer distributor—and taking out his stress on a punching bag, he also knew boxing was no life. Especially not when you had a family to provide for. So he was okay with his decision to stop boxing. Wasn't he?

Who was he kidding? The decision to leave his boxing career behind still ate away at him like tiny maggots on a piece of rotting flesh. It didn't help that on the rare occasion he *did* get to Mahoney's, both trainers and fighters alike often asked him, when was he coming back, when could they count on him for a match or two, when could they get him a fight, when *in hell* was he gonna get over the civilian life and come home? The questions were endless.

And while Tony loved hearing the comments from world-class fighters about his abilities, it served only to depress him even further because the answer was always the same. *Never.*

Not only had he promised his mother that he wouldn't fight again because she couldn't take the constant injuries he received to his face, but he also had other commitments now, other priorities that took precedence over boxing. No matter that he was good at it.

This led Tony to thinking about Laura and the kids. He loved them with all of his heart, or at least as much as he was capable. Yet something kept tugging at him, something that he kept to himself, something that kept him from giving himself completely to his family. What it was, he wasn't sure.

Maybe it was the sensation of time running out, the time to make good on the promises he had made to himself when he was a teenager—which was that he would become something so he could repay his parents for all their hard work and their sacrifices during his childhood.

All Tony knew was that when he got to Mahoney's gym in Philly, his soul came alive. One whiff of the sweat and leather, a glance at the punching bag, the speed bag, the canvas, and his heart would start racing faster in anticipation of the beating to come—that which he would inflict on his sparring partner and those punches that would tumble down on him.

When he walked into a gym, Tony could feel his muscles tense in response to the adrenaline and the blood that rushed through his body, feeding his very core, until he thought he would explode from the excitement.

He shook his head. No amount of explanation could ever make anyone understand it. You *couldn't* understand it unless you were a part of that world. He had tried to talk to his father and his mother and, later, Laura, about his feelings, but they had all looked at him as if he was crazy.

He didn't have an answer except to say that he was good at it, and he liked it. At the time, he thought he had been a very lucky man to find something he was talented at *and* that he enjoyed.

Overhearing fighters say things like *If he don't ever come back, that's fine with me,* and *That bitch can fight* had not only boosted his ego but given him the respect he craved.

Maybe that's what was nagging him. That he wasn't fighting anymore. But did he blame Laura and the kids? He didn't think so, but who knew? He was tired of trying to figure it out. Best to beat it out on the pavement.

"Screw it," Tony muttered and took off on the straightaway of Quincy Hollow Drive, heading toward Quiet Road, which would bring him home.

As he approached the small three-bedroom house he shared with Laura and the boys, he slowed to a jog, then a walk. He felt better now than he had when he'd gone out, but then he always did.

Tony lifted the latch of the gate that held the chain-link fence together, whistling to let their dog, Blue, know he was in the yard. The dog came racing around the corner of the house. A mix of husky and wolf, Blue had belonged to Tony since he was a puppy.

Tony squatted and scratched the dog's head and ears. Blue pushed his way into Tony, almost making him fall on his ass.

"Okay, okay, that's enough now. I gotta go see the other half of the family," Tony told the dog, giving him one last scratch. He stood up and stretched, arching his back and, for the first time, reveling in the late-afternoon sun.

Yeah, I definitely feel better, he thought. *Musta just been in a funk and needed to get out.*

Tony walked up the short path to the front steps and pushed open the front door.

"Hey," he yelled. "Daddy's home."

When he got no response, he listened. He heard voices in the kitchen and the soft clunk of a glass being put down on the small dinette table they used for their meals.

"Hey," Tony said. "Where are my fans to greet me when I come in? I work hard, and I expect—"

Laura sat at the table, gently touching William's arm, her face only inches away from the boy, a towel in her hand stained with red.

Danny, the younger of the two, was fast becoming the big brother to William, always ready to protect and defend his older sibling.

At birth, William's central nervous system had been damaged, resulting in a mild form of cerebral palsy. Fortunately, the only real thing that was affected was William's balance. To look at him was to see a perfectly normal, healthy young boy of eleven. It was only when he walked or tried to keep up with Danny or his friends that you could tell something wasn't quite right. It was, Tony knew, the reason he sympathized with William.

"Hey, what's goin' on?" Tony asked.

Laura looked up at the sound of Tony's voice.

Tony walked over and knelt by Laura and William.

"Hey, what's up?" Tony asked again, putting his hand on William's knee. His heart clenched when the boy immediately covered Tony's hand with his own.

"Nuthin' Dad," William said, swiping at his face with the back of his hand.

"Would someone please tell me what's goin' on? Why is William crying?"

Danny came around from where he had been sitting and stood by Tony, his brow creased.

"You know Tommy, the boy who lives behind us?"

Tony stood up and shook his head.

Danny rolled his eyes, as if realizing he was talking to a young child.

"Dad, Tommy is a boy who lives behind us," Danny said impatiently. "Anyway, Tommy and some other boys were making fun of William. They pushed him down and beat him up, but he's okay. He's tough, right, William?" Danny said, glancing at his brother while at the same time putting his hand on his brother's shoulder.

"By the time I ran up, they had taken off. I'm sorry I couldn't get there in time, Dad." Danny hung his head as if ashamed he hadn't been able to defend his older brother.

Tony looked down at Danny, amazed at how mature the boy was for his age. At only nine years old, Danny clearly felt the need to be grown up enough to take on bigger, older kids because his brother couldn't. But hell, Tony had felt that way too.

"Tony, what are you gonna do?" Laura asked, her hazel eyes brimming with tears, challenging Tony to both stay and go fix the problem.

TONY TANCREDI AND CINDY L. O'HARA

Tony looked at the ceiling, his hands tensing and flexing, embracing the old rage he used to feel as a kid, remembering a time that seemed not so long ago, when boys like Tommy had made fun of *him*. He tried to suppress his anger, lock it back up in the spot in his chest where it seemed to bloom the fiercest, but he knew it was too late.

Finally, he looked down at Laura and said, "I'm going to go talk to our neighbor."

Only then did Laura push back from the table, her long brown hair swinging as she did so.

"Now, Tony, please don't do anything stupid," she said, rising from her chair and simultaneously clutching his arm.

Without answering, Tony shrugged off Laura's hand, turned, and headed out the back door, letting it slam closed. He stomped through the backyard. When he got to the chain-link fence, he put one hand on the large knob that held the gate, pushed off with his feet, and launched himself neatly over the top, his feet never touching the wire. To anyone watching, it was a stunt worthy of an Olympic gymnast.

Tony, however, had only one thing on his mind, and that was getting to the neighbor's house behind him. His hands continued to clench and relax. Tony recognized that his body was readying itself to fight and protect itself from harm at the same time. He tried to control his breathing, to temper his anger, but he knew it was no use. Once the rage started building inside him, the only way to get rid of it was to let it out.

When Tony got to his neighbor's back porch, he didn't bother with the steps. In one motion, he pulled the screen door open with such force that it ended up off its hinges, although he took no notice of this.

He had one thought, and it was that he could not, under any circumstances, kill the father of the boy—which was exactly what he wanted to do, what he knew he was capable of doing. But what he could do was put the fear of God into him, which was what he intended to do.

Tony strode to the table, grabbed the father by the neck with one hand, lifted him off the chair, and kicked it aside hard enough to topple it over. Still holding the man with one hand, Tony walked him over to the kitchen wall and slammed him up against it. The man's feet dangled an inch off the ground. Although Tony's biceps burned from the effort of holding up what he estimated to be about a one-hundred-and-eighty-five-pound man, the pain felt good. So did the screams coming from the man's family. It meant he was being taken seriously.

"If I ever see your kid on my street again, I'll come back and make you a cripple! Are we clear on that?" Tony yelled into the man's watermelon-red face. All that came out was a slight gurgling noise. The man was now turning purple, yet Tony refused to let go.

He shook him once for emphasis. "Well?"

The man gave a barely perceptible nod, all the while clawing at Tony's hands, begging with his eyes to be released. Tony let him drop to the floor. The man lay hunched over, rubbing his throat and coughing. His wife ran up and stooped beside her husband.

"What are you?" she screamed. "Some kind of animal?" She rubbed her husband's back.

"Yeah, you could say that. And by the way, I've been called worse, lady. I'm assuming we understand each other?" Not waiting for an answer, Tony stepped through the now open doorway, where the screen should have been, and bounced down the three steps toward home.

When he got to his back fence, he opened the gate this time and let himself in. Tony strolled leisurely across his small backyard, lighthearted and in no particular hurry. He walked up the back steps and into the kitchen.

"Tony, what did you do?" Laura asked. "I could hear the screams all the way over here with the door closed." She stood at the sink, one hand cocked on a hip, a dishtowel hanging from her other hand.

"I just talked to him. We've agreed that his kid shouldn't play on our street anymore. I don't think William will have any more problems with Tommy." Laura just shook her head, sighed, and turned back to washing the dishes.

After answering endless questions from the boys about what had happened next door and assuring them that no, he hadn't kicked anybody's ass (even with all the screaming? Danny had asked), Tony thought it would be a good idea to take the family out to dinner. He thought he might take them to Luigi's—a small as-yet-undiscovered Italian restaurant just around the corner from the house.

Tony supposed the restaurant could be dubbed a hole-in-the-wall, but he preferred to think of it as quaint. The portions tended to be family-size, the owner catered to them, and the food was exquisite. Plus, it wasn't too expensive—yet.

"Hey guys," Tony said. "How 'bout we eat out tonight? I was thinkin' Luigi's?"

"Yeah!" William and Danny chorused. "Can we, Mom? Can we?"

Laura had wandered into the living room, wiping her hands with the blue-and-white-striped dishtowel she had been using to dry the dishes, and leaned against the wall, smiling. "Sure," she said, looking at Tony and tossing the dishcloth onto the couch. "Why not? Your daddy owes us a dinner, I think."

An hour later, when Tony, Laura, and the boys walked up to the restaurant, Luigi, the owner, greeted them, his arms outstretched and a large grin lighting up his fleshy face. Thumping Tony soundly on the shoulder with one hand, Luigi grabbed Tony's other hand and gave it a vigorous shake while pulling him close in a bear hug.

"Hey, Tony, how you doin'? You no come by for months. What gives?" Luigi asked in his thick Sicilian accent. Before Tony could respond, the large Italian had squatted down to study the boys.

"And these leetle fellas, they get so big, so fast." Luigi stood up. "Hey, you know who would love to see you?" Both Danny and William looked up, trying to see the proprietor's face over his substantial waist, and shook their heads.

"Giovanni, the chef. He miss you. Why don't you go help him in the kitchen?"

"An' as for you two, don' worry. The boys, they will be fine. Enjoy a nice glass of wine on me, a few minutes alone, and then I'll send them back out."

Luigi pulled a chair out for Laura, unfolded her napkin with a flourish, and placed it on her lap. He then began barking orders at the waitresses to bring bread, wine, and antipasti for the couple.

"You know," Laura said, watching Luigi follow a waitress into the kitchen, badgering her the entire time. "I could get used to this."

"Yeah," Tony agreed, breaking off a piece of bread and soaking it in the small plate of olive oil that seemed to have appeared out of nowhere. "Me too." He looked at his wife and smiled. "Wine?"

"Sure," Laura answered. "I wouldn't want to upset the owner of the restaurant." She smiled back.

"Hey, I wanted to remind you that Wendy's wedding is next Saturday, in Philly."

"Oh yeah," Tony said, taking a sip. "What time do you have to be there?"

"All the bridesmaids are supposed to be there around three o'clock. The wedding's not 'til seven though," Laura replied. "Then after the reception, we may go to another club in town."

"What club is that?"

"I dunno." Laura soaked a piece of bread. "Some after-hours place that one of the groomsmen knows about, or belongs to or something."

"Huh," Tony grunted. "Whatever you say, dear." He winked at his wife across the table and reached for her hand.

TONY TANCREDI AND CINDY L. O'HARA

THREE

THE SHAMROCK CLUB, a nightclub located on South Hampton Road in the heart of Northeast Philadelphia, was indistinct from other clubs in the city save for one thing—it was the only place to go after all the other bars had signaled for last call, and as such, it catered to a select type of clientele, including other club owners, bartenders, waitresses, big-breasted girls who made their living showing off their tits to traveling salesmen, and blue-collar workers on payday.

The Shamrock was set back from the street and was virtually unseen by passersby because of the large parking lot separating the two. This afforded almost complete privacy to anyone who wanted or needed it, which of course made it a favorite of both the Irish and Italian mobs.

As Tony pushed his way through the thick steel doors and stepped onto soft light-colored carpeting, he wondered briefly why a club would need such protection.

Although lighting was kept to a minimum, it was easy to take in the surroundings, thanks to the mirrored walls covering the entire bar. Tony imagined this gave the manager and owner the ability to see what was going on in any corner of the room.

Tony made out two long dark bars situated at opposite ends of the room, a hardwood dance floor in the middle, and a DJ booth, as well as a door leading to a back room. He headed for the bar closest to the front door.

"What can I get 'ya?" the bartender asked. Tony leaned up against the railing.

Before he could answer, someone yelled, "Holy Christ, I can't believe this. He'll have a Jack and ginger, ain't that right, Ton? It's on me." A lanky figure slid off a barstool.

Now who the hell would I know in a place like this? Tony thought, watching the man walk toward him. When the figure walked out of the shadows, Tony couldn't believe whom he was looking at.

"Sam Grozzi!" Tony exclaimed. "How the hell are you, man?"

Tony grabbed his childhood friend's hand and pulled him in close, slapping him on the back at the same time. He was as Tony remembered him—average height, stringy blond hair, thin frame, mustache, and still gnawing on a toothpick that would switch nervously from one side of his mouth to the other.

"What's it been? Four, five years?" Tony asked, drawing away to look at his friend.

"Yeah, sumpthin' like that."

Tony took in his friend's pinstriped dark suit and leather loafers. Sam had never had much in the way of clothes or money when they were growing up, but clearly, something had changed.

"So what's goin' on?"

"Nuthin' much," Sam replied. "Managing this club, trying to keep the riff-raff out. You know the drill."

Tony nodded sympathetically.

"How 'bout you?" Sam asked. "What brings you into a club like this?"

"Just waitin' for Laura, my wife. She was in a friend's wedding tonight, so she and a bunch of other people should be showin' up soon."

"Huh. So whatdaya up to these days?"

"Oh, you know," Tony said. "This and that, working construction mostly."

"That pay okay?"

"Yeah, you know, it's all right." Tony looked around the room, at the bar, at the dance floor, everywhere but at his friend. "Laura and I do okay."

"Well, you know, if you're interested in makin' a little cash on the side, we could always use somebody like you around here to help clean things up."

"Ah, I don't know, Sam. I'm not a bouncer. I quit fightin', and I'm married now. I got two little boys, and I don't wanna get into that. I'm really tryin' to settle down."

Sam chuckled and switched the toothpick from left to right.

"Ton, who you tryin' to kid? It's me, Sam. You're never gonna settle down. I *know* you, man."

"Well, I'm tryin', Sam."

"Look, Ton," Sam said, putting an arm over Tony's shoulder and guiding him away from the bar. "I'll pay you more than all the rest. I'll pay you fifty bucks a night instead of the usual forty you'd get at any other bar in the city."

"I don't know Sam—"

"Plus, there's an added bonus," Sam continued quietly, as if Tony had never spoken. "Look at it this way, you can fuck and fight all you want."

Tony looked at his friend, eyebrows raised.

TONY TANCREDI AND CINDY L. O'HARA

"I gotta tell ya, Sam. I can't believe I'm havin' this conversation with you. All I wanted to do was come in, have a drink, and enjoy a few minutes to myself before the rest of the yahoos from the wedding party arrived. Now you're offerin' me a job?"

"Just lemme introduce you to someone." Sam looked up and yelled across the bar. "Hey, Joe, if you gotta minute, could you say hello to a friend of mine?"

A thin but well-muscled man emerged from a dark corner. The most interesting thing, Tony noted, was that he was wearing a very smart felt fedora, with the brim pulled low on his head. "Joe," Sam said. "This is Tony Tancredi—the fighter I mentioned to you a few times. We went to high school together."

Joe did not extend his hand, and Tony got the feeling this was normal, that Joe was used to being deferred to. Instead, Joe looked Tony up and down, giving a slight nod to Sam.

"So, Joe, can I hire this guy to bounce, or what? We could really use him around here."

Joe turned to Sam, effectively dismissing Tony, and said, "Sure, Sam. If you can vouch for him, sure."

Joe had spoken for the first time, and Tony realized he liked the soft, almost-silky voice that came out. It in no way matched the person he was looking at, yet he liked it.

"Now, gentlemen, if you'll excuse me, some other, uh, customers need my attention."

"Sure, Joe, thanks," Sam said, watching his employer move away.

"Now he's a character," Tony commented.

"Joe? Yeah, sumthin' like that," Sam said. "So, Ton, whatdaya think of the offer?"

"I don't know, Sam," Tony said, putting his hands in his pocket and looking down at the floor. Hemming and hawing, trying to buy some time, Tony finally said, "The money sounds good, but I gotta be honest, I'm really tryin' to do the right thing here, ya know?" He looked up at his friend of more than half his life.

"So do the right thing," Sam said, spreading his arms out wide, palms up. "Who's stoppin' you? I'm simply presentin' you with an opportunity. Tell ya what," Sam continued. "Talk to—sorry, what's her name again?"

"Laura."

"Right. Laura. And see what she says. But at the very least, give it a try. If it doesn't work out, it doesn't work out. No harm, no foul. Whatdaya say?"

Tony looked at his friend and smiled, thinking that if he had wanted to, Sam could have had a great career in sales. "I say I'll talk to her when she gets here, but I gotta warn you, if I were a bettin' man, I wouldn't play the odds on her sayin' yes to this."

"Great," Sam said. He embraced Tony. "That's all I wanted to hear. Now I bet you could use that drink right about now, huh?"

After discussing Sam's offer throughout the entire week after the wedding (endlessly, it seemed to Tony), he had convinced Laura that the money would help and that it would only be one night a week, two tops. She couldn't argue that an extra fifty or a hundred bucks paid under the table wouldn't come in handy, so she had finally relented and given her okay, albeit grudgingly.

Plus, he had told her, if it didn't work out, then he would just quit. That helped.

But as Tony looked in the bedroom mirror and straightened his tie, he had a feeling he was going to enjoy his new job.

His thoughts were interrupted when both William and Danny wandered in.

"What are you doin', Daddy?" Danny asked.

"Yeah," William echoed. "Why are you getting so dressed up to go get ice cream?"

"Hey guys," Tony said, glancing down at the boys before looking back at the mirror. "Daddy's not gonna be able to take you out for ice cream tonight. I would've thought your mom would have told you that already."

"No," Laura said, leaning against the doorframe. She crossed her arms defensively. "I thought I'd leave that to you."

Tony gave Laura a withering stare before squatting so he could be at eye level with his sons. "Look, guys," Tony said, shifting his weight from leg to leg so as not to wrinkle his pants, which had taken him half an hour to iron. "Daddy got a new job, and it starts tonight. I'm really sorry about not being able to go get ice cream, but your mom'll still take you, right, honey?" Tony looked up and smiled. Laura glared back at Tony before the boys turned their faces toward her.

"Of course I'll take you. You know, guys, this new job that Daddy has won't be forever. He's just trying to bring in a little extra money."

"For presents? For us?" the boys yelled.

"Sure," Tony said, amazed at how the boys—most children, he supposed—were fine with things as long as it meant they got gifts.

"Yeah!" William and Danny whooped.

"So we're good?" Tony asked, getting up. He straightened the creases in his pants.

"Yup," the boys said in stereo.

"Okay, now get outta here and go get ready so your mom can take you out."

"'K, Dad." The boys ran out of the room, but Danny stopped short. "Hey, Dad?"

"Yeah, Danny?" Tony asked, trying not to sound as exasperated as he felt. He didn't want to be late his first night.

Sounding wise beyond his years, Danny said, "Good luck tonight. You're gonna do great." Then he promptly ran out of the room and after his brother.

Those simple words from a nine-year-old boy tugged at Tony's heart and would have made a better man reconsider what he was doing. But Tony knew he was not that kind of man.

He checked his appearance one last time. Satisfied, he headed toward the front door, brushing past Laura on his way out. Laura turned and trailed her husband.

"Tony?"

"Yeah?" Tony stopped at the front door, facing her. *Would he ever be able to get out of this damn house?* he wondered.

Laura stepped in close and straightened a tie that had already been straightened about thirty times. Without looking at Tony, she said, "Promise me you won't hurt anyone?" She looked up at her husband's face.

"What do you mean don't hurt anyone?" Tony asked, shocked. "What about me gettin' hurt? This ain't like the ring, honey."

"I know, but I don't have to worry about you," Laura said, looking Tony in the eyes. "I know *you* won't get hurt. It's everybody else I'm worried about."

Tony shook his head and smiled before leaning in and kissing his wife. Then he headed out the door to his new job.

FOUR

AS TONY DROVE down Route 1 toward Philadelphia, he thought about what he was getting himself into. He knew the drinking wouldn't be a problem (it never had been), or the fighting—although Tony suspected that Sam couldn't wait to see him knock somebody out. In his opinion, if the fight wasn't in the ring, it really didn't mean much. In this case, it should be just punching out a few drunks and smacking a few wise guys around to take care of any problems.

No, the fighting and drinking wouldn't be a big deal. His, he knew, was a different kind of addiction, a different temptation. The real test would come when faced with the girls. How he handled that aspect of the job would be . . . well, interesting, Tony thought. Based on past experience, he didn't think it was going to go very well at all.

"Can't worry about something that hasn't even happened," Tony mumbled to himself as he turned onto South Hampton Road and into the club's parking lot. He found a dark unoccupied corner in a lot that was virtually empty since most of the clientele wouldn't arrive until after one in the morning.

When he walked into the Shamrock Club, the first thing Tony heard was the familiar voice of his friend Greg, from high school. He hadn't known that he worked here.

"Wait until you see this guy hit," Greg said. "He can knock you out with either hand. I've seen him do it plenty of times."

"Well, if this guy is so tough and hits so hard, why the hell did he quit fighting?" asked another bouncer.

"Hey, Greg, how ya doin'?" Tony walked up, interrupting the conversation.

"Hey, Ton, I was just tellin' the guys here about that last fight I seen you in. That's okay, right?"

"I guess," Tony said. "What the hell do I care what you tell 'em? Long as you make me look good." Tony laughed.

The other bouncers laughed nervously.

"So it was at the last fight this guy had," Greg said, pointing at Tony. "And he got beat up so bad that when he got home, his mother passed out. When she came to, she cried for two days, and Tony hadda promise that he would never fight again. Idn't that right, Ton?"

"Yeah," Tony said. "I took a pretty good ass whippin' that fight."

"Tony, tell 'em from the beginning. I mean, I was there and all, but tell 'em what happened that night."

"I don't know, Greg. No one wants to hear about that shit—war stories and all."

"Come on, man," said Monte, another bouncer.

Tony sighed and moved up to the bar so he could lean on the railing.

"Have we got time?" Tony asked Greg.

"Hell yeah, we got time."

"Well, the shit started at the weigh-in," Tony began, getting comfortable with the story. "See, this was the Golden Gloves, and my trainer knew I was s'posed to fight the guy who was four and oh, and the commission wanted me to fight the guy who was fifteen and one because they had seen my first fight and thought it would be more competitive.

"Anyway," Tony continued, "it didn't make any difference to me who I fought, 'cuz I knew that I could win. Well, I fought the guy with the better record, and I don't think he missed a punch the first two rounds. I mean, my face was a mess—especially my right eye. If it was a pro fight today, they woulda stopped it."

"No shit," said Monte, transfixed.

"Toward the end of the second round, this guy hits me with a left hook to the kidney, and I gotta tell ya, I'd never been hit with a punch like that before. Finally, the bell rings to end the second round, and I stumble back to my corner on rubber legs that wouldn't work, gasping for air," Tony paused, warming to his story.

"Well, my trainer, Jake, knew just what to do." Tony looked down and chuckled, remembering vividly that moment. He looked up and gazed at the faces of the bouncers surrounding him, all of them waiting expectantly.

"So Jake grabs this handful of ice." Tony turned his palm up, as if he were holding ice in it. "Reaches his hand down into my cup and puts the ice right on my nuts." Tony had turned his palm facedown and cupped his balls.

A collective groan went up from the bouncers, who all grabbed themselves in sympathy.

"No fuckin' way," Monte yelled, smiling.

"Yup," Tony said, laughing.

"Then what happened?" Monte asked.

"Jake tells me to take a deep breath, which I can't help but do 'cuz I got a fuckin' ice pack on my boys, right? Then he asks me if I want to stop the fight. At this point, my right eye is closed except for a slit, and the doc comes into the ring. I beg him to let me go one more round, and he does."

As the story continued to unfold, Tony could still see the crowd on its feet as the bell rang to start round three. He could hear his father screaming, "Box and protect yourself!" And he could feel each punch of his opponent's glove hit his skin.

"At the time, I'm thinkin' if I can just hit him once, I can knock him out. It was about halfway through the third round when he seemed to be getting tired. Unfortunately, it was from beatin' my ass." Tony smiled.

"With about thirty seconds to go, I finally land a left hook, knocking him into the corner. Before he can fall to the mat, I put my left shoulder under his chin and pin him in the corner and begin clubbing him in the head with my right."

"It was a beautiful thing to watch," said Greg, smiling.

"So the crowd's on their feet, screaming. Everyone's goin' friggin' nuts, and the ref comes up behind me and grabs me in a headlock, trying to pull me away. But all I can think about is all the punches this guy threw and how messed up I was, so I'm not stoppin'."

Tony paused and looked around at his audience, making sure that everyone was paying appropriate attention.

"Well?" Monte asked impatiently, breaking the silence. "What the hell happened then?"

"Finally, the ref is able to pull me off the guy, the whole time screamin' at me that I was crazy, that I was gonna kill the fighter if I didn't stop, that he was out and just to let him fall down. Then the ref raised my hand in victory.

"I tried to get out of the ring to tell my dad I was okay, 'cuz I knew he was feeling every punch I got hit with, but Jake, my trainer, dragged me back to the center of the ring so the crowd could see me.

"When I finally get out of the ring and find my father, he tells me it was one of the greatest fights he's ever seen. His only regret, he said, was that I had to take a beating like that.

"So I head back to the dressing room, where a friend of the guy I just fought comes over to my side and accuses me of being on drugs 'cuz he, says, and I quote, 'Nobody could take a beatin' like that and come back and win unless they were doin' some shit.' At this point, that's the last thing I wanna hear, 'cuz I knew I'd never done drugs once I started fighting, right?"

It was a rhetorical question, but he was quickly learning that Monte, though generally quiet, usually had something to say.

"Well, seems to me like it would be a natural question," Monte said.

"Yeah, Monte, well, you weren't there," Tony snapped. He was starting to lose his patience with the younger, bigger man.

Tony put Monte at about six-foot-two and more than two hundred pounds. This meant that the dark-haired Irishman had him beat in size, but not by strength—not by a long shot.

For a moment, the two men looked at each other, until Monte finally said, "Well, I'm just sayin' it *could* be a logical conclusion—not in your case, maybe, but in somebody else's."

Tony gave the big man an out by turning away.

"Well, *I* knew I had never done drugs." Tony looked pointedly at Monte. "So I stand up and tell this guy's friend, 'Oh yeah? You think I'm on sumthin'? Well, I still have plenty left in me.' Then I knock *him* out!"

"Holy Christ!" said one of the other bouncers, eyes wide. Surprisingly, Monte kept his mouth shut.

"Well, I wanted to get back out there and watch the next fight, 'cuz my friend Tommy was fighting in the light heavyweight finals. And as I'm sittin' at ringside with ice on my eye, the guy I just fought comes up beside me and puts his arm around me and says he's sorry about his friend.

"He tells me he's gonna turn professional in two months, that I'm the baddest white boy he's ever seen, and when I turn pro, not to call him for a fight. It was a great compliment, 'cuz this guy messed me up. So we both laugh and say good-bye and say we hope we won't meet again. And that's it."

"So you never turned professional," Monte asked quietly.

"Nah," Tony answered. "Greg told you I promised my mom I wouldn't have another fight in the ring, but after that fight, for the next five or six years, all the main trainers and promoters tried to get me to turn professional. I hadda say no, though."

"Hey, Ton, you ever wish youda done it? Turned pro, I mean?" Greg asked.

"Ah, I try not to think about it. What would be the point?"

"Well, *I* know you coulda been champ."

"Shoulda, woulda, coulda. Let's change the subject," Tony said, suddenly depressed. "Whatta I gotta do here tonight?"

"So lemme get this straight, Ton, you give up a kick-ass boxing future becuza your ma?" Monte asked.

Tony turned on Monte. Greg put a hand on Tony's shoulder.

"I got this, Ton. Why don't you go see what Sam wants you to do tonight."

"Yeah, okay."

Tony turned and stomped off toward his friend.

Greg backhanded Monte on his shoulder. "What the hell's the matter with you, man? Don't you know when to leave well enough alone? Couldn't you see he was gettin' pissed and didn't wanna talk no more?"

"Look, I gotta work with the goombah, and I'd like a heads-up on what makes him tick."

Greg steered Monte to the back room. "Let's go in here. I don't want him walking up on us. Besides, everyone'll think we're just doin' a line."

"Hey, I *could* really use a bump if you got one, Greg."

"You know sumpthin'? You're a pain in my ass, Monte." Monte smiled.

"Yeah, but I'm *your* pain in the ass. Besides, it's all work-related—the story and the bump—and it'll help me be a better bouncer."

Greg pushed open the door, then walked behind Joe's desk and took a seat. Monte sat across from him looking, Greg thought, very much like a schoolboy waiting for class to start. Greg reached into his pocket and dug around for some meth. He pulled the drugs out triumphantly.

"I've known Tony since high school, okay? Even then, he always talked about what great parents he had and how close they were. He could never understand when someone would say they hadda fight with their old man or their ma. He was given up for dead when he was born, and his parents had already lost a baby before him."

Greg chopped the meth into a fine line.

"Then at five—or was it six, I don't know, whatever—he got some disease in his leg. Doctors told his parents he'd never walk again without a brace or sumpthin'. I guess the doctors told his parents he should go into the hospital, but they wouldn't hear of it. Said they'd give him better care than a hospital ever could. Well they did, and he obviously beat the damn thing."

Greg leaned back.

"He promised himself he would pay his parents back someday. He was a helluva baseball player in high school, and everyone thought he'd go pro, but it just didn't happen. I guess he really felt like he let his parents down when he realized the baseball thing wasn't gonna work out. Said if he *did* make it, he was gonna buy his parents a big house, tell his dad he'd never have to work again, that kinda thing. That's the stuff he'd tell us all through high school."

"So then what happened?" Monte asked.

"I don't really know. I lost contact with him for a while. Then I hear he's becomin' a fighter. So I go to his fights, and we meet again. And he was great in the ring—all action. He never stopped throwin' punches, never backed up. Then all of a sudden, I find out he quit boxing. I was at that last fight. It was brutal, his face was a bloody mess. As cut up as he was, even that couldn't stop him and he managed to knock the guy out in the third round with a wicked left hook. But I heard when he got home, his mother took one look at him and boom, passed out right on the kitchen floor. Story goes he got so scared that when she came to, he promised her he'd never fight in the ring again. It's a shame too, because in my opinion, he coulda been champ. And I'm not the only one who thinks so.

Everybody from the neighborhood was shocked. After that, I lost contact with him again. Then, what, ten, twelve years later, he shows up here." Greg stopped and looked at Monte. "Now that you've done almost all of my shit, story time's over."

"Thanks, Greg. I feel better already."

"Yeah. I'm sure you do, dickhead. Now get outta here and go do some work, will ya?"

Greg opened the door for Monte, who practically waltzed through.

"I'm gonna go see what Sam and Tony are doin'. Why don't you go move the speakers closer to the DJ booth."

Monte's smile faded. "Hey those fuckers are heavy, man."

"Well, look at it this way—with all the shit you just did, they should feel like nothin' to you."

Greg turned and headed toward Sam and Tony.

"Hey guys, what's up?" Greg asked.

"Nothin' Greg. I was just tellin' Tony here that I was gonna put him on the door collectin' money," Sam said.

"Yeah, that'd be good."

Sam looked at Tony. "No matter what anyone tells you, everyone pays five bucks to get in," said Sam. "We're also gonna give you a clicker to count all the people who come into the club."

"When *do* people come into this place?" Tony asked.

"This is an after-hours club, and we get all the people who come here after every other place closes. The clients have to sign a book, and nobody gets in unless they're a member or are with a member. Got it?"

"Yeah," Tony answered. "So we don't get busy until 1:30 or so?"

"Yeah, that's right."

Just then, a figure appeared from the back room and strode purposefully toward Tony, Sam, and Greg. Tony recognized Joe from meeting him the week before, and this time, Tony noted, Joe shook hands with everyone and said hello.

"Hey, Sam, we gotta go," Joe said.

"Yeah, okay." Sam turned back to Tony. "You okay? You got it?"

"Yeah," Tony answered.

At midnight, Tony and the other bouncers began setting up outside, which included rolling out the ramp that would take people inside, putting a table by the door with a sign-in book, and placing a velvet rope along the ramp to form a line. Around one, just as Sam had predicted, people started trickling in—many heading straight for the back room, not even stopping at the bar for a drink. Although Tony was curious about what went on in that room, he also decided that it was none of his goddamn business.

Almost half an hour later, as Tony was making change for a pretty blonde, he was bumped so hard that the change fell to the ground. Just as he turned to snap at whoever had run into him, Greg raced out to the parking lot along with a couple of other doormen. Puzzled, Tony watched the scene unfold.

Shortly after Greg and the other two bouncers had cleared a parking spot, a long silver Lincoln Town Car with tinted windows pulled into the space. When the driver's door opened and a thin leg in pinstriped pants came out, Tony knew it was Sam and Joe.

Sam opened the back passenger door. From there, Joe emerged wearing a dark suit, complete with felt fedora.

Joe approached the club, and Greg halted the line to let his boss pass. Before he did so, though, Joe stopped, extended his hand, and asked Tony how he was doing, if everything was going okay.

"Fine, sir. No problems," Tony mumbled, confused and uncomfortable with the pomp and circumstance that preceded his boss.

Who the hell is this guy that everyone treats him like friggin' royalty? Tony wondered.

As soon as Joe got two or three steps into the club, the crowd engulfed him. Tony caught sight of Joe, who seemed to be working the room, offering a word or two here or there—especially to the ladies—before finally disappearing into the back room.

TONY TANCREDI AND CINDY L. O'HARA

By two thirty, the club was jammed, and a line had formed around the corner. Madonna screamed that she was "like a virgin" (although Tony suspected that ship had sailed quite a long time ago for the blonde starlet) through loudspeakers from the DJ's booth.

As the song came to an end, someone yelled.

"Hey, there's a fight outside in the parking lot!"

Since Tony had been standing inside the door, he hadn't seen anything going on.

Immediately, Tony shoved the money and the clicker that he had been holding into the hands of the first person who was walking by, who happened to be his boss, Joe.

"Here, take this," Tony said, bolting down the ramp, elbowing people out of his way.

When Tony got to the parking lot, he could see his friend Sam on the ground, curled into a tight ball, one beefy guy on top of him, another standing over him, ready to kick him in the head.

Next to Sam was another bouncer going at it with another guy. Out of all of them, Tony knew that the bouncer could handle himself a while longer but that Sam was in more serious trouble.

Tony quickly hit the guy who was about to kick Sam in the head with a left hook. The man went down and never moved. Tony then moved toward the guy who was straddling Sam. Tony reached to grab the back of the man's shirt with the intention of dragging him off of his friend, but he needn't have worried. When he saw Tony stalking toward him, he stopped beating Sam and put his hands up to ward off any blows. Tony then faked a left and hit him with a right. The man was out cold before his ass hit the blacktop. Tony then turned his attention to the third guy, who wisely took off running.

As Joe approached, Sam mumbled through bleeding lips, "You see why I wanted to hire this guy, Joe?" Sam looked up, smiling lopsidedly, blood oozing down his chin.

Joe nodded and handed Tony back the money and the clicker.

"Damn, I've never seen anybody hit like that. Nice work," Joe said.

"I'm just doin' what you're payin' me to do," Tony replied, dusting himself off and putting out a hand to help his friend up off the ground.

"Thanks, Ton," Sam replied, spitting blood and drool onto the stained pavement, a thin red stream hanging from his oversized lips. He wiped it away with the sleeve of his jacket.

"Son of a bitch!" Sam yelled. "This is a three-hundred-dollar suit!" Tony looked at his friend's clothes, which were indeed torn and shredded in places. He tried to wipe the smirk off his face, but could feel that he was only slightly successful.

"Hey, let's look at the big picture here," Tony answered, gently patting his friend on the back. "You're fine, and you only slightly got your ass kicked."

"Yeah, okay, but couldja do me a favor and wipe that friggin' smile off your face?"

"I'll try. Now let's go back inside and get you cleaned up," Tony said, guiding his friend to the club entrance. "What was all that about, anyway?"

"You don't wanna know," Sam said, and Tony left it at that.

By the end of the evening, word around the club had spread that a new bouncer had been hired and he wasn't taking shit from anyone. While pleased, Tony knew from experience that it was better to remain humble than let it go to his head and get cocky.

"Hey, Ton," Sam called from where he was sitting at the bar, nursing a rum and Coke. "Come 'ere a minute."

"Yeah, Sam?" Tony asked, sauntering up to his friend. For once, Sam was minus his toothpick. Tony realized his friend looked odd without it. "What's up?"

"Joe wants to see you in the back room."

"Oh yeah? Do I just walk in, or what?"

"Well, I'd knock first." Sam laughed. "Ya never know what could be goin' on in there—*if* you know what I mean." Sam winked. "Damn, that hurts."

Tony lowered his head so Sam wouldn't see the smile that threatened to turn to laughter and headed to see Joe.

As he was about to knock on the door, he stopped. Inside, he heard Joe explaining what he had seen in the parking lot to whoever was in the room with him.

"I swear to God, it was like steaks being slapped on a tile wall. I shit you not. The friggin' idiots were still out cold five minutes later. We had to wake 'em up."

Tony tapped lightly on the door.

"Yeah?" Joe yelled. "Come on in."

Tony opened the door.

TONY TANCREDI AND CINDY L. O'HARA

"We're done here, right, boys?" Joe asked the other two occupants.

The bartenders nodded and brushed past Tony.

"Wanna stick around and have a drink? No obligation. You can leave if you want to."

Although tempting, Tony thought it best that he call it a night.

"I appreciate the offer, Joe, but I think I'll head out. Maybe another time."

"That's fine," Joe said. "See you tomorrow night."

Tony nodded and backed out the door.

When he got home, Tony entered his bedroom as quietly as possible and eased himself into bed, trying his best not to wake Laura.

Although half asleep, Laura reached for Tony, gently feeling his hands and face.

"Were you in any fights tonight?" she asked groggily. "Are you okay?"

"I'm fine, baby. Just fine."

Tony hoped he wasn't lying.

FIVE

TONY LINED UP the mud pans for the blocklayers, telling himself that working at the club was no big deal, just a way to bring in some extra cash, and that he could take it or leave it at any time. But the truth was that when Wednesday or Friday rolled around, he'd be absolutely giddy during the day—like a damn kid in a candy store—because he knew he'd be going to the club later that night.

Why he felt more at home in the Shamrock than he did with his own wife and kids, he didn't know. He just knew it to be true.

I guess part of it has to do with all the trim I could get, Tony thought ruefully as he wiped the sweat off his forehead and took a momentary break from the grueling work.

Tony bent over and picked up the gallon jug of water and guzzled, letting the cool water dribble from his mouth. Wiping away the water from his lips, he continued to think about being at the club and what drew him to it. While the women were definitely an added bonus, more than that was that he impressed the other bouncers. They liked his style and what he could do with his hands.

Of course, Laura wasn't too keen on him being away from home so much. Which led him to his current problem. Joe had asked him if he could start working at the club Saturday nights as well as the other two nights, and he was dreading telling his wife about it. True, the money was coming in handy, but Tony didn't think he could sell Laura on a third night by using the money angle. That song and dance was getting old. Nope, he'd have to come up with something new and fresh, something she couldn't say no to. What that was, Tony hadn't figured out yet.

"Hey, Tancredi!" Tony was jerked back to the construction site by the voice of his boss, Ron. "Are you gonna get back to work today or continue to stand there and soak up the sun, princess?"

Tony hated his supervisor. Not because he was a prick (he was), but because he was an asshole with a chip on his shoulder and just enough power to make his life miserable.

Tony sighed, put down his jug of water, and picked up the hammer and nails he had just set down on a two-by-four.

"Hey, Tancredi, come 'ere a minute, would ya?" Ron yelled.

"Ah hell, now what?" Tony muttered under his breath, setting down the tools he had just picked up.

"Yeah, Ron, what's up?" Tony asked, walking over to where his boss was standing.

"Lucky you. I need some supplies from the house over in Pine Run. I need you to take a truck and go get 'em for me. Here's a list of things I need. Think you can handle bein' in an air-conditioned truck for a while and out of the sun?"

"Yeah, Ron. I think I can handle it," Tony said, grabbing the list out of the super's hand.

"Hurry it up, will ya? I ain't got all day," Ron said, flipping him the keys. "Take that truck over there." He pointed over his shoulder to a beat-up white Ford F-150 that had seen better days.

Tony walked over, hopped into the old truck, and headed over to the supply house.

Pine Run was a housing development built in Newtown, Pennsylvania, in the early '80s by Tony's boss—Dave Shenk. The community catered to the middle and upper classes with homes that were two stories and more than thirty-five hundred square feet—that is to say, fairly large. Some had pools, some didn't; but all had neat, well-manicured front lawns and big backyards that, if pool-less, contained patios and decks for entertaining.

On the rare occasion when Tony had to come over to pick up supplies, he had always been impressed by the community and thought that someday he might move Laura and the kids here.

As Tony turned onto Evergreen Street, he glanced to his right. There, a woman sat in the dirt, knees tucked under her, one gloved hand holding a trowel, the other pushing dirt around. Her long blonde hair was tied back in a ponytail. The scene would have been unmemorable except that when she looked up at the sound of the truck rumbling down the street, Tony couldn't take his eyes off her.

Of all the women Tony had seen in his lifetime, never before had he seen anyone as stunning as the one he was looking at now. In those few seconds, he was able to take in that she was tall, long-legged, and had full, pouty lips.

Tony surprised himself by waving at her. She waved back tentatively, and then turned back to her gardening.

One day, when Tony pulled up to the supply house, a woman yelled down the block. At the sound of the voice, he turned. The woman Tony had seen in the garden stood at the edge of her yard, an empty leash in one hand while a barrel-chested white dog rushed toward him.

"Sasha, come back here!"

"Whoa there, Sasha," Tony said, leaning down and grabbing the dog's collar. He needn't have worried because the dog stopped directly in front of him, plopped down, and rolled over on her back, exposing her pink-and-white belly. At this, Tony promptly squatted and began rubbing the dog's stomach.

"Sasha, bad dog! Thanks so much—uh . . . I'm sorry, I don't know your name."

"It's Tony." Tony stood and stuck out his hand.

"Well, hi," she said softly. She took Tony's hand and lightly shook it. "I'm Diane."

"Diane, it's nice to meet you," Tony said.

"Yeah, you too," she said. She shifted her weight from foot to foot and looked back at the dog.

"I don't know why she takes off like that."

Tony looked into Diane's green eyes, willing her to look back at him.

"Me either," he said. "Maybe she's trying to break the ice for us. So that we can do more than wave at each other when I come over here."

"Yeah, maybe," Diane said, smiling. "I swear, my baby listens to me better than she does." Tony inhaled sharply when he heard the word *baby*. Shit. *Of course, she's got a family, you dickhead,* he thought.

Diane pointed at the dog, who was now sprawled contentedly on her back, tongue lolling out of the side of her mouth, spit dribbling onto the driveway. Diane bent and snapped leash to collar. "Come on, girl. Playtime's over."

"What kind of dog is she?" Tony asked, not wanting the moment to end. He bent and scratched behind the dog's ears. "A husky?" he asked, looking up at Diane.

"Close. She's a Samoyed. And a damn stubborn one at that," Diane said.

"Ah, she's just doing what dogs do—run."

"Well, thanks again. I really appreciate it, Tony."

"Well, I should get back." Tony stood up, hitching his thumb behind him toward the supply house.

"Yeah, I . . . I mean, we'll get out of your hair. Thanks again, and don't be a stranger."

"I won't," Tony said, meaning every word of it.

A week later, as Tony was in the midst of showing the cleaning crew which house he needed done, his boss, Ron, pulled into the job site and yelled from his truck, "Hey, Tancredi!"

"Yeah, Ron?" Tony yelled back.

"I need you to go over to Pine Run and do some work for me. The guy who was supposed to go didn't show up today. Lazy bastard."

"Sure, boss. Where do I need to go, and what do I need to do?" Tony asked.

"Here's the address. It's on Evergreen Street. Name's Diane Stanton. She called and says the cement in her fireplace is coming out, so she needs some pointing work done. You got it?"

"Yeah, boss, I got it."

Tony couldn't believe his luck. He was actually going to see Diane for more than a few brief moments in a driveway. He didn't know what to expect—if anything—but he was happy nonetheless. No, correction, he was ecstatic.

As Tony pulled the beat-up Ford into Diane's driveway, he tried to calm himself. His heart racing, he put the truck in park and leaned his head on the steering wheel. *Just get in, do your work, and get out*, Tony thought, taking deep breaths.

When he thought he was under control, he pushed himself up to a sitting position. He grabbed his tools and bucket of cement from the back of the truck, walked up to her front door, and rang the bell.

When Diane opened the door, her eyes widened in surprise.

"Tony? What are you doing here?"

"The guy who was supposed to show up didn't, so you get me." Tony smiled, trying very hard not to pay attention to the cutoff shorts and the too-little tube top that Diane was wearing.

God, she's gorgeous, Tony thought.

"Oh. Okay," Diane said, flustered. "Well, come on in. I'll show you what needs to be done." She stepped back from the door so Tony could enter.

"Gimme just a minute, would you?"

"No problem," Tony said.

While she was gone, Tony took in the house—the fresh flowers sitting on the kitchen table, magazines stacked neatly on the coffee table, the carpet that still had vacuum lines in it, and the faint hint of lemon.

When Diane reappeared with a baby in her arms, Tony tried not to let his disappointment show.

"Who's this little guy?" Tony asked.

"My son, Matthew," she replied, rubbing the baby on the back. "Here's what needs to be done." Diane brushed past him into the living room and pointed to where cement was indeed falling away.

"This'll be easy," Tony said, running his hands over the surface.

Tony bent, taking his time to blend the cement and water. He stood and slathered the mixture on the pieces of fireplace that were coming unglued.

The baby began to whimper.

"You okay in here, Tony? I gotta go get the baby his bottle."

"Yeah, I'm good, Di," Tony replied, then mentally cursed himself for using her name so casually.

When Tony was satisfied that he had applied enough of the mixture, he went over it with a trowel, smoothing the cement so it was even with the rest of the fireplace. When he was finished, he stood back and surveyed his work.

It had taken all of twenty minutes to accomplish. Sighing, he picked up his bucket and trowel and headed into the kitchen.

"All done," Tony said from the doorway. "Good as new."

"Thanks so much, Tony," Diane replied, glancing over her shoulder from the sink, where she was running a bottle under cold water. "I swear I'll never figure out how long to heat these things."

Tony smiled, put down his bucket, but said nothing.

Just then, the baby spat up on Diane's shoulder.

"Oh crap. Tony, could you hand me a paper towel?" Diane asked, glancing back.

"Sure," Tony said, walking over to the opposite counter. At the same moment that Tony ripped the towel off the roll and turned to hand it to Diane, she turned away from the sink and toward Tony, effectively bringing them within inches of each other.

Impulsively, Tony leaned in and kissed Diane on the lips.

Diane stepped back, eyes wide.

"What the hell are you doing?" Diane said.

Tony put his hands up and backed away.

"Diane, I'm so sorry. I don't know why I did that. You gotta believe me. I've never done anything like that in my life. Please. I'm really sorry."

"What kind of woman do you think I am? Who the hell do you think you are anyway? I could have you fired for this."

Tony put his hands down and picked up his equipment.

Tony couldn't look at her, but he had to ask. "So are you gonna get me fired?"

"No, Tony, I'm not."

Tony left, closing the front door softly behind him.

Two days later, Ron came up to Tony and said, "I need you to go over to the supply house and pick up a couple of things."

"Well, I would, Ron," Tony said, "but I don't want this mud to dry before I get the windowsills in, so I gotta get to it now. So I don't really think—"

Ron put up his hand as if to stop traffic. "Save it, Tancredi. I don't know what the hell's goin' on, or why you're suddenly not interested in goin' to Pine Run, but I need some shit from the supply house, and everyone else is just as busy as you are, so you're it. Take the truck and be back as soon as possible. Got it?"

"Got it," Tony replied, his shoulders sagging. He took his time cleaning the trowel, then laid it facedown so that it was perched precariously on the bucket.

"Tancredi! Damn, let's go already. Jesus!"

"Yeah, I'm comin', Ron."

Unable to prolong the inevitable, Tony trotted to his boss, grabbed the keys, and jogged to the truck.

Ironically, as Tony turned onto Evergreen Street, Diane was in the same position she had been the first time Tony had seen her—on her knees, hands in the dirt, gardening.

At the sound of the old truck, Diane turned and waved at Tony. He waved back.

"Ah shit," he muttered.

Tony continued past Diane's house and pulled into the driveway of the supply house. After parking, Tony jumped out. Diane called to him from her yard.

"Hey, Tony . . . come here a minute, would you?"

"Great," Tony said, looking up at the sky. "Just what I need." He wondered if he could get away with pretending that he hadn't heard her, and decided that he couldn't. He walked slowly toward her house. When he got close, he stood at the edge of her lawn.

Diane walked down to meet him, taking her gardening gloves off as she did so. "Walk me to the door?" Diane asked.

Tony nodded and fell into step with her.

"Tony, why don't you come over to the supply house anymore? Or when you do, why don't you wave to me? Say hello?"

"I would think the answer is pretty obvious, Diane," he said, looking at the ground.

She stopped on the small front stoop and cocked her head, a quizzical expression on her face.

With her arms crossed, she said, "But I told you it was okay, that it was fine."

Tony continued to stare at his feet. Had he been five-years-old, he would have dug his toe into the ground like a kid who had been caught in a lie.

"Yeah, okay," Tony said, turning to walk away.

"And, Tony?"

He sighed and turned around. Diane stood inside her front door, a smile playing on her lips.

"By the way, that kiss? It wasn't so bad."

With those words, she closed the door, leaving Tony standing on her walkway, utterly perplexed.

TONY TANCREDI AND CINDY L. O'HARA

SIX

AS TONY DROVE home from work Friday afternoon, he puzzled over Diane's last remark. What the hell did it mean?

Although he was still excited about going to the club that night, he also had to admit that it had lost some of its appeal. If Diane was truly interested, all of a sudden, the potential trim that would be available to him wasn't so important.

Miles later, he pulled up to his house, but he still didn't have any answers.

"So," Laura started, looking at her husband, "what's wrong?"

"Huh?" Tony answered. "I'm sorry, honey . . . what did you say?"

"I said, what . . . is . . . wrong?" Laura drew out the words.

Tony snapped out of his reverie. "What makes you think anything's wrong?"

"Oh, I dunno," Laura said. "Maybe it's the half-glazed expression in your eyes when I'm talkin' to you, like you're a thousand miles away, or the way you're just staring down into your plate of spaghetti instead of eating with your normal frenzy—you know, little clues like that."

"I'm sorry, babe," Tony apologized, laying down his fork that still had noodles twined around it. He looked at the utensil as if seeing it for the first time, never remembering having scooped up the pasta in the first place.

Oh boy, Tony thought, *I'm really losing it.*

"I'm just tired, that's all," he said, still contemplating the food in front of him.

"Are you sure?" Laura asked, reaching out and touching her husband's forearm. "'Cuz it seems like there's more to it than just bein' tired, like you have the weight of the world on your shoulders. I gotta tell you, Tony, I'm worried about you." Laura looked at her husband, her eyebrows knitted together in concern, and worry clouding her eyes.

"Honey, I'm fine," Tony assured her, finally looking up. He didn't really believe the lie he had just told, but he hoped she'd buy it. "I just . . . I guess I don't like how late I've been getting home from the club, and I don't want to do that tonight. You've been so good about it, and I guess I'm feelin' a little guilty."

"Oh," said Laura, removing her arm from Tony's and sitting back in her chair.

"Well, as long as you call me from the club and tell me you're gonna be late, I don't mind if you stay and have a couple of drinks to wind down."

"Well, you know, Joe *has* asked me to stay a couple of times, and I've always said no, until last week when I felt obligated to stick around. You know, I just don't want him to take my refusals the wrong way," Tony replied, once again playing with the pasta on his plate.

"Yeah, okay, I get it," Laura said. "You should stay for a while after work. It's fine, really." Laura smiled, leaning forward and patting Tony's arm.

"It's not like you're out sleepin' around, right?" She smiled and laughed, digging into her spaghetti with renewed gusto.

Tony jerked his head up, realizing that Laura had been teasing him. He smiled back at his wife of five years and wished he could share the joke.

That night, as Tony kissed Laura on the cheek and left for the club, he felt guilty for fantasizing about Diane. The emotion was so completely foreign to him that at first, he couldn't put a finger on what it was, or why he was so down. Normally, he was bouncing out the door. After all, he'd had too many girlfriends to count and had rarely been faithful to any of them, so why should this be any different? he asked himself. But Laura *was* different. She was such a good person, and he had hoped that this time, he'd be able to change. So far, though, he was down for the count—with both girlfriends and the wife.

When Tony pulled into the Shamrock's parking lot (his head so filled with thoughts about Diane and Laura that he had taken to talking to himself out loud on the way), he headed straight for what he had come to think of as *his* spot.

He took one last look in the side view mirror and adjusted his tie. He opened the door and carefully stepped out, adjusting his pant legs as he stood up and tugging the bottom of his suit coat and sleeves. Satisfied that he was wrinkle-free and well-pressed, he strode purposefully toward the club—all thoughts of Diane and Laura gone.

As Tony walked through the steel double doors, an imposing large man blocked his way. Not fat, necessarily, but definitely thick. Tony put him at six-foot-four and somewhere around 250 or 260 bills.

"Hey, Ton," Greg greeted Tony, who had to inch his way around the man. "I'd like you to meet Doc. Last name's not important." Greg smiled from his spot behind the bar.

The big man turned and extended his hand toward Tony as he walked up. "I've already heard a lot about you. Nice to meet ya."

"Yeah," Tony said. "Likewise. As big as you are, maybe there won't be as many fights around here."

"Yeah, well, we'll see," Doc said, breaking the handshake. "Hey, Greg, I'm gonna go take a leak. I'll be right back."

As Doc walked away, Tony found himself curious about the name. "So, Greg, what's up with his name?"

Greg smiled and said, "He got that because when he comes to see you, you're usually gonna need a doctor when he's done."

Tony looked at the man's retreating back, nodded, and smiled. Doc was his kind of guy.

Over the next hour, the rest of the staff and bouncers straggled in—some still hungover from the night before, but most ready to face the night ahead.

"All right, guys," said Greg. "I'm sure everyone has met our new doorman and all-around bouncer, Doc. So let's get things set up on the ramp."

Just as Tony and some other bouncers started readying the club for the regular Friday-night crowd, Sam's black Lincoln pulled up to the front, presumably with Joe in the backseat. Doc lumbered over and opened the back door for Joe. The two men shook hands, and to Tony's surprise, Joe clapped Doc on the shoulder as if greeting an old friend. By this time, Sam had gotten out and been included in the tight circle. To Tony, the three men appeared well acquainted. As many answers as Tony got to questions he had about the club and its personnel, a dozen more popped up each night he was there. Like a good soldier, though, he knew enough not to ask.

"Hey, Sam," Tony said.

"Hey, Ton, how's it hangin'?"

"Oh, you know, a little of this and a little of that . . ."

"Yeah, I know whatcha mean." Sam laughed and moved toward the bar.

"Hey, Sam, I kinda' got a situation goin', on and I want to talk about it, see what you think."

"Sure, Ton, anytime. Take a walk with me to the back room," Sam said, smiling, the ever-present toothpick doing its shuffle.

Tony often wondered if he kept the same toothpick in the entire day and night, or if he switched them after a few hours. He'd never actually *seen* Sam take it out, and Tony didn't think it a good idea to ask. You never knew what was going to set Sam off.

"So this woman—"

"Don't most good stories start out that way? It's how they end that's a bitch."

"Yeah, well, anyway, this woman . . ." Tony continued to tell Sam from beginning to end about Diane, about the kiss, about how he had avoided her for an entire week, their last encounter, and, finally, Diane's enigmatic remark.

"This woman, she hot?"

"Hell, yeah," Tony replied, offended that his friend would think otherwise. "I don't fuck ugly women. You know that. In fact, this woman is so gorgeous that's she's way out of my league. Which is why what she said is so weird. She couldn't possibly be attracted to me. Could she?"

"I don't know, Ton," Sam said, all trace of humor gone. "There's no accountin' for taste. Maybe she's into ugly sons of bitches!" Sam laughed merrily.

Tony balled up his fist and cocked his right arm as if to hit his friend, but couldn't keep up the pretense because he was laughing so hard.

"Besides," Sam continued, "didn't you tell me something about bein' married when you started this job?"

"Hey, I've been pretty good so far. I turned down lots of pussy since I've been here."

"Yeah, but you haven't turned down *all* of it from what I'm hearin' around here."

"Well, I've turned down a lot more than you have. I don't think you've missed a turn yet. And how is *your* wife these days?"

"Hey, don't bring her into this. You only turn it down because you're so damn fussy." Sam turned at the sound of Joe calling his name.

"Time to get back to work, I guess."

Just after midnight, Greg handed Tony the bank so he could collect the cover charge from the customers. Tony looked down the thick line of people who were already standing around, waiting to be let in, amazed because by two, the throng would still snake down the length of the building and continue around the corner. Tony shook his head and got ready to start letting people in. Suddenly, he heard his name being called from the parking lot.

"Tony, come 'ere. I gotta talk to you," Laura yelled.

Just then, Greg clapped Tony on the shoulder, easing past him. "I got her Ton, just stay on the bank."

Greg then rushed up to Laura and led her inside. "You don't ever have to wait in line to see Tony. You're his wife. Come right in."

TONY TANCREDI AND CINDY L. O'HARA

"Thank you," Laura said, visibly shaking. As she neared Tony, she opened her mouth to speak, then abruptly closed it.

Tony knew then that something was terribly wrong.

"Tony, I'm sorry, your sister's been taken to the hospital. She's having trouble breathing. That's all I know."

"Holy Christ," Greg said. "Tony, get outta here and call us as soon as you can. Let us know what's going on. I'll tell Joe and Sam. If there's anything—I mean *anything*—we can do, let us know."

"Thanks, Greg, I appreciate it," Tony said, shoving the money he had collected at his friend.

Tony raced to his car, calling back for Laura to follow him. He wished he was already at the hospital and by his parents' side. He tore out of the lot, tires squealing, smelling the noxious residue of rubber and smoke.

He kept Laura in sight as she ran yellow lights and pushed speed limits as far as she dared. When they finally pulled up to the front of Northeastern Hospital, it was in a red zone reserved-for-emergency vehicles and authorized personnel. Before the car came to a stop, Tony jumped out, running, shouting back at Laura to park both cars.

When Tony pushed through the heavy hospital doors, a large woman dressed in white with a name tag that read "Joan" greeted him.

With no preamble or attempt at diplomacy, Tony yelled, "Marie Tancredi was just brought in here. Where can I find her?"

The woman calmly looked Tony up and down. "Well, let's start with what was the problem? Then I can tell you where she was taken and what floor."

"I don't know. My parents brought her here because she can't breathe! Listen, lady, I don't have time for this shit. Now where the hell is my sister?" Tony slammed his hands on the desk for emphasis, the loud *thwack* sending ripples through the coffee that was sitting by her papers.

"Oh yes, I see it here on the chart," she said instantly. "She's in cardio on the fourth floor."

Tony raced to the bank of elevators to the right of the desk, bobbing and weaving between visitors and patients as if he were a football player trying to make the winning touchdown. Finally, Tony skidded to a stop in front of the aluminum doors that would take him up to see his sister, his Marie. One opened just as Tony reached for the Up button. He stepped in and frantically punched the number 4, at the same time stabbing repeatedly at the button that would close the door. The trip took only seconds but felt like a lifetime.

When the doors slid open, Tony raced toward the nurses' station. His father leaned against the desk, badgering the nurse on call. Tony glanced to the right. His mother stood off to the side, nervously shifting from one foot to the other. One look at his mother's face told Tony all he needed to know—that this situation was far more critical than Laura had let on.

When Tony reached his parents, he grabbed his mother. "What do we know so far?"

Tears wet her eyes and threatened to spill over, but to her credit, she held on and kept them at bay.

"What we know is that she was having trouble breathing, and we brought her here to the hospital. They gave her oxygen and took her away, and that's *all* we know."

Tony turned to his father. He put a hand on the aging man's shoulder. "Dad, they only know what the doctors tell them. Don't keep asking them about Ree. They'll tell us as soon as they know."

Tony's father nodded and allowed himself to be led away to the waiting room.

In the small dimly lit room sat a dozen chairs, covered with faded, green fabric that did nothing to hide the stains. It was Tony's experience that chairs like these decorated hospital waiting rooms across the country. Wholly uncomfortable, they reminded Tony too much of his childhood and how filled it was with memories of rooms just like the one he was in now. He wondered what the stains were, then decided that he really didn't want to know.

As the clock ticked by molasses-slow, the wait for information seemed interminable. At some point, Tony noticed, Laura had arrived, but he made no move to touch or greet her. He was too consumed with what was going on with his sister. Laura kept her distance, giving him the space he needed.

When he looked up again, Laura had her arm draped over his mother's shoulder and had pulled her into the crook of her neck, comforting her in the same way a mother comforts a child. Laura's lips moved softly as she did her best to calm his mother's fears and provide her some words of encouragement. For that, he was grateful.

Less than an hour after he had arrived upstairs, a doctor who looked ten years Tony's junior walked up to the family, a clipboard in his hand. Tony leaped up and met the doctor halfway, ignoring the outstretched hand.

"Hello, I'm Dr. Sharif," the young man in white said. "Let's get right down to it." He looked at Mary and Anthony, and the couple stood.

TONY TANCREDI AND CINDY L. O'HARA

"Your daughter Marie has blood clots near her heart, and we're going to have to operate as soon as we can."

Mary's hand flew to her mouth, and she sank into Laura.

"Doctor, she's only twenty-two, how can she have blood clots?" Tony asked. "Isn't that something that usually happens in older people?"

"Yes, but she told us she's been taking birth control pills. The jury's still out, but some studies indicate that they can cause clots. What I need you to understand is that this is a very serious operation, and we need to get started as soon as possible. If you could sign these forms, we can begin."

He handed the clipboard to Tony, who looked it over before passing it to his father.

His father signed his name and handed the papers back. "Doctor, what are her chances?"

Tony had never heard his father's voice shake except in anger. In fear, it took on a whole new meaning. Tony realized he hated the tenor of that voice.

"Sir, I'm not going to mince words. She's young and strong, and that's in her favor. I would say she's got a 60 or 70 percent chance of making it."

The older man nodded and shuffled toward his wife and daughter-in-law. He made no move to sit down, however.

Satisfied that it would be all right to leave his family for a few moments, Tony strode after the doctor, who was deep in conversation with a nurse.

"Excuse me, Dr. Sharif, how long do you think this operation will take?"

The nurse murmured something to the doctor and quietly left.

"It's hard to say, Mr. Tancredi. We won't know until we get in there. If I had to hazard a guess, I would say anywhere from four to six hours. Now if you'll excuse me?"

"Thank you, Doctor. Oh, one more thing—"

"Yes, Mr. Tancredi?" the doctor asked through gritted teeth. Tony knew he was trying the doctor's patience but didn't care. "I know I don't have to tell you this, but please give it your best and keep us updated every chance you get."

"Of course. Now I have to go."

As minutes stretched into hours inside the hideous waiting room, Tony pondered his life and where it was headed. He thought it appropriate that the room he was sitting in smelled of death and despair. Everything seemed so unimportant now. He sat with his head down, elbows propped on his knees, fingers interlaced, contemplating some crumbs littering the pale beige carpet. When he finally looked up at his family, he saw that they too were all staring into space, lost in their own thoughts, probably contemplating the same things he was.

After what seemed like days, but were actually only six hours, the doctor emerged from the operating room, the starch white uniform he went into surgery with now a coat of red. Tony knew it was his sister's blood. He froze, unable to speak or move.

"Oh dear God!" Mary screamed, rising halfway out of her seat.

"Ma'am, it's okay," the doctor said soothingly. "Marie's in recovery, and she's doing fine."

This time, all of Laura's strength couldn't keep his mother from collapsing to the ground on her knees. Mary sat that way, rocking back and forth, unable and unwilling to get up.

Ignoring his mother for the moment, Tony jumped up from the chair and grabbed the doctor's still-gloved hand, realizing too late that it too was covered in Marie's blood. "Thanks, Doc. Thanks very much."

The doctor placed his other hand atop Tony's. "Your sister did great. She's a strong young lady and lucky to have a family who cares so much about her."

Tony's eyes filled with tears at the words.

"You can see her in about an hour. I'll come and get you when it's time."

Only after the doctor was gone did Tony allow himself to hope that things might turn out all right after all.

TONY TANCREDI AND CINDY L. O'HARA

SEVEN

T HE PINE RUN development, muddy after so much rain, licked at Tony's truck as he pulled up to one of the unfinished homes.

He sat for a minute, pondering whether to eat lunch in the truck or get out and go find the rest of the crew. After weeks of making daily trips to the hospital, Tony found it difficult to make the easiest of decisions.

Just then, one of the blocklayers appeared at the driver's-side window.

"Hey, Ton, why don't you come and eat out back with us instead of sittin' out here worryin' about everything?"

"Yeah, what the hell. Let's go."

Tony and the man next to him (for the life of him, he couldn't remember the man's name) shuffled along to where the rest of the crew was eating, trying hard to stay atop the planks that had been laid down as a pathway for the workers.

"So how is Marie doin'?"

"Oh, ya know, it's just a day-to-day thing. Tryin' to put one foot in front of the other, man. Know what I mean?" Tony answered.

"Yeah, I do."

"We're hopin' she'll be home soon."

"Huh. Well, I hope everything works out for her and your family, man."

With nothing left to say, Tony and the blocklayer walked on and joined the rest of the crew for lunch.

Tony looked at his watch and stood.

"Well, guys, I hate to break up this little party, but I gotta get back to work."

"Yeah, okay, Ton. We're right behind you."

He thought after having eaten that he'd feel better, but instead, he felt more tired than he had when he sat down.

It's all this damn running around, Tony thought. *It's killing me.*

Then Tony stopped.

"What the hell," he muttered. "Marie's sittin' in a hospital bed, and I'm sittin' here complainin' about how tough I got it. What an ass."

Just as abruptly, Tony forgave himself his egotism. Tony knew that his thoughts came from a place of helplessness and guilt over his own childhood illness and all that his parents had already been through. Now Marie was in the same place, a victim of circumstance. Just like he had been.

So quit acting like you're *the one suffering,* a voice whispered.

"Yeah, you're right," Tony muttered again to no one in particular.

One who was not complaining, Tony realized, was Laura.

Strangely, the stress of the situation helped him to appreciate Laura and all that she did for him and his family. He didn't know what he would do without her. When she wasn't working at the bank or tending to the boys, she was cooking extra meals to take to his parents or stopping by to straighten up their house.

At home, Tony noticed extra bags of fresh fruits and vegetables, milk, and bread and butter that he knew she would later drop off to fill his mother's refrigerator. On days when she was going to the hospital, Tony knew she was sure to include one or both of his parents by picking them up on her way, or dropping them off on her way home. Tony marveled at her stamina, often jealous that she seemed to be managing everything so effortlessly. He, on the other hand, was struggling at both his day and evening jobs.

Because he had to juggle his time at the current construction site and the hospital, Tony found his relationship with his supervisor, Ron, quickly heading south.

The club was different. He felt closer to the men there than he had to anyone in a long time.

He looked forward to going to the club more than ever, often wondering on his drive there what hapless idiot would invoke his rage. And no one at the club ever said anything, thus giving him permission to let loose on the clientele—as long as it was justified.

Tony recognized that his temper and anger were taking on a life of their own. Like a giant balloon, he knew that unless something changed, he was going to pop.

As he entered the hospital later that evening, Tony told himself that he had to get a grip, if only for a few moments in front of his sister. But when he pushed open the door to the room, Tony knew that today would not be that day.

Marie sat up in bed, her brown hair fanned out against her pillow, framing a face that blended with the whiteness of the sheets and pillowcases because of its paleness. Tears coursed down her cheeks.

Tony immediately hurried to her bedside and sat down, all weariness gone.

"Ree, what's wrong?" Tony asked, taking her hand in his. He was shocked by how cold it was.

"Oh, Tony, a male nurse had to take some blood today . . ."

"Ree, that's their job. That's what they have to do."

Marie shook her head in frustration. "Don't you think I know that by now?"

The sting of her words was like a slap in the face. "Ree, I'm sorry—"

"No, *I'm* sorry, Tony. They've taken blood before, and it's never really hurt, but this guy kept digging into my arm. Just digging, digging, digging, and it felt as if he was chopping up every vein in there with a blunt knife. God, it hurt so bad!" she cried, tears streaking her face.

"He told me I was a big baby."

"Ree, what's this guy's name? What's he look like?" Tony asked quietly, pulling at a stray fuzz on the blanket covering her legs.

"Tony, don't do anything stupid. I'm sure it was nothing. Besides, I don't know his name."

"Then what does this guy look like?"

Marie looked away. "He's about your height, but Spanish-looking. That's all I know."

"Marie, I gotta go, but I'll be back tomorrow."

"Tony, please." Marie grabbed his hand.

"Ree, I'm gonna make sure this guy never comes into your room again, but I need you to do me a favor and not say anything to anyone about this. Okay?"

Marie nodded silently.

Tony kissed his sister's forehead. "Get some rest, Ree. I'll see you tomorrow."

"Okay," she whispered, sinking back into her pillows and closing her eyes.

Tony watched his sister for a moment, and then closed the door softly as he left. His next stop was the nurses' station, where he asked the nurse on duty who had been in his sister's room earlier taking her blood.

"Let's see, Mr. Tancredi . . . that would be Mr. Flores," she answered, looking through a stack of papers that were pinned down by a clipboard.

"Do you know where he is right now by any chance?"

The nurse looked up at Tony quizzically, the clipboard in her hand.

"I just want to thank him personally for taking care of Marie. That's all." Tony smiled.

"Oh." The nurse relaxed. "He's on the fourth floor finishing his rounds, I believe."

"Thank you."

On the next floor, Tony systematically checked each room, looking for Mr. Flores. About halfway through his search, Tony overheard conversation from down the hall. Luckily, whoever was speaking was at the far end of the floor, away from the elevators and the nurses' station. Tony waited outside an empty room next door, hoping that Mr. Flores would work his way down, not up, thus passing Tony in the process.

Tony's luck held, and not a minute later, he saw a Hispanic man dressed in white, backing out of the room. As Flores turned to continue his rounds, he came face-to-face with Tony, almost running into him.

Looking surprised, Flores asked, "Can I help you?"

The accent was soft, almost unnoticeable, Tony thought, taking in the Spanish man's height and weight in a matter of seconds.

"Yeah," Tony said. "I was wondering if I could talk to you for a few minutes. I'm Marie Tancredi's brother. You took her blood today?"

"Oh sure," Flores answered. "I remember her."

I bet you do, Tony thought.

"How can I help you?" Flores asked, looking puzzled.

"Our business is best done in private," Tony replied.

With one hand on the door to the room he was standing in front of, Tony quickly snaked his other hand onto the back of Flores's neck and guided the man in. Tony softly closed the door behind him, at the same time shoving the Hispanic man into the room. Flores's eyes widened in shock.

"What's this about?"

"Do you *like* hurting people, Mr. Flores?" Tony asked quietly, looking at the floor.

"Mr. Flores, I asked you a question."

Before he could respond, Tony grabbed the man's throat and slammed him against the wall so hard that the man's teeth chattered. Tony thought he might have left a mark on the wall with this one.

"If I *ever* find out that you were inside my sister's room again, or if you so much as breathe a word of this little encounter to anyone, someone will come back, and when he's done, even this hospital won't be able to help you," Tony whispered into Flores's ear. "You know what *I* look like, but you won't know the next one. Do I make myself clear?" Tony shook the man by his throat for emphasis.

TONY TANCREDI AND CINDY L. O'HARA

Flores nodded as much as he could, before Tony threw him to the floor and walked out of the room.

The following week, Marie started showing signs of improvement, giving Tony hope that she might actually make it out of the hospital sooner than expected.

It was with this thought in mind that Tony entered Marie's room one bright August morning.

"Hey, Ree, how ya doin'? You ready to get out of here yet?" Tony asked.

His sister looked up at him, smiling. "Nah, I think I'll stick around for a while longer. I kinda like the food. The chef here's better than you." Her eyes twinkled brightly—something Tony hadn't seen in weeks.

Tony liked seeing his sister smile. It was a good sign. He took in his sister's appearance, noting that she looked healthy. "I'm sorry I got here late, Ree," Tony said, leaning down to kiss her cheek. "But work, you know."

His sister waved away his apologies.

"How you doin', Ma?" Tony turned his attention to his mother, who was sitting by his sister's bed, holding her hand. His father was in a far corner chair, thumbing through the *Philadelphia Inquirer*.

Before she could answer, Marie's surgeon stepped into the room.

"Mr. and Mrs. Tancredi? I was wondering if I could speak to you a moment."

Both Tony's mother and father looked up.

"Sure, Doc," Tony's father said, smiling. "Talk away."

The doctor cleared his throat. "I think it best if we speak outside."

His father's face fell. "Mom, Dad, stay here. I'll do this."

Tony then walked to the door, opened it, and stepped through. When both men were outside the room, Tony looked the surgeon straight in the eye, bracing himself for the bad news to come. He knew that nothing good ever came from having to have a private conversation with a patient's doctor outside their room.

"So what's wrong?" Tony asked, dispensing with the preliminary bullshit that he suspected was coming.

"Mr. Tancredi, we've found new blood clots in Marie's legs, and because of their location and their size, we feel that removing her leg would be in her best interest, that ultimately it will be what will save her life. I'm sorry."

Tony was speechless.

"Do you have any questions?"

Tony could only shake his head. "Could you please come into the room and explain everything to my parents and my sister? I don't think—"

"Of course," the doctor said, squeezing Tony's shoulder.

Before Tony followed, he took a moment to get himself together. He looked up, took a deep breath, and let it out. Only moments ago, he had been so happy. He put his hand on the doorknob and stepped into the room.

When he entered the room, the doctor was explaining the procedure to his parents and sister.

Surprisingly, Marie remained still, not shedding a tear. Tony marveled at this. He couldn't tell whom he hurt for more, his sister or his parents. He swore to God that if things didn't change soon, he was going to snap. He didn't know how much longer he could hold it together—and he knew that he hadn't been doing all that great of a job to begin with.

"So, Doc, what's the next step?" Tony asked.

"Well, Mr. Tancredi, we'll take some more X-rays just to be sure we know what we're in for, get the results back, and go from there. We should know more in a couple of days."

"So there's a *chance* that you, um, might not have to operate?"

"There's always a chance, Mr. Tancredi, but as trite as it might sound, I always tell people to expect the worst and hope for the best. I'm sorry I couldn't deliver better news." He turned toward Marie. "You're going to be fine, young lady, one way or another."

For the first time, tears filled her eyes.

Two days later, Tony and his family were back in Marie's room, waiting to hear what the doctor had to say.

When the doctor finally walked in, his eyes locked on Tony. "I'll get right to it. The X-rays showed that we do not have to remove Marie's leg, but we will still have to operate to remove the blood clots."

Tony turned to his father and grabbed him in a bear hug.

After a few moments, however, Tony broke the embrace, clapping his father loudly on the back. When Tony looked around the room, Laura and his mother were doing the same.

"Ahem," the doctor cleared his throat.

Tony had forgotten he was still there.

"While that news is good, there, unfortunately, is more."

The small amount of hope Tony had just been given, he knew, was going to be shattered by whatever the doctor said next. *Damn*, he thought, *why can't we catch a friggin' break lately?*

TONY TANCREDI AND CINDY L. O'HARA

"What is it, Doc?" Tony asked, stuffing his hands in his pockets, waiting.

"The operation is still risky because in order to remove the blood clots but keep the leg, we need to stop giving Marie heparin, the blood thinner that is currently preventing her from getting more blood clots."

"And why do you need to stop giving her the heparin?"

"Because if we don't, she'll bleed to death on the operating table. Look, folks, here's the problem—put simply, we have to stop giving Marie the very thing that is preventing her from forming more clots so she won't bleed out during surgery. However, by stopping the drug, more clots may form. It's a chance we have to take, though. We have to treat what's going on right now and worry about what may happen later. Any questions?"

"No, Doc, you've been perfectly clear. Can you give us a few minutes?"

"Of course," the doctor said, turning to go.

"Oh, Doc, one thing. When would you operate?"

"Tomorrow, Mr. Tancredi." He turned and continued out the door.

No one said a word. There was really nothing to say.

For the next twenty-four hours, Tony and his family became fixtures in the waiting room—a place he hoped he would never be a part of again.

When it was time for Marie to go into surgery, Tony and his family squeezed into her room. His mother whispered words of encouragement while his father just touched her hair, her face, her hand.

At the last minute, Tony bent down and whispered into his sister's ear. "You're going to do great, kid. When you get outta here, I'm going to give you the biggest damn party Philly's ever heard of!"

He squeezed her shoulder and allowed the nurse to wheel her away.

Later that day, the doctor came out of the surgical room, declaring the operation a success. When pressed, he said Marie had done well enough that he thought she would be able to go home sooner than expected.

For the first time since this whole sorry mess had started, Tony felt the tiniest glimmer of hope that his sister would get out of the hospital alive.

EIGHT

THE NEXT DAY, Tony returned to the construction site where temperatures that stretched into the nineties made the sweat roll off his body in sheets. As he picked up the plastic gallon to chug water from, a car came speeding through the site. It braked to a stop so quickly that dust rose. After the dust settled, Laura's car appeared.

Puzzled, he stared as his wife and sons got out of the car, all of them weeping. The jug slipped from his hand, the water cascading and splashing his boots and feeding the dry, dusty earth.

Tony knew then that Marie had died.

Tony's knees buckled, and he fell to the ground. Tony's chin dropped to his chest as if his head was too heavy to be held upright. Tears coursed down his face. His shoulders hunched and shuddered as he let his grief take its toll. For a moment, that morning's breakfast of Cheerios started to snake its way up from his stomach to his throat, but thankfully, he was able to shove them back down into his gullet. Tony shook his head, as if by doing so, it would cheat death and bring his sister back to life. When he had nothing left, he rose and dragged his feet toward Laura, the tears continuing to stream down his sunburned cheeks.

When they came together, Laura touched Tony's hand. "Do you need to sit down again?"

Tony shook his head, still unable to speak. He took a deep breath and blew it out. "Let's just go. I need to be with my parents."

Laura, Tony, and the boys then headed to the hospital. Silence filled the car.

The ride seemed endless to Tony. Normally, he would have insisted on driving her car or taken his own, but when she had asked if he wanted to drive, his answer was to get in the passenger seat.

Worried, Laura continued to glance back and forth from the street to Tony.

Laura pulled up to the front entrance of Northeast Hospital to let Tony out. Almost before the car came to a stop, he had the door open and his foot skating along the ground, waiting for the car to come to a halt.

When Laura stopped, Tony pushed himself up and out and wordlessly slammed the door. With the car idling behind him, Tony slowly but determinedly walked up to the place that had just changed his life forever. Like some monster's gaping mouth, the hospital doors slid silently open, engulfing Tony.

He headed to the now-familiar bank of elevators, in no hurry to get to where he was going, and pushed the button for the fourth floor. As the elevator came to rest at his stop and the doors parted, the first thing Tony noticed was that he could see into Marie's room. The second thing was that her face hadn't been covered. In fact, it appeared as if she was simply sleeping. She looked that serene and peaceful. The grief Tony had been able to keep in check flooded through him, and he ran from the elevator to his sister's room, bumping into interns and nurses, almost knocking over a cart of something—he didn't know what, didn't care.

When he arrived by Marie's bedside, Tony leaned over the bed and took his dead sister in his arms. Her skin against his felt cold and doughy. Her arms hung limply by her sides like the arms of some large rag doll.

"Marie, I love you so much," Tony whispered, hugging her to him. He kissed her face, her closed eyes, her lips. "And I'm so, so sorry. I'm sorry I haven't been here for you, that I couldn't help you."

"Mr. Tancredi?" A nurse gently placed a hand on Tony's arm. "May I cover her up now?"

Tony looked blankly at the nurse, unable to process the words coming out of her mouth. He looked at her, and then gazed back at his sister lying lifeless in his arms. Reality washed over Tony like a cold shower, and he shook his head. Marie was dead. He remembered that now.

"Not yet, please," Tony answered, tenderly laying his sister on her bed. Tony sat, holding Marie's hand and talking to her for the better part of half an hour before covering her up.

When he was finished, he called for a nurse. He stood, looking down at his sister. Silently he turned away. He had said everything he needed to say.

From the doorway, Tony watched the young intern with curly black hair roll Marie to the elevator that would take her to the morgue. As the doors slid silently closed, Tony whispered a final good-bye and headed to the waiting room to see the rest of his family.

After an hour of hugging and comforting one another in the cold, sterile sitting area, Tony decided it was time to leave and started herding everyone toward the elevators.

Once downstairs, he announced that he would be going back to his mother and father's house, and that everyone should follow him back there to discuss arrangements. No one questioned Tony's direction and authority, and if anyone had been asked, they would have said they were thankful someone was making the decisions. Tony knew he had to be businesslike now. Weeping and grieving would have to wait. The problem was that his brain and his body weren't on the same page.

Mentally, Tony mulled over the things that needed to be done for Marie—the flowers, the casket, and the cards that had to be ordered—yet he was so damn exhausted. He didn't know how he was going to get through this and remain sane. In fact, sanity was so far out of reach that he couldn't even fathom it. He knew he was on shaky ground, and that he had to hang on for his mother and his father, but a part of him craved to dive into the deep, dark hole of depression that was calling him, staring at him with its open mouth and welcome relief of solitude and quiet, where no one needed anything or wanted anything from him. Tony knew it was just a matter of putting one foot in front of the other, that people were depending on him; but right now, it all seemed so monumentally overwhelming, and truth be told, he didn't give a damn.

As he and Laura drove back to his parents' house, Tony wondered why God would choose to inflict such pain and suffering on such good, hardworking people. It just didn't seem fair. Hadn't his parents paid their debt to God threefold with Tony's birth and all that they'd had to endure? Then again, when doctors had said Tony would probably be crippled for the rest of his life? Hadn't his parents been through enough? This was the second child God had taken from them. This was too much. It was just too much.

Tony shook his head as if to rid the thoughts from his mind, but they just kept coming, coming, coming even as the car rolled along to his parents' home.

Like high-speed pictures from a camera, unbidden images and thoughts swirled through Tony's head—of Marie as a child, of him and his sister laughing in a park, and then of Marie lying cold and dead in a hospital room—so that he felt nauseous and dizzy.

"Tony, are you okay?" Laura asked, concern lacing her question.

"Yeah, why do you ask?" Tony replied, never taking his eyes from the passenger-side window.

"Because for a minute there, you looked as white as a sheet."

"I'm fine, Laura. I mean, I'm just peachy for just having lost a sister."

Laura remained silent the rest of the way.

When she pulled up to the curb, Tony looked at the place that held so many fond memories for him—and not just him but for everyone in his family. In the past, and even now, relatives always ended up at this house for holidays or special events. He knew they would still come, but now there was a void, and he knew that nothing would ever fill it.

Tony sighed and pushed open the car door. The queasiness he had felt earlier had subsided, although it still lingered somewhere between his stomach and his throat. He tried not to think about it as he slowly climbed the four steps. He paused on the porch before opening the screen door. Laura and the boys trailed after him.

"Dad, Mom?" Tony called out.

Tony's father appeared, a dishtowel in his hand, slowly, almost absentmindedly, drying a teacup. Both puzzled and curious because for the life of him, Tony had never seen his father pick up a towel, let alone dry a dish, he asked, "Whatcha doin', Dad?"

"What's it look like I'm doin'? I'm drying a cup for some tea for your mom. She's upstairs lying down. Come on in." He turned and walked into the kitchen.

Tony followed his father. "Hey, Dad, when you're done with that, I thought we could go to Dejaccomo's Funeral Home and start making some arrangements for Marie."

The only indication that his father had heard was a slight nod, which, had he not been looking, Tony would have missed.

Dejaccomo's had been in the neighborhood ever since Tony could remember. His father and Mr. Dejaccomo (as a child, Tony never knew the man's first name, and so he would forever be Mr. Dejaccomo) had been friends for years, had grown up and gone to school together.

On the rare occasion when Tony had to attend a funeral for one of his father's friends or a relative, he remembered Dejaccomo's as a plain small brick building, with only a few rooms inside.

The funeral home that Tony and his father drove up to now, however, was a large Tudor-style building dressed in white, with two columns holding up a covered walkway.

Business must be good, Tony thought sarcastically, still unable to comprehend that he was here.

The two men stepped through the double doors and waited as a bell chimed softly in the background.

Within seconds, a smaller-than-he-remembered, well-dressed man appeared.

Tony had met Mr. Dejaccomo on many occasions as a boy, both at his parents' house and in the funeral home, but thought it funny meeting him again as an adult. At the time, in his child's-eye view, Mr. Dejaccomo had seemed so tall and robust, but standing in front of him now was an older gentleman of average height and build, with dark hair and clean-shaven olive-tinted skin, dressed immaculately in a dark blue three-piece suit.

"Hey, Angie," Tony's father greeted his old friend with the pet name he had been allowed to use for years, opening his arms wide. Everyone else Dejaccomo associated with, however, knew better and referred to him by his full name of Angelo—when allowed.

The two men embraced. Then Dejaccomo took his friend's face in his hands and kissed each cheek soundly. Embarrassed to be witness to such a private moment, Tony looked away and eyed the funeral parlor, taking in the tasteful, muted décor, the plush carpet, and the fresh flowers that seemed to be everywhere, their sickly sweet scent filling Tony's nose and wreaking havoc with his already-questionable stomach.

Tony wandered away from his father. After a few minutes, Tony drifted back, just in time to hear Mr. Dejaccomo expressing his condolences.

"I heard the news, Antonio," Dejaccomo said, addressing the elder Tancredi in a thick Italian accent that, Tony noted, had not lost its richness over the years. "And I am so very, very sorry. They are just words, I know, and they won't bring Marie back, but I wanted you to know that me and my family are sick with sorrow."

The small man gripped his friend's hands in his. When Tony looked from his father to Mr. Dejaccomo, he saw that tears shone brightly in both of their eyes.

Tony's father sniffed loudly and nodded.

"I appreciate that, Angie, and I know you and Teresa thought of my daughter as one of your own. That means the world to me, to us, you know."

Dejaccomo listened and nodded.

"Look, Angie, we don't have a lot of money, but I want the best I can afford for Marie. I wouldn't normally ask for anything, but money's a little tight, you know?" Tony's father looked down at the carpet and away from the small Italian man.

"Hey, Antonio?" Dejaccomo said softly. When Tony's father still did not look up, Dejaccomo repeated it, a little more loudly. "Hey," he said sharply.

TONY TANCREDI AND CINDY L. O'HARA

Tony held his breath and waited. No one spoke to his father in that tone of voice. Not family, and certainly not friends. Amazingly, however, Tony's father looked up, like a small child who had stumbled upon the reality that the world was a cruel and bitter place. Like a deflated balloon, all signs of caring gone, the elder Tancredi lifted his head slightly and looked at his friend.

"Antonio, don't you worry. Marie will have the very best, and even if you had all the money in the world and tried to shove it in my hand, I wouldn't accept a dime from you." Dejaccomo wagged a finger at his friend.

"I don't know what to say, Angie."

"Hey, this is not for you. This is for Marie. So as sad an event as this is, we are going to send her off in style. Yeah?"

"Thank you, Angie. Thank you very much."

The funeral parlor owner waved his hand. "No thanks are necessary, Antonio. Now let's go see what we can find." With that, Tony and his father followed Dejaccomo to the back room to pick out a casket for Marie.

On the drive home with his father, Tony inadvertently passed the Shamrock Club, not realizing that the club was only half a mile from the funeral home. Tony made a mental note to call Greg and let him know what had happened. He knew that he should stop and tell everyone in person, maybe even have a drink or two, but he just didn't have the energy.

Silence filled the car, and yet it was louder than anything Tony had ever heard. The unspoken words between him and his dad screamed volumes, yet it was not entirely uncomfortable. If not for the circumstances, Tony would have thoroughly enjoyed this time with his father.

When they arrived back home, Tony called Greg at the club and told him what was going on.

Yes, Tony said, he was fine, and no, he didn't need anything, but thanks anyway—just some time off.

After hanging up, Tony didn't know what to do. Everything had been taken care of at the funeral home, his mother was still asleep, and his father had gone upstairs to join her. Laura and the boys had gone home as well, so there was really nothing to do. Tony decided he would try to get some sleep. Within minutes of lying down on his mother's sofa, his eyelids started to droop. His last thought before he gave in to sleep was not of Marie, but of Diane.

From somewhere in his dream, a doorbell rang—which was strange, he thought, because his dream was of the beach. *Where the hell would a door be on the beach?*

As Tony struggled to rise to the surface through the waves of dreams and sleep, he realized that the sound he heard was someone ringing the doorbell of his parents' house. When Tony glanced at the clock, it read an hour later than when he had lain down. He felt like it had been only minutes.

Rubbing his eyes with one balled-up fist and wondering who the hell was ringing the bell, he stumbled to the front door. Jerking it open, Tony started to rant, but fell silent at the sight. In front of him stood Greg, Monte, and a handful of other bouncers from the Shamrock.

"What the—"

"Ahem," Greg cleared his throat. "We're all real sorry about you and your family's loss, Ton. I don't know if it's a good time or not, but we all wanted to stop by and give our condolences." A murmur of assent rose from the men surrounding Greg. Tony was touched beyond words. "Hey, you guys wanna come in? Have a beer or sumthin'?"

"Nah, Ton," Greg answered, smiling. "You and your parents got enough goin' on that you don't need a bunch of yahoos getting drunk in your livin' room."

Tony laughed and nodded. He hadn't realized how much he'd missed his coworkers.

As his friends turned away, Sam and Joe pulled up to the curb. Tony invited them in, and they accepted. After handing out cold beers, Tony took a seat opposite Joe in the living room and waited for him to speak.

"Tony, I wanted you to know how sorry I am for your loss. It's never easy losing a family member, even harder when it's your baby sister, I imagine."

Tony remained silent, fearing that to speak would start a flood of tears he couldn't stop. Instead, he gazed into the bottle of amber liquid in his hands.

Joe continued, "In honor of your family, I'm closing the club this weekend. I didn't want you to have to worry about working, or even think that was on my mind. That's really all I came here to tell you."

Tony was speechless. He knew that closing the club for a day, let alone an entire weekend, would cost Joe thousands of dollars.

"Joe, I don't know what to say. I'm touched, but really, you don't have to do that."

Joe got up from his chair and said, "Yeah, Tony, I do, and I did. It's done. That's what family does for one another. Thanks for the beer." Joe turned and walked out the front door, with Sam trailing after him.

It was minutes before the enormity of what Joe had just done hit Tony.

The next day found Tony running from the funeral parlor to his parents' house and back, trying to tie up loose ends. As he drove past the club on South Hampton Road, something caught his eye.

Curious, he pulled into the Shamrock's parking lot and up to the steel double doors. He stared in wonder at what was hanging there. Someone, presumably Joe, had hung a large wreath on the door. Across the wreath, a banner read "Closed Due to Death in the Family" in big, bold black letters.

Tony sat there, stunned. With his car idling and tears streaming down his face, he tried to pull himself together before heading to the funeral home. He knew then that he would be forever grateful to Joe for showing so much respect to a family he hardly knew.

NINE

TO TONY'S SURPRISE, many of the bouncers from the Shamrock arrived to help set up for the wake the following afternoon.

When they came in, they did so toting a wreath the size of a small man (both in height and width), bursting with dozens of pink, yellow, peach, and cream roses. Tony didn't know if Joe knew the flowers were Marie's favorite, but he suspected that he did. He had long stopped questioning how extensive Joe's knowledge was or how far his arm reached. With no time for pity or grief, Tony thanked the boys and helped to manhandle the massive wreath to a spot by the casket.

Once that task had been accomplished, Tony looked around—at the chairs that had been set up, the dark room that was given light by the hundreds of flowers blooming from dozens of arrangements, and, finally, Marie in her casket.

Tony walked over and looked down at his sister, lying quiet and peaceful. He still couldn't believe he was here. God, he missed her. He touched the white box and lightly ran his hand down the length of it. Yes, they had done well for his little sister. And wherever she was, Tony hoped she was without pain. He smiled and turned away.

After the wake, Tony found Joe at the entrance to the funeral home, shaking hands and talking to guests. Puzzled, Tony approached his boss.

"Joe, I just wanted to thank you for the wreath. You didn't have to do that. You've done too much already," Tony said.

"Tony, when are you going to understand that you are like family to me? In my opinion, the wreath wasn't enough, but it's a sad time for everyone, so I did what I thought I should—out of respect for you and your family. I hope I didn't overstep my bounds."

"No, no," Tony said hurriedly.

"Okay, then. I've invited all of your friends and family to the club for food and drinks after the wake. I understand this is a personal and very difficult time for you, but if you and your parents feel up to it . . ."

"Joe, I don't know what to say. Thank you. Thank you very much. Of course we'll c-c-c-ome," Tony stuttered.

"Good." Joe smiled, nodding his head slightly at Tony, while at the same time touching his fedora in respect. As Joe walked away, Tony's only thought was that someday maybe he could repay his boss.

For two weeks, Tony stayed at his parents' house and avoided the world. He refused to answer the phone, he didn't go to the club, he didn't go to the construction site, and he barely had enough strength to get out of bed. But despite being so goddamn tired, he soldiered on—for his parents' sake. When he told his father that he would be staying with them at their house, his father had tried to put up a fight, but Tony could see the relief in the older man's face. He had told his father it was so he could help, in case anyone needed anything, but Tony knew that staying with his parents was as much for him as it was for them, that he was taking solace from just being in the presence of his family; and after two weeks, he believed it might actually be working—for both of them.

Through Laura, Tony learned that Dave, the owner of the construction company, was becoming disgruntled that one of his best employees was not yet ready to get back to work, but Tony didn't give a rat's ass what the owner thought. He'd go back when he was goddamn well and ready, when it suited him, not when someone else thought he should.

"If Dave calls, tell him I'll be at work on Monday morning," Tony told Laura over the phone. "I'll call Ron too. Oh, and . . ."

"Yeah, Ton?"

"I'll be home tonight."

Tony could feel Laura's smile through the wires.

When Tony returned to the construction site the next day, the only thing that helped was Diane.

As perverse as it was, Tony couldn't wait to see her.

Fortunately, fate was on his side; and on his first day back, he had to run to the sample house for some supplies. This would, he hoped, give him the opportunity to see Diane.

He needn't have worried. The minute his truck pulled into the driveway, a door slammed from somewhere in the neighborhood. When he looked up, Diane raced down the sidewalk toward him.

Breathless from running the short distance, Diane said, "Tony, I'm so sorry to hear about your sister. Ron, your boss, told me. How are you doing?"

The concern in her face and eyes almost brought Tony to tears—not for Marie, but because people whom he barely knew continued to shower him with kindness. While Tony was thankful, accepting help or sympathy was not familiar to him, and so was uncomfortable.

"I'm okay—better than I was, I guess," Tony replied uneasily.

"Hey," Diane said, recognizing and easing Tony's apparent awkwardness. "I know you're in a hurry, but I'm making cheese steaks for lunch. Lemme get you one to take with you."

"Oh, don't do that," Tony started, but stopped because she had already turned and was running back to her house. Tony shook his head, sighed, and leaned in to hit the automatic garage door opener clipped to the driver's-side sun visor.

"Women," Tony muttered to no one in particular. He headed up the driveway and started loading supplies into the truck. When he had finished, Diane walked toward him at a more moderate pace, a brown paper bag in her hand.

"Here you go," she said, holding the sack out like a child offering a parent a present that she had worked especially hard on. The top of the bag was folded over precisely two times, and the lines were completely straight. He took the bag, their hands touching momentarily, sparking another short burst of electricity.

"Thanks, Di. I really appreciate this," Tony said.

"No problem," she answered. "If you like it, I'm having meatball sandwiches tomorrow." Without waiting for a reply, she turned and began the short walk home.

Tony stood in the driveway, watching her leave, shaking his head in puzzlement. Like most men, he thought if he lived to be a hundred, he would never understand women.

Back in his truck, he stared at the brown paper bag as if it contained a bomb. Tony sat for a moment, unsure whether to try the sandwich now or later. His stomach gave a loud rumble, effectively making the decision for him. *Can't hurt to take a bite*, Tony thought. Although he tended to be critical of other people's cooking, he found the sandwich quite tasty.

Go figure, the woman can also cook. He chuckled to himself as he pulled out of the driveway and headed back to the construction site with the supplies, the sandwich never making it back into its brown paper home.

Later that day and into the next, Tony worked tirelessly at the construction site, pushing his body beyond its limits, abusing it so he wouldn't think about Marie or his parents. When others took breaks from the unheard-of one-hundred-degree heat wave that plagued most of the northeast, he continued to work tirelessly at his many tasks. Whatever the job, Tony volunteered. He knew that the physical torture he was putting himself through was just a way of stopping the torment, of staving off the depression that seemed to be forever sitting there, waiting for him, calling to him like a siren.

Late Wednesday afternoon, he finally realized what had been eating at him all week. He had told Sam he would be back to work at the club tonight. On any other day, he would have been glad to be going, but Tony knew these men, and he knew the situation would be awkward. He thought the best thing to do would be to defuse any discomfort at once.

With this thought in mind, Tony walked into the club that night. Immediately, he knew he had been right to suspect they would be somber out of respect to him and his family. But Tony also knew that he couldn't allow it, that this was a place of business—a very profitable business, he reminded himself—and bartenders and doormen couldn't go around acting as if, well, as if someone had died. He owed it to Joe to end this pall that hung over the club.

"Hey guys," Tony said. "If I could just have everyone over here for a minute, I'd appreciate it." The men who were setting up and readying the club for opening came over. "I just wanted to thank you all for your support and respect during this difficult time for me and my family. It means the world to me. But the time for mourning is over. We need to get our heads out of our asses and try to have some fun again. So let's knock off this somber bullshit and get this club ready to open." With those words, smiles reappeared, and laughter rippled through the group. Some even came up and slapped him on the back before returning to their duties.

Tony was grateful that his little speech had worked for his friends. He, on the other hand, would just have to fake it.

The next day Tony was back at the supply house on Evergreen Lane. He was only mildly surprised to see Diane wander out and head toward him. Still in her long white robe, her blonde hair was disheveled from not yet having seen a brush. She walked to Tony. He wondered how someone could look so beautiful so early in the morning without any makeup.

"How was lunch yesterday?" Diane asked.

As Tony went back to hunting for the mud pans he needed, he mumbled that the sandwich had been wonderful. When she didn't respond, Tony looked up apologetically, "I'm sorry, Di . . . it was great, really. I'm just in a hurry. The boss needs me to get back to the site."

"Sure. I understand. But if you have time, meatball subs are still on the lunch menu. Stop by if you can."

Tony climbed into the truck and slammed the door, wanting more than anything to make that lunch date. "I'll try," he said, knowing he'd do more than that.

On the ten-minute ride back to the construction site, Tony chewed on a few of the dozens of questions that swirled through his head, not the least of which was *Why? Why him?* She could very well have any man she wanted, so what in the world would she want with him? Then Tony's mind started walking down a completely different road, one that said she hadn't asked him *in* for lunch, but just to come by. Maybe she was just being nice. When Tony almost ran a stop sign a mile from the site, he thought it best to put the questions to bed—at least until this afternoon—and focus on getting back to work in one piece.

When noon finally rolled around, Tony still hadn't decided if he should go to Diane's, but curiosity won out over common sense. Grabbing the keys to one of the dinosaurs off the hook in the front office, he jogged to the truck, hopped in, and pulled out of the lot before anyone could ask any questions, anxious to get where he was going. Pulling into her driveway, Tony was still uncertain about whether to go up and ring the doorbell or to wait in the truck. He was torn between being respectful to a married woman and yet assuming she had meant that they would be lunching together inside.

After a few minutes of feeling like a complete idiot for sitting in his truck in ninety-degree heat, Diane came to the truck door and looked at Tony.

"What are you doing just sitting there?" she asked. For that, he had no answer. When he didn't reply, Diane said, "This isn't curbside service, you know. Come on in."

Tony whispered a silent thank-you to a God he had recently begun doubting and climbed out of the truck. Although he'd been to her house once before, he was still amazed at how tidy everything was, especially with a baby in the house. He looked over and saw that she had set the table, even adding a small vase full of flowers. Still uncomfortable about what to do or where to go, not knowing whether he should sit right down or stand, he chose to stay in the front foyer.

For lack of anything else to say, Tony asked, "Where's the baby?"

"Taking a nap," Diane said. From the kitchen, utensils clinked together, a cupboard door shut softly, and plates clacked as they were piled, one on top of the other.

Tony stood in the front hall, wondering whether he should take his boots off so he wouldn't track dirt all over her white carpet. Since he didn't see any other shoes by the door, he supposed it would be okay to venture in. Still unsure, he undid the laces and stepped out of the shoes, hoping that she wouldn't assume he was making himself at home, but rather, was being courteous. He then wandered into the living room, figuring that he'd made it this far, he might as well go all the way in. The pun was not lost on him, and he suppressed a laugh. Unwanted fantasies raced through his head—of him and Diane lying naked together, their sweat-soaked bodies becoming one. He stopped the barrage of images by asking a question as she set the table. "So what does Paul do for a living?"

"Well, when he's not asking me why can't I look like this woman or that woman on TV, he runs a garage," she answered, laying down a silver fork on a yellow napkin.

Tony was dumbfounded. "Does he say that to you?"

"Yes," she paused. "Yes, he does."

"How could he possibly question how beautiful you are? You're the most beautiful woman I've ever seen."

"Well, Paul certainly doesn't think so, but thank you," she replied. "It's been a long time since I've heard that." Tony ached to hold her in his arms.

"So you're the assistant superintendent at the construction site?" she rushed on.

"Yeah, I'm the guy who makes sure all the work gets done by the subcontractors," he answered, pulling out a chair for Diane to sit down. Diane sat and thanked Tony. Throughout lunch, the two chatted and made small talk; but to Tony, it was as comfortable as putting on a favorite old pair of jeans.

"I'd love to stay and talk—well, forever—but I should be getting back."

"Of course," Diane answered. She pushed back her chair, stood, and followed Tony to the door.

"Thanks again for lunch. It was great. Really." He reached for the doorknob. "Di, what's the matter?" Tony gazed at her crestfallen expression, wondering what he could have possibly done to offend her.

"What? You're not going to kiss me today?"

Tony was speechless, his whole body rigid except for his knees, which had started to shake. He gazed into her green eyes, then ever so chastely, like a sixteen-year-old, gave her a peck on the lips. When Tony pulled away, he saw only disappointment. He then took her face in his hands, took her lips in his mouth. She sighed as he moved his lips to her cheek and down her neck. Unexpectedly, Diane grabbed Tony and kissed him hard, her tongue pushing its way into his mouth. The pleasure Tony felt was excruciating.

A wail echoed from a back room, signaling that the baby was awake. Breathless, Tony pulled back.

"I'd better get back to work."

"Yeah. Me too," she said, gesturing toward the nursery.

Tony smiled and asked, "Should I stop by tomorrow?"

"If you want to."

Like some bad scene being played out in a B-movie, Tony replied, "Not unless you want me to."

"Tony, we could do this all day . . . stop by tomorrow," Diane said, touching his hand.

Tony nodded, turned the handle, and walked into the blistering sunshine.

TONY TANCREDI AND CINDY L. O'HARA

TEN

FOR THE REST of the day, Tony was useless, doing the bare minimum to keep Ron off his back at the construction site. By the time the day ended, Tony had envisioned a million different fantasies, and almost all of them ended with him and Diane in bed together. Tony knew that he had a good body, but it wasn't as if you'd find him modeling in a catalog or magazine. Besides, Tony reasoned, lots of guys had a good body, and were a hell of a lot more handsome. So again, he had to ask himself, *why?* This lone question nagged at him, and as much as he tried to put it out of his head, the more it ate at him.

At quitting time, the one thing that helped put his mind at ease was replaying the moment over and over again. It brought a smile to his face every time.

The next morning found Tony already dressed for his day job, sitting at his small kitchen table and wolfing down his eggs and toast, hoping to avoid Laura. Unfortunately, she walked in before he could get out of the house.

Coffee in hand, Laura sat down across from Tony and took a sip of the hot liquid. "Things must be going better at work for you," Laura stated. "Or are you just glad it's Friday and you get to go work at the club tonight?"

"Come on, Laura, you know the club job is just extra money for us and that I can take it or leave it." Tony refused to look at her, guilt washing over him. Instead, he continued to stare at his plate, absentmindedly sopping up runny yellow juice with his toast.

"Yeah, but I'm sure those girls flirt with you, and some of them, I'm sure, try and go a little farther. You know, you have that look about you when you get all dressed up."

Annoyed at the turn the conversation was taking, Tony finally looked up. "I don't know what look you mean. All the guys have to get dressed up, members of the club as well. It helps with the image. You know, keeps out the low renters and some of the troublemakers."

"Well, maybe some night I can go to the club and see for myself what goes on there and how many girls come on to you."

Tony got up, roughly grabbing his plate, spilling egg yolk onto the tablecloth. "I'm sure it would be fine," Tony said, rinsing his dish and giving it a couple of shakes. He set the dish in the drainer and turned to Laura. "I've even heard some talk about having a night for wives and girlfriends."

Tony walked up behind Laura and placed his hands on her shoulders, massaging them gently. "I don't know why you worry. I just do my job and rarely talk to anybody—male or female. Funny, everyone always asks why I'm so serious and why I never smile. Does that sound like someone who's trying to make it with the women there?"

She looked up at Tony and smiled. "That just makes you seem that much more mysterious to the ladies."

Tony laughed and said, "I can see that I just can't win here. I'm going to work. I love you. Now kiss me good-bye."

On the ride to work, Tony reflected on his conversation with Laura. She really didn't deserve to be treated this badly. She had done nothing wrong in her life except to get married to a son of a bitch who couldn't keep his dick in his pants if his life depended on it. Tony comforted himself with the knowledge that the girls at the club were just toys, something to collect, like trophies.

But the situation with Diane was different. That was getting serious, and Tony knew it could get far worse—or better depending on how you looked at it. As he pulled into the lot of the construction site, thinking about Diane brought a smile to Tony's face so that he was practically bouncing up the steps to the trailer.

"Hey, Ron, what's up for today?" Tony asked, trying not to appear too eager.

Without looking up, Ron replied, "I need you to go stake out a job in a new development. It's over in Great Falls."

"But that's all the way on the other side of town," Tony said, hearing the whine in his voice.

Ron looked up. "Yeah. So? You got a problem with what I'm asking you to do?"

Tony sighed, resigned to not seeing Diane until Monday. "Nope, just pointing it out, is all."

"Good. Then get outta here," Ron said.

On his way out, Tony let the door of the trailer slam shut.

What had started out as a potentially great day was quickly turning to shit, Tony thought. Without warning, his anger quickly evaporated, and Tony found himself profoundly sad and missing his sister.

TONY TANCREDI AND CINDY L. O'HARA

For the first time since he had started working at the Shamrock, he found himself wishing that he didn't have to go.

"Hey, Ton, what's with you?" Sam asked, approaching Tony.

"Whatta ya mean?" Tony asked, his best fake smile in place.

"Well, if you were to ask me, you look like you been up two or three days and ran out of meth."

Tony didn't answer right away.

"Hey, I know when sumthin's buggin' you." Sam switched the toothpick from left to right seamlessly.

Tony confessed he had just been thinking about his sister.

"Ah," Sam said. "Tell you what, come to the back room in about ten minutes and I'll have something for you. Fix you right up."

Sam approached a few clients—one at the bar, another who was hanging out by the DJ booth, still another who seemed to be engulfed by an entourage of people made up primarily of beautiful young girls who couldn't possibly have been old enough to get into the club. Watching Sam work the room, Tony wondered what kind of white rabbit his friend was going to pull out of his hat this time.

After a few minutes, Tony walked to the back of the club and knocked, once, twice on the black-painted door.

"Tony, say hello to Victor," Sam said, his skinny ass precariously perched on the corner of Joe's desk. Tony frowned in worry, his immediate thought being that Joe wouldn't approve of where Sam's ass had come to light. Still considered the new kid on the block after six months, however, Tony also didn't think it prudent to mention it to his friend.

Instead, Tony turned his attention to the only other party in the room.

"Victor." Tony stuck out his hand. "It's my pleasure to meet you."

The man, well dressed in a three-piece black suit, met Tony's hand with his own.

"Man, I've heard a lot about you," Victor said, his thick Philly accent making him sound tougher than he really was—at least in Tony's opinion. Victor gripped Tony's hand and squeezed before letting go. "It's really good to finally meetcha."

Tony remained silent, waiting to see how this would play out.

"You, my friend, are a man I do not want to get on the wrong side of."

Still Tony waited.

"Look, Sam told me your problem, and can I just say that I am very sorry to hear about yer sister, but I have a solution, should you wanna, um, take advantage of it."

Tony looked at the man, still not uttering a word. Victor continued. "I have some meth, and if you want to do some—maybe just enough to get you through the night—I'm your man. I don't sell it. I just give it to friends and hope that you will consider me a friend someday."

Tony knew right then that he didn't like this dressed-up piece of shit.

"Well, Vic-tor," Tony enunciated, "I don't pick my friends by what drugs they lay on me, but thanks for the offer."

"Hey, Ton, Victor's a friend, and he's just trying to, ya know, help you out, make you feel better."

Tony knew when he was being played, and Sam had put him in a tough spot. If he refused, Tony knew that Sam would find a way to work it into a conversation with Joe. On the other hand, if he went ahead and did a little, Tony would maintain his reputation among the boys in the club and feel better at the same time.

Besides, Tony reasoned, he'd been around drugs since he was a teenager. Although he was strictly a weed man, and even then only on occasion, his friends had dabbled in meth, coke, and hash. Back then, he had always refused his friends' offers because he couldn't fathom putting anything up his nose or putting a needle in his arm. So when Sam hopped gracefully off the desk and he saw the small white mountains of precut lines that lay on top of the desk, he thought he had a way out—one that would allow him to keep his dignity and reputation intact and still decline graciously.

"Hey, Victor, I appreciate the offer, and I'd love to take you up on it, but I don't do anything that goes up my nose. It's not personal, I just can't stand it. But thanks anyway." As Tony was about to turn away, Victor reached into his pocket.

"Not to worry, my friend. Just break off a piece of this and eat it." He opened his palm, and within was a chunk of meth the size of a golf ball. Victor broke off a piece and handed it to Tony.

"Some for now, and some for later if you want."

Stuck, Tony took what was offered and quickly pocketed the drugs. "Thanks, man."

With the business completed, Victor hurriedly left the room.

Tony turned on his friend, barely containing his rage. "What the hell did you tell him?" Tony shouted.

TONY TANCREDI AND CINDY L. O'HARA

Sam raised his hands defensively. "Nothing! Just about your sister. Whatever else he heard, he heard in the club or on the streets."

"Damn, Sam!"

"Hey, Victor's got a lot of money. His family's rich, and he just likes being a part of the club clique. He's harmless."

"Harmless? With the amount of shit he has on him, if he gets popped in here, the man's not gonna believe he just gives shit away!"

Joe walked through the door.

"You know, Sam"—Joe walked to his desk and thumbed absentmindedly through a ream of papers neatly stacked in the middle—"I think Tony's on the money with that guy." Joe looked up. Like a scolded child, Sam looked down.

"And," Joe continued, "from here on out, he don't bring that shit in here. I mean, not in the club at all. You got it?"

Joe turned to Tony. "Tony, you know him now. You make sure it don't happen again." With that, Joe turned back to thumbing through his papers.

Tony didn't know if he was being punished or promoted. He had his answer when Joe said, without looking up, "It's nice to see someone thinking about the club instead of themselves for a change."

The next night, Tony felt like shit and knew he must look like it too. The meth he had done the night before had certainly made him feel more upbeat and helped him forget about his sister, but it had also kept him up all night. As a result, he hadn't slept at all, and now here he was, sitting in the club parking lot, a complete disaster. Tony didn't know how he was going to make it through the night. He glanced at the little plastic bag lying on the seat next to him, the tan rock-shaped substance calling his name. Tony knew he couldn't take the drugs inside the club (per Joe's orders), so he took the meth out of the bag and broke off a small piece. He placed some in his mouth. He then grabbed his suit coat, slammed the car door shut, and began the short walk to the club.

Always one of the first men there, Tony felt like a new man as the other bouncers began drifting in.

"Hey, Greg." Tony laughed. "You look like shit, man!"

"Ah, eat me, Tancredi."

"Ah, I'm just playin' with you, Greg. You look as bad as I felt ten minutes ago."

"What do you mean *felt*? If you got some stuff, you better hand it over, dickhead!"

"Here." Tony tossed him the bag. "You can give it to whoever wants it."

"So, big shot, you're one of us now? I knew it wouldn't take long. You always were a team player. Oh, by the way, Joe thinks it's time that you carry a gun like the rest of us."

"Okay, but just one—not four or five like you, you crazy bastard."

"Hey," Greg said defensively. "You never know when you'll need an extra."

"So," Tony continued, "how do I go about getting one? Oh, and I guess I'll need a permit too. I gotta go to Doylestown to get it, right?"

"Some of us have permits, and some of us don't. You don't have a record, so you'll be able to get one pretty easily. Sam's gotta friend coming in tonight to have a gun customized for you."

"Well, just make sure it's not a cannon like you got. A .38 caliber snub-nosed will do just fine."

"Friggin' girl. Get a real gun." Greg chuckled.

"Yeah, yeah," Tony quipped, unable to keep from smiling.

After six months at the club, Tony shouldn't have been surprised that he was being told to pack a gun of some kind. Almost all the bouncers carried a wide assortment of weapons—from knives and guns to blackjacks and stun guns; he had seen it all. With the clientele the Shamrock attracted (everyone from bartenders and strippers to drug dealers to real and wannabe mobsters), Tony knew it was simply a matter of protection, a way to be ready for anything. If, God forbid, one of the bouncers came up on the short end of a fight, losing would send the wrong message.

And although most of the people who came to the club were already drunk or high or both from being out all night at other clubs, when you walked into the Shamrock, you left your attitude at the door, or you'd find yourself back in the parking lot when you woke up. A weapon helped underscore how seriously the bouncers took their job and how loyal they were to Joe.

Tony's thoughts were interrupted when a dark blue Cadillac Fleetwood pulled up to the front entrance at precisely 11:00 p.m. Tony figured that Joe was inside, but didn't recognize the car or the beautiful brunette who got out of the driver's side. As was the custom, many of the patrons surrounded Joe as he walked into and through the club. The young brunette remained attached to him, an arm linked through his.

Tony didn't know the girl's name, but what he did know was that he had never seen a girl drive his boss around. Curious, he walked to the bar to ask

TONY TANCREDI AND CINDY L. O'HARA

Greg or Sam who the broad was, but before he could utter a question, Joe walked up and introduced him to Nicky.

Tony knew enough not to stare—it would, after all, be disrespectful—but he did accept her hand and told her it was nice to meet her, before excusing himself.

A little later, a girl yelled. Then a man's voice roared, "Shut the fuck up!"

Tony ran to the front of the club where the noise was coming from and saw Joe and Nicky in a heated argument. In an act of defiance and frustration, Nicky threw her drink precisely where Joe was standing. Not only did glass shatter everywhere, but whatever pink concoction she had been sipping splashed onto Joe's cream-colored pant leg. The new suit was one of Joe's favorites, Tony knew, and from the deep shade of purple that was quickly taking over Joe's normal complexion, he was ready to explode at Nicky's infraction.

Tony cut in, trying to defuse the ticking time bomb by saying that he would pick up the mess, that it was no problem, but Joe stopped him.

"No, Tony, I'll clean it up," Joe said, putting his hand on Tony's arm.

"Really, Joe, it's no problem." Tony continued to pick up the large chunks of glass.

"I. Said. I. Got. It. But thanks." Tony detected the subtle yet firm change in Joe's voice and knew he had been given a warning, one that he should take seriously. Tony knew that Joe could have thrown his weight around or shown off, but that wasn't Joe. It became clear to Tony the type of man he was working for, and he liked what he saw.

Later that night, Sam introduced Tony to a tall redheaded Irishman who went by the name of Kevin. Tony concluded that he was about six-foot-one and lanky, but not at all athletic. The small paunch that hung ever so slightly over his belt told Tony that the man enjoyed more than an occasional beer.

"He'll be starting next week," Sam said.

"Yeah, okay. Looking forward to working with ya."

"Yeah, looking forward to working with you too. I've heard a lot about you," Kevin replied.

Tony nodded at Kevin, feigning the social niceties, but all Tony wanted to know was *would this guy cover his back, and could he take care of himself in a fight?* He wasn't sure about either of the answers.

After meeting Kevin, Tony walked to the bar for a drink. He leaned against the brass rail and looked around. The night so far—minus a couple of hiccups—had been relatively uneventful, which gave Tony more time to pick the girl of his choice for a quickie, which was now becoming a weekly event. Luckily, most of the girls would come up to him, because despite his reputation, he was not the type who would approach a woman and start talking to her. He had only to wait to see which one it would be.

No sooner had he finished this thought than a big-titted blonde strode confidently up to Tony and started chatting with him. Within five minutes, Tony knew this would be the one.

By the time the evening ended, so had the meth he had done earlier. Now Tony was exhausted. Even his bones felt tired. All he wanted to do was go home and sleep—preferably without the aid of a Valium or some other sleeping pill, which was also quickly becoming a habit.

When he opened the door to his bedroom, however, his eyes widened in surprise. A normally dark room was alight with candles—dozens of them. Sitting propped up in bed, wearing a sheer negligee, was Laura. Inwardly, Tony groaned. Of course, she'd want to make love *tonight*, Tony thought. Knowing Laura would not be put off, not tonight, Tony smiled and walked to the bed, silently hoping his dick would rise to the occasion—again.

Tony slept the entire weekend, never getting out of bed until it was time to go to work Monday morning. He knew Laura was concerned about him, but was certain she thought he was just tired from working two jobs.

On his way to the construction site, Tony mentally kicked himself for taking advantage of her. *But she just makes it too damn easy*, he thought, immediately shifting the blame elsewhere. He didn't deny his contribution to the situation, but he also thought that if she weren't so gullible, he probably wouldn't be doing the things he was doing—at least not as often.

He sighed. Who was he kidding? She was the best person he knew at the time he married her. And since he thought he'd never find anyone he would or could love (let's be honest Tony-boy), he married the best girl he could find. But it was so unfair to her. Mentally he cursed the tiny (annoying) voice in his head that kept adding commentary to his thoughts.

He knew that he could keep the club girls from Laura, but Diane was going to be the real problem. If Di was truly interested, he knew his marriage was in trouble. He had become completely overwhelmed by her—and yet, at the same time, she intimidated him.

You'd think by now that a thirty-five-year-old man would know when he's in love, Tony thought. But all he knew for sure was that Diane was all he thought about.

ELEVEN

WHEN TONY ARRIVED at the site, Ron was waiting, a list in his hand.

"Tony, you gotta go to Frost and Watson's for some lumber. We're short on two-by-fours and two-by-sixes. They know you're comin' so head out and get back ASAP."

"Sure, Ron. No problem."

Tony enjoyed going to the lumberyard because he knew most of the men there, knew they were all good, hardworking family men. And they usually let Tony get his own materials even though they were supposed to do it. He supposed it was to cut down on theft or some shit, but hell, it was less work for them when Tony helped himself, and Tony didn't have to wait around until someone was free to help him. He was in and out, and everyone was happy. He was also acquainted with the owners of the lumberyard, Don Watson and his partner, and knew they liked him. Hell, they must like him, or they wouldn't keep offering him a job every time he stopped by for supplies. Or maybe it was just that they disliked Dave, the owner of the company Tony worked for now. The truth was Dave *was* a crazy bastard who acted more like Hitler than Ghandi.

After grabbing the materials he needed, Tony headed back to the site, promising himself that he would go see Diane at lunch. He hadn't seen her since last Thursday and didn't have her number.

As noon approached, Tony took off in one of the company trucks and drove over to Pine Run. *God, I hope she's home,* he thought. When Tony drove by her house, Diane was taking some groceries out of her car. Tony slowed to a crawl and leaned out of the truck window. "Need some help with those?" he asked.

Diane smiled and motioned her head toward the house. Tony pulled in behind her car, quickly shut the beast down, and practically fell out of the car in his excitement to get to her. Just as Tony was walking up her pathway, his arms laden with groceries, he saw Dave, the owner of the construction company, drive slowly by before speeding away. Tony knew then that he was in trouble. He had heard, on more than one occasion, that at Diane's settlement, Dave was trying to get into her pants and had made a fool of himself in the process. (*Like you got room to talk, asshole,* piped up the little voice in Tony's head). He sighed. This time the voice was right. Hell, Tony probably would have given her the house for free if he had owned the company.

Knowing it was too late to worry, he went into Diane's house. He set the bags down carefully on the kitchen counter, but couldn't shake the feeling of being seen by Dave.

"Tony, what's the matter?" Diane asked.

"I think I might be in trouble, maybe even fired."

"What? What are you talking about?"

"My boss, Dave Shenk, just drove by and saw me going into your house."

"Oh my god! What can I do? Who can I call?" Diane ran her fingers through her hair nervously. "This is awful. I'll feel terrible if you lose your job because of me."

"Don't worry about it. The only thing that would bother me is if I wouldn't be able to see you every day." Tony grazed her arm lightly with his fingertips.

Diane looked away. "I don't know, Tony. I'm so confused. I know that I like it when you're here. And I love the way you kiss me, but we're both married with kids. Doesn't that bother you?"

"Of course," Tony lied. "But I know how I feel about you. Just what *is* it that you want with me anyway, Di? Why did you even let me kiss you last time if you weren't interested?" Tony tried to capture her gaze, but she avoided him.

When she finally looked up, she said, "Maybe this should stop before I let myself go."

"You mean you've been holding back? You have feelings for me but just didn't want to tell me?"

Diane nodded and stepped closer to Tony. "I don't know what I want, or what I'm doing. All I know is that I want you to kiss me and go back to work. It may be for the last time, or it may not, but that's what I want."

Never one to disobey an order, Tony complied. As he leaned in to kiss Diane, he whispered, "Okay, I'll do whatever you want. Always."

When Tony got back to the site, he parked the old truck and got out. He was dying to ask Ron if Dave had called, but knew that it would be suicide to do so. Tony got his answer when his boss remained tight-lipped and distant the rest of the day. Tony knew then that Dave *had* called and told Ron what he had seen. What Tony didn't know was how the situation was going to play out.

By midweek, no one had said anything, and Tony thought things might actually be okay. His theory was supported when Ron asked him to run over to the sample house to get some materials the crew needed.

If Dave intended to fire me, he wouldn't be sending me back to the place that he saw me, would he? Tony thought as he bounced along in the truck. For the first time in a long time, Tony's little voice didn't have an answer.

"Sure, *now* you're quiet," Tony said.

When he arrived at the supply house and opened the garage, he groaned. The steel support beams he needed weren't where they were supposed to be, and he had to reorganize almost the entire garage just to get to them. The entire process took about an hour. After much maneuvering, Tony finally got what he needed. As he hauled the first beam out to the truck, something black and shiny sat atop the hood. Unable to look at what it was until he set his load down, he lugged the beam to the back of the truck bed and dropped it, a loud *clang* echoing throughout the neighborhood.

Tony walked to the front of the truck, curious about what was lying there. What he picked up was a forty-five record. It was REO Speedwagon's "Can't Fight This Feeling." Tony didn't have to play it; he knew the words by heart. In fact, everyone did, because it was the number one song in the nation. Tony was torn between running to Diane's house and staying where he was. The wise course of action would be to stay put, but Tony was not a wise man—he knew this. The decision was made for him when he glanced down at Diane's house and saw an unfamiliar car parked in the driveway—her husband's, presumably. Tony took in the rest of the house and glanced at the second floor. There he saw Diane sitting in the window, looking down at him. The look on her face told Tony all he needed to know. Had her husband not been home, they probably would have run to each other like some scene out of a bad movie.

Wishing that the moment could end on a more romantic note, Tony continued to load the support beams into the back of the truck. This time, however, the columns felt as light as air.

That night, Tony wolfed down his dinner, anxious to get to the club to talk to someone about Diane. He didn't care who, anyone would do. He shoveled mashed potatoes into his mouth and followed it with great gulps of milk.

"Hey, big man, what's the rush? Your stomach's not going anywhere." Laura smiled and handed Tony a napkin so he could wipe his mouth.

"Thanks, hon." Tony took the napkin and dutifully wiped his lips. "Sorry, babe. Something's going on at the club, and I gotta get there early. I don't know what it is. I was just told to show up earlier than normal."

"Oh, okay," Laura replied, hurt. "It's just—"

"Just what?" Tony asked suspiciously. He asked more out of expectation than curiosity.

Laura sighed and covered Tony's hand with her own. "I just never see you anymore."

Tony removed his hand, a stab of guilt piercing him. "But I'm pullin' in good money, right? You don't mind that, do you?"

Laura shook her head. "No, of course not. But sometimes I wonder if it's worth it. That's all."

Tony shoved his chair back, the legs scraping against the linoleum floor; grabbed his plate and glass; and stomped to the sink. By way of an exclamation mark, he poured his fork and knife off of his plate so they clanged against the stainless steel. He then dumped the rest of the dishes into the sink, the glass rattling enough that Tony thought it might break.

"I've gotta go," he said.

"But, Tony, I was just saying—"

Tony slammed the door behind him, cutting off the rest of what Laura had to say.

As Tony drove down Roosevelt Boulevard toward Southampton Road, he raged.

"I don't need this shit right now!" he yelled and banged his hand on the wheel for emphasis. The adult in him knew his anger at Laura was primarily due to guilt over Diane, but the child in him was unwilling to control it. Like a spoiled little boy who had been told he couldn't have what he wanted, he had exploded at the one person who loved him unconditionally. After riding out the storm of emotions, Tony made a note to call and send flowers to the house—after he talked to someone about Diane.

Tony figured that someone would be Greg since he was always the first one into the club. For that, Tony was thankful because Greg was the one person he could talk to.

When Tony pulled into the parking lot of the Shamrock, he had only to wait a few minutes before Greg pulled in behind him. Greg got out of his car, juggling a large cup of coffee with one hand, while slamming the door shut with the other. Tony got out as well and quickly fell into step with his friend.

TONY TANCREDI AND CINDY L. O'HARA

Greg glanced up, surprised. With no attempt at preamble, Greg asked, "What the hell you doin' here so early?"

"I just need to talk to somebody about somethin', and I guess you're it." Before Greg could answer, Tony continued. "Remember that girl Diane I told you about?"

"Uh-huh," Greg grunted, fumbling the key to the club into the lock. "The Miss America that's too good for you?"

"Yeah. Well, it looks like she's really into me, and we're gonna start a relationship," Tony said, trying unsuccessfully to hide the excitement in his voice.

"You know," Greg said, heaving open the heavy front door and waiting for Tony to walk in ahead of him, "I don't care how good-lookin' this bitch is, you're never going to find a better woman than the one you have. That would be Laura I'm talkin' about."

Annoyed at hearing his wife's name, Tony bristled. "Greg, don't tell me—"

But Greg put his hand up. "No, lemme finish. You mess around with these little *puntas*, these whores, in the club, and I know they don't mean shit to you, so it don't bother me as much, but now you tell me you're gonna get serious with this woman—what's her name? Diane? You know what? You're lucky I'm not Laura's brother or father." Greg got directly in Tony's face and pointed his finger for emphasis. "I know I can't beat you with my hands. Shit, I don't know anybody who could do that, but I sure would put one in the back of your friggin' head if I *were* one of them," Greg said, making his thumb and forefinger into the shape of an L, as if holding a gun.

"You don't have to make me feel any worse than I already do, Greg, but you can't tell me that if you ran into your personal dream girl, you wouldn't take a shot at it."

"Whatever. I've had enough of this shit. I know I'm talkin' to a brick wall. I got my own problems and a shitload of work to do before we open without havin' to listen to your bullshit. Come on over here, *lover boy*, and help get things set up. And by the way, how the hell did you meet this girl anyway? I never see you talk to anyone in here. These bitches walk up to you night after night, and the more cold you act, the more they want you. Then at the end of the night, you get your pick of any of them. How's that work?"

"Let's just drop it," Tony mumbled.

Later that night, Tony stood at the bar surveying the crowd, watchful of the clientele and trying to predict who was going to get out of hand next. For now, everything was relatively quiet and peaceful. The sound of a heavy glass being plunked down in front of him startled Tony out of his reverie. Behind the bar, Greg poured two fingers of some amber liquid into the large shot glass, all the while talking to Tony without actually looking at him. His gaze remained transfixed on the pour.

"Hey, about earlier tonight, you know that no matter what, I always have your back. Me going off about that Diane shit—"

"Greg, you don't have to say nuthin'. I know exactly where you were coming from." Greg looked up at Tony. "And it goes without saying that I know I can depend on you no matter what the situation. So let's just drop it, okay?"

Before Greg could reply, the phone began its high-pitched ring. Greg answered with the standard "Shamrock Club" while Tony continued to sip his drink, uninterested in the conversation.

"Sure, Joe, I'll tell him to be there. Yup, right away."

"What's up?" Tony asked.

"That was Joe," Greg said, taking a napkin from underneath the bar and grabbing a pen that was resting close by. "He wants you to go pick him up."

"But I don't even know where Joe lives. How come I'm going?"

"Because you're the only one here, and I can't leave," Greg replied, still scribbling furiously on the napkin. "Here's how you get there," he said, tossing the napkin at Tony, who looked at it blankly. "Better get going."

Tony nodded and headed out the door of the club.

During the few minutes it took to get there, Tony tried to calm his nerves. Despite the shot (Tony thought that alone would have helped), his heart sped up, and little beads of sweat popped out on his forehead like tiny pimples.

As he pulled up to the house he had been directed to, he parked and listened to the engine idle. Unsure whether to honk the horn (he didn't think too long about this option, guessing correctly that Joe probably didn't want to be summoned this way) or go to the door, Tony was relieved of having to make a decision when the door to the house opened and Joe kissed someone good-bye. Having seen the protocol that was expected of his drivers, Tony hopped out, ready to open the back door for Joe. As his boss approached, he extended his hand in greeting. "How you doin' tonight, Ton? You hungry?"

As if on cue, Tony's stomach rumbled. He remembered that he had only gotten to eat a few bites of his dinner at home before he had thrown the rest down the garbage disposal in a childish fit of anger. "Actually, I am, Joe. That would be great. Thanks."

"Great! How about D'Lu Lu's?"

"Sure, sounds good," Tony answered, opening the car door for Joe, wondering at the same time where the night was headed.

TWELVE

ON THE WAY to the restaurant, Tony let Joe take the lead in conversation, which consisted mostly of directions on his boss's part. Their destination was located on Buselton Avenue in Northeast Philly—an area with various bars and restaurants catering to people from all over the world and, consequently, all ethnicities. Ironically, it was also home to one of the oldest churches in America—Lower Dublin Baptist Church.

Tony pulled up to the front of the restaurant. Inside, people looked out their window expectantly at the sleek white Cadillac that had just arrived. When the car came to a halt, Tony immediately stepped out and started around to the passenger-side door to let Joe out. Before he got there, Joe swung open the door and stepped out. When Joe approached the patio, doormen began gently pushing people to the side, clearing the way. Tony watched all of this with fascination, not only unable to believe what he was seeing, but knowing that for one night, he was a part of it as well, simply by association.

When the two men finally got inside and were seated, Joe introduced Tony to everyone who stopped by, including the restaurant staff. Tony had never felt more important in his life. He took in the superb dinner and free-flowing wine, the beautiful women who seemed to know Tony's name, and the fact that there were never fewer than two servers at the table hovering discreetly, waiting for their slightest request. He absorbed it all and reveled in it.

"Mr. B., may I get you some more wine?"

"No, Gussy," Joe replied to the maitre d'. "Tony and I have to get going, but everything was magnificent—as always. Thank you." Joe leaned over to Tony. "Did you enjoy the wine?"

"Very much so. Thank you."

"The reason I ask is that it came from my personal wine rack downstairs. I'll show it to you some other time, but right now, we have to get over to Club Ciao next door."

Tony almost choked on the mouthful of red liquid he had been swirling in his mouth. It was true that the wine had been one of the highlights of the meal, but what if he hadn't liked it? What if he had said it was just okay? What if, what if, what if, what the fucking if? Thankfully, he hadn't been lying, but

Holy Christ, what a land mine he could have stumbled onto. When the bill came, Joe took it, looked at it, and began fishing in his pockets for the wad of cash that was always there. Tony subtly watched Joe peel off three $100 bills, and then add another as a tip. Joe handed the check and the money back to the waiter, then wiped his mouth with the linen napkin and pushed his chair away from the table, signaling it was time to go.

Club Ciao was an elegant establishment and did well because of the spillover from D'Lu Lu's. It was, most people knew, a place favored by Jewish girls looking to hook up (usually for only a night) with Italian lovers. The door, painted red, was at street level, but the actual club was up a flight of stairs.

For most, a ten-dollar cover charge got you into the club, but when Joe and Tony approached, the doorman nudged people in line aside so they would have a clear shot to the stairs. For the favor, Joe shook all the doormen's hands, palming twenty-dollar bills into them as he went. When they finally made it to the bar, Joe's drink (a vodka martini with two onions, not olives) was already waiting for him. The bartender turned to Tony. "What can I get you?"

Tony asked for his usual Jack and ginger ale and turned, watching the crowded dance floor. For the next hour, Joe and Tony made idle conversation, talking about everything and nothing. Breaking a lull when both men were enjoying the comfortable silence, Joe told Tony he was going back to the phone by the men's room to call the Shamrock Club, just to check on things. Tony promptly followed his boss, keeping an eye on the crowd, making sure no one got too close.

Once there, Joe told Tony to go ahead and call the club.

Tony listened to the phone ring, once, twice. Then he heard a familiar voice.

"Hey, Monte, it's Tony. I'm with Joe, and we're at Club Ciao, and I was just makin' sure—"

"Hey man, cool hat. Can I try it on?"

"No, sir. I don't let anyone touch my hat," Joe answered politely.

"Yeah, everything's okay here," Monte continued. Momentarily distracted, Tony looked at the black receiver in his hand as if it were a snake and remembered that he had called Monte. "Hey, Monte, hold on a minute, wouldja?"

"Sure, Ton." Monte paused his monologue.

Just as Tony turned to assess the situation, the drunk who had asked about Joe's hat began reaching for it. Without thinking, Tony hit the asshole with a right, knocking him across the hallway and into the men's room door. Tony waited to see if the man would get up, the phone dangling loosely by his side.

When he was sure the drunk was going to stay where he'd fallen, Tony put the phone back to his ear. "Now what were you saying, Monte?" Tony asked.

"Hey, greaseball, did you just hit somebody?" Monte yelled into the phone.

"Yeah," Tony said.

"Holy shit! I heard it all the way over here at the club!" He laughed.

"Monte, I gotta go," Tony said and hung the receiver back in place.

Joe smiled at Tony, then looked down at the man Tony had hit. He was propped against the door like a broken puppet, his arms and legs bent haphazardly.

"Well, we certainly can't leave this guy here," Joe said.

"How about if we drag him into the men's room and sit him up on the shitter and close the door?" Tony suggested.

"Sounds good to me," Joe said, leaning down to grab the man's legs.

Tony took the arms and lifted him, both men crab-walking into the men's room. Tony prayed to God no one was inside. Luck was with them, and the bathroom was empty. Without setting the drunk down, Tony kicked a stall door open and inched his way into the tiny space, trying to make himself as small as possible. Finally, Joe and Tony were able to maneuver their load onto the toilet, where they propped him up. Their goal accomplished, Joe and Tony backed out of the stall and closed the door.

"Think I'll wash up," Joe said, looking at Tony.

"Good idea," Tony agreed.

When he had finished drying his hands, Tony grabbed the door handle and opened the door slowly, sticking his head out and looking from left to right. Satisfied, he walked through, with Joe following close behind.

"I could sure use my drink right about now," Joe whispered into Tony's ear.

Tony remained silent, but nodded in reply.

After what seemed like miles, the two men finally reached their spot back at the bar. As they sat sipping their drinks, one of the bouncers approached Joe and politely told him that someone had knocked out a cop in the men's room.

TONY TANCREDI AND CINDY L. O'HARA

"It's up to you whether or not you'd like to stay Mr. B.," the bouncer said, implying that Joe and Tony would be on their own when the man woke up.

With just a nod, Joe indicated it was time to leave.

Comfortably settled back in the car and speeding toward the Shamrock Club, Joe told Tony he had done the right thing by hitting the cop.

"Man, that guy must have been out all that time. It had to be fifteen or twenty minutes. When you hit 'em, they don't wake up," Joe commented thoughtfully.

"Maybe he was drunk or sumthin'," Tony answered, looking in the rearview mirror at his boss.

"Drunk? Shit! That's about the eighth or ninth guy I know you've put to sleep! I've heard from the guys at the club you're really getting a reputation around Northeast Philly."

"Well, maybe if I do it enough, people will stop screwing around in your club, and eventually, I won't have to do that."

"I also heard you do all right with the sweethearts in the club."

"All the doormen do okay in that department, don't they?"

"Yeah, but they have to work a little to get 'em. I heard they just come up to you and you take your pick. This true?"

"Well, whatever goes on, I hope it stays here. I'm married, you know."

Joe waved his hand as if shooing away an annoying fly. "Well, I am too. Most of the guys who work at the club are. And you never have to worry about anything getting out. These guys would never get anyone in trouble. They know better."

When Tony pulled into the parking lot at the Shamrock Club, one of the bouncers was waiting and immediately opened Joe's door and helped him out. Another began clearing a path. Tony reached for the handle to open his door, but as if of its own accord, the car door was opened for him. In the light of the outdoor parking lights stood Greg. He did not look directly at Tony, but rather somewhere over the top of the Caddie.

Tony stepped out.

"Whatdaya waitin' for, a friggin' invitation? Let's go," Joe said. He took Tony's arm and led him toward the club. Joe introduced Tony to some of his friends, people that Tony had seen in the Shamrock but never actually met. These men were part of Joe's inner circle of people whom you didn't approach unless they needed something.

Finally in the club, Tony relaxed. He was in his world now, one that he felt comfortable in. Tony thanked Joe and tried to excuse himself to go back to work, but Joe stopped him. "Where do you think you're going? You *are* working. Stay here. From what I hear, if any trouble starts, I'm sure you'll be the first one in—as always."

"Well, you know how quick things can happen around here, and after the way you and the guys have treated me lately, I feel like the least I can do is be the first one in when there's trouble."

Joe gave Tony a quick nod of approval.

As the night wore on, Tony found himself enjoying Joe and his friends, their camaraderie and the ease with which they spoke to one another. The nervousness he felt earlier in the evening soon began to melt away, and for the first time in a long time, he thought he might actually be able to be a part of something larger than himself, *and* that it could be a possible road to repaying his parents for all they'd been through. As if fate had been privy to his thoughts, Joe introduced Tony to one of his friends whom Tony had seen in the club earlier that night.

Of average height and weight, with the most remarkable thing being that he wore glasses, Tony found the man so nondescript as to be almost invisible, and so one of the least intimidating people he had ever met.

"Tony, I'd like you to meet Francis, although most of his associates and friends call him Wolfie."

Tony stuck out his hand in greeting. "Pleased to meet you, Wolfie."

"And I you," he replied softly, taking the offered hand. "I understand from Joe that you may be able to help me with a matter that I'm having trouble, er, correcting," Wolfie asked, releasing Tony from his grip.

Tony found the rhythm of Wolfie's speech mesmerizing and caught himself leaning forward to catch everything he was saying.

"I'm sure you know Gary. He's a bartender here," Wolfie continued.

Tony nodded. Gary was a nice kid whom Tony knew of only by name and face, not through interaction.

"Well, he's my son, and it seems that some gentlemen he flagged from the club last week wrecked his car. I happen to know their names and that they will be at Rose's Bar next Wednesday night—a week from today—playing in a dart league."

Tony remained silent, listening. "I need you to teach them a lesson, so to speak, and you can take whomever you need to in order to accomplish your, um, task."

"Okay," Tony said hesitantly. He looked at Joe, but Joe was already talking to another patron.

It seemed that Wolfie didn't need to ask Joe for permission for Tony to take some doormen with him when he went to Rose's next week. This left Tony, once again, with more questions than answers about how things operated at the club, but he knew enough not to ask.

As the night wore on and the clock ticked toward 2 o'clock, the club was unusually busy for a Wednesday night. Distracted by the number of people in the Shamrock, Tony paid attention to everyone and no one. He then located each and every other doorman—Monte, Greg, and Doc. These men were, in Tony's humble opinion, the best in the business, although he wouldn't have been caught dead saying so. Tony let his gaze linger on one particular area of the club that remained off-limits save for a select few of the clientele. While most of the regulars and guests knew not to go near the door next to the DJ booth because *that* door led to the back room, one or two idiots occasionally wandered too close. The area in question was reserved for Joe's friends and girlfriends and the doormen's girlfriends—club policy. But for those who didn't know or, God forbid, actually sat down, they were removed. More than one drunken fool had found out the hard way that no good ever came from going to that particular section of the club, nor was it even healthy to stare in that direction—especially if girls were there. Any girls sitting in that part of the bar were off the market.

As Tony made his rounds at the opposite end of the club, Wolfie and a well-dressed man stood close together, their heads bent deep in conversation. In the exact moment Tony was watching, he could have sworn he saw Wolfie hit the man with a left hook to the kidney, although it was hard to tell through all the smoke that was a permanent part of the Shamrock.

When the man fell, Monte and Doc appeared out of nowhere, grabbed the fallen man, and quickly took him outside. The entire event had taken less than two minutes. Tony's first thought was that Wolfie had thrown one hell of a punch, but as Tony got closer, blood drops on the floor led to the back door. When Tony looked up, he saw Wolfie hurrying out the front.

Tony stood, dumbfounded, rooted to the spot.

Wolfie had stuck the guy.

THIRTEEN

SNAPPING OUT OF his stupor, Tony immediately jumped in to help the other two bouncers drag the bleeding man outside, where, for lack of a better place, they propped him up in his friends' car.

Done with dumping the body, the three men hurried back into the Shamrock Club, where they began clearing out the clientele. Tony suspected this was so that if the cops came in asking questions, the club would be empty.

Finally, at 3 o'clock, with no sign that anyone would be stopping by, Greg, Doc, Monte, and Tony finished closing up and headed out to the parking lot.

"Helluva night, huh, Ton?" Greg said on the way to his car. He got out his keys, jangling them to get the right one.

"No shit."

"I'm beat," Greg added, stretching his arms over his head. "I'll see you Friday, right?"

Tony nodded, climbed into his Cadillac, and drove home.

Two hours later, with little sleep and not enough coffee in the world to wake him up, Tony was on his way to stake out a house with his super, Ron. As they bounced along in one of the old trucks, Ron glanced slyly at Tony. "You going to lunch at Diane's house today, lover boy?"

"Yeah, why? You want something?" Tony asked, shifting in his seat, uncomfortable with the turn the conversation had taken.

"Yeah, sure. A sandwich would be nice."

"You got it," Tony said, wondering what Ron was up to, but too tired to care.

At exactly noon, Tony arrived at Diane's house, his energy renewed at the prospect of having lunch with one of the most beautiful women he had ever known.

When she opened the door, Tony inhaled sharply. Clad only in a small bikini that accentuated her full breasts and narrow waist, she told him to come in.

"Lunch today is lox and cream cheese on rye toast," she announced.

Tony followed, quipping that he usually ate that for breakfast.

Diane stopped and turned. "Well, I chose this because it's easy to get ready, and I didn't know if you'd show up."

"I'm sorry, Di. I didn't mean anything by what I said."

"Apology accepted. Now get over here and kiss me."

In two long steps, Tony reached her, grabbed her around the waist, and kissed her, tasting her lips. He couldn't believe how badly he wanted this woman. He pulled away, breathless.

"We should eat," Diane said.

After lunch, Diane and Tony moved to the couch and continued to kiss, both pawing and fondling each other frantically. When they pulled apart, Tony asked Diane when he could see her away from the house.

"*That's* why I made lox," Diane said. "So we'd have longer to kiss."

Tony rolled his eyes. He couldn't believe that he was trying to get this woman into bed, and still all she wanted to do was kiss.

"Well, I'm glad you were thinking of us," Tony said. "So when do you think you can get away?"

"I don't know, Tony. As soon as I can get out of the house, I will."

Unsatisfied, but unable to do anything about it, Tony looked at the clock. "I hate to go, but I should get back."

Diane rose from the couch.

Tony grabbed her fingers and walked to the front door. "Thanks, Di, for everything," Tony said, refusing to let go of her hand. He leaned in to kiss her gently good-bye and was surprised when she kissed him hard on the mouth, pushing him against the front door.

Tony felt himself grow hard, which only excited Diane more. Panting, her nipples erect, she continued to grind against Tony, pressing herself into him. Realizing they were only a kiss away from sleeping together, Tony gently pushed Diane away.

"Di—"

"I'm sorry. I just . . . I've forgotten what it's like to feel passion like that."

Unable to speak, Tony fumbled for the door handle behind him. "I should go," was all he could manage.

"I know. It's okay," Diane said. "I'll see you tomorrow."

Tony walked slowly to his truck, willing his dick to go down. When he got in, he looked up to wave good-bye, but she had already closed the door.

When he arrived at the construction site, Tony felt more composed and was ready to get back to work. Collecting his things, Tony went to find Ron.

"Hey, Ron," Tony said. "Here's your sandwich."

"What? You don't have one for me?" The owner, Dave, eased out from behind the wall of a house that was almost finished. Tony knew then that Ron had set him up and that this was his last day on the job.

Before Tony could answer, Dave told him to go to the office.

"Get your check and get the hell out of here, Tancredi." Tony looked at Ron, who avoided eye contact. Tony turned and, without a word, stomped to the office.

After getting his check, Tony drove to Diane's house to get her phone number, lost in his own thoughts and trying to figure out how he was going to tell Laura he had lost his job because he'd been caught trying to fuck one of the customers.

When he arrived, Diane opened the door.

"Di, I need to get your phone number."

"Sure, come in. Tony, what's wrong?"

Tony told her what had happened.

"Di, it's okay," Tony said gently, not sure at all that he was telling the truth. "I'll call every day, and no matter what my new job is, I'll somehow get here to see you."

Diane sniffled. She told Tony that she would try to get out to see him as soon as she could.

"I know you will, honey." Tony opened his arms, and Diane walked into them. He hugged her tight. "Lemme give you the number to the Shamrock Club. You can always get in touch with me there." Unwilling to break the embrace, Tony finally pulled away. "I gotta go," he said, still holding her arms. "I promise I'll call as soon as I can."

"I know," Diane said. "Can I do anything?"

Tony dropped his hands and shook his head. "Nah. I'll be okay. Somehow, I always seem to land on my feet."

He left Diane's, ironically feeling worse than when he had gotten there. Maybe, he reasoned, it was because he wasn't entirely sure he had told her the truth when he had said he would see her again. After all, he didn't know where his next job was going to be, or what he was going to be doing, and that depressed him. He also had no idea in hell what he was going to tell Laura.

Driving home, he had an idea. He thought he'd stop by the lumberyard, see if they needed any help. Don, the owner, had always been kind to Tony and told him that he could come by if he ever needed anything. Tony thought it might be time to take him up on his offer.

When he pulled up to the site, Don was pulling out. Tony motioned for Don to roll down his window. "Hey, Don, you got a minute?"

"For you Tony? Of course." Don opened up the door to the truck he was driving and got out. "What's up?"

Tony recounted what had happened earlier, minus Diane, saying only that he had been fired and he wasn't sure why. Embarrassed, Tony looked at the ground and asked, "So I was wondering if you might need any extra help around here?"

"Hey," Don said sharply.

Tony looked up.

Don clapped him on the shoulder and said, "You start here Monday at seven. Talk to Mark when you get here. He's head of the union, and he'll hook you up." Then Don walked away.

"Thanks, Don," Tony yelled at the man's back. Don acknowledged him without turning around by raising his hand in the air in reply.

Tony couldn't believe his luck. Within two hours, he had lost a job he hated but had gotten a union job. And if the guys at the yard weren't talking out of their asses, his new job—his new *union* job—would pay more and require fewer hours. Now he couldn't *wait* to get home. Laura would be thrilled. Plus, with the additional income, he could also start helping his parents more, maybe even become a union steward. His father would love that.

As a thirty-year member of the Teamsters, his dad would have loved to have been the head of the union. Unfortunately, he had never even come close. But who knew what this would lead to. Although he had no aspirations of becoming union steward, he knew that it would, more than anything else, please his father, which of course, was what he lived for.

With the rest of the day off, Tony drove home, thinking he might take a nap and catch up on some much-needed sleep before he went to the club that night.

As soon as Tony walked into the Shamrock later that night, Sam walked up to him and told him to go pick up Joe.

Confused, Tony said, "Okay, but what am I gonna do about working tonight?"

"You'll be with Joe most of the night and then come back here around one or two in the morning."

"Okay."

"Oh hey, Ton, I almost forgot. Take this."

Tony turned back and reached for the object in Sam's hand. "This is from Victor. He was here last night, waiting for me in the parking lot."

The chunk of meth that Sam cupped stared at Tony like something alive.

"You might need this if you're going to be with Joe all night. It'll help sober you up before you get back to the club."

Tony took the drugs, broke off a piece, and handed the rest back. "Here, take some for the guys."

"I already did." Sam laughed. "I didn't think you'd mind. Don't worry, I'll tell them where it came from."

Tony waved his hand away. "That doesn't matter. You know I don't care about that shit."

"Yeah, I know. Okay, get outta here. Joe's waiting."

During dinner, Tony confided to Joe what had happened earlier in the day.

"Sounds like everything worked out and you still get the girl," Joe said, smiling, twirling his pasta with a fork. "So lemme ask you," Joe said, still playing with the food in front of him. "Talk is this girl is so beautiful you think she's too good for you. Why don't you invite her to the club and let me and the boys be the judge?"

"Yeah, okay," Tony said. "I'll call her in the morning."

After dinner, Tony and Joe walked over to Club Ciao to meet Joe's girlfriend, Nicky, and some of her friends. Tony knew that Joe had numerous girlfriends, but Nicky was the one he cared about.

Before going upstairs to the club, Joe pressed a twenty into each of the bouncers' hands.

"I'm expecting a lady friend and some of her girlfriends. When they get here, let 'em up."

Both bouncers nodded, hastily stuffing the money into their tuxedo pants while simultaneously allowing Tony and Joe to pass. Just as Tony and Joe started to climb the stairs, a voice called to Joe from somewhere behind them. It was Nicky and her friends. With just a nod to the bouncers, Nicky and her entourage were allowed in, and a path was cleared.

When the group reached the top, they were met with the loud *thump*, *thump*, *thump* of a song that was mostly bass and little else.

"Joey, let's dance!" Nicky squealed, grabbing Joe's hand.

"Baby, I need a drink before I do anything, and besides, you know I don't dance. But go, have fun."

"Joey, you're such a party pooper! You never wanna do anything!" Nicky whined, hands on her hips and pressing her full lips into a pout.

TONY TANCREDI AND CINDY L. O'HARA

Joe sighed. "Look, baby, I've told you before, I'm an awful dancer. But you know I love watching you. So please, I have some business to take care of. Go, enjoy yourself. Here's some money. Treat yourself and your friends to a good time. I'll catch up with you in a little while."

"Okay," Nicky said, placated only slightly by the cash that she kept fingering. She turned to her friends. "Let's go."

With Nicky taken care of, Joe and Tony walked to the bar. Tony surveyed the clientele and noticed three guys staring at Nicky and her girlfriends. Unsure of what to do, Tony finally pointed to the three men.

"Hey, Joe, you want me to take care of that situation over there?"

"I was wondering when you were gonna ask. Thanks, but I'll take care of it," Joe said, slipping off his barstool. Tony had no idea what Joe was up to, but followed his boss anyway. Standing shoulder-to-shoulder with Joe, Tony glanced at his boss. Tony's eyes grew wide, and he had to stifle a laugh.

Joe opened his jacket. With his hands on his hips and his dick hanging out, Joe said, "Are you staring at my girl or my dick? Because either way, you're going to get hurt if you don't find something else to look at."

Tony just looked impassively at the three men, who in turn had the sense to look horrified before turning away.

Joe zipped up and turned to Tony. "We're outta here," he said. "Let's go get Nicky and her friends."

Tony chuckled and followed his boss.

As the group barhopped throughout the night, the entire party—including Tony—was showered with attention wherever they went.

Yeah, Tony thought, *I could get used to this.*

FOURTEEN

ON HIS WAY to the lumberyard Monday morning, Tony realized that with everything going on, he hadn't spoken to Diane for two days. He made a mental note to try to get in touch with her sometime today.

When he pulled into the yard, promptly at 7 a.m., he went directly to the office to meet the general manager, Bob Keebe. Not knowing what to expect, Tony was not entirely surprised by the man sitting in front of him.

Bob was squat, with a bulbous nose that had a roadmap of red veins running over it, suggesting he loved some kind of alcohol. Judging by his gut, Tony thought, beer was his drink of choice.

Tony thrust out his hand and said, "Hey, Bob, I'm Tony Tancredi. Don Watson hired me Friday and told me to come by this morning."

Bob looked up from the mountain of papers he was sifting through and looked Tony up and down without extending his own hand.

"Don didn't tell me about you, but that don't mean nuthin' around here. After all, I'm just the general manager."

Not knowing what to say, Tony remained silent before letting his hand fall to his side.

Bob then heaved himself up, the chair groaning in relief, and managed to squeeze himself by Tony.

"Come on. I'll take ya around and introduce you to these yahoos I call employees."

Bob grabbed his clipboard and consulted it as if it were the Holy Grail. "Okay. I guess for now you can just work in the lumberyard. Then at some point, you'll make up lumber loads for the contractors.

"Until you get comfortable doing the loads yourself, you're gonna spend about a month as a helper on the forklift. Got that?"

Tony nodded as he kept in step with Bob. For a fat man, he walked surprisingly fast.

The first person they stopped in front of was Mark Chambers. A tall, medium-built man with glasses, who looked, Tony realized, a lot like Clark Kent.

Mark stuck out his hand and gripped Tony's in a firm shake. "How's it goin'?"

"All right," Tony replied.

"If you two ladies are done chitchattin', I've got other shit to take care of. Mark, take Tony here around and introduce him to the rest of the dickheads who work here, wouldja?"

Watching Bob retreat, Mark said, "That guy's a shithead."

Tony smiled, trying not to laugh out loud because it was as if Mark had read his mind. Tony knew then that he and Mark would get along great.

"Let's go meet the guys."

As they walked, Mark gave Tony the rundown on some of the crew he would be working with.

"Hey guys," Mark asked, walking up, "where's Murray?"

One tall well-muscled man with glasses pointed toward a forklift that had just pulled into the lumberyard.

"He's over there."

"Thanks, Pete. Guys, this is Tony. He's starting today, and I'd appreciate it if you'd show him at least a little more respect than you show me." The men laughed. "Shit, that won't be hard," one man boomed.

"I gave everything I had to your girlfriend—if you know what I mean," another said.

"Johnny, everyone knows what you mean, you friggin' idiot," Mark said, smiling at his crew. "Okay, back to work, everybody. Break time's over."

After the disgruntled rumblings died down and the men had disbanded, Mark and Tony walked toward the truck that had just arrived.

Inside the cab was a tall, thin man with sandy brown hair and a large, thick mustache.

"Hey, Murray, I want you to meet Tony," Mark yelled over the rumble of the engine. "He's starting today."

Murray shifted the heavy piece of machinery into gear to park it and jumped down.

"I know you, d-d-d-douche b-b-b-b-bag," Murray stuttered, landing neatly on his feet. "You u-u-u-sed to work for Dave S-s-s-s-shenk. What'd you do, get fired? 'Cuz I know you were working for him on F-f-f-friday." Murray let out a loud, sarcastic laugh, utterly pleased with himself.

"Murray," Tony said. "You are just about the funniest bastard I've been around in a long time."

Murray grinned like a kid who'd just been given the keys to the candy store.

"Okay, you two, if you're done kissin' each other's asses, there's a thing called work to be done," Mark said. "Tony, you stick with me the rest of the day. Murray, you finish up here."

"Sure, b-b-boss," Murray stuttered, which got Tony laughing all over again.

Walking away, Tony said, "All these guys seem all right."

"They are," said Mark. "They're the best. Every single one of 'em would have your back in a heartbeat."

"Good to know," Tony said.

Throughout the day, Tony continued to tag along after Mark, watching and learning the ropes of working in a lumberyard, which really wasn't much of a stretch from where he'd worked before.

During a rare moment of downtime, Mark and Tony took a break. Mark immediately took a pack of cigarettes from his shirt pocket and lit up.

"So," Tony asked, "what do you like to do when you're not here enjoying the sunshine and BS'in' with the boys?"

"Normal bullshit, I guess—hang out with the guys, watch the Eagles get their asses kicked, drink some beer, the usual stuff. Why?" Mark asked.

"Just wondered," Tony said.

"You play darts?"

"Nah, not my game," Tony replied. "Why?"

"'Cuz there's this great bar downtown called Rose's. I mean, it's just your normal sports bar, but it's got a pool table, a few dartboards, and pitchers of cold beer for a few bucks on Wednesday nights. What more could you ask for, right?"

All of a sudden, Tony was very interested in what Mark did in his off time and where he went. "So darts, huh?" Tony asked, trying to appear uninterested.

"Yeah, I'm in a league at Rose's, and we're always lookin' to pick up a player. Wednesdays is when we play, which is why beer's so cheap. You wanna come?"

"Nah," Tony said. "Well, maybe . . . you playin' this Wednesday night?"

"Yeah, we play every week, why?"

"Just makin' conversation," Tony said, trying to figure out how in the hell he was going to keep Mark from going to Rose's in a couple of days.

A dozen what-ifs raced through Tony's mind, one leading to another in perfect order. Questions like, what if Mark knew the men whom Tony was supposed to take care of for Wolfie Wednesday night? Or what if Mark was a friend of one or all of the men? Or what if Mark was *one* of the men? Question upon question continued to eat at Tony, until finally, he asked the only thing he could. "Any of the guys here play?"

"Nah, just me. These yahoos wouldn't know a dart from their dick."

TONY TANCREDI AND CINDY L. O'HARA

Tony laughed, then asked, "Hey, you ever been to the Shamrock Club?"

"Nah, never heard of it," Mark replied, throwing the remainder of his cigarette on the ground and grinding it with the toe of his boot. "Why?"

"Never mind."

"You know, you sure ask a lot of questions for no reason. What's up?"

"Look, Mark, I like you . . ."

"Ahhhh, I like you too, Tony," Mark said, putting his arm affectionately around Tony and grinning.

"Okay, asshole, knock it off. Look, everyone here seems pretty cool, but I gotta ask you a favor."

"Uh-huh, go on," Mark said, dropping his arm.

"I can't tell you why, but I need you to stay home this Wednesday night—or at least stay away from Rose's Bar."

Mark gave Tony a puzzled look. "Why?"

Searching quickly for a believable answer, Tony said, "I don't know. I heard there might be some trouble there Wednesday night, and trust me, you don't want to be there."

"How would you know that? What kind of trouble?"

"Mark, listen, just don't go there Wednesday night, okay?"

"Sure, Ton. Whatever you say."

"Okay, thanks," Tony said. "I guess we better get back to work, huh?" Tony asked, turning and walking away, anxious to put some distance between himself and Mark—at least for a few minutes.

"Yeah, I guess," Mark said.

FIFTEEN

"HEY, DICK, TONY Tancredi here, from the Shamrock Club. How you doin'?"

"Fine until now. What's up?"

"Look, I'm gonna be honest with you. I have some business I have to take care of there tonight, but I wanted to let you know so you wouldn't worry."

"You tell me you're comin' to *my* bar tonight to, quote unquote 'take care of some business,' and I'm not supposed to worry? What the fuck?"

Tony could almost feel Dick's blood pressure rising through the phone lines.

"Look, calm down. You're gonna have a heart attack, for Chrissakes!" Tony knew Dick, and at five-foot-eight and pushing three hundred pounds, the likelihood of a heart attack or something else just as fatal happening to the normally happy, easygoing bartender was not unlikely.

Tony continued, "I wanted to call you personally and tell you that you have my word that nothing is going to happen . . . *inside*, but I needed to let you know so you can keep your bouncers out of it—you know, so they don't get hurt."

Tony knew his reputation was starting to precede him throughout the Philly bars and nightclubs, so that bartenders, owners, and even staff members, had, at the very least, heard of someone working at the Shamrock who should be taken seriously.

"Yeah, okay," said Dick. "I appreciate the call, Tony. Thanks."

With that task accomplished, Tony had only to wait for Monte and Doc before heading to Rose's.

When Doc turned onto Roosevelt Boulevard, he circled the block three times before finally parking across the street.

"Okay, this is how it's going to play out," said Tony, turning sideways to look at both bouncers. "I've already called Dick and told him we were coming, and he said he'd make sure his bouncers didn't get in the way. I also told Dick that we wouldn't do anything inside, so I figure we'd take these guys out back and rough 'em up there—unless anyone has any objections or better suggestions."

No one did.

They climbed out of Doc's brand-new coal-black 1984 Cadillac Fleetwood.

"Nice ride, man," said Monte, slamming the rear door soundly.

"Hey, what the hell!" Doc yelled. "You wanna be a little careful there? This baby's brand-new, dickhead, and I'd like to keep her that way for longer than a few days. Know what I mean?"

"Ah, bite me," Monte replied.

"Hey, if you two goombahs are done announcing our arrival, can we do what we came here to do?"

"Yeah, yeah, yeah," Monte said. "Keep your panties on, dago."

"I would if I were wearin' any," Tony replied, smiling.

"That's just friggin' disgusting!" Monte answered. "Not to mention wrong. And let me add, something that I absolutely did *not* need to know."

They crossed the street and stood outside the bar.

"So everybody ready?" Tony asked one more time.

"Yeah, Ton. Let's get this over with," Doc said.

Tony opened the door.

Not wanting to stay longer than was necessary, he took in their surroundings.

Inside, Rose's was dark, save for the neon Budweiser sign that hung behind the oak bar. A four-leaf clover and other Irish memorabilia glowed unsteadily, blinking off and on, casting small shadows on the floor. Light also flickered from the four or five TVs mounted throughout the pub, one broadcasting an-Eagles game, the other tuned in to the Steelers.

Tony looked around and noted that the place was jammed with locals, more than he had expected for a Wednesday night—some playing pool, others watching the game, but most waiting for the dart league to start. With the back of his right hand, he smacked Doc on the chest and lifted his chin toward a trio of men standing around a waist-high table, intent on guzzling a pitcher of beer. One man in particular grabbed Tony's attention. He was louder than the others, and the way the other two men kowtowed to him told Tony he had to be the leader of the three.

Ignoring the oval faux leather barstools that were pushed to the side, the men opted to stand and drink their beer. This, Tony thought, would make their job a whole hell of a lot easier—nothing to get in the way of getting the men out of the bar.

Overhead, Jim Nantz called the play-by-play for the Eagles game, and from the corner jukebox, Bruce Springsteen screamed in his gravelly voice that he was "just tired and bored with myself."

Tony welcomed the noise as he eased through the throng of people. Monte and Doc followed two steps behind. They walked up to the table and surrounded it, encasing the trio.

"What's going on, boys?" Tony whispered, not really wanting or expecting an answer. "We need to talk to you—outside—and I think it's best if you don't make a scene in here, or it's gonna be a lot worse out there." Tony jerked his head toward the door.

The three men dutifully got up and did as they were told.

During Tony's discourse, Monte and Doc had positioned themselves directly behind one man each. When Tony nodded, Monte and Doc grabbed the man they were standing behind, wrenching one arm up their back and twisting the back of their shirt collar, shoving them ahead. Tony did the same, but in addition to twisting the leader's arm into an obscene angle that shouldn't have even been possible, Tony grabbed the man's long mulleted hair in one hand (business in the front, party in the back) jerking and yanking the kid's head just to the point that Tony could see the vein in his neck beginning to throb.

Just as they were about to leave, Tony whispered almost lovingly into the boy's ear, "Got anything to say now, tough guy?"

"Hey man, you gonna just stand there and let them do this?"

The bouncer looked blankly at the man. "Do what? They just wanna talk to you. Right, Ton?" The bouncer laughed and winked at Tony.

"Right. That's what I was tellin' him."

As they neared the front door, Tony said, "Hey, stupid, get that for me wouldja?" With that, Tony shoved the kid forward, releasing his grip just enough to let the boy's head bang soundly against the bar door, hard enough for it to open. Stunned, the boy stumbled out, his knees beginning to buckle.

"Oh no, no, no," Tony said. "Not yet, you don't." Refusing to let the kid fall, Tony continued shoving him until he had joined Monte and Doc, who already had their victims down on the ground.

Tony then released his grip—at which point the boy's legs gave way, and he collapsed like a broken doll to the asphalt.

They then began beating and kicking the boys, their hard-toed shoes connecting with ribs, balls, knees—any place they could find.

"This is from Wolfie," Tony yelled, stomping on one boy's dick. "He sends his regards!"

TONY TANCREDI AND CINDY L. O'HARA

The beating continued for the next couple of minutes until Tony finally signaled that it was enough. As the three boys writhed in pain, Tony squatted by the leader of the three. The boy's face was marred with bloody cuts, scratches, and scrapes that would take more than iodine to heal, and one eye was ballooned shut. A bruise on his cheekbone was already beginning to turn purple, and Tony wouldn't have been surprised if he hadn't broken a rib or two. He smiled, leaned down, and in a soft voice said, "I'm going to say this once, so pay attention, you little prick. The next time you and any of your friends think about causing any problems at the Shamrock Club, remember where it got you." Tony stood, looking at the mess he had created of the boy's face and felt a sense of pride at a job well done.

"Hopefully, you've learned your lesson, but just so there's no misunderstanding between us, let me be clear." Tony had walked behind the boy. "Don't." Tony kicked him square in the left kidney. "Fuck." This time, Tony aimed and connected with the right kidney. He walked around to the front. "With." He delivered a swift kick to the stomach. The boy's hand instantly moved from the back where he had been holding his kidney, to the front. He grabbed his stomach and exhaled loudly, then groaned. "People." Tony took a couple of steps toward the man's feet, raised his leg, and brought his foot down with bone-crushing force on the man's ankle. Bones snapped under Tony's foot. This time, the boy screamed. Tony kept moving. "From the Shamrock." The last blow he delivered to the man's crotch. Tony turned and walked away, Doc and Monte trailing him.

When they returned to the club, Tony leaned on the bar and said, "Hey, Gary, call your dad and tell him everything is done."

"Sure, Ton," Gary replied, a puzzled look on his face.

Later that night, Wolfie walked into the Shamrock and headed straight to Tony.

"I just wanted to personally thank you for taking care of my family's problem. It means a lot to me."

Embarrassed, Tony said, "It was nuthin', Wolfie. Nuthin' I wouldn't have done for anyone in my family."

"Well, again, thank you. I'd like to buy you and your friends a drink."

"Sure."

Looking around the club, he spied Doc and Monte leaning against a wall in the corner of the bar, watching the club's clientele. He walked over to the two men. "Hey guys, how's it goin'?"

"Good, Ton. What's up?" Doc asked.

"Wolfie came by to thank us for the errand we did earlier. He'd like to buy us a drink to show his appreciation. I've already told Greg to take us off the clock for a few minutes, unless, of course, all hell breaks loose."

"Cool," Monte said. "I could use a drink."

"Amen, brutha," Doc said.

Tony, Doc, and Monte ended up taking the rest of the night off, drinking with Wolfie and recounting in excruciating detail what had happened at Rose's.

The next day at the lumberyard, before even punching in, his head hammering from the night before, Mark met Tony.

"I need to talk to you."

"Yeah, well, everybody needs sumthin'. Right now, I need a few dozen aspirins, my gallon of water, and more sleep, but it ain't gonna happen," Tony replied, sensing it best to avoid Mark for a while.

Tony hoped that his irritability was enough to keep Mark from pursuing further conversation. But as he turned away, Mark kept in step with him.

"Look," Mark started. "I did like you told me and didn't go to Rose's last night—"

"Good for you."

"But my sister did," he continued. "She called me at six this morning and told me that I missed a helluva show last night. Said these guys that looked like gangsters came in the bar and took out the players on the team who I don't like and beat the hell out of 'em. Said the other bouncers just stood around and watched, didn't make a move to stop it at all. Would you like to explain that, Chief?"

Tony stopped walking and turned to his friend. "Look, Mark, I've got a headache the size of Texas, I'm hungover, and I'm working off of about two hours of sleep. The fact is, I just heard some trouble could be goin' down, and I didn't want you to get involved."

Mark snorted a laugh. "Thanks for the concern, but I'm not buying it."

Thankful that Mark hadn't been there, Tony continued walking away. "Believe what you want, but that's it. Nothing more to it than that."

TONY TANCREDI AND CINDY L. O'HARA

SIXTEEN

THE LUMBERYARD, LOCATED on Lincoln Avenue in Newtown, took up the entire street and then some. With temperatures in the nineties and humidity to match, it was just hot enough to make working conditions miserable.

As the sweat poured off of Tony and dust and dirt rained down, he reflected on a conversation he had recently had with Mark.

Mark had said the workers were being taken advantage of by the owners, and *that*, more than anything else, rubbed Tony the wrong way and made him reconsider getting involved.

Mark was not only one of the crew but was the union steward as well, which meant he was head of the union for the forklift drivers and laborers. Tony knew the job was an easy one that consisted of handling minor disputes between owners and workers and making sure the employees were being treated fairly. But the word around the yard was that the owners weren't living up to their end of the contract. They weren't paying the men time-and-a half or double-time when required.

To make matters worse, Mark had said, the carpenters union and the teamsters weren't standing up to the owners either. Any time one of the workers or the union heads threatened to go to the business agent—the next person in the food chain of the union hierarchy—the owners would threaten that person.

"Threaten them with what?" Tony asked, curiosity getting the better of him despite his personal promise not to get drawn into whatever drama was going on in the yard. "The owners can't fire them."

"No," Mark said. "They'd never do that. They'd just make whoever was complaining so goddamn miserable on the job that they'd quit. And most, if not all these guys, need this job."

With nothing left to say, Tony just nodded in what he hoped conveyed understanding and sympathy. Mark hadn't pushed Tony, and then he just dropped it.

Now standing in the blazing sun with nothing to do but think, Tony wondered, against his better judgment, if he shouldn't give this situation some of his attention.

Who the hell was he kidding? Just by the amount of time he had spent thinking about it, he was already involved. Why not take it a step farther? He sighed and made a mental note to talk to Mark.

Having made the decision to do what he could for the men, whatever the hell that might be, Tony thought it would be easy enough to get the crew to rally behind him. A few of the guys from the yard had already been to the Shamrock Club, and Tony had made sure to show them a good time, for no other reason than he liked to take care of people he was close to.

Tony had helped Mark fix a little problem a while back. Tony smiled as he remembered how he had been able to get Mark a room at Caesar's in Atlantic City when they had been sold out.

In passing, Mark had told Tony that he was going to get engaged one weekend, and had wanted to take his girl to AC as a surprise but couldn't get a room. Tony told Mark to give him a day and he'd see what he could do.

Mark just laughed and said, "What the hell can you do? They're sold out."

"Just gimme a day," Tony replied.

"Whatever. Hey, Ton," Mark said, turning back. "You pull this one outta yer ass, and I'll owe you one!"

Tony just smiled.

That night at the club, he went to Joe and explained the situation. Soon after that, the problem was solved. Not only would Mark have a room, Joe said, "I'll comp him so he doesn't have to pay a thing."

By the way, Joe asked, "Who's this for?"

Tony told Joe it was for the union steward at the lumberyard, a good guy. He wondered if Joe was going to renege on the room for some reason.

"The union stew? Why aren't you head of the union down there?" Joe asked.

"Ah, Joe. I don't want that responsibility. I got too much goin' on already. You know that. Besides, if I did ever become the head guy, and I'm not sayin' I am or would, it'd have to be because the guys up there *want* me to be."

"All right. But if you *do* ever decide to do this, I can take care of it in a day," Joe said. "All the union heads and business agents from all the unions are friends of mine and come into the club. In fact, the legal owner of the Shamrock Club is head of the plumbers union. So I'm just sayin' if you ever want to, you know, take over up there or whatever, I could help."

Tony stood in front of his boss, mulling over the information he had just been given. Tony knew the people Joe was referring to, not only by face when they came into the club, but as names from the past when his father worked as a teamster.

Tony was beginning to realize just who and what he was dealing with—and loved it.

That night, Tony lay in bed with Laura, the soft glow of the TV the only light in the room. Laura snored softly as Johnny Carson finished up his monologue. Tony got up and silenced Johnny with the flip of a switch, then climbed back into bed. Still not tired enough to sleep, his thoughts turned to his life and what had become of it in the last few months. He had gone from being a devoted husband and father to someone even he didn't recognize.

Most days (or nights), when he allowed himself to think about it, he justified his behavior by telling himself that he could walk away from this life any time he wanted to. He just didn't want to—nor did he see a need to. What he did on his own was part of what he had come to think of as his private life—and was none of anybody's goddamn business, thank you very much. And Laura never complained because the extra two hundred dollars a week more than made up for his absenteeism and indiscretions. Didn't it?

Ironically, though, Laura didn't weigh on his mind. Diane did.

For months, he had been trying to see her for more than a few minutes at a time, which always seemed to be limited to quick meetings at night. On those occasions, she would make excuses to her husband about needing to get some air or wanting to go for a walk. Tony would then pick her up around the corner from her house, where they would go park for fifteen minutes and kiss like love-starved teenagers before he dropped her back off again. It was, Tony thought, ridiculous, not to mention frustrating.

No matter how much pussy he was getting at the club, it wasn't the right person—it wasn't Diane.

One night, as he drove to her neighborhood, he vowed that he was done begging. He had asked her on more than one occasion to come to the club so he could introduce her to his friends and then take her to a hotel where they could be alone, but she always declined.

Selfishly, and not without a little vanity, Tony reasoned that if he could get her to the club, she would see other women coming on to him, and that would spur her to give in. So far, though, she was digging in her heels, telling him the reason she was holding out was not because of some misguided sense of loyalty to her husband, but to her kid.

While Tony said he understood her reasons (he didn't), and that he didn't like to give ultimatums (he did), he argued that everything was getting to be too much for only a few minutes of her time a week.

Tony remembered one night just last week. They parked just around the corner from her house, but instead of the usual groping and grabbing, he and Diane had sat and argued about when she could come to the club. In the end, she said she would think about his offer. With her hand on the door handle, she turned and asked, "Can you come by for lunch tomorrow?"

Puzzled, Tony said, "I think so. If you don't hear from me, I'll be there." Tony thought he could manage it by asking to take a longer lunch and offering to let them dock him for the extra time off.

Typically, lunch breaks were only half an hour, but if Keebe let him go, he calculated that he could make it to Diane's house in fifteen minutes. Leaving the same amount of time for the return trip would give them half an hour to be together.

Not wanting her to leave on the remnants of an argument, Tony leaned over and gently kissed her on the lips. "I love you, Di."

Taking a deep breath, she whispered, "I love you too." Then she pushed on the door handle and climbed out of the car. She lifted her hand and waved good-bye. Tony did the same, put the car in gear, steered the car toward home.

Once there, Tony finally fell asleep, his dreams colored by a woman with long blonde hair and green eyes, holding a baby who looked an awful lot like him.

The next day at the yard, when Tony asked Keebe about taking an extended lunch, the general manager's only response was, "Don't make a friggin' habit of it."

Elated, Tony practically ran to his car, fumbling for his keys, almost dropping them in his hurry. He jammed it in the lock and, in one motion, opened his car door and slid inside. Tony peeled out of the lot, leaving billowing clouds of dust in his wake. Anyone watching would have wondered what in the hell had gotten into him.

Driving as fast as the speed limit would allow and taking corners on what felt like two wheels, Tony made it to Diane's in approximately twelve minutes. There, he squealed into her driveway, leaving skid marks as he did so. Tony threw open the car door and practically fell onto the driveway in his impatience to get to Diane.

Taking a minute to get his breathing under control, he waited a beat, then rang the bell.

As if she had been waiting by the door, Diane pulled the door wide open so he could come in.

"Hi," she said shyly.

"Hi," Tony replied, stepping into the foyer.

Diane closed the door behind him and started for the dining room, where she had lunch set up.

For Tony, food was (almost) as important as, certainly sometimes even better than, sex. So when he saw the meatball subs—the buns toasted to a crisp golden brown and the provolone cheese melting, mixing atop the tomato sauce and meatballs—he practically groaned in anticipation.

"Honey, you made my favorite," Tony said.

"Here, sit down and eat while I clean up the kitchen."

Tony pulled out a chair and sat. He snatched the blue linen napkin from beside his plate and gave it a crisp shake. Tony picked up the first sandwich and bit down. He let some of the tomato sauce dribble down his chin, not caring that he was making a mess. The food exploded with flavor, and although Tony would have loved to have taken his time and savored each crumb, he also wanted to have as much time as possible with Diane. So when she wandered into the dining room, wiping her hands on a dishtowel, and saw that he had wolfed down two meatball subs in approximately five minutes, she said, "Like 'em, didja?"

Tony could only nod, feeling a bit sick at having eaten so much, so quickly.

He pushed back from the table and quietly burped into his palm. Diane giggled.

After excusing himself, Tony walked over and took her hand, intent on taking her into the living room so they could be on the sofa. Instead, Diane withdrew her hand and roughly pushed Tony against the dining room wall. At the same time that her lips crushed his in a hard kiss and her tongue pried open his mouth, her hand traveled down to the top of his shorts, fumbling with the button. She then unzipped his cutoffs, gently slipped her hand inside, and massaged him until he was hard. While her hand continued to squeeze and tug, she gently bit Tony's lip. She let go and whispered into his ear, "I don't want any other woman near you."

Then Diane got down on her knees and took Tony in her mouth. His hands flat against the wall, Tony couldn't believe what was happening. He closed his eyes and fell into the moment, groaning as he began to climax.

When she was finished, Diane got up and asked, "Was that okay for you, honey?"

Tony's eyes opened. *How could she be serious?* he wondered. But Tony could see she was and that she needed some assurance.

"My god Diane, how could you even ask that? It was incredible!"

"Really?" she asked, like a small child waiting to be praised.

"Honey, I swear to God, that's the best it's ever been for me. I promise, no other women—ever." As soon as the words were out of Tony's mouth, he wondered how true they were. The old, familiar pang of guilt that was such a part of his everyday life now returned. It was immediately washed away, though, by the very mundane thought of having to get back to work.

"I'm sorry, Di, but I've gotta go. I'll call when I can."

She nodded in understanding. "It's okay, really," she said, walking ahead of him to the front door. Tony trailed her, loath to leave, but knowing he had to get back to the yard.

Before stepping outside, he chastely kissed her on the cheek while rubbing her arm. "I'll call, okay?" he said, pulling back and searching her eyes. In them, he saw nothing.

"Okay. Now get outta here," she said, smiling.

Tony stepped outside, and the door closed softly behind him.

He took a moment to stretch, letting the sun wash over him. With a large grin on his face, he climbed back into his car and headed to the lumberyard.

This time, the soft hum of the radio kept him company as he drove down the street toward work.

TONY TANCREDI AND CINDY L. O'HARA

SEVENTEEN

THE NEXT DAY, Tony used a few minutes of his lunchtime to call Diane from the lumberyard. Given what had happened yesterday, Tony felt justified in asking her (more like begging, really) to come to the club this weekend. Before he could get the words out, however, Diane said she had told her husband that she would be going out with the girls and wouldn't be home until 2 o'clock.

Tony was speechless. When he recovered, he blurted the first thing that came to mind.

"Diane, you've just made me the happiest guy in the world! I'll see you Friday, okay?"

Diane laughed. "Okay, it's a date."

When Tony hung up the phone, he let out a whoop of joy so loud that Mark, who was walking by, stopped and asked, "What's up, Chief?"

"Mark, my man, I just got some really great news!" Tony said, pounding his friend on the back.

"Oh yeah? What's that?"

"Well, that I can't tell ya, but trust me, it's good, and I appreciate you bein' happy for me!"

"Whatever you say, Ton."

"So whatdaya have goin' on this weekend?" asked Tony, falling into step with his friend and colleague.

The two men chatted comfortably as they walked to the forklifts to continue their day.

When Friday finally arrived, the first thing Tony did after walking into the club was to announce that Diane would be coming in that night. He hadn't wanted to tell anyone beforehand because he knew he would've heard about it all week long. He also called Joe and told him that Diane would be coming to the club and he wouldn't be able to pick him up that night.

"Really?" Joe said. "We finally get to meet the mysterious Diane? Well, after the buildup you've given this woman, I'm not goin' anywhere either. I wouldn't wanna miss this."

Tony wondered if he'd overdone it by talking so highly of her, but then immediately dismissed the thought as ridiculous.

Throughout the night, Tony waited for Diane to show up. They hadn't set a time, so Tony didn't know when to expect her. In a moment of panic, he thought, *What if she can't get away or something else happens that she can't show? Then what'll I tell the guys?*

As Tony paced, Greg finally marched up to him and said, "Will you go sit down and have a drink, for Chrissakes! You're making me nervous!"

"Damn," said Doc, walking up. "I've never seen anything make Tony so uptight. Look at him. He's always so cool. This is great, watching him sweat!"

"Shut the hell up, you guys. I'm nervous enough as it is. At least that Irish piece of shit, Monte, is late, as usual, so I don't have to listen to him too. And by the way, when you see her, you'll know why I'm like this. If you guys knew what she did to me a couple of days ago—"

"Well, why don't you tell us, my little greaseball." Monte walked up, a large grin plastered on his face.

"Nope, I'm not sayin' any more about her until you see her for yourself. Then we'll see what all you tough guys have to say."

As the bouncers' voices continued to heat up, everyone trying to talk over one another, Sam and Joe walked into the club. All conversation ceased.

Joe took one look at Tony and said, "Why don't you take the night off and leave with her after I buy you both a drink and we get a look at her."

"Joe, really that's not necessary—"

Joe raised his hand. "I don't want to hear another word. Oh, and don't let her walk through the parking lot alone. Make sure you or one of the other guys meets her."

Angry with himself for not thinking of that very thing, Tony said he would do it.

"Have the parking spot at the front door cleared and let her park there in my spot. I'm not going anywhere until she leaves with you anyway," Joe said, smiling and winking at Tony.

Feeling grateful, as well as humbled, Tony did the only thing he could think to do, which was to say thank you.

As Tony watched Diane pull into the parking lot, he could hardly contain himself. He waved at her to park in the front of the club. Just as Tony started out the door, Greg (all 160 pounds of him) breezed past.

"Just stand there and look pretty, wouldja? I'll go get the lady fair and bring her to you."

Tony did as he was told, amazed at his friends. After taking heat from everyone only hours before, here they were—at least here was Greg—trying to make him look good in front of Diane.

Greg opened the car door and took Diane's hand, helping her out of the car. She nodded her thanks and turned toward the club, while Greg walked a respectful step behind. When she crossed the threshold into the club, she kissed Tony lightly on both cheeks. Greg tried not to gape and continued to eye his friend.

"Thanks, Greg." With his hand pressed lightly to her back, Tony walked Diane slowly through the club.

Diane played the room to perfection, her hips swaying gently to the music as she walked, her yellow dress (which was just short enough in both the front and back to give people a glimpse without a show) clung in all the right places.

Tony marveled at her confidence, watching her strut through the club, as if she were on the catwalk, modeling for Dior and Versace. She reached back so that Tony could lightly hold her fingers.

When Tony glanced around, all eyes were on Diane—men with girls, who didn't care if they were caught looking, couples, single women, it didn't matter. Everyone watched as Diane and Tony parted the crowd.

Wanting to show the utmost respect, Tony took Diane to Joe first before introducing her to anyone else.

"Welcome to our club," Joe said. "Please. Sit down." "Gary!" Joe yelled, settling into his chair.

"Yeah, boss?" Gary yelled back.

"Give this beautiful lady whatever she wants—and oh, Tony too, I guess." Joe winked at Diane.

"I thought Tony was a little too nervous tonight, but now I understand why," he said, smiling.

"Here you go, boss." Gary brought the drinks and set them down.

As she brought the glass to her lips, Tony noticed her hand was shaking ever so slightly. "Tony's so silly sometimes." She took a sip of the white wine, and then leaned in so that her full breasts were nearly touching Joe's hand, talking as if Tony weren't there. "I'm sure he could have anyone he wants in here."

"Well," Joe said, never taking his eyes off of the woman in front of him. "I don't know how he could be interested in anyone, anywhere, after being with you."

Diane smiled at the compliment and sat back in her chair.

As the night wore on, Tony was anxious to get out and spend some time alone with Diane, but he was also hesitant to leave his coworkers and friends with so many people crowding the club. Joe had long ago excused himself and gone to the back room, and everyone else seemed preoccupied, but fine. Making the decision to leave, Tony decided he would go say good night to Joe and thank all the bouncers—especially Greg.

Tony whispered to Diane that they would be leaving soon, after he made his rounds. She nodded and smiled. "Make it quick," she whispered into his ear.

Groaning, Tony shook his head in wonder at this woman he felt he was just beginning to know.

As Tony drifted away from her, a tall, well-dressed, and well-built man entered the club. The man took one look at Diane and made a beeline for her. While Tony couldn't tell what was being said, the man reached out to touch Diane's leg.

In seconds, Tony closed the gap between himself and the man who was touching Diane. Tony grabbed the guy by the throat and shoved him up against the closest available wall. The man's feet dangled like a rag doll's, inches from the ground. It was, Tony thought, eerily similar to what he had done to that spic Flores and the idiot from his neighborhood. Tony repeatedly bounced the man's head off the wall, his skull making a sick, crunching noise as it banged back and forth like a tennis ball.

"Get him before he breaks that guy's neck!" Greg yelled.

As Tony started to throw a right, Monte grabbed Tony's arm, but it was as ineffective as a gnat trying to stop an elephant, as evidenced when all of Monte's 220 pounds went flying against the wall.

"He's lost it!" Greg shouted. "We gotta talk to him! Doc, try and get this asshole away from him!"

Finally, Diane screamed, "Tony! Stop it!"

By now, the poor, hapless man was starting to lose consciousness.

As if in a daze, Tony yanked his hand away in disgust, looking at it as if it were something foreign to him.

"Ton, come on, man, it's okay. It's over," said Doc, gently putting his hand on the back of Tony's neck. Tony allowed himself to be pulled away from the man, who by now was slumped on the ground.

"Monte," Greg said. "Get this guy outta here." Monte nodded, rubbing the back of his head, which had begun to throb from where it had connected with the wall.

"What the hell's going on here?" Joe strode up to Tony. Tony refused to look Joe in the eye, mumbled that the guy came into the bar and harassed Diane.

"How?"

"He touched her leg," Tony replied.

Trying not to smile, Joe pulled Tony aside and said, "Tony, it's okay. Don' worry about it. In fact, why don't you and your lady go have some quiet time together."

Tony nodded, only wanting to put as much distance as possible between himself and the club.

"And one other thing," Joe said before releasing his grip on his protégé. "Take this."

Joe handed Tony a small metallic object. "This is the key to my suite at the Hilton. You can't take a lady like that to just any hotel." Joe winked slyly at Tony, who remained speechless.

Finally, Tony recovered enough to say, "Joe, what if you hook up with something you like?"

"Lemme tell you, after seeing Diane, I don't think anything is going to look good to me tonight. Nope. I think I'm just gonna go home, jerk off, and go to sleep." Then Joe laughed and walloped Tony on the back. "Now get outta here!"

With that, Diane marched past Tony, who was doing his best to stay in step with her. Monte and Doc followed a respectful few feet to the rear.

On the way out, Diane started in. Because she was ahead of him, Tony caught only a few words at a time. He wasn't sure if she knew that he couldn't hear her, but he didn't think it best to correct her.

"I can't believe—" Then the crowd and music drowned out the rest of her sentence.

"Behaved like some wild—"

Tony was saved from her one-sided conversation when Monte interjected.

"Damn, dago! I can't believe how strong you are! I'll never try and stop a right hand of yours again!"

"And *I* can't believe what a monster you can be!" Diane continued. This Tony caught with perfect clarity.

"Ah, Diane," Doc said. "He just got a little excited, is all. I hope you can forgive him. He was only protecting your honor."

Unmoved, Diane opened her own car door, plopped down in the seat, and slammed it shut.

EIGHTEEN

O N THE WAY to the hotel, Diane remained silent, emotionally spent from what she had just witnessed at the club. She wondered if she hadn't gone completely off the deep end to get involved with a man like Tony. Yet here she was on her way to a hotel to sleep with him—and happy to be doing so. Her husband was such a prick and didn't treat her well (not that what she was doing made it right), yet still she questioned herself as to whether or not she was being completely selfish.

Until now, she had justified her behavior by consoling herself that this affair was only harmless kissing (okay, a little more than kissing, let's be honest), but after tonight, she wondered if she'd be able to live with herself. After agonizing over this throughout the week, she still didn't have an answer. Now having seen how Tony could act when provoked made the decision of whether to go through with tonight that much more difficult. Although, she had to admit, Tony's behavior had turned her on back there. Her husband certainly would never have done what Tony did, fought for her honor. Instead, Paul probably would have wondered (out loud) why the hell the man at the club would have wanted to touch her anyway.

Diane sighed. If not for her son, she would have left her husband a long time ago.

Tentatively, she rested her hand lightly on Tony's leg while still staring out through the window at the darkness.

"I'm not condoning what you did back there, and I better not ever see that again."

Tony remained silent, but quickly covered her hand with his. "I know. I know."

For the first time in a week, Diane felt at peace with her decision.

When they arrived at the hotel, two doormen greeted them by opening their car doors. As they walked through the lobby of the Hilton, Diane stared in wonder at the exquisite wall hangings and ornate furniture decorating the large room.

"This is stunning," Diane murmured, unable to keep from commenting.

"Uh-huh," he muttered, pressing one hand on her back while steering her toward the bank of elevators.

Once inside, Tony relaxed slightly. He pressed the number 4 and stepped back, reaching for Diane's fingers. When the elevator arrived at their floor, Tony stepped ahead of Diane. Still not saying a word, they walked toward the suite. Tony inserted the key into the lock and pushed open the door. Diane eased past him, taking in the room.

Atop the coffee table sat a large arrangement of red roses, with a card poking out of it.

"Tony, you didn't have to do this."

Although he could have taken credit for it (he assumed Joe had sent them and knew his boss wouldn't care if he did), he said, "Uh, I wish I could take credit for those, Di, but it wasn't me."

"Oh, well who then?" She plucked out the card and opened the envelope. "Ah, Joe. How sweet. Tell him they're lovely when you see him."

"I will," Tony replied, his gaze continuing to sweep the room. Soon, he lighted on something Joe had provided for *him*, and walked to the ice bucket that was sitting on a bedside table in the large master bedroom. Beside it was a card that read simply, "Enjoy."

While Tony popped the Dom Perignon, Diane called to him from the other room. "I'll be right in."

"Okay," he said.

"Hi," she whispered. She walked over to him, her hips swaying back and forth.

Without a word, Tony kissed her gently on the lips, then a little more urgently.

Although she thought they would both be ravenous for each other, ripping and pawing at each other's clothes (and from Tony's hard-on, she didn't think she was far from the truth), they were actually moving quite slowly, almost as if in a dream.

As they continued to kiss, the champagne forgotten, Tony slipped the dress over her head. She undid the buttons on his shirt and ran her hands over his chest.

Gently, Tony eased her onto the bed and slowly slipped her white silk panties down her legs. He gazed at her full breasts, then let his gaze roam up and down her body. Still, he remained silent.

Finally growing uncomfortable under so much scrutiny, Diane said, "Why are you just looking at me? Is something wrong?"

"God no, Diane. How could you think that? You're perfect."

"Well, what then?"

"It's just I can't believe we're finally here. I've fantasized about this every day since I first saw you in the garden, and I don't wanna rush this."

Diane nodded in understanding. She then fixated on Tony's manhood, which by now was throbbing with anticipation. Her breathing had become erratic. She panted, "You've told me so many times how much you love me . . . now I want you to show me."

Tony complied by bending down between her legs and gently parting them. He began exploring her with his tongue. After she came three or four times, she whispered, "I want you inside me now."

In only a few moments, they came together.

When they were done, they held each other tightly.

"I love you, Tony," Diane whispered against his shoulder.

"I love you too," Tony said, holding her away from him to get a better look at her.

Although Diane had her head bent, one tiny tear escaped and leaked down her cheek.

Concerned that he had done or said something wrong, Tony asked, "What's the matter?"

Diane shook her head.

Tony waited, holding his breath. Unable to wait any longer, Tony asked, "What?"

"It's just, I have never, you know, trembled like that before, never lost control like that. Wherever you took me, I want to go back there again."

Exhaling, Tony gripped Diane by the shoulders and waited until she looked him in the eyes.

"From this point on, you are my life, Diane. This is what love is supposed to feel like."

For the next three hours, they made love continuously, stopping only long enough to drink from the champagne glasses and nibble on the fruit and cheese resting on the opposite table.

At that moment, Tony fell completely and madly in love.

After being together at the hotel, Tony began calling Diane every day from the lumberyard. Although they could only talk for minutes at a time, Tony feigned understanding but, in truth, was enormously frustrated.

"I'm just sayin' I don't understand why you don't leave him."

"I promise, Tony, when the time is right, I'll leave."

"Well, when then?"

"When. The. Time. Is. Right. I can't tell you any more than that, and I have to tell you I don't like being pressured."

"Yeah, well, I don't like waiting."

"You know, maybe we better hang up before you lose your temper."

To that there was silence, then the irritating, tinny *beep, beep, beep* signaling that Tony had hung up the phone.

That night on his way to pick up Joe, Tony reflected on his conversation with Diane earlier that day.

Should I put more pressure on her or less? Back off or keep pressing the issue? What's gonna get her to move her ass? He just didn't know. He thought maybe Joe would have some ideas. That led him to think about Joe and their relationship. Tony knew it was really Joe's reputation that got them into clubs and impressed women. He was simply riding Joe's coattails, but he didn't care. It was a ride he never wanted to stop, let alone get off of, because it only kept getting better every day.

Besides the women, Joe had also taken to buying him hundred-dollar shirts and thousand-dollar suits.

"You gotta look good if you're gonna hang around with me," Joe had said on one occasion. "But not *too* good."

As he pulled up to Joe's house, he smiled at the memory.

"Guess it's back to business," he said to no one in particular. He got out of the car, straightened his pant legs, and strode up the walkway to get Joe.

"So, Joe, where we headed tonight?"

"I thought we'd hit Club Ciao again. Friday night means more girls to round up and take back to the Shamrock."

"That the place I hit the cop?"

"The one and the same."

Tony pointed the car toward Oxford Avenue in Northeast Philly.

When they pulled up, the line (which was made up of mostly women) wound past D'Lu Lu's and around the corner. Tony and Joe bypassed the clientele (with Joe pressing twenty-dollar bills into waiting hands as he went), until they were seated at the bar, a drink placed neatly before each of them.

Looking around, Tony's gaze settled on a short thin girl with long brown hair, not so much the color of a mouse but rather like the color of faded, sun-kissed flowers. Why she stood out, Tony couldn't say. After all, she wasn't stunning (at least not in a Diane kind of way), but instead, she had an understated elegance that attracted Tony.

"You like what you see?" Joe asked.

Embarrassed at having been caught, Tony mumbled, "Yeah, I guess. Just checkin' out that little brown-haired girl over there."

"So why don't you go up and buy her a drink?"

"Ah, Joe, you know I don't do that."

Joe sighed. "Yeah, I know. That's why I'm gonna help you out. Make this easy on you. I know the girl she's with. Hey, sweetheart," Joe yelled to a passing waitress. "Do me a favor, wouldja? Give those two girls over there whatever they want, on me. And here's something for yourself."

The waitress nodded once, tucked the money away, and hurried off to fill her drink orders.

The waitress delivered the girls their drinks and pointed discreetly toward the two men who were standing in the corner as their benefactors.

"Hey, Joe. How are you?" gushed the platinum blonde. She kissed Joe on both cheeks. "Thanks so much for the drinks. This is my friend Melissa."

"I'm good, Tiff. Thanks. Oh, this is my friend Tony."

"Hi, Melissa." Since Melissa didn't extend her hand, Tony kept his left hand securely in his pocket.

"Hi. Thanks for the drink. Are we done here, Tiff?"

"Uh . . . sure. Thanks again, Joe."

"No problem. Hey, Tiff."

"Yeah?"

"If you and Melissa are lookin' for sumthin' to do after hours, stop by the Shamrock. Drinks are on me."

"Thanks, Joe. We're not sure what we're doin' yet, but we'll *definitely* keep it in mind. Right, Melissa?"

"Yeah. Whatever. Can we go now?"

"See ya later, Joe. Maybe."

Tiffany gave one wave good-bye before the crowd on the dance floor engulfed her.

"Well, I think that went well. Don't you?" Joe smiled widely.

"Shut up. I could've screwed things up that much, Mr. Personality. Didja see that? She hardly even looked at me. And she couldn't wait to leave. What the hell was that all about?"

"That's what I'm sayin'," Joe laughed. "We're outta here. Let's head back to the Shamrock. And who knows. Maybe she'll show up after all."

"Yeah. Whatever. I'll betcha a dinner she don't."

"Ton, my man. You're on."

When Joe and Tony returned to the Shamrock, Tony drifted away from Joe to find Greg.

"Hey, Greggie-boy, how's it goin'?" Tony asked, loudly pounding Greg on the back and smiling.

"Hey, dago? Been drinkin' wine again?"

"Nah . . . okay, maybe a little," Tony said, annoyed at the question. "Whatdaya care anyway?"

"'Cuz, asshole, when you're drunk, you won't fight. You're worthless to me. Hey, Joe," Greg yelled. "Take him in the back and straighten him out will you?"

Joe laughed. "Yeah, come on, Ton. I'll take care of you." He led Tony by the nape of the neck to the back room. Over his shoulder, he yelled to Greg, "I'll see what I can do with him. You don't think my bodyguard would get drunk or mess with girls while on duty, do you?"

Greg shook his head in disgust.

When they reached the back room, Joe said, "You can do some of that stuff if you want to straighten out." Joe shoved his hand into his pants pocket and pulled out a chunk of meth.

Tony held out his hand and turned to leave.

"Where you goin'?" Joe asked.

Tony turned back. "Outside."

"Nah," Joe said. "You can do it right here if you want. Long as it's just you and me."

Tony proceeded to break off a small piece and pop it into his mouth like a stick of Juicy Fruit. Minutes later, Tony felt clearheaded and sober.

Just then, the phone rang. As Tony was about to turn and head back to the club, Joe held up a finger, signaling Tony to stay. Joe's entire end of the conversation amounted to, "Come on down. I'll be here."

When Joe hung up, he looked at Tony and said, "I'm expecting some company in the form of a man named Chas. If he ends up coming in, there's probably gonna be some trouble, so I'll need you to stay close to me."

Tony nodded, knowing better than to ask what was going on. If Joe had wanted him to know, he would have told him. Joe described the man who would be coming in and what he expected of Tony.

"I understand," Tony replied. After all, this was why Joe paid him.

"I'm gonna go tell the other doormen to come get you when they see Chas in the parking lot," Tony said.

Joe nodded absentmindedly.

When Chas entered the club, he did so with a very large, very well-muscled man who Tony assumed was the man's bodyguard. Intrigued, Tony moved to get a better a view and took in the man's large biceps, which barely fit through the shirt he was wearing. Although he outweighed Tony by fifty pounds, Tony was still confident that he could win any fight against him.

As Chas and Joe discussed business in a corner of the club closest to the back door, Tony kept a watchful eye and a respectful distance. When the conversation became more heated, Chas's bodyguard began moving a little too close to Joe.

Tony drifted toward the three men, and when he was directly beside the large bodyguard, he lightly rubbed one of the man's huge arms.

"Hey, big guy, how 'bout you and me take a walk over to that dark corner and talk about your big muscles?"

The bodyguard's face turned red, and he moved to do as Tony asked.

"Hey!" Chas said sharply. "Don't go anywhere with him, or you won't be coming back!"

"But, boss, I can handle this goombah."

Chas continued to shake his head. "I know who he is, you don't. Now stay here, and don't move."

Sensing how badly the other man wanted to fight, Tony patted his cheek like a dog who has done an especially good trick and said, "Good boy. That's good advice."

When Joe and Chas concluded their business, they shook hands uneasily. Chas motioned for his bodyguard to follow him, and as the two men stalked through the club, the bodyguard made one final attempt at respect by stopping and looking back at Tony.

Tony strode up to the bodyguard. "I'll see to it that Chas gets home safely if you want to meet me in the parking lot."

Just then, Joe walked up and put a hand on Tony's arm. "Tony, you got in his head. Let it go. He blinked. You didn't." Tony nodded, and the bodyguard backpedaled out of the club, the two men never taking their eyes off each other.

TONY TANCREDI AND CINDY L. O'HARA

NINETEEN

LATER THAT NIGHT, after almost all of the regulars had wandered out, the employees and a select few (mostly girls), stayed for drinks.

"So what's up for you tonight?" Joe asked. "You gonna see Diane?"

"Nah," Tony replied. "Not tonight. Gonna just go home, I guess." Tony couldn't believe how utterly awful that sounded. He must have looked as depressed as he felt about having to return home to a wife who loved him (although that was becoming more and more questionable every day) and kids who still thought the sun rose and set on his say-so, because Joe said mildly, "Well, if you don't feel like goin' home, you can come over to the Lair."

"The Lair? What the hell's that?" Tony asked.

"Just a little place I keep on Larkspur when I don't go home and I don't go to the Hilton."

After Joe had chosen his pick of girls to come with them, they stopped at the Squire—a small club located around the corner from the Lair—to get some booze. Although it had already closed, Joe knocked, identified himself, and the door quickly opened.

Ed, the bartender, asked Joe what he needed and quickly gathered together the items. Joe tucked the torn brown box under his arm, trying to hold it together while not letting any of its precious cargo break, and thanked Ed.

"No problem, Joe. Anytime."

Having gotten what they came for, Tony and Joe left through the back door.

"This place, the Squire, is on our side, and we can get what we want there, whenever we need it," said Joe.

"It's also a contact point to get in touch with me, and eventually you, in due time, when you're ready for that."

Tony didn't reply but couldn't help but wonder what Joe meant.

The Lair was unlike anything Tony had ever seen—or smelled, for that matter.

It was not a clean, well-lit place, but instead—with no other delicate way of putting it—was a shit hole. It was the type of place used strictly for sex, drugs, and partying, with little thought to cleanliness.

But when he spied two girls kissing in a corner, their tongues making lazy circles in each other's mouths, and their hands groping each other's tits, he thought he might be able to get past what little inhibitions he had left.

With all that was going on around him, Tony knew he should have been much happier than he felt. Yet he wasn't.

Annoyed at his mood, and unable to figure it out, he sulked in the corner, passively watching the blonde and the brunette get it on.

As he focused on the dark-haired girl, he thought how much she reminded him of the girl from Club Ciao. She had never shown up at the Shamrock, and Tony was insulted.

Determined to put her out of his mind (and thankful to have pinpointed his irritability), Tony threw himself into what was going on around him.

Besides the two girls whom he had seen when he first walked in the door, half a dozen other couples made out in various corners of the large living room.

Looking around, Tony wondered what he should do. Joe motioned for him to sit down on a sofa in a corner of the room. It was, Tony saw, the perfect place to see everything that was going on. As Tony and Joe leaned back and watched the two girls together, three other women came over to Tony. One straddled him and started grinding against him, while the others leaned in on each side and began touching and caressing him until he thought he would explode.

The rest of the weekend was more of the same, ending in a blur so that by the time Tony stumbled up to his house early Monday morning, he was spent.

Later that day, on his way to the lumberyard (despite his exhaustion from the weekend's debauchery), Tony reveled in the cool fall weather. He rolled down the driver's-side window of his white Caddie and listened to the DJs on WMMR spin the Eagles' "Hotel California."

As Tony banged his left hand on the side of the car in time to the music and listened to Don Henley sing "You can get anything you want, but you can never leave," Tony thought how apropos the song was to the weekend he had just had.

With a smile, Tony pulled up to the yard, his exhaustion forgotten, and to no one in particular, he said, "It's gonna be a good day."

"Hey, Chief," Mark groused. "What the hell are you so friggin' happy about?"

TONY TANCREDI AND CINDY L. O'HARA

"Ah, nuthin'," Tony said. "Just thinkin' about the weekend. But I'm glad you're here. I wanna ask you sumpthin'. Do you notice Keebe gettin' a little attitude toward me?"

"Hell, you know what's been goin' on. He's a dick to everyone. On top of that, he's a control freak. But now the men are starting to rally around you, and they know you can do things that I can't do. Plus, they know you're not afraid of Keebe. This makes you a very dangerous man, my friend—at least in Keebe's eyes. So do I think he's singling you out? Yeah, sure, I do."

"Huh." Tony pondered his next words. "I know he's not payin' you guys what he's supposed to on holidays and for overtime and stuff, and to be honest, I feel like it's a slap in the face to my old man—bein' that he was a union guy his whole life—when it actually meant somethin'. Ya know?"

"Yeah, man. I know." Mark looked up, his gaze transfixed elsewhere. "Maybe someone needs to man up around here." With that, he stalked toward the time clock, leaving Tony with a lot to think about.

That night, as Tony readied himself to go to the club, he ducked his hand in his left pocket, feeling for his keys and cash. Then he plunged his hand in his other pocket, fingering the meth he had stashed there. Since he had become Joe's unofficial bodyguard, he now found himself in the unique position of not only carrying everything for Joe and his friends, but also of distributing it to other people. Tony suspected the reason Joe trusted him was that he would never sell anything, but instead just hand it out discreetly to friends only.

And when people realized who the bagman was, Tony knew it made him look important, which was never a bad thing in his world. Everyone wanted to be his friend. He was the guy you had to go through to get anything.

So it was that one night, Tony was working at the club, and a girl no more than eighteen-or nineteen-years-old stood at the front of the velvet ropes, clamoring to get in.

"Go get Tony or Joe. They'll let me in!"

"Look, lady. I don't know who you *think* you are, but I'm not gonna—"

"Hey, Monte. I got this."

"You sure, Ton? I'd be happy to escort this . . . um . . . lady outta line."

"Nah. That's okay, big guy. I got it."

"So." Tony spun the ledger toward him to get a look at the girl's name. He remembered her from Club Ciao but, for the life of him, couldn't come up with a name. "Melissa, how come it took you so long to take Joe and me up on our offer to come see the club?"

With a "See? I told you so" look on her face, Melissa eased past Monte.

"Oh. Well, I've been down to the Shore with my parents and out on the boat a lot, just partying. You know how it is," she said, looking away from Tony.

Tony nodded sympathetically, although he did *not*, in fact, know how it was. "Well, I'm glad you finally made it. You look good," Tony said, eyeing her caramel-colored skin, which had clearly been browned by the sun.

Tony then steered her away from the door and brought her to Joe, who, of course, remembered her as one of the few girls who had stood Tony up.

"Joe, Nicky, this is Melissa."

"Hi," Nicky said, rising and taking Melissa's hand. "Pleased to meet you. Joe-Joe, Melissa and I need to go to the bathroom. Could we have a little coke to make the trip worthwhile?"

Joe looked sharply at Nicky, who had just breached a cardinal rule, which was that you didn't ask for, let alone do, any drugs that came directly from Joe or Tony—not unless you were a personal friend, which Melissa was not, at least not yet.

Instead of replying, Joe motioned for Tony to come over and whispered something in his ear. Tony stood and then sent Melissa to a friend at the other end of the club. With just a nod, Tony signaled that the girl approaching was to be treated well.

Tony soon found out just how well Melissa was treated when she came back, practically swinging a baggie full of white powder. Tony quickly strode up to her and gently, but firmly, grabbed her arm.

"Honey, you need to put that away," he said, guiding her to Joe and Nicky. "How much did that guy give you anyway?"

Melissa looked up at him adoringly through half-glazed eyes and replied, "A whole bag—after I told him I was your girlfriend." She giggled, wiping her nose as she did so.

Tony rolled his eyes. Before he could reply, Melissa went on, "You have such nice friends. Do they always do what they're told to do?"

Dodging her question, Tony asked, "Would you like to go to dinner tomorrow night?"

"I'd love to," Melissa crooned into Tony's ear. "Walk me out to my car, and I'll give you my number."

"Where do you have to go?"

"To another club. I promised some friends I'd meet them." She turned to Joe and Nicky, "It was nice meeting you. And thanks for—well, you know."

Joe nodded, and Nicky waved.

Trying to hide his disappointment, Tony walked Melissa through the club and out to her car.

"This is yours?" Tony asked, with more than a little surprise in his voice. They had stopped at a silver convertible Alfa Romeo Spider.

"Yeah. So?" Melissa asked defensively.

"No, it's great. It fits you," Tony said.

"I love my car. My grammy buys me something new every two years." Melissa tossed her purse into the passenger seat through the open top.

"We should all be so lucky. My grandma used to buy me a new baseball glove every year."

"Are you making fun of me?"

"Nope. I wouldn't do that." Tony smiled.

"Because I don't go out with guys who are wiseasses."

"No worries there," Tony said, thinking that there'd be a line as long as the club of people who would be willing to contradict *that* particular lie.

"You got something to write with?"

Tony fished around in his pocket and came up with a crumpled up cocktail napkin and pen.

Melissa recited her phone number and directions to her house.

"So you'll call?"

Tony promised he'd call tomorrow afternoon to set a time.

"Great," she said, kissing Tony chastely on the cheek. "You're sweet. I'll see you tomorrow." She opened the car door, plopped down into the driver's seat, inserted the key into the ignition, and roared out of the parking lot, leaving a bemused Tony in her wake.

TWENTY

THE NEXT NIGHT, Tony drove to the Churchville section of Bucks County—a quaint, well-to-do part of Pennsylvania, with homes that had a price tag of anywhere from three hundred thousand to four hundred thousand, a bit steep when you considered the average price for a home in 1984 was less than eighty thousand.

Impressed with the neighborhood, Tony pulled up to the two-story brick house and took note of the, not one, not two, but *three* cars sitting in the driveway—the least expensive being a Lincoln Town Car that still had paper plates.

Tony got out of his brand-new Cadillac, thankful for the purchase. At least he didn't feel *so* out of place.

He rang the bell, and when the door opened, he stood facing a petite well-dressed, dark-haired woman.

"Please, come in," she said, eyeing Tony coolly. "I'm Melissa's mother, Victoria." She did not offer Tony her hand in greeting. "Melissa will be down momentarily."

Tony stepped into the foyer, hoping that Melissa wouldn't take too long. He had a feeling that her mother didn't like or trust him much—of course she was right not to.

After only a few minutes, but what felt like a lifetime to Tony, Melissa glided down the stairs.

"My god, Melissa. You look beautiful," Tony said, staring at the girl.

Melissa blushed and murmured a thank-you.

"Come, Melissa," Victoria said. "Let me put this necklace on you. Tony, will you help me please?"

"Sure," Tony replied, not really knowing how it was that he could help.

When Melissa turned around and lifted her hair, Victoria slipped the necklace around her daughter's neck and asked Tony to hold one end so she could make sure it was straight. As Tony and Victoria fumbled with the clasp, Tony couldn't help staring at Melissa's neck.

Without looking up from her task, Victoria said, "You want to kiss her neck, don't you, Tony?"

Shocked at her boldness, as well as her accuracy, Tony just smiled.

"Oh my god, Mom!" Melissa shouted.

"Well," Victoria replied, adjusting her daughter's necklace. "I was right, wasn't I, Tony?"

Embarrassed, Tony said, "Yes, ma'am, and in the future, I will try and control my thoughts around you."

"Don't bother," Victoria replied. "I'll always see right through you. Consider that a warning." Victoria placed a protective hand on Melissa's shoulder.

"Mom," Melissa said, gently but firmly removing Victoria's hand. "We're going now."

"Fine. Tony, please do not keep my daughter out all night. Have her home at a reasonable hour—something before two in the morning, perhaps?"

"Of course."

As they left, Tony looked back to see Victoria staring at him, staring through him really, as if she had known Tony her whole life and could see all of his missteps and misdeeds.

He left Melissa's home feeling extremely uncomfortable under Victoria's watchful gaze.

Tony decided on D'Lu Lu's for his first date with Melissa—the same place Joe had taken Tony when Tony had first begun driving for him.

When Tony had called ahead to tell Gussie, the maitre d', he would be coming in and bringing a companion, Gussie had assured Tony he would be treated as well as if Mr. B. himself was there.

When Tony and Melissa arrived, Gussie had in one hand a large bouquet of flowers and in the other a bottle of red wine—all compliments of the house. Melissa smiled.

"Tony, this is so sweet. I can't believe you did this."

"Well, you know, from what I've seen, you're a little spoiled, so I figured I'd spoil you a little more."

Tony thanked Gussie and discreetly handed him a hundred-dollar bill, knowing that this was all going straight back to Victoria. Tony hoped it would score him some points with Melissa's parents because he had a feeling he was going to need all the help he could get.

After finishing dinner, Tony drove Melissa home. Tony turned onto Melissa's street and eased the car to a stop at the curb. After parking, Tony went around, opened Melissa's door, and helped her out. As Melissa breezed past Tony, his gaze came to rest on her ass. Tony decided that it was a good thing her mother had wanted her home early.

When they reached the front door, Tony kissed Melissa good-bye on the cheek.

"What the hell was that?" Melissa pouted. "I want you to kiss me."

"I just did."

"No. I want you to *really* kiss me."

Figuring that he didn't have much to lose (*except maybe a pair of your favorite testicles*, the little voice in his head whispered), he kissed Melissa full on the lips. He did, however, keep his tongue in his own mouth.

Half expecting the front door to fly open and Victoria to be standing there, Tony stopped before anything else could happen.

"Will you call me tomorrow?" Melissa asked.

"Sure," Tony said, wondering what the hell he was doing.

On the phone the next day, Tony confessed to Melissa that although he wanted to see her again, he was married.

"But I'm getting a divorce," he added quickly. (*You are?* the little voice piped in.) Even Tony was surprised at what might be termed a Freudian slip.

"When?" Melissa finally asked.

"Soon," Tony answered, hoping to buy himself some time.

"Fine. I'll wait," Melissa replied. "As long as you meet me for lunch a few days a week in the park that's down the street from where you work."

Tony was puzzled. "How do you know about that park?" he asked.

"Because I work right around the corner from the lumberyard, silly—at the law services building." Tony felt like he had just been set up. "Of course you do," he muttered under his breath.

"What was that?" Melissa asked.

"Nothing," Tony said. "Fine, I'll meet you a couple of days a week for lunch at the park." After all, Tony mused, what could it hurt?

"I said a *few* days a week, Tony."

"Fine," Tony answered, exasperated with the semantic word play. "A *few* days a week, then."

"Good. How 'bout Monday?"

Tony thought quickly, but couldn't come up with a reason not to see her. "Sure," Tony said, all of a sudden feeling queasy.

"Great! I'll see you then," Melissa practically chirped before hanging up the phone.

On Monday, Melissa pulled into the lumberyard, her Alpha Romeo humming quietly, the radio blaring Prince's "When Doves Cry." While

TONY TANCREDI AND CINDY L. O'HARA

waiting for Tony, Melissa thought about her feelings for this man she barely knew. She didn't know why she was attracted to Tony, but she did know she was hooked. Part of the appeal, she knew, was the club and the people he hung around. Lost in her thoughts, she didn't hear Tony approach until he opened the passenger door and slid into the seat next to her.

"Let's go."

Mistaking his shortness for urgency, Melissa had started to comply by putting her car in gear when she suddenly shifted back into neutral. "Hey, Fred!" Melissa yelled, standing up in the convertible and waving her arm in greeting.

Fred, one of the youngest guys on the crew at the yard, waved back hesitantly, a puzzled look on his face.

Tony tried to slide down in his seat before Fred recognized him. "Hey, Melissa. Hey, Ton."

"Hey, Fred," Tony said. "Just goin' to have a little lunch."

"Yeah. Okay. Whatever you say, Ton." Before turning away, Fred said, "Hey, goombah, should I tell Mark you're gonna be late?" A lopsided grin was spreading across his face.

"Nah," Melissa piped up. "I'll have him back on time."

Melissa waved one more time before throwing the car into gear and speeding out of the lumberyard. On the way to the park, Melissa explained that Fred lived with his parents, three houses down from her. "Isn't that funny?" Melissa laughed.

"Frickin' hilarious," Tony said. He sighed in resignation and turned his face up to the sun, relishing the warmth of the fall day.

When Melissa dropped Tony off, a few of the men had conveniently gathered at the entrance, smoking cigarettes and generally enjoying one another's company. Tony knew it was all an act.

"So how you doin', Big Daddy?" one of the men called.

Tony just shook his head as he approached the group of men. "Okay, guys, so I guess Fred told you."

"Told us what?" another man asked innocently. "Oh, you mean about Melissa being young, rich, and obviously hot? Yeah, he may have mentioned it." Laughter rippled through the group.

Figuring that he didn't have a choice and that he had indeed brought this on himself, Tony remained silent and let the men have their fun.

"Hey, Mack Daddy, so how old is she?"

To this, Fred piped up. "She's nineteen."

Another round of oohs and aahs rose throughout the group.

"Holy crap, I knew you were a lot of things, Ton, but I didn't know you were a cradle robber too." Another round of laughter followed.

Tony actually hadn't known Melissa was that young—not that it would have mattered, but it was good information to have. He filed it away, thinking it was as good a reason as any to keep her out of the Shamrock for a while. Besides, he didn't want to get too close to Melissa because of Di.

After making love with Diane, he found that for the first time in his life, he was losing his taste for other women (*no pun intended*, whispered the voice) and that he might actually be in love—an alien concept if ever there was one.

As the men continued their jabs, Tony tuned them out and let his mind wander to just what it was he wanted from Diane. What he wanted most, he decided, was for her to leave her husband. For this to happen, Tony thought, he would have to set an example. The only way to do that would be to leave Laura. By doing so, Diane would understand how serious he was about their relationship. Even as he was thinking this, he knew that leaving was the best thing he could do for his wife. Perhaps it was out of guilt for having cheated on her so many times or for not having been home in—well, ever, lately. Or maybe his feelings about leaving were just the coward's way out. Whatever the reason, Tony knew it was what he needed to do—for everybody involved.

"Hey, Ton? You okay, man?" Mark said, concern creasing his forehead. "We were just bustin' your balls. We didn't mean nuthin' by it."

"What did you say?" Tony asked. "I'm sorry, Mark. I guess I was thinking about something else."

"Nothin' important, but, man, for a minute there, you looked like you were going to pass out. You were as white as a sheet. You sure you're okay?"

"Yeah," Tony lied. "I'm fine. But if you yahoos are done here, I'm gonna get back to work."

"Okay," Mark said. "Sure. We should all get back to work."

With the men still snickering and making jokes, they finally broke apart, leaving Tony to ponder whether he was doing the right thing or not. In the end, he decided it was the *only* thing to do.

TONY TANCREDI AND CINDY L. O'HARA

TWENTY-ONE

THE SQUIRE, A sports bar located on Buselton Avenue in Philadelphia, was wedged in snugly between a deli and a greeting card store in a nondescript strip mall that could have been in anywhere-America. But Tony liked the place, ever since he and Joe had shown up one night and gotten a case of liquor, no questions asked. He also liked it because he knew, with just a nod of his head to the bartender, that no one would bother him. Usually, he would check in with whomever was working to see if there were any messages for him or Joe, but tonight, he wanted nothing more than to be left alone.

From his curt "Thanks" to the waitress who delivered his beer, to the dismissive wave he gave her when she approached to see if he needed anything, Tony hoped he wasn't being a total prick, but for once, he didn't really give a rat's ass.

He glanced at the clock over the bar that was in the shape of a basketball—a tribute to the Sixers, who as of late hadn't done squat except lose Tony a lot of money. The face read 10:02 p.m. He knew people at the Shamrock would wonder where he was, but again, on this night, he didn't really give a shit what anyone else needed or wanted.

Just when Tony thought he should probably get moving, Joe slid into the other half of the booth opposite him. He set his drink in the center of the coaster, covering up the Eagles insignia. Tony watched the coaster fade from green to a dead-faced gray as water from the glass settled on it.

"So I get this call from Harry, the bartender, about half an hour ago. Tells me that my main guy is actin' weird. Won't let anyone wait on him. Barely grunts a 'thanks' for the beer he's drinkin' and is generally actin' like a dick. Sound like anyone you know? 'Cuz it don't sound like anyone *I* know."

"Joe, I'm thinkin' about leavin' Laura and movin' into the Lair," Tony blurted.

Joe leaned in and twirled his glass between his fingers in a lazy circle. "Do I need to remind you that Di's married?"

"Your point?"

"All I'm sayin," Joe continued, "is that most women don't leave their family—"

"And I don't want this woman to, but, Joe, she said she loves me."

Joe stopped the glass, and then looked up. A smile played on his lips. "And how many times have *you* said that and didn't mean it?"

Tony looked away from Joe's penetrating gaze, formulating a response. Of course, Joe was right, but this was different, he reasoned. He looked back at Joe and said with what he hoped sounded something like sincerity, "Come on, Joe, what the hell else could she want with me? You've seen her—she could have anybody. Why wouldn't she be for real?"

Joe leaned back into the booth. "She might be," he conceded. "But all I'm sayin' is, be careful."

Tony nodded reluctantly. "Okay, Joe. Thanks for tellin' me how you feel."

"Well, just stay in control of the situation. You haven't even moved out of your house yet, and you're already makin' plans on how you and Diane are gonna ride off into the sunset together."

Tony remained silent, listening.

"And when you *do* put the pressure on her to leave, make her give you a date when she'll do the same."

Tony nodded at the advice.

"Hell, here I am telling you how to live your life when I'm a hell uva an example. Well, no matter what happens, you know I'll back your play whatever it is," Joe said. "And as for movin' into the Lair, that's okay with me too."

Surprised by his boss's candor, but pleased, Tony replied, "Thanks, Joe. I know you're only telling me what you believe is best for me."

"Damn straight."

"I'm still gonna take care of Laura and the boys—give 'em whatever they want or need."

"Is that to take care of them or you?"

To that, Tony remained silent, mostly because he didn't have an answer. Finally, he said, "So when can I move in?"

"Whenever you want."

"Great. Um—"

"Now what?" Joe asked, impatience beginning to creep into his voice.

"I was just thinkin'. If you don't mind, I'll have some carpenters come over from the lumberyard and do some renovations, maybe have a cleaning crew come in to get the place in order, if that's okay? Of course, I'll pay for everything," Tony said hurriedly.

"Yeah. That'd be all right, I suppose. Just one thing, you can't move or get rid of the china cabinet. That stays exactly where it is."

TONY TANCREDI AND CINDY L. O'HARA

"Sure, Joe. Whatever you say."

"I'll tell you why another time. But for now, this calls for a celebration. Let's go to the Shamrock, say hello to the boys, do a little shit, and tell them we're out for the night. I think this evening we should go somewhere different, maybe see if we can get some girls who don't know us. Whatdaya think about that?"

"What about the club?" Tony asked, vaguely concerned how his preferential treatment by Joe was going to affect his relationship with the other bouncers.

"They'll just have to handle it without you tonight. I'll tell 'em we got somethin' else to do."

"If you say so."

"I say so. Now let's get outta this joint," Joe said, ushering Tony toward the door.

In the car on the way to the club, Joe started in again.

"I think it's a good idea to move into the Lair. No matter how much you trust the person you're with, or the people you're dealin' with, you always need a back door. I guess it's come true for you quicker than you thought."

Tony pondered what Joe had said.

"Yeah, you're right. I guess the Lair's my back door."

After trying a few different clubs, Tony and Joe finally found one they liked in Warminster, a town in Bucks County. The pink neon sign over the door flashed that it was "Ladies' Night," and a smaller sign below stated ladies would drink for free until midnight. Tony glanced at the green neon numbers on the car's clock face. The time read 11:06 p.m.—a little less than an hour before the midnight deadline.

"What about here, boss?"

"Looks good to me," Joe said.

Once inside, in less time than it took to order a drink, Joe had charmed his way into the arms of two very lovely, very young ladies. Soon, the foursome piled into Tony's Cadillac, with Joe and his girl in the back and Tony and his girl up front.

"You know, I hope your friend is a gentleman and won't get out of line, because Lisa's not the type to fool around."

"Don't worry," Tony answered. "Joe's not like that. He would never make a girl do anything she didn't want to do. It's just not his style."

"Okay, good. Now what I want to do," Donna said, leaning over and whispering into Tony's ear, "is to do some shots when we get back to your place and then get crazy in bed. Think you're up for it?" She giggled quietly.

Tony just smiled and kept driving.

When they got to the Lair, they all sat at the kitchen table and drank shots of tequila.

"Hey," Donna said, starting to slur her words. "Do you guys have any pot?"

Joe nodded to Tony, who got up and went into another room to get the drugs.

Already more than drunk and having done meth earlier in the night, Tony declined the offer to smoke with them. When they were done, Donna got up unsteadily and asked Tony to take her to the bathroom, which was located just to the right of Joe's bedroom. Rather than return to the kitchen, Tony waited outside for Donna. She wobbled out moments later, bumping ungracefully into the doorjamb.

"Are you okay?" Tony asked. "Do you want to go back to your friend?"

Donna shook her head slowly, leaned in to Tony, and whispered, "Which room's yours?"

Tony pointed to a large master bedroom.

"Why don't you *show* me?"

Tony was more than happy to comply.

During the night, Tony managed to please Donna repeatedly. Before starting up again, however, Donna insisted on going to the bathroom to clean up. After a third round of fucking and trip to the bathroom, Donna came back to Tony's bedroom, and asked "Is your friend Joe always so neat and clean?"

Puzzled, Tony asked what she was talking about.

"Well, every time I pass his bedroom, I hear him shaving with his electric shaver."

Knowing that Joe had a briefcase full of dildos and vibrators in his room, Tony began laughing hysterically, almost falling off the bed.

"I'm pretty sure," Tony laughed, "that your girlfriend isn't as innocent as she would have you think."

"Whatdaya mean?"

Finally, Tony regained his composure enough to explain what was going on a mere two steps away. Once he shared the joke, Donna giggled at her remark.

"Guess I'll have to have a talk with her!" Donna said. They continued to giggle as they fell asleep, a soft whirring sound playing in the background.

When Tony woke up the next morning, his head throbbed as if someone were tapping out a beat with a ball-peen hammer. Looking at Donna, who was no more than a child, really, Tony felt only disgust at his actions from the night before. Loathing the person he had become, he promised himself that he was going to stop screwing around. Literally.

Determined to start at least one day off on the right foot, Tony tried unsuccessfully to rouse Donna, who was still sleeping.

"Hey, baby? Time to get up," Tony said gently. "I have some things I have to do, and you can't stay here." As he said this, he began picking up pieces of her clothing off the floor—a thong that had somehow maintained its perch on the bedside lamp, a bra off the headboard, one red shoe from under the bed—until after a few minutes, he felt as if he had gathered everything she had come with.

Finally, a semiconscious Donna mumbled something that sounded like "Fine" to Tony. She wrapped a blanket around her naked torso and tried to get up, but plopped back down on the bed. The second attempt proved more successful, and Tony almost cheered when she maintained a standing position. He handed her the clothes he had managed to gather. As she took the clothes from Tony, she let the blanket fall unceremoniously to the floor and began the arduous process of getting dressed. Tony waited patiently, trying not to snicker as he watched a still-drunk Donna hop on one foot while trying to insert the other foot into her thong panties. After almost falling (twice) and uttering a very unladylike word, she must have decided that it wasn't worth the effort, because she stuffed the panties into her small black purse and breezed past Tony.

Tony could only shake his head at what his life had become.

When everybody was up and dressed, Tony drove the two girls home.

"So," Joe said from the backseat, "where should we go for breakfast?"

TWENTY-TWO

O N A NIGHT that Tony should have been at the club, he was instead at the Hilton, making love to Diane for the second time that night. She rolled over and looked at Tony.

"So I know you're getting irritated with me because I'm not making the moves you want me to make fast enough."

"Listen, Di—"

"Wait. Lemme finish. You have a right to be frustrated, but I have to ask, when will *you* be moving out, mister?"

"Tonight, if it'll make you happy," he said, jumping on her interest.

"Tony, it needs to make *you* happy. Don't do it for me," Diane said, lightly tracing a finger along Tony's bicep and up to his shoulder.

It was all Tony needed to hear. "I'll do it tonight," he replied.

Diane gazed up at him, her green eyes searching his.

Before she could change her mind, Tony leaned over and whispered, "I love you." Then he gathered her into his arms and made love to her one more time.

After leaving the hotel, Tony went to the club to see Joe. He needed to get a key to the Lair so that when he told Laura he would be moving out, he would have somewhere to go.

When he walked into the Shamrock, Greg was behind the bar, mopping up beer and God knew what else, with a wet rag.

"Hey, Greg, where's Joe?"

Without looking up, Greg said, "He's in the back room. Is there a problem, Ton?"

"Yeah, but it's my problem, and I don't feel like hearing from you tonight."

Greg gazed evenly at Tony.

Tony regretted snapping at Greg, but he also knew how Greg felt about Laura. If Tony divulged why he needed to see Joe, he knew that Greg would give him shit about his decision. And to be honest, he just didn't want to hear it right now.

Instead of easing his friend's distress, Tony turned toward the back room to find Joe.

When Tony came out, Greg was still behind the bar, this time cleaning glasses and restocking the liquor.

For a moment, Tony thought he might just get in and get out of the club without anyone knowing of his plans, until Joe yelled, "If you're gonna live there, you need to get yourself a key made tomorrow."

"Sure, Joe." Tony quickly looked at Greg to see if he had heard Joe's words—but of course he had. From the look in his eyes, Greg had figured out what was going on.

As Tony passed the bar, Greg grabbed his arm, effectively stopping Tony in his tracks. They gazed at each other, but Tony was unable to hold his stare and looked away. Greg dropped his hand and gave Tony a push before going back to his task behind the bar.

When Tony arrived home later that night—morning, really—the house was still and quiet. Everyone was sleeping—except Blue, the dog. Normally, he didn't make a sound, but on this night, even the damn dog seemed to know Tony was up to something because he took one look at the startled Tony and started howling loud enough so both Laura and the kids appeared, groggy and rubbing the sleep from their eyes.

"Daddy?" William yawned. "What's going on?"

"Boys, go back to sleep. Everything's okay."

"You heard your dad," Laura said. "Nothing's wrong. Now back to bed." She gently herded the boys to their bedrooms, then turned and hurried down the stairs, practically taking them two at a time. When she reached the bottom, she strode up to Tony and took his hand, a worried look on her face.

"My god, why are you shaking, Tony? What's wrong with you? Did you hurt someone? Are they okay?"

The only thing Tony could think to do was to buy even more time, so he asked her to sit down on the couch with him.

"Look, honey, Joe and I are into something that will take a few months to sort out, and I have to move into the Lair so that I don't bring any trouble to our house." Tony just couldn't bring himself to tell her the real reason behind the move.

"I can't tell you what's going on because then you'd be involved," Tony explained. "If things go wrong with what we're doing and the cops start asking questions, wanna give you a lie detector test or something, you really won't know anything. Do you understand?" Tony looked at his wife of seven years, imploring her with his eyes to do what he was asking of her.

Laura, however, remained silent, gazing evenly back at Tony.

"I'll still come by and see you and the kids, but this could be some big money for us," Tony continued. Hell, if he was going to lie, he may as well lie big.

"I don't care about the damn money!" Laura said, her voice rising. "I don't like this, and I sure as hell don't like being kept in the dark." She gripped Tony's forearm.

Tony looked away, unable to witness the raw emotion etched on Laura's face.

"Tony, we already have enough money. We have everything we need and more. The only thing we need around here is you, and now you tell me you're moving out?"

A loud sniffle from the top of the stairs interrupted Tony's reply. He rose to see William, the older of the two boys, looking down at them, tears spilling from his eyes. Straining to keep his balance, William awkwardly navigated the steps until he reached the bottom landing. Without his shoes on for support, the cerebral palsy he had been afflicted with since he was a baby, threatened to topple him. But by the grace of God, William reached the bottom without falling. He then hitched his way toward Tony, whose face was also wet with tears at the sight of his son struggling to reach him.

"Daddy, I don't want you go anywhere without us," William hiccupped.

Squatting directly in front of the child, Tony said, "Some fathers have to go away all the time because of their job. This will only be one time for a few months."

While it disconcerted Tony that the ad-lib excuses and lies seemed to roll so easily off his tongue, he didn't have the luxury of thinking through the psychological complexities of how he could do this so easily.

Just as Tony began to pledge that he would come home as soon as he could, Danny walked up and joined his brother. Tony hadn't even heard him come downstairs. Unlike William, however, Danny refused to cry, and instead looked defiantly at Tony. He was, Tony remembered, more like his mother.

"I promise, boys, I'll be back home as soon as I can," Tony said, his legs beginning to ache from squatting in the same position. "I'll still see you during the week, and sometimes be here for dinner."

Tony could feel Laura's eyes burning right through him. When he finally rose and turned toward her, he expected Laura to (finally) lay into him. In the end, Laura withheld whatever she had been going to say—in part, Tony suspected, because of both her love for the boys and her desire to protect them.

Tony looked at her imploringly.

Sighing, she rose off the couch and walked toward her sons. Hugging each one, she then whispered something in each of their ears. Whatever it was, both boys dutifully headed upstairs, Danny following William to ensure that he made it without falling. Tony watched the scene unfold, surprised and saddened that neither boy looked back. It seemed they too knew of their father's sins and lies.

The next day, Tony moved out of the house he had shared with his family for the last five years, while the boys were at school and Laura was at work.

When he had gotten the last of his things into the Lair, he lay down on his bed, looked at the ceiling, and contemplated his life. For once, Tony was glad that the only mirrors in the house were in the bathroom and on Joe's bedroom ceiling because right now, he couldn't stand to look at himself.

Why, he asked himself, *can't I just be happy with what I have at home?* For once, the little voice that normally piped in with some sarcastic comment or other remained strangely silent, refusing to answer such an absurd question.

When Joe walked into the Lair, he gazed around and marveled at the renovation. Tony had installed a still-neutral but slightly darker carpet to hide stains, painted the entire interior of the house, and, as a final touch, discarded the tattered, worn furniture and replaced most of it with newer, albeit still-used, sofa and chairs.

The only caveat Joe had stipulated for Tony's project was that the old china cabinet would remain. The piece was chipped and marred in places, did not, and most likely would never, hold any china of any worth, and was, in Tony's opinion, one of the ugliest damn things he'd ever seen. Regardless of Joe's mandate, as the redecoration neared an end, Tony had broached the subject of replacing the china cabinet to Joe. Joe's response had been a firm no. Reluctant to question Joe's decision, Tony had just shrugged and accepted that the cabinet would be staying. Now, however, Joe told Tony to go and sit in either a chair or on the sofa and to look in the china closet glass. Obediently, Tony did so.

"What do you see?" Joe asked.

"Nothing but some crappy dishes. Sorry, Joe."

Joe waved his hand dismissively as if waving away smoke. "Look again," Joe said patiently.

Tony did, letting his gaze roam over the dishes inside, then the rest of the reflection. When he saw it, his eyes widened.

"Ohhh," Tony said. "I get it. From here, you can see the kitchen and what's going on."

Joe smiled and nodded his head.

Now it all made sense. Whenever Joe had guests over, he would call Tony into the living room, leaving an abundance of drugs on the table. While Tony had always complied, he had never understood the reasoning behind it. Now he did. From here, Joe could see who was trying to take something they shouldn't. To Tony, it was ingenious; he wondered how many other similar things in the Lair he hadn't been told about yet, how many other little tests he had been put through.

TONY TANCREDI AND CINDY L. O'HARA

TWENTY-THREE

TONY WALKED INTO the club and was greeted by the sight of Kevin, the redheaded Irishman Joe had hired a few months ago, leaning against the bar, no doubt embellishing bar fight stories to anyone who would listen. Puzzled that Kevin would be here on his off night, Tony looked around and noticed Greg wasn't in his usual spot behind the bar.

When Joe had hired Kevin, Tony had mixed feelings about him—nothing he could put a finger on, just a feeling that the idiot was bad for business.

Tony's opinion of the man was justified (at least in his mind) when one night, he leaned outside to check out the line into the club to make sure no one was getting out of hand. As he was glancing up and down, he spied Kevin showing off his gun to people, undoubtedly trying to impress girls—an obvious error in judgment since most of the bouncers, Kevin included, had records and weren't supposed to be carrying a fingernail file, let alone a piece.

That night, Tony tried to talk to Joe, but his reservations fell on deaf ears. For some reason, it was one subject that Joe wouldn't budge on. Tony didn't know if it was because Kevin was Irish or if there was some other unknown relationship, but whatever the reason, since then, Tony had made sure that the two of them worked on different nights, because to be honest, Tony didn't want to be around when the shit hit the fan.

Unfortunately, it looked as if tonight he'd have no choice. Curious about where Greg was and why he was working with someone whom he specifically made a point of avoiding, Tony sauntered over to Monte and asked, "How come Kevin's here and Greg isn't?"

"I don't friggin' know! What do I look like, Greg's mother? He had some personal thing to take care of, I think," Monte said.

Shaking his head, Tony sighed, resigning himself to working with the redhead. After all, it was just one night. What could happen?

When a slightly inebriated, unattractive girl wobbled up to Tony asking for Kevin, it was clear that the idiot had (somehow) picked up a girlfriend along the way. Without replying, Tony pointed to the end of the bar, where Kevin was leaning, surrounded by a few women. Tony hoped she'd give him hell. Without a second thought, Tony turned his attention to other parts of the bar.

The night, Tony thought, was turning out to be unusually quiet for a Friday, and just when he thought he might actually get done with his shift on time and without incident, he noticed Kevin escorting some kid who had too much to drink out of the bar. Although the drunk seemed to be complying, Kevin grabbed the kid by the back of his hair and slammed his head into the front doorjamb. The move made Tony wince in sympathy because surely, the boy would be feeling that particular bump in the night tomorrow. As quickly as it came, his sympathy was replaced by anger at Kevin's idiocy. When Tony realized Kevin's girlfriend was watching the entire scene unfold, he knew it was Kevin's way of showing off. Regardless, it was unacceptable. When Kevin strolled back in, Tony was there to greet him.

"What the hell was that all about?" Tony asked tightly, his voice barely concealing his anger.

"What?" Kevin asked innocently, his hands splayed out, palms up.

"You Irish piece of shit. You know what. That kid wasn't doing anything that would call for you to run his head into the door!"

Kevin shrugged and moved to turn away. "That was your take on it—from about twenty-five feet away."

Infuriated, Tony grabbed Kevin by the shoulder and spun him around.

"We have enough lawsuits around here that we don't need any unnecessary ones, you friggin' idiot!" Tony shouted, taking up all of Kevin's personal space.

Kevin merely smiled, turned, and walked away.

Disgusted, but unwilling to let the redhead goad him into doing something he would regret later, Tony turned and stomped purposefully to the bar for a drink.

The following Saturday night, three detectives showed up with four girls and a guy in tow. When the detectives asked them to point to the person who had hurt the kid, all of them looked nervously in Doc's way. The detectives approached Doc.

Tony was stunned. He knew what Kevin had done and couldn't believe that these kids were going to pin it on Doc. The two men were polar opposites, with Doc standing at almost six-and-a-half feet, weighing in at about 250 or 260, while Kevin was slightly shorter and lighter at just over six feet and about 220 pounds or so. And the hair—how could anyone mistake Kevin's flaming red for Doc's black Wolfman Jack-like hair? At a glance, one man looked very Italian, the other clearly Irish. Yet Doc was the one who was being identified. Tony knew then that something was wrong, just not what.

Later that night, gossip at the club was rampant about what had happened earlier. While Tony discounted most of it, one piece of information he overheard had made a lot of sense. The kid whom Kevin hurt was the son of the secretary to the state Attorney General. The state needed a suspect, and for whatever reason, Doc was it. He was being convicted before even being charged.

Instead of stepping up, Kevin remained silent—even though Doc had a wife and kids to take care of.

Out of a sense of honor, Doc never talked; and for his loyalty, Joe paid him handsomely by covering all his lawyer's fees, giving a monthly stipend to his family, and helping with anything else needed over the next few months.

While Doc's case ground its way slowly through the justice system, all of Joe's efforts were for naught when Doc was convicted of assault and sent away for eighteen months.

Not long after that, Kevin quietly disappeared.

TWENTY-FOUR

JOE SIGHED AND absently pushed some papers around on his desk, looking over the thousand things needing his attention, and not really interested in doing any of them.

Instead, he sat in his chair, steepled his fingers in front of him, and continued to think about Doc, wondering what he was doing at that moment. Finally, Joe shook his head, unable to envision his friend's new hell, frustrated he couldn't do anything for him.

His thoughts turned to Tony.

In his opinion, Tony's life was a train wreck—with him moving out of the home he shared with his wife and two sons just to be with a married woman, who, so far, had yet to make good on her promise to leave her husband. Although the situation with Tony didn't concern him (yet), Joe watched how his bodyguard was handling himself, in the same way someone else might watch a soap opera. It was enough to keep him interested, just to see how things would turn out.

Tony had been staying at the Lair now for a few months, with his blessing of course, and had surprisingly kept his promise to stay away from the drugs and women. Joe hadn't pushed the issue because Tony was still doing his job, possibly even better than in the past. Without alcohol or drugs in his system, Tony was clearheaded and professional around Joe's friends and in the other clubs they visited.

But the fighting, the ongoing in-club fighting, concerned Joe.

Of course, he hadn't known what to think when he hired Tony, but when he saw what Tony could do, how he could subdue anyone with his bare hands, he thought surely, the amount of fighting would go down in his club. Strangely, it seemed that Tony's reputation had pushed him to the top of some unseen list among barflies because the more his notoriety grew among the clubs, the more challengers he had.

Joe's thoughts shifted to Diane. An interesting woman (and beautiful, to be sure), but Joe couldn't bring himself to trust her. Of course, that was his general feeling toward most women, but in this case, he thought Tony a fool for believing a woman with a child would actually up and leave her husband for a new life with someone she had been screwing for only a short while—and a thug and a gangster too. No matter that the two were clearly in love. That was the stuff of romance novels, not real life. And although Joe would, on occasion, inquire about the situation, Tony had made it clear he was going to do exactly what he wanted.

Two quick raps on the office door interrupted him. Annoyed at the intrusion, Joe yelled, "Yeah?"

As if he had been privy to his musings, Tony stuck his head in the door.

"You too busy to talk?"

"Nah," Joe sighed, looking over the sheaf of papers splayed across his desk. "I don't seem to be getting much done anyway. Come on in."

Tony entered and softly closed the door behind him. He plopped heavily into one of the chairs, his entire posture one of frustration.

"So what's the matter with you?" Joe asked, pen poised in midair. "Lemme guess, is it Diane?" Joe laid his pen down and propped his elbows on the desk. He waited for Tony to continue.

When he didn't, Joe prompted him. "Sooooo . . ."

Still, his friend of less than a year did nothing but look at his feet.

Irritated, Joe said, "Look, Ton, I'm happy to talk, but it seems to me I'm the only one doin' the talkin' here. Now personally, I'd rather be chattin' with you than tending to this shit"—he spread his arms wide over the desk—"but if you're not gonna say anything, I've got a lot of people who would appreciate my attention elsewhere."

"I don't know what to do about Diane."

Joe didn't say a word, just gazed back at Tony. "Go on."

"I've moved out of my house, left my family, changed my life completely, but every time I ask her when she's gonna leave that friggin' idiot she's with, she tells me that she will when the time's right. At this point, though, I don't know if she ever will. I mean, it's been four months since we started seeing each other, and three weeks since I left Laura. Still, Diane hasn't done shit. So I'm thinking if she can't tell me by Christmas, at least what week she's gonna move out, then she's never going to."

Choosing his words carefully, Joe said, "Sounds realistic. Does Diane know of this deadline of yours?"

"Nah," Tony said absently.

"Well, let's say she *doesn't* leave—what's his name?"

"Paul."

"Okay, *Paul*. Let's say she doesn't leave Paul by Christmas. Then what?"

"Well, I thought it might be a good time to go back to Laura and the boys."

Although Joe had his thoughts on the matter, he was fairly certain Tony didn't want to hear them. Instead, Joe sighed. "Sounds like you've got it all figured out."

"So you think this sounds all right?"

Adopting what he hoped sounded like a sympathetic response, Joe said, "Sure. Whatever you think. I'm sure it'll work out."

To end any more talk about Diane, Joe asked, "So what are you up to tomorrow night?"

"Nuthin' much. Dinner at my folks' house, watching some college ball with my dad. Why? Do you need me?"

"Nah," Joe said. "I was just wonderin'. Have a nice time with your mom and dad. It's important you spend time with your family."

"Yeah. Well, thanks for listening, Joe. I really appreciate it."

"Anytime, Ton. You know my door's always open to you."

"You need anything?" Tony asked, moving to leave.

"Nah, I'm fine. Anyone needs me for anything, I'll be in here for a while, but tell 'em only if it's important. I gotta get a handle on this shit."

"Okay, I'll let 'em know," Tony said, closing the door softly behind him.

The next afternoon, Tony pulled up to his parents' white clapboard house, the same house he had grown up in. Before getting out of his car, he sat there, looking around at the old neighborhood, allowing the memories to flood over him. He didn't do this often enough, he thought, and he should. Everyone should take time to remember their roots, remember where they came from.

Luxuriating in the Indian summer, Tony took a deep breath of the crisp fall air. A few boys gathered in the street to play ball. Tony deduced that the boys were having a disagreement of some kind from the way one boy was waving his arms about wildly in front of the others. In time, though, everyone grudgingly took their places, and the game began. It reminded him of so many days and evenings he spent on this same street, doing that very same thing.

Wishing he could prolong his time outside, but knowing that his parents were probably expecting him, Tony gathered the bottle of red wine he had brought for dinner and the bouquet of flowers he had stopped to get for his mom. He managed to open the car door and step outside. Careful not to drop anything, he pushed open the unlatched gate with his foot and walked up the stone walkway. Climbing the three front steps, he fumbled with the door. He finally managed to open it and stepped inside.

TONY TANCREDI AND CINDY L. O'HARA

His mother stood there, smiling warmly.

"I saw you drive up." She opened her arms wide for a hug.

He kissed her gently on both cheeks. "These are for you, Mom," he said, handing over the large arrangement of flowers and the wine.

"Thank you, Tony. Such a good son." She leaned over the bright fall bouquet and breathed in deeply. "I love flowers. You're too good to me! Now go find your father. He's been asking for you. I think he's in the den, watching some game or other," Mary said, walking into the kitchen to find a vase.

Tony walked farther into the house, but didn't immediately do as his mother asked. Instead, he wandered down the hallway, looking at the numerous pictures of his family his mother had hanging there. He gazed at himself as a little boy, baseball bat in one hand and a bright silver brace on his left leg but, nonetheless, a huge smile on his face. He remembered that day and how happy he had been just to be outside, bat in hand. He moved on and looked at Marie, his baby sister—pictures of her as an infant, of her and Tony together when she was four-or five-years-old, and then the last picture to be taken of her before she had gotten sick and died. The photo showed Dad wearing one of those silly birthday hats, the kind with the thin rubber strap that always caught you under the chin just so, the number *58* emblazoned in bright red. Looking at the picture, Tony still couldn't believe his dad had actually put the damn thing on *and* had the good nature to wear it throughout the evening. That party, Tony remembered, had been at Casmiri's, one of his father's favorite Italian restaurants. More than thirty people were there that night—cousins, uncles, aunts, kids, and grandkids—and someone had captured Tony and Marie huddled together, laughing uproariously at something. He couldn't remember what.

That had been a good night. He had been happy then. Not that he was unhappy now, but at times like these, he did miss his Ree. He swiped at a tear before it could escape, and continued to move down the line of pictures. He stopped in front of one of his sister Kathy. A petite girl with dark brown hair and eyes, she had taken after their mother in stature and size. At least he still had her.

Like Marie, Tony loved Kathy and had always gotten along well with both of his sisters. He knew enough to know that he was trying to recapture what he had felt outside—the elation of being a child and growing up in this house with his family, in this neighborhood—but he found it almost impossible. If anything, this walk down memory lane was depressing him. Tony finally turned his back on his childhood—glad for the visit, but equally happy to leave the ghosts of his past behind—and went to find his father.

TWENTY-FIVE

TONY WALKED INTO the small den to find the television tuned to the Penn State / Boston College game, and his father rocking back and forth in yet another piece of nostalgia Tony recalled from his life here as a boy—his father's old, now-beat-up leather lounge chair. When it was new, it had smelled of oil and animal skin; and on the rare occasion when Tony had been allowed, he would curl up in it, the chair almost seeming to envelop him in its warmth and comfort him with its old-world smell.

"Hey, Pop," Tony said.

His father squirmed his now-considerable bulk out of the chair to a standing position. He grabbed Tony in a bear hug and clapped him loudly on the back. "Hey, Ton! I thought I heard you come in, but I wanted to give you and Mom time. I know how she is when it comes to you."

Tony smiled at his father, feeling better already. "How's the game goin'?" Tony asked, pointing to the television, where Joe Paterno, the coach of Penn State, was storming his way up and down the sideline, trying in vain to get a referee to change a ruling on the field.

His father gazed at the game. "Ah, so far so good. Penn State's up, but they just turned it over, so we'll see. Come on in and sit down. We have a few minutes before dinner, anyway."

Tony sat on the couch, happy to be in the present rather than the past, enjoying the company of the man who was most important to him.

Too quickly, his mother called them to the table. When Tony walked out of the den, he was hit with the smell of cooked noodles, fried onions and sausage, tomato sauce, and melted cheese. His stomach rumbled in response to the aroma. Breathing deeply, he took in the scent of warm bread and melting butter, and garlic—lots and lots of garlic. All thoughts of the football game fell away as he hurried to the dining room, again caught between the past and the present, memories of when he was a child being called to the table for dinner echoing in his head.

Tony managed to maintain his manners long enough to pull out his mother's chair, before finding his own seat and plopping down. He heaped his plate with his mother's steaming lasagna. To complement the meal, his mother had made homemade garlic bread, salad, and, for dessert, tiramisu. Tony piled his plate high with everything and dove into the meal with gusto.

"Oh, my Tony," his mother said. "I love when you come to visit. It gives me an excuse to cook."

"You don't cook for Dad anymore?"

"Not so much. Your dad doesn't eat as much as he used to, and with no kids to feed anymore, or dropping by,"—here she looked at Tony pointedly—"well, there's just no need."

Tony knew his mother was right. He didn't stop by as much as he used to, but with everything going on between his job at the lumberyard, Diane, Laura, and the club, he simply didn't have time. Of course, they didn't know about any of that, so instead of making excuses, Tony nodded sympathetically.

Wiping his mouth with the red cloth napkin his mother had laid by his plate, Tony said, "You're right, Mom. I haven't been by as much. I'm not even going to make excuses, just say I'm sorry."

She patted Tony's arm. "It's okay, Tony. I know you have things going on, that you're busy with Laura and the boys."

Tony felt another painful stab of guilt for the deception and outright lie he was telling his parents by keeping silent about his separation from his wife.

"Which is why your father and I have been talking about possibly moving to Florida to be with Kathy."

Stunned, Tony sat back, speechless. He stared at his mother, perplexed, and then slowly turned toward his father. "Pop?" Finally, his father looked up from his plate, his food untouched. All of a sudden, all that Tony had eaten threatened to come right back up. He had to suppress the urge to race to the bathroom, but managed to get control of his stomach enough to ask, with what he hoped was a neutral tone, "Why? What's going on down in Florida?"

His father said, "Your sister's having a rough time with her husband, Craig. I don't know if we can be of any help, but we figure just being there for moral support would be a good thing. Plus, we never get to see Jeff, our grandson, and since you're not around as much anymore—"

Tony realized that this conversation was extremely hard for his parents to have with him, and although he wanted to ease their distress, he couldn't just give his blessing without telling them about his reservations.

Tony said, "Hey, we all know why Kathy, Craig, and Jeff had to move to Florida, and I hate to see you guys being dragged into their situation just because Craig got drunk and stabbed someone one night." His sister's husband had, according to court records, allegedly stabbed someone over drugs, but had been released on bond. Instead of making his court appearance, however, he had skipped town with his family and moved them to Florida, where they were currently hiding out.

Having no education to speak of, and thus no way (or interest, for that matter) to earn a regular living, Craig had turned to selling drugs to make money. Tony had no doubt he was back to his same old routine of doing and selling whatever he could, as well as running around on his sister. No matter that Tony was doing the same thing, it was his sister who was at issue.

Tony supposed his parents had a point about their grandson; they could at least be there for him. When Kathy, Craig, and Jeff lived in Philadelphia, Tony had showered his nephew with presents and attention, had, in fact, loved him like a son. So he accepted that his parents' move would be beneficial for the boy. But the thought of not having his parents close to him, not being able to drop in anytime unannounced, once again made his stomach churn as if filled with acid.

He realized his parents were looking at him, waiting for him to answer. He had to fight the urge to rail against them for wanting to leave and in turn make them feel guilty for doing so. Asking his opinion was just their way of being considerate, of making him feel as if he was a part of their decision, when in fact, he knew they had already made up their minds.

"Well," Tony said slowly, "the change might be good for you, and who knows, maybe this is for the best. You can help the daughter you have, rather than thinking about the one you lost."

Immediately, Tony regretted the words, hearing the insensitivity in them. However, his parents seemed not to notice or care because neither one said a word.

Finally, his mother leaned over and kissed him on the cheek, her hand still on his arm. "Tony, I'm so glad you understand. It's not that we don't love being here for you and Laura and the boys, but . . . well, you have your own life now, and you're doing well. Kathy, on the other hand, needs us."

Tony nodded, not understanding at all, feeling his stomach roll threateningly. Trying his best to downplay what was going on internally, he excused himself from the table, muttering that he needed to use the bathroom. Abruptly, he pushed back from the table, almost knocking the chair over in his rush to put some distance between him and his parents. He managed to maintain his balance, however, and walked shakily out of the room.

Tony flipped on the light and turned the faucet to Cold, leaning heavily on the sink for support. Testing whether the water was indeed cold enough,

TONY TANCREDI AND CINDY L. O'HARA

he then splashed his face repeatedly, almost as if trying to wake from a bad dream—which, in a sense, he supposed he was. Finally, his heart and breathing slowed. He looked at his image in the mirror. His face was putty gray, his eyes sunken and haunted. He watched the water dribble down his chin and cheeks, staring at his eyes, and wondered why he felt so lost. After all, this was the natural progression of things, right? Kids grow up, move away, leaving the parents to . . . do what? Whatever the hell they wanted, he supposed. For his parents, it meant helping their children out whenever they could. He knew this was what his parents felt they had to do. Even as Tony recognized this, his inability for self-sacrifice left him incapable of supporting their decision, although he would never say so.

A soft knock at the door jolted Tony back to reality.

"Tony, honey, are you okay?" asked his mother.

"Fine, Ma. Just washing my hands. I'll be right out."

"Okay. Take your time. I was just starting to get worried, that's all."

"Everything's fine, Ma," Tony lied. "Be there in a minute."

His mother shuffled away from the door. Tony took one last deep breath before shutting off the water. Thankful that he had been able to hold on to his dinner and feeling a bit calmer than when he had first entered the bathroom, he turned the light off and went to find his parents.

When he got back to the dining room, he found his mother sporting her plastic yellow cleaning gloves, clearing the dishes from the table.

She looked up and smiled. "You okay?"

Tony glanced at the dish she was holding. It was his half-eaten plate of lasagna, now cold and congealing in its own sausage fat. Seeing this, his stomach gave a final burp of protest before going back to sleep.

"Fine," he replied. "But I'm gonna have to get outta here. I have to work at the Shamrock tonight."

"Ohhhh," said his mother. "Your father will be so disappointed. I know he was looking forward to watching the rest of the game with you."

"I know, Ma, but I can't miss work. I'll go say good-bye, then help you clear the dishes before I leave."

"Oh, don't worry about this." His mother waved her gloved hand at him. "I got it."

"You sure?" Tony asked.

His mother nodded, then stood on her toes to kiss Tony's cheek.

"You go. But say good-bye to your father," she reminded him.

"I will, Ma," Tony said, exasperation lacing his words.

His mother said, "Without the attitude."

Smiling, Tony said, "Yes, ma'am," then wondered if he was ever going to stop feeling like a boy trapped inside a man's body.

In the den, Tony's father had resumed his position in the leather lounger and was, when Tony walked in, yelling at the television. "That's bull!"

"How's the game goin'?" Tony inquired, smiling.

"Ah . . . okay," his father complained. "But the refs are a bunch of friggin' idiots. I swear they wouldn't know their ass from their elbow."

"Well, do me a favor, wouldja, and calm down. You're gonna give yourself a heart attack. Besides, I don't think they can hear you from here."

"Yeah, okay. Are you outta here?"

"Yeah. I gotta work at the club tonight," Tony replied, thankful he had an excuse to leave. All of a sudden, his parents' house seemed small and claustrophobic. "I'm gonna take off. Remember, take it easy."

With a barely perceptible nod, his father returned his attention to the Penn State game.

TONY TANCREDI AND CINDY L. O'HARA

TWENTY-SIX

O N EDGE FROM the earlier news about his parents, Tony had a feeling it was going to be a long Friday night. The only saving grace was that he would get to see Diane that evening.

"Hey, Ton," Greg yelled down the crowded bar. "Phone call."

Puzzled, Tony walked over and took the phone from Greg, who refused to look at him.

"Hello?"

"Tony? It's Di."

"Hey, honey. When are you getting here?"

"Well, that's the thing," Diane said. "I can't make it tonight. Paul's going out, and you know I don't leave the baby with anyone but family. Even if I *could* find someone to watch Matt, Paul would wonder where I'm going and who I'm going out with. I'm sorry, baby."

"Fuck sorry!" Tony exploded. "I'm tired of living by Paul's schedule, Diane. I've left my family. I've been outta my house for a month now. And what are *you* doing to get us together? I'm goddamn sick and tired of it."

"Tony Tancredi, you will not speak to me like that!" Diane snapped.

"I'll speak to you any goddamn way I want. It's not like you're my wife or anything. You're just the person I happen to be fucking. For now!" Tony let the threat hang in the air. "You know what? I don't want you here anyway. You'd just get in the way." Before Diane could respond, Tony slammed the phone down.

"Trouble in paradise?" Greg asked, drying a glass, a smile playing across his lips.

"Shut up, Greg," Tony said. He moved away from the bar. Tony knew he'd gone too far, and he'd have to call Diane back and apologize, but he was in no frame of mind to do so now.

Angry because he had devoted so much time to this woman, had, in fact, turned his life upside down for what appeared to be no reason at all; Tony was tired of her excuses. He had done everything he said he would, and then some. As promised, he had been clean for a couple of weeks now, had stayed away from alcohol, drugs, *and* women—not that he expected the Medal of Honor, but hey, it *was* a sacrifice on his part.

But tonight would be different. Tonight, Tony vowed, all bets were off.

Spotting Joe deep in conversation with Monte and Greg, Tony headed toward them. He knew the two bouncers were telling Joe about the conversation they had just overheard, and as Tony approached, all three men wordlessly slipped away. This served only to aggravate him even more.

"Hey, Ton . . . wanna get a bite and make the rounds?" Joe asked.

"Yeah, sure," Tony said. "I need to get outta here and have a drink. Let's go."

"Great. Come with me to the office."

Tony followed his boss to the back office. Joe split off a small piece of meth and put it in his mouth.

Joe looked at Tony questioningly. "You want some? I mean, I know you've been clean for a while, so I figured—"

"Yeah, why the hell not, right?" Tony replied.

A large smile lit up Joe's face. "That's my boy! He's back! Here. This'll make everything better," Joe said, breaking off a piece and holding it out to Tony.

Tony didn't know how much better the meth would make his situation, but he knew it would numb the pain and temper his anger.

Gladly, he took what was offered from Joe's hand.

After making the requisite rounds of different clubs, Tony and Joe finally got back to the Shamrock just after one in the morning.

"Place is crowded tonight, even for a Friday," Tony commented.

"Yo, Ton!" Monte walked up and leaned over so he could yell into Tony's ear and be heard above some band screaming from the speakers. "That kid, the one from way back in the summer who was screamin' for me to let her in, she's sayin' she's your girlfriend. You been holdin' out on us, dago?"

Tony knew that Monte meant Melissa, but he wasn't about to make the decision to let her in without Joe's blessing. Tony leaned close to Joe and said, "Boss, Melissa's here, and she wants to come in for a minute and talk to me. She's underage, so I won't let her stay. Is it all right?"

Without looking at Tony, Joe replied, "Yeah, go ahead. She might be just what you need tonight. Might make you forget about your other problem for a while." Tony knew whom Joe was referring to. He turned to Monte and nodded.

Tony watched Melissa weave her way to him. He knew she'd had too much to drink by the way she stumbled periodically in the few feet she had to walk from the front of the club to where Tony stood. If not for Monte gripping her forearm and holding her upright, Tony was sure she would have fallen long before she reached him. To her credit, though, she managed

TONY TANCREDI AND CINDY L. O'HARA

to look sexy and simultaneously stunning. Unlike the rest of the girls who were caked in too-dark makeup, with clothes looking more like lingerie than something you would wear out, Melissa wore only a hint of lipstick and a little black dress. It was a clingy little thing that showcased more cleavage than Tony knew she had and hit her midway down her perfectly shaped lean thighs.

To Tony, it seemed clear that Melissa had more than a dinner date on her mind.

When Monte finally made it to Joe and Tony, he released Melissa a little too soon, and she staggered into Tony's arms. "I'm a little . . . drunk," Melissa slurred. "And just messed up enough to tell you what I have been wanting to tell you for a while."

"What's that?" Tony smiled, looking down at the girl.

"That I need more from you—I mean more *of* you. I want more than talk from our relationship. And I don't care about your divorce or how long it takes. I wan' us to be together. Now."

Trying not to laugh at what was, for Melissa, obviously a serious monologue, he propped her up to a standing position and nodded. "I see," Tony replied. "Well, when would you like to start this so-called relationship?"

Joe spoke up. "Sounds like she means business, Ton."

Ignoring him, Melissa said, "My parents are down at the house on the Shore for the weekend, and I'd like you to spend the weekend with me."

"Really?" Tony said, pretending to consider the offer.

"I'm serious," Melissa said.

Tony raised his hands in defense. "Okay, okay. When I'm done here tonight, I'll come to your house. But you can't stay here until I'm done with my shift."

Melissa's face lit up. "Great! I'll see you about three or four in the morning," she said, turning (surprisingly well, Tony thought) on her heels to leave.

"Wait!" Tony said. Melissa stopped and turned. "Go outside and sit in your car. Monte will come out and give you something to sober you up. I don't want you driving home like that."

Melissa looked back, the shift in balance threatening to topple her once again, caught herself, nodded, and walked off.

When Tony pulled up to Melissa's two-story brick home at exactly four in the morning, one faint light peeked through a white lace curtain in an upper window. Although he had not been in her home long on their first and only date, Tony had noted the finery within, including the Persian rugs in the hall, and, although he was no expert, what appeared to be original portraits, by artists long dead, hanging on the walls. Clearly, her family had money.

He rapped softly on the front door so as not to wake the neighbors. To his surprise, it opened swiftly. Tony wondered if she had seen him drive up and had been waiting for his knock. It was a brief thought, replaced by instant longing when he saw Melissa.

Standing before him was not the drunken mess of a girl Tony witnessed at the club, but a young woman dressed in a black teddy that rested just at the top of her shapely legs. Underneath the lingerie, she wore black pantyhose, topping off the outfit with high heels that lent her short stature some height. Tony took in the woman before him, letting his gaze travel up from her black heels to her legs, lingering on her pert small breasts. She had combed out her chestnut-colored hair so it lay softly on her shoulders. Everything about her was a mystery, Tony thought. She appeared at one moment to be young and innocent, almost childlike, yet sultry and sexy the next. Without saying a word, Melissa shut the door, then took Tony's hand and led him upstairs.

Too soon, it was Monday morning, and the alarm clock signaled it was time to rise by buzzing loudly next to Tony's ear. Reluctantly, he stared bleary-eyed at the time. The numbers *5-3-0* stared back at him in blood red. Too much wine the night before and all-night sex had left Tony exhausted and unable to fully focus. The alarm clock continued its annoying sharp drone, until finally Tony rolled onto his back, one arm draped across his forehead, the other fumbling for the Off button.

Groaning inwardly, he somehow managed to swing a well-muscled leg over the side of the bed, to start the process of getting up. Slowly, Tony sat up, taking his time. He sat on the edge of the bed, trying not to wake Melissa.

"What time is it?" she murmured softly.

"Early," Tony replied. "Go back to sleep."

"Mmmm."

Glad she had apparently drifted off, Tony pushed himself out of the comfort of the warm bed and headed to the bathroom to take a shower. When he returned, Melissa was nowhere to be found.

He took one last look around to make sure he hadn't forgotten anything, then jogged down the stairs. He found Melissa in the kitchen making breakfast, a pot of coffee already brewing. Unsure of how to make a gracious escape, Tony said lamely, "Wow. Someone's been busy."

"Well, I thought you'd want to eat something before you left," Melissa said, scraping bacon bits off the bottom of the pan.

For lack of anything better to say, but wanting to make it clear that he had to leave, Tony said, "Well, it smells wonderful, but I don't really have time." Unused to being taken care of by anyone other than his mother, Laura, and, on the rare occasion, Diane, he was uncomfortable with Melissa's kindness and generosity.

"Don't be silly," she replied, dishing a heaping pile of scrambled eggs onto a china plate. "Of course you have time. You need to eat." She used a fork to pluck four pieces of bacon out of the pan they were sitting in, gelling in their own fat. As if on cue, the toaster gave a loud *pop*, and two pieces of golden wheat bread shot up.

"Butter?" Melissa asked.

With his stomach grumbling in protest at the thought of not being fed, and unsure of how to leave, Tony agreed to stay, by reluctantly taking the plate full of eggs, bacon, and toast, then sitting down at the dining room table.

"You really shouldn't have gone to all this trouble," Tony said, scooping a large forkful of eggs into his mouth.

"It was no problem. Really," Melissa said.

"Aren't you gonna eat?"

"Not hungry."

Shrugging, Tony continued to ravage the meal before him, finally giving in to his appetite.

"So I wanted to talk to you about your divorce."

Tony paused, his fork hanging in midair. "What about it?" Tony asked, not at all liking where this was going.

"It's just . . . I don't know, I thought after this weekend that maybe . . . ," Melissa stammered, wiping at some nonexistent crumbs on the white tablecloth.

"What?"

Blushing, Melissa said, "It's just that . . . I think I'm falling in love with you, and I just wanted you to know that whenever your divorce is final, I'm here for you."

Tony's first instinct was to snap at her, to tell her she was being ridiculous by mistaking great sex for love. But when he looked at her face and gazed into her dark brown eyes, he softened.

He wiped his mouth with the napkin, then pushed back from the table, the chair making a sharp, grating sound.

"Look, kid, I'm gonna be honest with you. I had a great time, but that's all it was—a great time."

While he didn't want to hurt her feelings, he didn't want her to get any misconceptions either. "I can't tell you what's gonna happen with my . . . divorce." Tony stumbled over the word. "For all I know, we may get back together. Now it really is time for me to go." He kissed her gently on the lips.

Unmoved by his speech, Melissa said in a clipped tone, "Fine."

Whether she was implying she was fine with the way things were ending, or whether she was okay with him leaving, Tony didn't know. But when he walked out the door, he comforted himself that he had never told Melissa he loved her and, by this slight omission, hoped she would get over him in the future.

TONY TANCREDI AND CINDY L. O'HARA

TWENTY-SEVEN

ANXIOUS TO PUT some distance between himself and Melissa, Tony skipped down the four front steps to the walkway, climbed into his Caddie, and headed to work.

While driving to the lumberyard, Tony realized he had not talked to Diane since he had blown up at her on Friday night. Panicking, Tony drove as fast as the speed limit would allow and finally made it to work. Once there, he parked, pulled his keys out of the ignition, and was out the door. Taking the few steps two at a time, he was in the office in moments.

Tony picked up the black receiver on the old rotary-dial phone and dialed Diane's number.

Just then, Bob Keebe walked in.

Frowning, Bob said, "Hey, Tancredi! This isn't your office, and these phones are not for your personal use unless it's an emergency. Is this an emergency?"

Tony was pretty sure that calling his mistress to lie about where he was all weekend didn't qualify, but he also didn't care. It had never been a problem before to use the phone on occasion; this was just Bob's way, Tony knew, of tightening his hold a little more on him. For the first time, Tony gave Bob the satisfaction of a response.

Although the words *fuck off* were dangerously close to Tony's lips, with monumental control and restraint, he instead said, "Hey, Keebe, don't start a war you can't win, and don't mention my personal life again!"

Bob smiled, turned, and walked away.

Mark said, "Hey, Ton. We were all punching in when we heard what you said to Keebe. Damn, Ton! No one ever talked to him like that before! It was like you challenged him or sumthin', and he actually backed down!"

The crowd of men murmured their assent. Fortunately for Tony, the men had gotten only one side of the conversation and hadn't been privy to Keebe's enigmatic smile. Tony didn't correct their impression. He let them think what they wanted to because, Tony thought, it might come in handy someday.

With the morning slipping away and Melissa coming by for lunch, Tony decided that his phone call to Diane would have to wait until he got back to the Lair.

The rest of the day flew by, and by quitting time, Tony was ready to head to his temporary home.

When he got back to the Lair, he found Joe sitting in a comfortable leather chair, his feet propped up, a drink in one hand and the television tuned to the local news.

"Hey, Ton," Joe said. "Wondered if I'd ever see you again."

Tony realized he hadn't seen or talked to his boss in more than forty-eight hours.

"Yeah, well, ya know—"

"Yeah, I know. Hey, Di called three times Sunday and once today. You should call her back."

"Yeah. I figured as much. I've been thinkin' about what to say to her—"

"Got any ideas?" Joe said, his eyes focused on the blonde airhead who was telling viewers what the weather was going to be like tomorrow.

"I don't know. I guess I'll come up with sumthin'."

Joe remained silent, and Tony took this to mean the conversation was over. He had a phone call to make anyway.

Tony walked to his bedroom and shut the door. He had to think of something believable, but for the life of him, he couldn't think what it might be. He knew Di would be beside herself. On more than one occasion, she had become irritated at the women at the club who hit on him. To this, she had advised that he should not let them get too close or touch him. It was pure and honest jealousy, and Tony recognized it for what it was, but now her inability to reach him over the weekend would only serve to fuel that particular emotion.

Basically, he was screwed.

After some contemplation, however, he thought he had it figured out. He would tell her that he was at his parents' house for the weekend because they had told him of their plans to move to Florida to help his sister. He had been devastated at this new development and had stayed with them, intending to phone her this morning. However, the argument with Keebe had gotten in the way, and this was the first opportunity he had to call. It was the best lie he could think of, and he hoped to God she bought it.

He dialed her number and listened to the shrill ring echo in his ear. As the line rang once, twice, then three times without anyone picking up, he thought for a moment he would get a reprieve. Then her voice, breathless from trying to get to the phone before the answering machine picked up, said, "Hello?"

"Hey, babe. It's me."

A chilly silence greeted him.

"Look, Di, I'm sorry I haven't called before now, but under the circumstances, I think it was best that we didn't speak."

The continued silence on the other end lent Tony the opportunity to explain himself. Warming to his story, he said, "I'm sorry that I upset you, but you have to understand where I was coming from. I've been patient as hell. I've upset my entire life, left my wife and kids, and then the few moments I count on seeing you, you cancel. I knew you couldn't just leave the kid, but it didn't make me any less pissed off."

He then launched into his story about his parents' move and the argument with his boss, so that by the end, Di was near tears with sympathy and compassion.

"Honey," Diane said. "I'm so sorry about your parents. I know how close you are to them. When are they leaving?"

"At the end of the month."

"Can I do anything?"

Tony smiled, inwardly breathing a sigh of relief. "Nah. I'm better now that I've spent some time with them. And I know I'm just being selfish by wanting them to stick around. They're doing the right thing."

Tony ended the call, but promised to phone later that night.

Tony lay in his bed, listening to the rain beat out a rhythm against the shingles on the roof. *Hell of a storm outside*, Tony thought. He gazed at the ceiling and realized that for once, he didn't feel like going out. He heard Joe in the bathroom, getting ready, his electric shaver making a distinct *hummm*. Tony smiled, remembering the joke he had shared not too long ago with *what the hell was her name?* He couldn't think of it now, didn't really matter anyway. It had been damn funny.

He swung his legs over the side of the bed, willing himself to get up and get going, but his mind had other business. He thought about his living arrangement and heaved a sigh. At first, the Lair had been exciting, but the attraction it had once held with all the chaos had worn off. *So now what?* Tony wondered. The only thing keeping him there was the hope Diane would finally leave her husband, but even that hope was slowly dwindling. When Tony insisted that Diane give him a date when she'd be leaving her husband, she had initially grown angry. Later, though, she had promised she'd think about it.

That'd be enough of a Christmas present for me, Tony thought.

With Thanksgiving less than a week away, Diane was still making excuses about why she couldn't leave. And the thought of spending the holidays at the Lair further depressed him.

In one particularly nasty phone conversation, Diane had said the main reason she wasn't leaving her husband was that she didn't want her son to come from a broken home. That, and she wanted to ensure there would be enough money for his college education—implying, Tony thought, that he couldn't provide for her and her son.

Tony had shot back that he would put enough money in the bank right then, in her name for her son's college, as well as for any children they would have together.

"Besides," Tony had argued, "you're going to get a divorce in the future anyway, with or without me."

Later, he had regretted making that dire prediction, but he truly believed it. She had hung up, and they had never spoken of that conversation again.

Now, Tony could only hope, if she loved him—and he truly believed she did—she would do the right thing.

Friday night at the yard was dead, and all the loads were done, with nothing to do but clean up. Tony had prearranged to see Di for about an hour if he could get there before her husband, Paul, came home.

Somehow Bob had learned of Tony's plans, however, and when Tony asked to leave, Bob said, "I'd love to let you go, Tancredi, but I've still got some things that need to be done."

Tony looked around at the stacked and bundled lumber, and the just-swept entranceway to the office, before replying, "Like what?"

"Never mind," Bob said. "You can conduct your social life on your own time, not mine."

Tony knew this was Bob's way of trying to show he was still in charge and he could control him in front of the few workers who were still around, but he had chosen the wrong day to do it.

With barely controlled fury, Tony said, "Okay, Bob! You wanna war? Now you've got one! Your worst nightmare is going to happen. I'll be the new union steward as of Monday morning!"

Bob threw back his head and laughed, his large gut jiggling. "Who do you think you are?" Bob asked, pretending to wipe away tears. "You can't find your business agent during the week, let alone on the weekend. And even if you could, what makes you think he'll make you steward?"

TONY TANCREDI AND CINDY L. O'HARA

"I could have done this a long time ago," Tony said. "For six months now, all the men have been asking me, begging me, to be steward. Well, as of Monday, they'll be *my* men, not yours anymore."

"Whatever you say, Tancredi. Whatever you say. Oh—and by the way, you still need to straighten out the big shed before you leave."

With a smirk, Bob turned and went back into the office.

TWENTY-EIGHT

WHEN TONY GOT back to the Lair that night, he found Joe sitting at the dining room table, an open ledger in front of him and a glass of some amber-colored liquid within arm's reach.

Without the usual preamble, Tony pulled out a chair and sat down. "We need to make some calls. I got a smart-ass general manager at the lumberyard, and I need to teach him a lesson."

Joe didn't even look up. "What? You want him in the hospital for a while?"

"Nah. Nuthin' like that. I need to be union steward by Monday morning."

Joe stopped what he was doing and looked at Tony. "Who's your business agent over there?"

"Some Jewish guy. Goes by the name of Alan Love. Hangs at the racetrack on the weekends. I see him there all the time."

"Okay," Joe replied. "Tonight at the club, I'll put the word out and have the other union heads go see him tomorrow at the track. That should take care of it."

Relieved, Tony said, "Thanks, Joe."

"You're welcome. But you know, you should have let me do this for you a long time ago. It doesn't look good, one of my guys not heading up the union where he works."

Feeling chastised, but nonetheless appreciative, Tony pushed back from the table and went to get a celebratory beer.

Tony waited at the entrance to the yard Monday morning, greeting the crew as they came to work. He gathered the men who were there and asked them to be at the office at around nine to see what was going to happen. Tony explained the situation and what had occurred over the weekend, although it was difficult because of all the interruptions and cheers from the group.

"So did Alan Love make you steward yet, or did I just miss it?" Bob asked. His smile lit up his face, crinkling the corners of his porcine eyes.

"Bob, you'll be the first to know." With an air of a confident man, Tony turned on his heels and sauntered off.

At precisely nine o'clock, Alan Love drove his white Buick Skylark into the yard, sending up a cloud of dust.

Love got out, put his hands on his hips, and looked around for Keebe.

Keebe emerged almost immediately from the office, making Love wonder if the man had been waiting for him.

"Well, hey there, Alan. To what do I owe the pleasure?" Keebe asked.

Uncomfortable in any other setting besides an office or board meeting, Love gingerly stepped toward Bob, trying to avoid getting dust on his pants' cuffs, at the same time smoothing the front of his navy blue suit.

Careful to leave his door open as an indication that he wouldn't be staying, Love looked blankly at the general manager's outstretched hand, but did not take it. "Bob, I just stopped by to inform you that Tony Tancredi is the new union steward of this yard, effective as of now."

"But . . . don't the men have to vote on it?" Bob said weakly.

"No," Love replied, taking off his glasses and holding them up to the sun to inspect them. He put them back on. "The contract now states that business agents appoint the steward—oh, hello, Tony."

"Hello, Alan," Tony said, sticking out his hand. Love looked at the proffered hand, hesitating only a second before giving it a quick shake, then letting go. Love made a mental note to wash himself thoroughly.

"Alan, if it will make Bob happy, I'd be glad to have a vote right now. If I get one person who disagrees with your decision, I'll decline the offer."

"That's awfully generous of you, Tony, but you don't have to do that," Love said.

"It's okay. Really. I don't mind."

"Okay, men, anyone here who does *not* want Tony to be steward, raise your hand." Love looked around the collected group, but not one hand was raised. "There you go, Bob. We did it your way, and everyone agrees. That should make you happy. And I think it was really nice of Tony to accommodate you. Shows a lot of class, don't you think, Bob?"

"Um . . . Alan, Tony, can I see you both in my office for a minute?" Keebe asked.

"Sure, Bob," Tony replied. "Let's go in and tell the office staff the news. In fact, I think I'll let you tell them. After all, you're the man around here, aren't you, Bob?"

Love gave an exaggerated sigh, but honored the request.

Once inside, Love said, "Okay, Bob. I'm here. What is there to discuss?"

"I just don't get it, Alan. I mean, Tony tells me Friday afternoon he's going to be steward on Monday, and here you are. You gotta admit that sounds a little suspicious."

"Bob, it sounds like you're suggesting I did something improper. Am I hearing you right?" Love took off his glasses and began polishing them, before putting them back on his rotund face. He took a step closer to Keebe and stared at him, waiting for his answer.

Keebe took what Love was sure was an unintended step back. "No, Alan. No. That's not what I'm saying at all. I'm just wonderin', who's callin' the shots around here? I mean, used to be it would take at least a week to get a new union stew in place, and Tony does it in a weekend?"

"Well, Bob. The truth is that the men have been complaining about you for a while now and have been begging me to make a change. I approached Tony months ago, told him what the men said. At the time, Tony told me he didn't feel he could give the time it required to do a good job. Whatever changed his mind is his business. I told Tony whenever he wanted to be steward to just tell me and I would make it happen. It's as simple as that. But he's standing right there." Love nodded toward Tony. "Perhaps you should ask him what his reasons are for taking on this new job."

Tony smiled at Alan, then looked at Keebe. "Well, Alan, I owe it all to Bob here." Tony walked over and slapped Keebe loudly on the back. "He knows what happened and why I decided to become steward."

"All right, then. I assume we're done here. Unless there's something else, Bob?"

"Well, I just don't get—"

Whatever else Bob was going to say was suddenly drowned out by a loud chanting coming from outside the office. Bob lumbered to the window.

"What the hell?"

Alan sauntered over, curious about what was going on.

"What the fuck do they think they're doin'? They're supposed to be working." Bob then waddled to the door as fast as his considerable bulk would allow and threw open the office door.

"Come on, Tony. I don't think we want to miss this." Alan smiled and held open the door.

Outside, Mark—the now-ex-union steward—had driven a forklift carrying a four-by-eight bunk of plywood over to the office.

"Hey, Ton. Get on, man."

"Okay, but as the new union steward, let me just say that this is the last time you're gonna tell me what to do." Tony laughed and climbed aboard.

TONY TANCREDI AND CINDY L. O'HARA

"Whatever, man." Mark raised the forklift to its highest point while the rest of the crew threw whatever grass and weeds they could pull from the ground, shouting, "All hail our new leader" and "Long live the king!"

Alan smiled at the scene as Bob began flapping his arms wildly, demanding that everyone get back to work or they would be fired.

Still laughing, Mark lowered Tony to the ground, but before anyone moved, they looked to Tony for approval.

"Okay, guys, we've proven our point. Let's get back to work," Tony said. He turned to Keebe. "I'm going to walk Alan to his car, Bob, and then I'll get started."

Bob's answer was to stalk back into the office and let the door slam behind him.

"That went well, I think," Love said with a smile. He began the short walk to his car.

"Yeah. Whatever. I'm over him," Tony said.

Love stopped, keys jangling from one hand, his other arm propped on the open door, "So why didn't you tell me of your connections before?"

"It wasn't important before, but now it is—for the men and for me. The company wasn't going by the contract, and the men were too scared to say anything. Now that shit is over. So now that you know what I can do, can I depend on you?"

"Absolutely," Love replied. "Anything you need. In fact . . ." He leaned into the car and came out with a pen. Then he reached into his jacket pocket and fished around until he found what he was looking for. "Here's my home phone number," he said, scribbling on the back of a business card. He handed it to Tony. "Oh, and, Tony, I don't need any of those guys coming to see me again."

"Understood. Thanks, Alan."

Love dove into the comfort of his car and sped away, his only desire to get as far away from the lumberyard as possible.

The next morning, Tony found himself standing in front of Jack Watson, the owner of the lumberyard. The scene reminded Tony of his Catholic school days, when he had gotten in trouble, except then it had been Sister Agnes.

"So . . . Tony, is it?" Watson questioned.

"Sir, with all due respect, I believe you know my name." Tony knew it was Watson's business to know who his employees were. After all, you didn't get to be a millionaire a few times over by being careless or oblivious.

It was Tony's opinion that because Watson had been wealthy for so long (or perhaps it was just his nature to be a dick), the man had completely lost touch with reality.

Tony recalled one instance in particular when Watson had told Mark, the former union steward, to go out and buy two cases of beer for the men. To cover the charge, Watson had handed Mark a five-dollar bill. Mark had looked at the money blankly before trudging off on his errand. Mark had paid the balance out of his own pocket, afraid to correct the owner's error. When Tony learned what had happened, he was enraged. Yet at the time, he too had done nothing except to reimburse Mark from *his* own pocket.

So it wasn't without a certain degree of irony and pleasure that Tony stood placidly in front of his boss.

"Look, Tony, I don't know who the hell you *think* you are, but lemme tell you this, no one—not you or anyone else—is going to tell me how to run my yard. I don't care what the fucking contract says!" Watson pounded his fist on his desk for emphasis, his voice rising with each word.

Tony leaned over the desk, his knuckles making indentations on inch-thick reports that were lying there. Tony's nose was just inches from the owner's face. "Well, *Mr.* Watson, let me tell *you* something. You will go by the contract, or I'll close every goddamn lumberyard in Philadelphia and Bucks County, and you can explain to the other owners why you don't have to go by the contract and they do." He kept his anger in check and, by doing so, made his voice even more menacing than if he had yelled back.

Watson rose to his full five-foot-six-inch height, hitched up his pants, and said with a smirk, "Even *I* don't have that kind of power, let alone a nobody like you."

Tony stood upright as well and said, "If you'll let me use your phone, I think I can convince you otherwise."

"Sure, go ahead. I gotta hear this," Watson said smugly. Tony dialed the number he had long ago committed to memory. "Hey, Joe? I'm here at the lumberyard, and I got an owner who's telling me that he doesn't have to go by the contract. He says no one's going to tell him what to do. I was hoping you could help me persuade him it's in his best interest to honor the contract."

"Sure, Ton. I'll call all the union heads, the carpenters, teamsters, laborers, and roofers and tell them to give him a call."

"Yeah," Tony said. "That should do it. Thanks." Tony placed the receiver back in its cradle, not saying a word, letting the tension between the two men build.

TONY TANCREDI AND CINDY L. O'HARA

"Well?" Watson asked impatiently.

"Within an hour, you'll be getting a call from the various union heads, and they'll explain to you what'll happen if you keep running things the same way you have been for the last few years. I think when you get those calls, you'll change your mind about how you run your business. I'll keep the union heads from doing what they tell you will happen when you change how things are done around here, and when you start treating these men with the respect they deserve."

Tony then walked to the office door. He turned back and said, "I should have expected this from you. After all, you trained Bob, and he had to find out the hard way that I mean what I say, because neither of you know who the fuck you're dealing with."

Tony stepped out of the office and closed the door gently behind him.

TWENTY-NINE

INSIDE, WATSON WATCHED through the window in horror as the scene unfolded. Large SUV's began arriving, blocking the front of the yard so no one could come in to get their load. Consequently, those customers who had been inside couldn't get out—everything playing out in a more public manner than Watson could have imagined. Well muscled men, union goons to be sure, got out of their vehicles; the men just stood around, leaning against the office. Even Watson could appreciate the amount of damage these men were doing to his business, just by being here. Once word got out, he would be a laughingstock.

Just as he was contemplating what to do, his phone rang shrilly, startling him and breaking the impenetrable silence. Although his office staff was inside with him, watching what was taking place, no one dared say a word even as curiosity, he knew, was running at an all-time high.

Watson reluctantly picked up the phone.

"Jackie, my boy, how's business?" boomed the voice on the other end. Watson recognized it as Joey Mulligan, a union head who represented the Teamsters Local 107 in Philadelphia. "It's all right," Watson said tentatively.

"Really?" Mulligan continued in his too-loud voice. It was as if Mulligan thought they were speaking internationally and had to yell to be heard. "'Cuz that's not what I heard. I heard you were havin' a little trouble over there this mornin', and that can't be good for business."

"Well, we're managing," Watson replied, trying vainly to sound more confident than he felt.

And so it went. For the next two hours, he fielded similar calls from union heads representing roofers, carpenters, and laborers, until finally, seeing no other option, he banged the phone into its cradle and grabbed his coat and briefcase, then stalked out of the office, slamming the door behind him.

"Mornin', sir," said one of the men outside the office, actually tipping his hat to him.

"I've nothing to say to you, *gentlemen*." Watson hurried past them to his car.

The men just grinned, although Watson thought he heard one mumble under his breath, "I bet you don't, asshole."

Watson whipped back around. "What did you say?"

"Nothing, sir." The man just looked back at him, still smiling.

Quickly, Watson opened the door to his black 1982 Rolls-Royce Silver Spur.

Keeping his focus straight ahead and refusing to acknowledge the many eyes he knew were watching him, he guided the car slowly through the lumberyard until he came upon the enigmatic Italian man who was his employee and currently making his life a living hell.

Watson rolled down his window only long enough to snap, "I'll honor the damn contract." Without waiting for a response, Watson pressed the gas pedal enough so the car jumped. He sped out of the yard, leaving a dusty cloud in his wake.

Tony smiled, savoring his victory. His euphoria was short-lived, however, when he realized someone was going to have to pay for his boss's embarrassment, and he knew that person was surely going to be him.

Tony groaned to himself. He had just read this morning that snow was expected later this week, which meant he'd be shoveling all the steps to the office, the mill, and all the bunks of lumber in the yard. He also knew Keebe would, upon Watson's instructions, happily give him every menial task that needed to be done, just to try and break him. He made a silent promise that like those little neighborhood bastards from his past, he would never let Keebe or Watson see his frustration. For them, he would always have a smile on his face and a just-another-day-at-the-office kind of attitude.

THIRTY

WHILE CHRISTMAS SHOPPING at Neshaminy Mall, Tony's eyes were drawn to the perfectly windexed glass case in the jewelry store that had not a streak on it. From hours of constant polishing, it shone in a way that should not have been possible. Under the bright fluorescent lights, the jewels inside sparkled and twinkled like tiny stars, all of them beautiful in their own way. Like energetic small puppies in a pet store, each one seemed to cry, *Pick me. Pick me. Take me home.* From rubies to sapphires to emeralds, all the colors of the rainbow were represented. Standing in front of the case, Tony didn't know which to choose. Would Diane prefer diamonds or emeralds as a Christmas present? Or maybe neither, maybe rubies would be a better choice? Just as Tony decided to elicit help from one of the many clerks who were hovering among the cases, because the choice was too much for one man, he heard a familiar voice behind him.

"Tony, is that you?" said someone with a soft Southern accent.

He looked up to see a man and woman who lived, if memory served, about eight houses up from Diane. The elderly couple, Tony remembered, had moved into Di's development from Georgia and, although pleasant, had always asserted that the South had so much more to offer than the North, including more temperate weather. This lecture usually came up after the first snowfall.

After a couple of years, though, they had gotten used to the freezing winter temperatures and snow that often accompanied the sometimes-sub-thirty-degree nights. Because of their age, neither was able to shovel their walkway or drive. One day, seeing Ted struggling in vain to clear a path from his car to the mailbox, Tony had driven up with a backhoe and cleared the snow from their driveway. They had been so grateful that he had continued to do so until the day he left the construction company.

"Hey, Ted. Linda." Tony smiled, genuinely glad to see them. "How are you?"

"Fine, Tony, fine. And you?" Ted asked.

"Good, good," Tony replied. "So how is everyone else in the neighborhood? Treating you well, I hope?" Having not spoken to Diane in more than a week (*try two*, the little voice piped up cheerily), save for small snippets of conversation that had found her running out the door to this place or the other, Tony thought Ted and Linda might have seen her. (*So this is what it's come to,* the little voice whispered. *Fishing for information from a couple of old farts?*) Tony ignored the voice.

Ted laughed. "Oh yeah, everyone's fine, although if you're looking for gossip, you're talking to the wrong one. Linda's the one who tells *me* what's going on."

Tony turned to the older woman and waited. Linda then gave a synopsis of the neighbors that, Tony thought, would be worthy of any policeman on crime scene detail. When she failed to mention his mistress, however, Tony inquired, "And what about Diane and Paul? How are they?"

Suddenly, Linda's face lit up. "Oh! How could I neglect to mention them?" Linda drawled. "Diane's pregnant with their second child. They're hoping to have a girl this time."

With those words, Tony's stomach clenched, then lurched as if he had just stepped off a forty-foot building, falling to his death. Unable to catch his breath, he put one hand on the jewelry case behind him to steady himself, leaving a distinct handprint on the shiny glass. It was all he could do to hold on to the contents of his stomach.

"Tony, are you okay?" Linda asked. "You look so pale."

"I'll be fine, but suddenly, I'm not feeling very well. I need to go." He stumbled away, barely remembering to grab the brightly wrapped packages he had just bought for Laura and the boys.

Tony heard a distant "Merry Christmas!" as he trudged, one foot in front of the other, through the mall.

Somehow he managed to make it to the parking lot. He found his car, dropped the packages, and then threw up. In the midst of one particularly violent episode, he was sure that the next thing he would see would be his intestines. Gripping the door handle with one hand, Tony waited for his stomach to rid itself of the snack he had just eaten, taking note of the small bits of hot dog and French fries, colored red from ketchup, clinging to the hem of his jeans. When the nausea subsided, the dry-heaving began, leaving Tony in a cold sweat. After what seemed like hours, but had probably only been a few minutes, Tony felt he might actually be able to stand upright.

Careful to avoid the chunks of vomit that now smeared the blacktop, he loaded the packages into the car and slowly slid into the driver's seat, not entirely sure his stomach was done with him.

He placed his forehead on the steering wheel, willing the thoughts and questions to stop flying through his head like some mad pilot on a kamikaze mission. He knew the child wasn't his because before he had married Laura, he had gone to his doctor for a checkup. He had mentioned that he would soon be getting married and hoped to have children at some point. Familiar with his childhood history, the doctor had asked to run some tests. The results were disappointing. Because of all the X-rays he had received as a child, the doctor had told Tony he was basically sterile, that it wouldn't be impossible to have children, but he would require some medical intervention to do so. Tony had shared this knowledge with only Laura and Joe, and of course, his parents.

So it was with a sense of morbid pleasure that Tony knew Diane was most likely, at this very minute, wondering whose baby it was.

As his thoughts turned to Diane and the time they had shared over the last six months, Tony felt hot tears course down his cheeks. Suddenly, without warning, he began wailing—an inhuman cry of pain and sorrow. Angry at himself for having let his guard down and allowing himself to fall in love, he began banging the steering wheel repeatedly with his hand, the pain never registering.

Finally spent, Tony let his head fall back against the headrest and waited for the tears to stop.

Tony sat in his car for the next two hours, recounting painful memory upon painful memory of his time with Diane—the first night they made love, the first time he had seen her in her garden, even the arguments brought a fresh round of tears. Grief turned to rage, and rage turned to embarrassment at not seeing this coming. How many times had he asked, no, begged, Diane to leave her husband? How many times had he offered to set her up in her own place, start a college fund for her son, whatever she needed? And she had always politely declined. He banged his hand against the steering wheel again, welcoming the pain.

Tony remembered one conversation when, after a couple of glasses of wine, Diane had explained her marriage was a sham, that she and Paul had gotten together because of their respective parents' wishes. She confessed she had never loved her husband and that hers was a marriage of convenience. She knew this. But she hadn't wanted to disappoint her parents, so even when she had acknowledged her lack of feelings toward her soon-to-be husband, she had convinced herself it was the right thing to do at the time.

"I don't know what the fuck she thinks she's doing bringing another kid into this world, but I sure as hell ain't stickin' around," Tony said to no one in particular. For once, the little voice in his head, which usually had a running commentary going, was silent. Then he realized that Diane had never asked him to stay.

"I gotta talk to Laura. See if she'll take me back." Again, the voice remained mute. Tony took this as a good sign indicating he was making the right decision by ending his relationship with Diane and asking for Laura's forgiveness.

"Thank God it's Christmas," muttered Tony, already formulating a plan to get back into Laura's good graces.

He could count on one thing—Laura's sentimentality during the holidays would go a long way in persuading her to let him back into her life. He would simply play on her emotions, and the boys' too, of course. They would want him home for Christmas as well, and Tony was sure she would do it just for them, if not for him.

He wiped away the last of the tears and drove to the Lair for what he hoped would be his last night.

The next morning, Tony sat at the all-too-familiar dining room table in the Lair, rehearsing his speech to Diane before calling her, when the door opened. Sam walked in. His ridiculously large grin and bright eyes indicated, to Tony at least, that he was still high from the night before. Tony groaned, knowing Sam was going to want to joke around, a thing he was in no way prepared to do.

"Heeeeyyyyy, Tony, *my* man! How the hell are you?" Sam slurred, stumbling up to Tony and slapping him soundly on the back.

Before Tony could reply, Joe came up and put an arm around his friend.

"Sam. Why don't you and I go have a little chat," Joe said.

"Yeah, sure, Joe. Anything you say." Sam's smile faltered a little, and his eyebrows came together in what Tony assumed was worry. The requisite toothpick Sam always had in his mouth began to do its shuffle more rapidly.

The night before, expecting to have the house to himself, Tony had been surprised to find Joe at the Lair. He knew he'd have to tell Joe about Diane, and although he had tried to remain cavalier, he couldn't maintain his casual attitude. He had finally broken down. Joe had then done the one thing he was capable of doing, which was to listen. Tony had talked for hours to Joe, about his feelings for this woman, about how much pain she had caused him, and ultimately about his decision to return to his family.

Near the end of their conversation, Joe asked, "So when are you moving home?"

"As soon as Laura lets me," Tony had replied.

Joe nodded in understanding.

Tony picked up the phone to call Diane, glancing back toward the closed bedroom door where he assumed Joe was probably imparting the gist of their conversation from the night before to Sam and implying that everyone should leave Tony alone for a while. His speculation about what the two men were discussing was confirmed when the bedroom door opened and a now-sober-faced Sam walked out, placed a hand on Tony's shoulder, and left.

Tony listened to the dull steel-like ring on the other end, his stomach clenching and unclenching in a syncopated rhythm, his heart hammering an accompanying, albeit offbeat, tempo.

"Hello?"

Tony took a deep breath and said, "Di? It's Tony. Don't say anything. Just listen."

Silence as thick as a wool blanket greeted him.

"I know you're pregnant. But you don't gotta worry about it being mine because I'm sterile from all the X-rays from when I was a kid. I always wondered if I should tell you, but now I know that I didn't matter to you. I guess you were too busy screwing your old man to give a fuck what was going on with me. What did you need, Di? What was it I didn't offer to do for you or your kid? Let me ask you this, Di, did I ever matter to you? Or was I just a diversion for a bored housewife who couldn't get her husband's attention. You know what? Maybe Paul was right to compare you to those other women. Maybe you're not nearly as pretty as you think you are. When you two get divorced, remember what we could have had together."

"Tony—"

Before he heard what she had to say, Tony slammed the receiver into its cradle.

TONY TANCREDI AND CINDY L. O'HARA

THIRTY-ONE

A FEW MINUTES later, Joe walked out of the bedroom. Seeing his friend sitting morosely at the dining room table, Joe stopped, pulled out a chair, and sat down.

"So. How'd it go?"

"It went . . . as well as could be expected, I guess," Tony answered.

"Hey, Tony." When his friend did not reply, Joe slammed both hands down on the table, making it jump. "Hey!"

Tony looked up, his eyes wide.

"I'm talkin' to you. Now I was fine listenin' to you last night and givin' you some time to sulk. But when I ask you a question, I expect you to fuckin' answer me. You got it?"

Tony nodded.

"So let's try this again. How. Did. It. Go?"

Tony heaved a sigh. "I told her I knew she was pregnant, but that she didn't have to worry, that I was sterile—"

"That's not what you told me, though. You said the doc told you that you *could* have kids, but you'd have to see him first, right?"

"Yeah. I can have kids, I'd just need some help."

"Sounds like a built-in protection system to me. Probably saved you a ton of money in child support payments." Joe laughed.

When Tony remained silent, Joe started squirming uncomfortably, the joke clearly falling flat.

"Well," Tony said after a few seconds, "I guess if I wasn't sterile, you'd have to pay half the payments since you provided half the girls for me." Tony smiled.

Joe grinned back, and the tension that had just filled the air dissolved. "So now what?"

"So now I go and buy the biggest friggin' diamond I can find and hope to hell that Laura lets me move back home."

"Diamonds, huh?" Joe rubbed his chin thoughtfully. He pushed back from the table. "Come on."

"Where we going?" Tony asked, puzzled.

"I gotta friend who can help you. That okay with you?"

Tony considered the offer for a beat, and then replied, "Sure."

They drove to Carlo's Custom Jewelry on Buselton Avenue in Northeast Philly.

On the way, Joe filled Tony in on the owner's history, which was a bit sketchy. "The better to fit in with the likes of me and the rest of my crew," Joe said with a laugh.

"Carlo and I go way back. We grew up in the same neighborhood but lost touch for a while. Then I find out he's in the joint for armed robbery or sumpthin'. When he gets out, he shows up on my doorstep. Literally. He asks if I could help him out, which I do. And for my money, I get a good price on jewelry and don't gotta pay for labor. It's a—whadda ya call it—mutually beneficial relationship."

When they entered the shop, a short, stocky olive-skinned man with battleship gray hair—what was left of it—was deep in conversation with another customer.

"Look around, Ton. See what you like," Joe suggested.

While Tony wandered off, Joe browsed the cases of diamonds, rubies, sapphires, and emeralds glittering up at him. Bored, he drifted to a small corner of the store devoted to what appeared to be antique necklaces, rings, and bracelets. He gazed through the shiny glass at the vintage baubles and thought briefly about buying something for Nicky, but dismissed the idea. She'd been a pain in his ass lately, so why the hell should he buy her a present?

Shortly, the bell over the door tinkled cheerily, signaling the customer had left. Joe walked over to Carlo and embraced him in a bear hug that seemed to go on for several seconds. Joe held his old friend at arm's length.

"I was hoping you could take care of my good friend here, find him a diamond ring for his wife."

Carlo turned toward Tony, then back to Joe. "*This* is the guy you been tellin' me about?" He hooked a thumb at Tony. "He don't look so tough to me. He is too pretty, yes?"

Tony laughed uncomfortably.

"Yeah, well, he gets ugly real fast when he wants to. So can you help Tony out?"

Carlo stared at Tony thoughtfully, his left hand propping up his right elbow while one finger did a tap dance against his lips. Suddenly, the finger stopped in mid-tap, and Carlo's eyes lit up brightly. "I got just the thing for you," he said.

When he came back, he held in one hand a small drawstring pouch, in his other a square of material. He strode to a window case and motioned

Tony and Joe to follow. There, he placed the square of dark purple velvet under one of the few Tiffany lamps decorating the tops of the cases. Then with large fingers that looked like plump sausages, he opened the pouch. He gently shook the bag until the contents tumbled out and fell softly onto the square. Under the glare of the light sat a flawless two-karat teardrop diamond ring. For a moment, no one said a word.

Mesmerized by its beauty, Tony said, "I'll take it."

"I told you he'd find you sumthin'," Joe said.

As Tony pulled up to his home on Quiet Road—the same one he had, until recently, shared with Laura and the boys. (*Until you fucked everything up and went after a woman who used you and then threw you away like so much garbage, a bored housewife looking for a little fun until she could get knocked up by SOMEBODY and have another kid, a woman who—*)

"Shut up!" Tony screamed at the voice in his head. God, he hoped this worked, he thought, rolling the platinum diamond ring between his fingers. He looked away from the jewel and watched small flurries of snow land softly against the car's glass.

He gazed one more time at the diamond, turning it so it caught the last rays of the dying December sun, and watched the waning light make pinpoints dance and twinkle in the ring. He sighed and said one more prayer to a God he had long ago dismissed, then reached for the small purple velvet box sitting on the passenger seat next to him. He opened it and carefully wedged the diamond into place, then snapped the lid closed, pocketing the box.

"Here we go." Tony bent his head against the snow and icy wind that had picked up and was now threatening to become something much more than some pretty flakes blanketing the ground.

Tony walked up the two steps and tried the door handle, expecting to be able to walk right in, but it was locked. He fumbled in his pocket but realized he didn't have his keys on him—and he didn't have the faintest idea where they could be. In all the madness of the last few months, he doubted he'd be able to put his fingers on them. He'd have to get another set made—if, that is, Laura took him back. Unsure of what to do, he finally knocked lightly, tentatively. When no one came, he rapped more loudly.

"Coming," Laura yelled.

She flung open the door. Her eyes widened in surprise, but then quickly clouded with anger.

"Hey, honey."

"Tony. What are you doing here? And don't call me honey. I'm not one of your honeys. I'm your wife, remember?"

"What the hell's that s'posed to mean? I know who you are, and don't I still live here?"

"That depends, how long you gonna be here this time?"

Tony got ready to snap a reply at her, but suddenly felt deflated. After everything he'd been through, all he wanted to do was come home.

"Look, Laura, I don't wanna argue. I wanna talk—about us. About this damn job at the club. About me and all the shit I've been going through since I started at the Shamrock. I'm tired, babe, and I don't want there to be any more secrets between us. I wanna come home." He looked at her imploringly, hoping his sincerity would at least buy him a ticket inside. He fingered the ring box in his pocket.

Laura gazed back at him levelly, one hand on the door, the other on her hip. Her answer was to step aside and open the door wide.

Tony sat at the small dinette table in the kitchen the next morning, the *Philadelphia Inquirer's* sports page opened in front of him. He savored the quiet of being the only one awake and thought about last night. He and Laura had talked about *almost* everything, well into the morning—something they hadn't done since they had begun dating—with Tony editing certain details of his time away, of course. For her own good, he had told himself.

Finally, after a bottle of wine and a large pepperoni pizza from Salvatorri's and what seemed like rivers of tears, rants and raves, and even discussions of *feelings*, for God's sake, he had worn Laura down, and she had agreed to a trial return. It was then that he had reached into his jacket pocket and brought out the small velvet box.

When she opened it, she was speechless. And just when he thought she couldn't possibly have any more tears left in her, she looked up at him, her eyes welling.

"Oh my god, Tony. It's . . . it's beautiful. I don't know what to say."

"Say I can stay." He took the ring, set the box aside, and grasped her left hand. He gently slid the diamond on her finger and brought her fingers to his lips. He gazed at her. "I'm sorry. For everything."

That had sealed it. After that, they had made love right on the living room floor, not even making it to the bedroom. When neither one of them had anything left to give, they slowly gathered up their clothes. She led him to their bedroom upstairs, and he'd had the best night's sleep he'd had in months.

Although he would have said anything to get back in her good graces, including that he would consider quitting the Shamrock, he didn't believe he could actually go through with it. The club gave him the space he seemed to need from Laura and the kids and fed something in him they couldn't—although what that something was, he still didn't know.

Frustrated about not being able to pinpoint what the hell was wrong with him when it came to his family and his *other life*, as he had come to think of the Shamrock and his crew, he started thinking about another problem, which was Keebe.

Keebe was still doing his best to make life as difficult as possible for him by giving him any menial task he could think of.

Fed up with thinking about problems he couldn't do anything about, his thoughts turned to the upcoming Christmas party he was throwing the men.

When Tony was appointed union steward, Keebe's first order of business had been to uninvite the workers to the annual company Christmas party, in the hopes, Tony supposed, that the men's loyalty to him would cost them the few bones they were thrown throughout the year. Keebe had been practically giddy when he had hung up the flyer announcing that the Christmas party would be for office staff only. Tony responded by placing a large poster board of a sign underneath Keebe's that read,

Union-only Christmas Party to be held at the Shamrock the Friday before Christmas. Free food. Free drinks. Lots of dancing girls. Come one, come all.

Tony smiled at the memory of Bob walking by and ripping the poster down, stomping on it as if it were a bug, flapping his arms like some mad chicken. Of course, it hadn't mattered. Most of the men had seen it, and those who hadn't had heard about it.

As Tony flipped to the next page of the newspaper, he shook his head and grinned.

"Ah, Bob. You're just a poor, dumb bastard who doesn't even realize how far in over your head you are."

THIRTY-TWO

FRIDAY NIGHT OF the Christmas party, Tony was at the Shamrock taking care of last-minute details, including making sure the local strip clubs had sent over the girls he had handpicked for his crew.

"Hey, Greg," Tony yelled. "Where's Jeannie?"

Without looking up, Greg yelled back from behind the bar, "In the back, doing somethin' or other!"

"Well, tell her to get the hell out here!"

"Tell 'er yerself! I got my own shit goin' on here tryin' to get ready for this goddamn party *you're* throwin' for *your* boys!"

Choosing to let Greg's rebuke go, Tony walked over to try to appease his friend. Since he had broken up with Diane and moved back in with Laura, the tension that had previously existed between the two men had disappeared, and things were now back to normal—for the most part. Greg knew about Melissa but, for some reason, seemed a bit more accepting of her than of Diane. Tony suspected it was because Greg knew the fling with Melissa was just a temporary distraction.

"Sorry, Greg," Tony apologized.

Greg looked up at Tony and pulled himself up from where he was squatting behind the bar, counting the number of bottles he had for the night. "Ah, that's all right, man. I know you're stressed. I'll go check on Jeannie and tell 'er to get her ass out here."

Relieved, Tony thanked his friend before turning back and addressing the rest of the girls.

"Okay, ladies, so here's the deal. I've told my crew they can touch you, but they gotta keep their dicks in their pants. If somethin's goin' on that you don't like, tell them—don't ask—tell them to stop," Tony intoned, pacing up and down the line, like a general readying his troops for battle. Only, *his* army had tits the size of Texas and asses that could crack walnuts.

"I've already told these guys that if you have to ask them twice, they're going to regret it. Also, I know we're all here to have fun and make some money, but don't get out of hand trying to make a few extra bucks. You know Joe and I'll take care of you, so do me a favor and tone it down. Any questions?"

The girls shook their heads. They were all there as a favor to Tony and knew it would serve them well later when they wanted or needed something from the Lair. Although he trusted the girls (as much as he could trust girls whose primary job was to interact with a pole and get middle-aged men's rocks off), he had asked Monte and Sam to show up so Joe knew nothing improper went on between the girls and his men.

"Okay, that's it. We'll be opening up here in about twenty minutes." The girls then wandered off to take care of what they needed to before the party started.

During his short monologue, Monte and Sam walked in. Tony stomped to the bar, where the two men were chatting with Greg.

"Hey, Monte. I need a favor. Melissa knows about this party, but she doesn't know about the girls. She probably won't show up, but if she does, keep her outta here if the girls are still around. It'll just make things easier for everybody, if you know what I mean."

"Sure, Ton," Monte replied. "Whatever you say."

"Thanks, man."

"You got it."

The party lasted until midnight and, by Tony's estimation, was a rousing success. Neither the girls from the strip clubs nor his men from the lumberyard had gotten out of hand. And by all accounts, everyone had a great time.

He walked to the bar and signaled for Greg with a nod.

"One Jack and ginger. Just like ya like, Ton."

"Thanks, Greg."

"That was quite a party. Seems like everyone had a good time."

Tony took a sip of his drink and pursed his lips. He braced himself for the initial explosion of warmth in his chest before the hot liquid continued its travels to his gut.

"Well, I better try and get these yahoos outta here so I can get going with Joe. Thanks for the drink, Greg."

Without replying, Greg moved off to attend to another customer.

Tony took one more sip from his glass before heading to check on the girls, most of whom were taking a cigarette break in a corner of the club.

When Tony walked up, he asked, "Did you ladies make enough money tonight?"

"Oh yeah, Tony. Plenty," they echoed, their bleached, bottle-blonde heads nodding in unison.

"Well, thanks very much for coming out. I know you made these guys' night. You've worked hard, so have a drink on me, and if I don't see you, have a merry Christmas."

"But, Tony," purred one particularly large-breasted redhead, strolling up to Tony and curving her body into his, looking every inch the cat who had just finished eating the whole fucking canary. "We haven't given you *our* Christmas present yet."

She toyed with the lapel of his dark suit, and when Tony looked down, she looked up with an innocent, doe-eyed expression. Tony couldn't help but grin. Although he tried to decline, his attempts were halfhearted at best, and the girls knew it. After three drinks that had more Jack in them than ginger, his ability to refuse much of anything (let alone discern between what was and wasn't appropriate) had, like Elvis so many years ago, left the building. As the girls pulled Tony toward the ladies' room, he tried to protest that what was about to happen wasn't necessary, but the girls would hear none of it.

Throughout the club, cheers and laughter from his men egged him on, and with such an audience, Tony felt as if he didn't have much of a choice. *What's a fella to do? The only thing I can.*

Within seconds, the girls had pushed Tony into the bathroom and had him pinned against a white porcelain sink, his dark, Perry Ellis pants around his ankles. Tony had time to note that the sink felt deliciously cold against his bare ass, before completely giving in to all of the squeezing, pulling, and tugging going on down south. Just as Tony felt himself about to climax, a loud pounding on the door of the bathroom interrupted the intimate party.

"Yo, Ton!" said Monte.

"What!" Tony yelled.

"Melissa's at the front door, and she's pissed because I wouldn't let her in."

"Fuck!" Tony muttered under his breath. "Okay, Monte. Tell her I'll be right there!"

"Okay, but she's hot and wants to know what's going on in there that she can't come in."

"Well, fucking stall her!" Tony yelled. To the girls, he said, "Okay, ladies, let's hurry this little reunion along." Tony smiled. He leaned his head back, closed his eyes, and with his fingers clenching the sink, embraced the convulsions that rippled through his body only moments later.

A few minutes later, Tony walked out of the bathroom, trying to adjust his tie and put himself back together, before finally mumbling, "To hell with it!"

TONY TANCREDI AND CINDY L. O'HARA

Through a fog of alcohol, Tony found Monte and asked where Melissa was. Monte pointed outside.

Tony walked unevenly out the door, weaving unsteadily and feeling a lot like Bambi on ice. He looked around for Melissa's trademark silver Spider but couldn't find it. Two loud honks from her mother's white Cadillac Allante told Tony where she was. With both doors open, the inside light illuminated Melissa. Tony staggered over to the car and plopped into the passenger seat. Tony tried to close the car door, but after a couple of unsuccessful attempts that nearly sent him tumbling to the blacktop, Melissa said, "Just fucking leave it."

Melissa narrowed her eyes. "Look at you!" she shouted. "Now tell me, what the hell was going on in there?" Then she spied something on Tony's shoe and shrunk back, horrified. "Oh. My. God!" Melissa drew out the invective. "You're such a pig! I can't believe you. You're so drunk you spit on your own shoe!"

Puzzled and at a loss for words, Tony looked down at his black Italian loafers, where a small thick white glob had come to rest. Realizing that what Melissa was pointing at was, in fact, *not* spit but some other bodily fluid entirely, the laughter began softly within before, like a wave, it built to a crescendo, causing his ribs and abdomen to begin to ache from the effort.

Of course, Tony's continued laughter and inability to enlighten Melissa about the source of his amusement only served to further infuriate her.

"Stop laughing!" Melissa screamed. "What the hell is so funny?"

Still unable to control himself, Tony could only shake his head, tears welling in his eyes.

"Hey, Ton. Everything okay in there?" Monte asked, walking up to the car.

Still giggling, Tony replied, "Hey Monte, I'm so drunk I spit on my own shoe!" At this, Tony stuck his shoe out of the open door to show Monte what was on it, which incited a whole new round of laughter—this time from both Tony and his friend.

"What the hell is so funny about him spitting on his shoe? That's just plain sick!" Melissa yelled.

Still wiping the tears from his eyes, but regaining a degree of control, Tony told Monte to close the Shamrock and tell his men he would see them at work on Monday.

Unable to reply, Monte nodded.

"Sure, Ton," Monte finally said between chuckles.

"I'll be back to take Joe on his rounds."

Monte walked away, raising his hand to show he understood, his shoulders shaking from the laughter still racking his body.

Finally, Tony turned to Melissa, and with a level voice, said, "Look, I'm sorry, honey, but I gotta go to Joe's house and pick him up. Why don't you go hang out with Nicky for a while and come meet us at the Shamrock later? Say around two?"

"Fine. Get out."

Realizing he wasn't going to be able to placate her right now, Tony complied and almost spilled onto the pavement. Catching himself just in time, Tony stumbled out of the car ungracefully and slammed the door. Melissa floored the gas pedal, causing the Allante to jump forward into the night, leaving Tony standing in the parking lot, just shaking his head.

TONY TANCREDI AND CINDY L. O'HARA

THIRTY-THREE

A T D'LU LU'S that night, Tony and Joe sat back and enjoyed a glass of the Bordeaux Gussie had just opened from Joe's private cellar. Although the wine was excellent, it barely made an impression on Tony's palate.

"How is it?" Joe asked.

"Huh?"

"The wine. How is it?"

"Oh. Fine. Fine."

"Fine? That's a frickin' 1966 Rothschild, my friend, so I can assure you that it's more than just fine. At five hundred dollars a bottle, it fuckin' better be better than fine. What the hell's wrong with you?"

"Joe," Tony said, taking a sip of the rich, flavorful red wine and realizing that it was quite good. He didn't know if it was five-hundred-dollars good, but he supposed it was better than fine. "I gotta ask you something."

"So ask," Joe said, swirling the dark liquid in his glass.

Tony put his elbows on the table, the better to have a quiet conversation. "To be blunt, what the hell's going on with you? You're starting to worry me. Is it the drugs?" Before Joe could reply, Tony continued. "Look, Joe, you're losing a lot of respect among people who used to look up to you. Nothing makes any sense anymore. So what gives?"

Joe sighed heavily. "Well, Ton, it's the club. Money's coming in, but it's not coming to me. It's going to the lawyers and payoffs to keep people off my back and out of court. But some money's missing, and I think I know where at least some of it's going."

Puzzled, Tony leaned back.

Looking down at his clasped hands, Joe said, "I really think the bartenders are overdoing it. All bartenders cheat, I know, but I think ours are taking advantage of me."

"Whatdaya mean?" Tony asked, unable to keep the disbelief out of his voice.

"Look, I didn't wanna believe it either, Ton, but it's true. I can't say why they're doin' it, but they are. Maybe it's all the gambling that goes on in the place—I don't know. If that's the case, I gotta take part of the blame for getting 'em hooked. It's the only thing I can come up with. And

I know some of 'em are up to their eyeballs in debt, because their bookies tell me so."

"Well, sure they gamble. Hell, we all do. Even I put some money down on the occasional football game."

"But you don't handle the money in the club. Look, I know you don't know this," Joe said, leaning in, "but I gave all the bartenders a lie detector test, and they all failed. Even Sam failed, and he's the manager! What the hell am I supposed to think?"

Floored, Tony sat back and took in this new information. Tony shook his head. "It's not right, Joe. The way you treat your employees, they should be kissing your hand every time they see you. You'd think they'd at least be scared of you. I mean, it isn't like they don't know who you are."

Joe waved his hand dismissively.

"Maybe at one time, but not so much anymore. Besides, gamblers are sick. The stealing itself is gambling, and they love it, it gets them off, just like betting does."

Gussie arrived with two steaming plates of linguine and clams, bread and salad.

"So what are you gonna do?" Tony asked when Gussie had moved on. He broke off a piece of bread and soaked it in olive oil and pepper.

"Well, I'm seriously thinking of closing the club. I'm not getting any younger, and Audrey's thinking of adopting a child."

"That's great," Tony said, feigning enthusiasm. "Well, whatever you decide, I hope we'll still be able to hang out together. Once in a while at least."

Joe smiled. "Hey, I'm not going into hiding or dying. I'm just gonna take the pressure off a little. Going out every night is getting old."

Shocked and dismayed that his nightlife might be coming to an abrupt end, Tony said, "Maybe we could cut it down to just two or three nights a week. That way, the wives would think we were really trying to make things right, and we could still get outta the house."

"Maybe," Joe said, twirling his pasta with his fork.

But something told Tony Joe had already made up his mind and their conversation was just a formality.

After dinner, they made their usual rounds, but Tony noticed things were different. For one, Joe seemed more like himself, as if confessing his future intentions had lifted a great weight off his shoulders. He was happy and effusive, buying rounds at the bars they visited, clapping owners on the back, and flirting with any woman who happened to walk within hearing distance of him.

Tony, however, was quiet and sullen. Quite frankly, he couldn't fathom the idea of a life of domesticity, one that didn't include fighting, women, drugs, and alcohol every night. In fact, the life Tony led now was its own drug, and he had to admit that he was addicted to it. But, Tony reasoned, what he was doing was simply a means to an end. While he had achieved much during his tenure with Joe, he still hadn't done the one thing he had set out to do in his life—to pay back his parents for taking care of him when he was a kid. Until he could do that, he would always be a failure in his own eyes. When Joe turned to Tony and said it was time to go back to the club, Tony nodded, thankful the night was coming to an end.

Two weeks later, Tony was at home, actually *enjoying* a rare moment alone with Laura, when the phone rang.

"Hello?" Tony answered.

"Ton? It's Sam. You gotta get your ass to the club. Now! Joe's gone crazy, man!" In the background, glass shattered, wood hit wood, or at least it *sounded* like wood hitting wood, and the cherry on top of it all were the shots being fired.

"I'll be right there!"

"What's wrong, Tony?" Laura asked.

"I don't know, honey. It's Joe. Something's going on, and I'm really sorry, but I gotta go to the club," he explained, looking for his keys.

With unusual understanding where the club was concerned, Laura placed Tony's keys in his hands, kissed his cheek, and said, "Go."

Moved beyond words, Tony returned the kiss and whispered "Thanks" as he hurried out the door.

When he arrived at the club, Tony's first thought was, *So this is what temporary insanity looks like.* In a corner, Joe's 195-pound frame teetered precariously on the chair he was standing on. What struck Tony was not that the man was standing on a chair, holding a .357 magnum and systematically shooting up his own bar, but the way Joe looked. Like Tony, Joe took great pride in his appearance. He was never without his signature hat, and was always impeccably dressed in some designer label. Sometimes it was Armani, sometimes Perry Ellis, and other nights called for Lagerfeld. However, the man standing before him now was a shell of the person Tony knew. This man wore no hat, and his hair stood up as if he had just tumbled out of bed. He looked unwashed and unshaven and, Tony noted, appeared to have left his pants elsewhere. The only saving grace was that Joe had left his shirt on—whether by choice or simple forgetfulness, Tony didn't know. It remained to be seen whether or not Joe even had underwear on, and Tony silently thanked God for the shirttails that hung to his mid-thighs.

Spying Tony, Joe's face darkened. "Whadda *you* want?" Joe slurred drunkenly. "Money? I ain't got any. Drugs? All gone. Girls?" Joe swiveled his head one way, then the other, almost upsetting his balance on the chair. "Nope. No girls either. I got nuthin'. I'mmmm allll . . . tapped out." Joe opened his arms wide, the gun dipping dangerously from his listless hand.

"Joe, I don't want anything from you," Tony said. He edged closer to his friend. So far, Joe didn't protest. Out of the corner of his eye, Sam stood in a far corner, worrying his toothpick like some kind of rosary bead. He continued inching his way toward Joe.

"Ahhhhhhhhh, everyone wants something from me, Ton," Joe said sadly. Somehow, he managed to get one foot to the floor without falling from the chair, the other foot following, stomping heavily. Once both feet were planted, Joe's ass plopped into the hard-backed chair. He put his elbows on his knees and shook his head, the gun lolling between his legs. At least, Tony noted, it was pointed down and no longer at anyone or anything. For the moment, the wind had gone out of Joe's sails.

Tony knew what this was all about. Rather than take out his anger and frustration on his employees, he had taken it out on himself and the club that he loved so much. These people, the same people who were stealing from him, were his family; and he would never hurt them—not over money, not over anything.

Finally, Tony managed to shuffle his way toward Joe so he was standing directly next to him. Tony squatted and put one hand on Joe's back. With the other, he gently took the gun, flipping the safety on as he did so.

"Joe, I know what this is about," Tony whispered. "It's gonna be okay. We'll figure something out. Together. But now it's time to go home."

Joe nodded and without protest allowed Tony to heave him up. Once he had Joe in a standing position, Tony tucked the gun into the back of his waistband, pulled his shirt out of his jeans, and led his boss out the door.

TONY TANCREDI AND CINDY L. O'HARA

THIRTY-FOUR

DESPITE HAVING GOTTEN home at two in the morning after Joe's destructive spree from the night before, Tony got up early and made coffee and breakfast for Laura.

Tony had finally been able to get Joe out of the club and into bed at the Lair around midnight, but then had gone back to the Shamrock to check on Sam. When he got to the club, Tony surveyed the damage and then stayed and helped Sam clean up as much as possible. They finally left the club together, with Tony assuring Sam he would have his crew come in after work on Monday and fix the place up—as much as they could anyway. Sam nodded, deferring to Tony and his decisions.

When Laura walked into the kitchen, Tony kissed her and poured her a large cup of steaming, hot coffee, to which she added a generous helping of cream. Tony then began telling her what had happened the night before, as well as Joe's reasons for what he had done. Laura listened, her brow furrowed, the cup inches from her lips, untouched.

"Is Joe okay?" Laura asked. She finally took a sip of the hot liquid.

"Yeah. He's just upset," Tony replied, scooping some eggs and bacon onto a plate. He held them out toward his wife, but Laura shook her head.

"Well I, for one, am glad to hear the club is closing and Joe's moving on to other things. And"—she took another tentative sip—"I think it would be great if he and Audrey adopted a child. It would give them something else to focus on besides that damn club."

Offended at Laura's remark, Tony tried defending his decision to work at the Shamrock. "Hey, the club wasn't all bad. It got us lots of extra money and things we wouldn't have been able to afford like that little rock on your finger."

"Don't get me started," Laura snapped. "It was more trouble than it was worth. We would have been fine without all that stuff. Which, by the way, cost this family a lot more than the diamond on my finger or your new car. Let's just leave it at that."

Laura went to take another sip, grimaced, and dumped what was left in her cup down the drain.

Tony knew when not to push his wife, so he let the subject of the club drop.

"Anyway," Laura continued, "I have some other interesting news. Danny just got promoted to assistant manager at the store. Isn't that great?" Laura smiled.

Actually, Tony thought, that *was* some good news. Their son Danny was the younger of the two boys and had exhibited some behavioral problems in high school. Nothing much, as Tony recalled, mostly just cutting up in class, always wanting to be the center of attention, things like that. It hadn't been as if he were bullying other kids or taking their lunch money. And because Danny's transgressions had seemed particularly benign, Tony hadn't given what the teachers and principal said much weight and had instead adopted a "boys will be boys" mentality.

To Tony, everyone was too touchy-feely these days anyway. All he *did* know was that high school had not been the easiest road for his younger son. So to hear that he seemed to be doing well at his current job was a godsend.

"This calls for a celebration," Tony said. "Whatever restaurant you want to go to, we'll go."

Laura beamed. "Well, I guess I'll have to see what four-star restaurants are in town."

"Whatever you want, honey. Whatever you want." Tony hugged Laura and, for the first time in a long time, enjoyed the feeling of having a family.

The next morning, he was sitting at the kitchen table, flipping through the *Philadelphia Inquirer*, thoroughly bored. Soon, however, his attention focused on a small article on pro boxing making a return to Bensalem. The article went on to list the boxers who were appearing and noted that the fight was to take place this Friday night. Knowing what a fan of the sport Joe was, Tony thought this might be just the thing to get Joe out for the night.

He picked up the phone and dialed Joe's number. When Joe answered, Tony told him about the fight, and Joe agreed to go. Hanging up the phone, Tony smiled. Finally, he had somewhere to go and something to do.

The rest of the week dragged slowly by until Friday arrived, in what seemed like three lifetimes to Tony. That night, Tony picked Joe up at the Lair in the same way he had picked him up a thousand nights before, reflecting on how good it felt to be going out again with his old friend. The feeling was short-lived, however, when Tony pulled to the curb and Joe climbed into the front seat. "Joe, whatdaya doing?"

"I'm gettin' in the friggin' car. Whatdaya mean, what am I doing?"

"No, sorry, I just—well, you *never* ride in the front. I just thought I'd be driving you there. Like old times."

"Hey, Ton, I'm not your boss anymore, remember? Those days are over."

"Joe, you'll always be my boss."

Joe smiled broadly. "Now let's go see some guys beat the hell out of one another!"

When they arrived at the arena, Tony breathed in deeply the scent of sweat and desperation, of spilled beer and cheap cigars that always seemed to accompany this world. He looked around and, even above the din, could hear the shrill, high-pitched whine from the sound system before someone adjusted the feedback, of ice tumbling into buckets, and of trainers shouting for their fighters.

Like a kid in a candy store, Tony was even more excited than he had thought he would be. He hadn't realized how much he missed this part of his life. As he steered Joe toward their seats and edged through the throng of people who crowded the aisle, Tony was surprised at how many people he knew and, more importantly, how many remembered him. At least half a dozen men he had sparred with, trained with, or even fought. During these brief encounters, he shook hands or offered or received a warm hug or a good-hearted slap on the back in memory and appreciation of a time past.

Finally, Tony found their seats. A couple of phone calls had netted them seats only a few feet away from the ring. Tony had done this not only to impress Joe but to be closer to the action. *Hell*, Tony thought, *if I can't be in the ring, I might as well be as close as possible.*

"So," Joe said, gazing at the ring, "I see you still have a lot of connections here."

"I guess," Tony replied, only half listening to his old boss, so enthralled was he with all the familiar sights and sounds. Tony leaned forward, his elbows resting on his knees, his fingers interlaced.

Just seeing the boxing commission executives and judges all deep in conversation and recognizing some of the refs, was just too much for Tony.

Before he could tell Joe he was going to go say hello to some people, Joe looked at Tony and said, "Get outta here. Hell, you're making me excited just sitting next to you. Go do whatever you need to do before you explode. I'm gettin' tired of watchin' that knee bounce up and down."

With a wide grin, Tony thanked Joe and assured him he would be back soon.

Tony moved easily through the mass still crowding the aisle, heading to the fighters' locker rooms. He recognized the fight promoter standing outside. An old friend of Tony's, his eyes lit up when he saw Tony. The promoter gave him a hug and invited him in to say hello to the fighters. When Tony entered, he was greeted by the sound of fists hitting the slap pads on their trainers' hands, quickly followed by loud voices barking orders and corrections.

Some things never change, Tony thought. He looked around at the familiar scene of trainers giving last-minute instructions, corner men yelling for more ice for their buckets, commission officers checking the wrapping on fighters' hands and scribbling their names on the wrap, signifying that the gloves had been checked.

By now, Tony was euphoric at being in his old world. After a few more handshakes and introductions, Tony excused himself with the pretense of getting back to his seat. In reality, he wanted to let the fighters get back to their routine. If it were up to him, he would have stayed for hours. As he left, he allowed himself to fantasize that he was walking to the ring, his trainer's hands on his shoulders, following behind him. It felt good.

The moment was short-lived however, when, as Tony approached his seat, some meathead was talking to Joe and waving his arms wildly. Tony felt the old adrenaline rush that always happened in situations like these, his blood racing through his body as his heart pumped and tried to keep up. Joe looked around, for him, Tony assumed, probably worrying about what Tony would do. As Tony stomped through the crowd, elbowing people to get out of his way, Joe managed to get the attention of an usher, who quickly removed the drunken man before Tony could get there.

Good thing, Tony thought.

When he got back to his seat, he asked Joe, "Everything okay? You all right?"

By asking, Tony hoped to put Joe at ease. Tony knew, at heart, that Joe was a diplomat and preferred passiveness to violence, although Joe obviously wasn't above employing the latter when need be.

"Yup," Joe said. "No problem." Joe grinned, and they settled back in their ringside seats, waiting for the fight to start.

TONY TANCREDI AND CINDY L. O'HARA

THIRTY-FIVE

TONY SAT ON the edge of his seat, the nervous energy returning in full force.

When the bell rang to start the first fight, Tony's muscles flexed and relaxed with each punch thrown. It was as if he was in the ring fighting.

After the bout ended, Tony turned to Joe and said matter-of-factly, "I need something to take the place of the club for excitement in my life."

Joe gazed back at his friend and replied, "Why don't you become a fight promoter? Hell, with all the people you know in boxing and all the people we know, promoting could be just the thing you're looking for."

Joe rubbed his chin thoughtfully and said, "I'll help you in every way I can. Ticket sales would be easy with all the nightclubs and bars we know because they could all sell tickets for you."

Tony's mind started racing with possibilities. This could work, he thought. This could really work. "Joe, I'll be right back."

Joe's only answer was a slight nod, the black fedora he wore bobbing once.

Tony hurried over to the boxing commissioner and asked him what was needed to become a promoter in Pennsylvania. After Tony gave the commissioner a quick rundown of his background, the man told him what paperwork to fill out.

"When that's done, stop by my office with a cashier's check for thirty grand as collateral, and you can have yourself a show."

"Thirty grand huh? Okay, thanks."

A piece of cake, Tony thought. Except for the money. Now where to get the thirty grand?

"So?" Joe said. "What'd he say?"

"Huh?" Tony asked, the amount of money needed still ringing in his ears. "Oh," Tony said. "Ah, I'll tell you about it later. The fight's about to start."

On the way home, Joe *did* elect to sit in the backseat, although Tony barely noticed. In no time at all, Tony pulled up to the curb outside the Lair and, as if he were on automatic pilot, hopped out and opened Joe's door.

"Hey, Ton," Joe said. "You don't have to do that anymore. I only rode back there to leave you alone, let you think about this idea you have."

"Joe, I'm sorry, I—"

Joe held up his hand. "Tony, you're my friend, and there's nothing to be sorry for. I'm here to help you if I can. Thanks for a great night." Joe slammed the car door, smiled, and turned toward his second home.

Tony watched Joe let himself into the house, and when he was sure everything was all right, he got into his Cadillac and pointed the car toward home.

When he arrived at his house, one dim light shone from one of the windows facing the street.

Once inside, he eased up the stairs, trying not to wake Laura if she was sleeping, then quietly opened and shut the bedroom door behind him.

"Hi, honey," Laura said, putting down the book she had been reading. She sat propped up, with a pillow behind her, her brown hair flowing over the white case. Tony thought she had never looked more beautiful. He wondered (again) why this wonderful, breathtaking woman wasn't enough for him. But before he could explore that line of thinking too much, he strolled over to her and kissed her on the lips.

"Now what was that for?" she asked, smiling.

"Just because." Tony sat down next to her on a corner of the bed. "Hey, I'm glad you're up. I wanted to talk to you about something I'm thinking about getting into."

"Tony—"

"No no no. Sorry, nothing like before. This is clean, and I think I'd be good at it."

Laura relaxed. "What is it?"

"I think I want to try my hand at being a fight promoter. I talked to the boxing commissioner, and he told me what paperwork I needed to fill out and how much money I'd need to start."

"Oh, Tony, that sounds wonderful. But how much money are we talking about?"

"Thirty grand."

Laura's eyebrows rose skeptically. "That's a lot of money. Where would you get it?"

"I don't know," Tony answered. He got up and paced the room restlessly. "The thing is, the money's gotta be clean. If the boxing commissioner even has a hint anything shady's going on, he'll yank my license."

TONY TANCREDI AND CINDY L. O'HARA

"Well," Laura said, putting aside her book and turning out the light. "I'm sure you'll think of something. For now, though, why don't you come to bed? Maybe, letting off a little, um, steam will get the creative process started. If you know what I mean."

Tony did know what she meant, and for the first time that evening, he didn't think about fighting or money or paperwork or boxing commissioners. *That* could all wait until tomorrow.

The next night, Tony met Joe at the Squire and explained the financial situation to him.

"Ton, you know that I would give you whatever you needed if the club were still open, but now I really don't have any income. But," Joe said, "give me a couple of days, and lemme see what I can come up with. Meet me back here Wednesday night."

"Thanks, Joe. I really appreciate it. One more thing," Tony said, looking down at his hands.

"What?"

"The money's gotta be clean. The commission would never give me a license to promote if they thought . . . you know what I'm tryin' to say."

Joe fondly slapped his friend's cheek a couple of times. "Don't worry about it. It'll be as clean as a newborn baby's butt."

On Wednesday evening, Tony walked into the Squire and found Joe sitting at the end of the bar, a drink in front of him, the television tuned to a football game. Without looking at Tony, Joe asked, "How much do you need to make up the difference?"

"I have about thirteen or fourteen thousand, but would need some of that for expenses to get things started. Now that I think about it, I would probably need the whole thirty thousand."

"Well, I've talked to Paddy Vitallo. You remember him? He owns two restaurants—La Familia and Vitallo's. I never told you this, no reason to really, but he owns the Lair too."

Tony nodded. "Yeah, I really liked that guy. I remember helping him one night when we were having dinner at his place and those two clowns thought they were going to give him some shit while he was eating with us."

"Yeah, that's right. Do you remember what he said to you after you knocked those two out, picked 'em up, and threw 'em in the dumpster out back?"

"He said if I ever needed a favor, to just let him know."

"That's right. And when I explained your situation to him, he said he would be glad to help as long as he gets the best ringside seats."

Tony smiled. "Hell, he can sit *in* the ring if he does this for me."

"I set up a meeting for tomorrow night at La Familia. I told him to make it cash, and you can get the check yourself."

Tony shook his head in disbelief. "Damn, Joe, the club is closed, and you're still doing favors for me."

Joe put a hand on Tony's shoulder. "Just because I'm not your boss anymore doesn't mean I can't help you. When I can help you, I will." Joe removed his hand and took a sip of his drink before turning back to Tony.

"You put yourself in some tough situations to protect me back in the day, and I won't forget it."

"You'll always be my boss, Joe. I just hope someday I can repay you for all the things you did for me."

Joe grinned. "Ah, fuhgedaboutit."

"So who do you like in the game?" Tony asked, pointing at the television.

"Gotta go with the home team, my friend."

"I think that's a mistake, but it's your money."

For the next hour, they sat watching the Dallas Cowboys thoroughly beat the shit out of the Eagles in the first playoff game of the season, content in each other's company.

The next night at Paddy Vitallo's place, Tony and Joe ate and drank with abandon, enjoying several antipasti between them—salad, bread, and, for the main course, bucatini, a tasty homemade pasta topped with mushrooms, prosciutto, bacon, and peas. As always, Paddy remained a gracious host, catering to Tony's and Joe's every wish. Three hours later, over coffee and tiramisu, Paddy sat down and discreetly handed Tony a black leather pouch.

Tony's only acknowledgement of the exchange was a slight nod. He knew enough not to insult the owner or Joe by counting the money in front of the men, knowing it would all be there. Tony looked around once, then subtly stuffed the two-inch-thick pouch in to the inside pocket of his suit coat. He looked at Paddy and leaned forward, the better to be heard only by Joe and the restaurant owner, both elbows resting on the table. "Thanks a lot, Paddy. I really appreciate this."

Paddy sat back and waved his hand. "You do the favor for me a long time ago, I do the favor for you now. We're, how you say, even, *capice?*"

TONY TANCREDI AND CINDY L. O'HARA

Tony nodded and grinned.

"There is, however, the matter of the seating arrangements." Paddy smiled.

"Paddy," Tony said, "my seating chart will revolve around you and your guests. You can sit wherever you want."

"Ah, you are a good man, Tony Tancredi. I always say, 'A sign of a good man is when he takes care of the people aroun' him.' You are that kind of man, Tony."

Tony didn't know about that (in fact, he was pretty sure it wasn't the case), but he did know he had thirty thousand dollars in his pocket and the opportunity to start a new chapter in his life. What happened next—at least if his life was any indication—he was pretty sure, was going to be interesting.

That, he thought, was worth the price of admission.

THIRTY-SIX

THE NEXT MORNING, Tony sat at the desk in the den, a pencil poised over a piece of paper. He had gotten home late the night before. After telling Laura about his idea, he had been too excited to sleep. Not even the two-hour lovemaking session with Laura had made him drowsy. He had wandered downstairs into his den, and when he sat down to make some notes at his desk, he looked at the clock blink bright red. It was 3 a.m. When he looked up again, he was shocked to see the numbers had flipped from three to 7:15 a.m. He hadn't moved all night. He looked at the pages he had created. To-do lists were scribbled haphazardly all over the paper, even into the margins. The phone sat next to him. He knew it was too early to start calling anyone, so he got up and stretched, clasping his fingers together and bending his shoulders first right, then left. He listened to his back protest from being in one position for so long. As his muscles lengthened and reawakened, he realized his ass was asleep. Without warning, what felt like a thousand pins and needles hit his ass and hamstrings simultaneously, so that he almost doubled over.

Better take a break. I'll start hitting the phones at eight, he thought.

By then, most of the front office help would be in at places like the Philadelphia Convention Center, the Philadelphia Armory, and various other places he thought he could put on a show.

With so much to do, Tony thought it would be best to have the show in a couple of months.

He decided to set the date for March 20. By having it then, it would, Tony figured, allow people to recover from Christmas and feel like they could start spending money again.

At exactly eight o'clock, Tony called all the arenas in the area he could think of, even high school gyms. For the most part, he was told to call back in a couple of months. Discouraged, but not disheartened, he called the Armory back since he hadn't been able to reach anyone there the first time. He had to jump through a few hoops to find the right person, but finally, persistence paid off, and the booking agent said he could accommodate Tony.

Two hours and more than a dozen phone calls later, he had secured the Philadelphia Armory for his show.

Tony's next phone call was to Joe.

"Hey, Joe. I got the Armory for the fight."

"That's great, Ton. So when's the fight?"

"I was thinkin' of havin' it on March 20. Gives people time to get some money in their pocket after Christmas. Whatdaya think?"

"Sounds good. What's next?"

"Well, I'm gonna need some help promoting this thing, and I thought you might be able to help me out with that—seein' as you still have connections and all."

"I'd be glad to, Ton. If you want to, you can call Greg and Monte and the rest of the old crew—you know, to help keep things in order. I'm sure they'd love it."

"Thanks, Joe. Yeah, I think I'll do that."

"Hey, Ton, I gotta run, man, but keep me in the loop, and you can be sure I'll help any way I can."

"Thanks, Joe. I 'preciate it." Tony hung up the phone and turned back to his to-do lists.

With the most important task out of the way, he pulled the promoter application to him and began filling it out. Putting on a professional boxing match was more work than he had imagined, but he loved every minute of it. Although it was only January, he figured he had at least a few months of work ahead of him, getting approved for his license, printing up the flyers, and finding fighters who would commit. Because of his connections and his matchmaker, Mickey, as well as knowing all the fighters in Philly, Tony didn't think it would be a problem to get fighters on the card.

Later that evening, Laura walked up and rested her arm lightly on the back of his shoulders. "Whatcha doin?" Laura asked.

Tony didn't look up. He liked the feel of her body pressing close to him, but he also didn't want to stop working on his list of preparations.

"Just tryin' to get some kind of seating chart going here."

"Anything I can help with?"

"Nah. But thanks anyway."

"Well, how much longer are you gonna be?" Laura asked, pressing herself more firmly against him.

"Not long," Tony said, finally taking his eyes off the paper. He looked up at his wife and realized how beautiful she was. She must have just gotten out of the shower, because even from his seat, he could smell soap and flowers and shampoo. *No*, he thought, *I won't be long at all.*

"Seein' how you look, I promise I'll be up soon."

"Okay. Well, hurry it up, mister. It's past midnight, and I won't wait forever."

"Yes, you will," Tony replied automatically, then immediately regretted the words.

Laura looked back at him, then sighed. "Sadly, you're probably right. Okay, *hurry.*"

Tony turned back to the seating chart he had drawn, and as he was scribbling in names, he came to his old friend Dick Williamson. Tony paused, his pencil poised over the chart of the arena. He absentmindedly bobbed the eraser back and forth against his lip in concentration.

It wasn't that Tony didn't *want* to put Dick up front with Joe and the rest of the boys—he did—but was he *deserving* of having a ringside seat? Tony didn't know. Sure, Dick had done more than his fair share of work helping to promote the show, and he was basically a good guy, but Tony kept going back to his friend's attitude about black people. One night over drinks, Dick had actually said that the only thing blacks were good for was beating the shit out of one another and fucking—not necessarily in that order.

Tony let it go because Dick continued to down gin and tonic after gin and tonic, so anything Tony would have said would have fallen on deaf, drunk ears. Besides that, he knew Dick's attitude had been born in prison, where he had spent some time. Later, Tony had tried to convince Dick that not all black men were like those he met in prison, but Dick remained resolute, even going so far as to call Tony an idiot, a fuckin' idiot, to be exact—something that hadn't sat well then and didn't to this day.

As Tony sat bobbing his pencil against his lip, he thought this might just be the time to teach Dick a little lesson about respect. Call it winning one for both white *and* black men.

The Friday night of the show, Tony was backstage barking orders and delegating tasks to anyone happening too close to him when Monte sidled up to him.

"Hey, Ton," Monte said, interrupting Tony. "Wanted to let you know that Dick's here."

Tony smiled. "Thanks, Monte."

Tony had been able to get most of the old crew together to help him with security and usher people to their seats. He trusted them and, more importantly, knew that they were well-armed and would be ready for anything. Having them there calmed Tony because he knew his show was in good hands.

TONY TANCREDI AND CINDY L. O'HARA

Hearing that Dick had arrived brightened Tony's mood instantly. He backhanded Monte on the chest. "Come on. Time to have some fun." Monte shrugged and followed Tony.

Tony stood in the entrance to the dark tunnel, looking out over the sea of plastic chairs the men had set up only a few hours before. Monte stood just slightly behind him. Tony scanned the aisles looking for Dick, at the same time listening to the crowd chant for the show to start. Their words could be heard even above the loud music thumping from stereo speakers Tony had placed around the arena. From the bleachers to the seats, it looked like it was a full house. Above all the noise, Tony heard whistles and catcalls and finally spied a beautiful young blonde girl who couldn't have been more than twenty-one years old at the entrance to the arena. Gracing her arm was a middle-aged man of about forty-five or fifty, who was no more than five foot eight, on a good day. His gray hair was cut short, almost to the point of him being mistaken for someone in the military. He was dressed smartly in what Tony suspected was some designer suit he had gotten at one of the hundreds of discount stores in the area.

"Watch," Tony told Monte.

Near the entrance, Dick handed his tickets to Mickey, one of the ushers.

Mickey led Dick up one aisle, carefully studying the ticket and the row numbers. Mickey stopped so unexpectedly that Dick almost ran right into him. So busy was he soaking up the atmosphere, nodding to people he recognized, and generally making an ass of himself, at least in Tony's opinion.

Tony watched Mickey stop about ten rows back from Joe and the rest of the boys, then heard Dick's voice continue to rise above the crowd, the music, *and* the catcalls.

"No no no no no! My seats are down there with those guys at ringside." Dick pointed to Joe and the rest of the crew.

As Tony and Monte wove through the crowd, Tony saw Mickey pointing to, first, the tickets, then the seat. In response, Dick gesticulated wildly, his arms waving above his head.

Tony walked up just in time to catch the tail end of Dick's tirade to the usher. Tony made a mental note to give the boy an extra hundred for all the trouble Dick was causing him.

"I don't fuckin' care what the damn tickets say," Dick growled. He grabbed them from Mickey. "Go get Tony, the promoter. He'll take care of this."

"Right away, sir." Mickey turned, almost bumping into Tony.

"I got this, Mickey. Thanks. Come see me later. I have somethin' for you. In the meantime, take the rest of the night off and enjoy the show."

"Thanks, Ton." Mickey smiled.

"No problem. Thanks for your help." Tony then turned his attention to Dick.

"Whatdaya lookin' at?" Dick yelled to a number of people who were staring at him. Even his date stood a few steps away.

"What seems to be the problem, Dick?" Tony asked.

"Hey, Ton. Thank God you're here. Your little prick of an usher tells me these are my seats. But that can't be right. There must be some mistake. My seats are down there with Joe. Right?"

Tony looked at the tickets Dick handed him, knowing full well what seat Dick was in. For Dick's benefit, he pretended to study the ticket and seat numbers.

"Well, Dick, I don't see the mistake. You're in the right spot. See, the row and seat numbers match up. Here's the thing. When I was doing the seating chart, I remembered how you felt about blacks, how much you hate them. So I thought I'd be sensitive to your feelings and put you far enough away so you wouldn't get any of their sweat or blood on you—which could definitely happen if you were sitting ringside." Tony smiled benevolently. "You can thank me later." Tony winked at his friend.

Dick's face darkened. Tony couldn't keep a straight face any longer. He slapped Dick on the back. "Next time, maybe you'll be a little more open-minded."

"Yeah yeah yeah," Dick nagged.

"Here's what I'm gonna do. I gotta go take care of a thing. Sit here for the first fight, then if you're a good boy, I'll move you down to ringside."

Looking dejected, Dick plopped down in his seat, barely giving his date room to pass. Tony leaned in. "I'm not gonna have a problem here, am I?"

Dick shook his head and kept quiet.

"Good." Tony walked away, hoping he had taught his friend a lesson, but somehow doubting that he had.

As the show drew to a close, the commissioner and his staff, along with the Atlantic City fight crowd, congratulated Tony and wished him continued success.

TONY TANCREDI AND CINDY L. O'HARA

THIRTY-SEVEN

"**H**EY, HONEY, WHY don't you bring that bottle of wine into the living room." Tony sat on the couch, a pen in one hand, a legal pad in the other. He had taken a week off from everything boxing and was just now sitting down to run the numbers, comparing the cost of the show and how much he had made. He discovered that he had actually lost money—something he expected going in. *Funny, though*, he thought, *I couldn't give a rat's ass. It was a helluva show, and I had way too much fun doing it*. For the first time, Tony thought he might have stumbled onto something he could be good at, something (legal) he could point to as a symbol of his success and, more importantly, would help him to take care of his parents when and if they ever needed it.

His thoughts were interrupted by the loud *brinnngg* of the telephone. Tony snatched up the black receiver.

"'Lo?"

"Hello. This is Mr. Stark at Shopper's Grocery Store. I'm Danny's manager. I'm sorry to bother you, but I was wondering if you'd seen Danny today?"

"No, Mr. Stark, I'm sorry. I haven't seen him, but hold on a minute, and lemme let you talk to his mother." Tony held the phone away from him and yelled to Laura, "Honey, can you pick up the phone in there? Danny's manager is on the phone."

Tony waited a beat until he heard Laura pick up and then gently put the receiver down, wondering what the hell was up.

A moment later, Laura walked in, the wine in one hand and two glasses in the other.

"Well, that was strange."

"Yeah, what was up?"

"I don't know. He never really said. Just wanted to know if we'd seen Danny. When I told him we hadn't, he hung up." She sat down on the couch but made no move to put the wine or the glasses down. Tony took the items from her and placed them on the side tables.

"I'm sure everything's fine," Tony said. He began tearing the seal off the wine. "Probably just a scheduling mix-up or something."

"Yeah, probably." But from the tone of her voice, Tony could tell she didn't think so—and neither did he, although he would never say so out loud.

Ever since he had gotten his promotion to assistant manager and moved out of the house, Danny had been hard to reach and hadn't come home as much. Tony didn't *think* it was unusual, but then again, he knew he wasn't exactly a litmus test for normalcy.

A knock on the door stopped Tony from further thought. Tony and Laura looked at each other, then at the door.

When Tony opened it, he wasn't surprised to see the tall, muscular cop filling the doorway, but he was taken aback when the officer asked if Danny was inside. It was the second time in less than two minutes that someone had asked about Danny's whereabouts. Tony knew then that whatever was going on couldn't be good.

"No, sir," Tony said. "We don't know where our son is, but please come in."

The officer stepped inside. He removed his hat, scanning the room. He said, "Mr. Tancredi, your son is a suspect in a robbery."

Laura's hand flew to her mouth. Immediately, she stood up from the couch.

"That's impossible, Officer. Our son would never do that."

"I'm sorry, ma'am, but according to our report, Danny and a friend allegedly took twenty-five thousand dollars from Shopper's Grocery Store. Would it be okay if I took a look around?"

Both Tony and Laura nodded.

Satisfied that Danny wasn't at home, the officer thanked them for their cooperation and requested they call if Danny contacted them. "Look, you seem like nice folks, so let me give you some free advice. The best thing your son can do right now is to turn himself in. Once he crosses state lines, it becomes a federal matter."

"Oh my god," Laura whispered.

"We'll call if we hear from him," Tony assured the officer. The policeman nodded, turned, and left, leaving Tony and Laura alone and speechless.

Three weeks later, Danny called. By sheer luck, Laura answered the phone. Before she could begin asking questions, however, Danny told her he was fine, he was in Texas, and he wanted to turn himself in. By the end of the short speech, both he and Laura were crying.

TONY TANCREDI AND CINDY L. O'HARA

"Mom, I'm scared. I know what I did was stupid. I don't even know why I did it, but—"

"Okay, baby. We're gonna take care of this," Laura replied, tears streaming down her face.

Silence greeted Laura, and the only indication her son was still on the line was the soft hiccups and occasional sobs from Danny trying to get control of himself.

"Mom, I need Dad to help me turn myself in."

"Sure, baby. Anything you want. Give me a number, and I'll call you back."

Danny did so, and Laura promised to call as soon as she could.

When Tony wandered into the kitchen a few minutes later, Laura recounted what Danny had told her on the phone.

"So lemme get this straight," Tony said. "Danny steals twenty-five grand, runs off to friggin' Texas with his friend—who, by the way, we have no idea who he is—then calls asking for my help, but doesn't even have the decency to ask me himself?"

Laura remained mute. She had been so worried about her son, and so glad he had called, she had momentarily forgotten he was accused of a crime.

Laura put her hand on Tony's forearm, trying to calm him down. "He was scared to talk to you, honey. You should've heard him on the phone. He was crying. He said he was sorry and knew he made a mistake."

"What the hell can I do?"

Laura looked down at the floor and shook her head. "I don't really know, but you know people, and if you want to help him, you can. I need you to do this, Tony. For me. For Danny. For our family."

"If it were up to me, I'd let the kid go to jail just to teach him a lesson."

"But you won't do that."

"No. I won't. But I won't promise you—or him—anything either. I don't know what the hell I'm gonna be able to do—if anything."

"Understood," Laura said, gently kissing Tony's cheek. "Thank you."

"Okay. I'll do whatever I can to help him. I'm sure there will be a trial, and our only hope is to get to the judge."

Laura looked up at her husband as if seeing him for the first time. "Tony, I'll die if I see him in handcuffs, if I have to see them take him away like that. Maybe in some crazy way, all those nights you spent away from this family will help us now." She lowered her head to his chest. "I don't know who you are on the streets or what you can do, but if you have any power at all, please use it to help our son."

"I promise I'll do whatever I can to help Danny."

Alone in the den, Tony kept glancing at the phone. The obvious thing to do was to call Joe with this new problem, but Tony knew this would be the biggest thing he had ever asked of his old boss. Tony didn't know how high Joe's contacts went, but he was sure his son's current problem would test them.

When Tony finally mustered enough courage to call Joe and ask if they could meet, stating he had a problem he needed to discuss in person, Joe was more than willing to help. Joe told Tony to meet him at the Squire the next evening.

At the Squire the next night, Tony laid out detail after painful detail for Joe and a mutual friend from Bensalem, Detective Bobby DeSanto. All agreed that Tony's problem was a difficult one, if not impossible.

"If I'm hearin' you right," DeSanto said, "you want no cuffs in the courtroom and a suspended sentence? I know some people in Bristol who owe me, but this is over the top, Tony. They could get in big trouble. I could maybe get 'em to keep the cuffs off, but the judge? I could lose my job just for sniffing around that one."

"Bobby, you know I'm no saint," Tony said. "But this could really help me with my marriage, get my wife close to me again. Whatever you can do for me, I'll appreciate. But I don't want you risking your job over this, either."

"Ah, man," DeSanto said. "Now you're bringin' the wife into this. We've been friends for a long time. You've done me some solids, and this is the first time you've ever asked for anything. You're a stand-up guy, Ton—for a *goombah*, that is. If I can help you out, I will. Now if you gentlemen will excuse me," DeSanto said, getting off his barstool, "I've got some calls to make." He squeezed Tony's shoulder, then turned and shook Joe's hand. "Joe, always a pleasure."

Joe nodded, and DeSanto walked out of the bar.

Tony looked morosely into his untouched familiar Jack and ginger.

"Hey, Ton, don't look so serious. Things may not be as bad as they seem. I may be out of business, but I'm not out of friends," Joe said almost in a whisper.

"What are you talking about, Joe?" Tony asked, in no mood for Joe's inferences.

TONY TANCREDI AND CINDY L. O'HARA

"Look," Joe said, "just pick me up tomorrow night. We'll get a bite to eat and talk some more." He got off his barstool. "Oh, and Ton?"

"Yeah?"

"Wear something nice. We're going out after we eat."

Joe turned on his heels and wended his way out of the bar.

Puzzled, and more than a little interested, Tony downed his drink in one gulp, followed the path his two friends had taken through the patrons, and headed home.

THIRTY-EIGHT

THE NEXT NIGHT, Tony picked up his old boss promptly at nine o'clock.

"Where to, Joe?"

"Michael O'Malley's."

"Why do we gotta go to Irish pubs all the time? The food sucks, and the drinks are even worse."

"Well, our next stop will be of the Italian variety, my friend. But for now, you'll just have to put up with some of O'Malley's famous Irish stew and a glass of their finest scotch."

"Whatever. That shit all tastes like piss to me. I'll wait 'til we hit the Italian joint and get a nice glass of wine."

Tony pointed the car toward Buselton Avenue and said little the rest of the way.

When they finished their meal and the waitress had cleared their dishes, Joe sat back in the booth, twirling his glass of Connemara Irish Whiskey.

"Tony, I'm gonna take you to meet someone who could help you with your problem." After his pronouncement, Joe downed the dark amber liquid, slammed his hands on the table, and rose to leave.

In the car, Joe directed Tony to a well-known shopping center on Knight's Road in Bensalem and instructed him to leave any weapons he had in the car. Although unnecessary, Tony still carried his knife and gun when he was with Joe—more out of habit than anything else.

Tony looked at his boss. "Why? Who the hell is in there?"

Joe gazed back at Tony. "Just do what I said. This guy you're meeting knows you're coming and knows your problem. He's an old friend of mine. His name's Giacomo Victorino." He slowly drew his index finger across his upper lip to indicate mustache. The inference was typically used by Irishmen to identify Italian men and the club they belonged to.

When they entered the bar, Joe whispered into Tony's ear. "Show this guy the utmost respect."

Annoyed at having to be told something that was inherent, Tony said, "They told me that when I met you, and I think I did okay."

Before Joe could reply, a thin olive-skinned man approached. Tony took in the man's indistinct black pants, black button-down shirt (with the top button done), and dark green sweater that hung down to his hips and had seen better days. The sweater was so out of place it looked more like it belonged on a grandfather than on this man who made Joe so uneasy.

When the man saw Joe, he smiled. The two men shook hands and hugged. Then Joe introduced Tony.

The man turned to Tony. "It is my pleasure to meet you. Joe has told me a lot about you. Then of course, what I hear on the streets. Joe is lucky to have such a man. Trust and loyalty are not things you can buy. In these days, it is hard to find men like you. Everyone talks too much, if you know what I mean."

Tony nodded, knowing not to interrupt him. When he had finished, Tony said, "It is very nice of you to say such things to me, Mr. Victorino."

The man smiled, showing even, white teeth. "My friends call me Gino. Now I understand you have a problem you would like to discuss with me."

"Yes, sir, I do."

"Well, let's take a walk, and we will discuss it. Joe, if you will excuse us." It was a statement rather than a question. "Please enjoy yourself by having a drink at the bar. It is, of course, on the house."

Joe nodded his thanks and turned away.

Tony and Gino left the bar and continued their stroll down the sidewalk of the shopping center, careful to speak in soft tones.

Tony knew Gino was aware of his problem and was equally confident he could help Tony if he chose to do so. It was just a matter of whether Gino liked him or not.

"Please, tell me of your problem."

With infinite care, Tony explained the situation to Gino, leaving nothing out. Throughout the one-sided conversation, Gino frowned. When he had finished, Gino said, "That is a sad situation, but not an impossible one. When the trial is set and you know the judge, bring me his name."

Tony's shoulders relaxed, and he exhaled.

"Thank you, Gino. If any money is needed, please tell me, and I'll get it to you."

Gino stopped, put a hand on Tony's arm, and looked him in the eye. "I do not do favors for money. That would be business. What you *can* do is be my friend. Come into my club once in a while and have a drink with me."

"Of course," Tony replied. "I am forever in your debt. Whatever I can do for you, please ask. You have no idea how much this will mean to his mother. And of course, to me," Tony added.

Gino smiled widely. "I would be honored to meet your wife. I look forward to it."

Tony knew that Gino expected to meet Laura the next night as a sign of respect, and his statement was simply a reminder.

When they returned to the restaurant, Tony glanced around, out of habit. At first, nothing seemed amiss, then Tony spied a face at the bar he remembered from the Shamrock—someone he had thrown out of Joe's club for trying to deal drugs. The man was talking to the guy next to him, pointing to the television set above the bar, which was tuned to a baseball game. To anyone watching, it would look like two friends enjoying a game on a Saturday night. From experience, however, Tony knew otherwise.

Tony said, "Gino, this is none of my business, but I assume you don't allow drug dealers in your club?"

Gino looked back at Tony, horrified. "Absolutely not!"

The man stood up and waved to Gino.

"The one who just waved to you, he's the dealer," Tony said. "They're going into the bathroom. If you come with me, I'll prove it to you."

Gino's face reddened, giving his olive skin a sunburned glow.

Tony gave the two men a minute or two before entering the bathroom. Gino waited by the door.

Tony saw two pairs of legs in one stall. Suddenly, Tony kicked in the stall door. Both men held small baggies that contained a fine white powder, and rolls of cash. The dealer immediately recognized Tony.

"Hey man, I don't want no trouble."

"Who the fuck is he?" his client asked.

"Just give him the shit and shut up," the dealer said, his eyes wide.

"Why? Is he a cop?" asked the idiot.

"No," the dealer replied. "Worse. He don't have no rules, and if you mess with him, you're gonna wake up in the hospital—if you wake up at all! Now fucking give him the shit!"

Reluctantly, the man handed over the drugs to Tony.

Tony said, "You're both very lucky tonight. Just leave. I don't want to dirty Gino's floor with your blood. But if I ever see either of you in here again, I promise, you won't be leaving on your feet." The words, spoken so softly, sounded menacing.

TONY TANCREDI AND CINDY L. O'HARA

The two men scrambled over each other trying to get out of the bathroom. As Gino and Tony walked back to the front of the restaurant, Gino placed a hand on Tony's shoulder. Joe stared at Tony and Gino, trying to keep the amazement off of his face.

"He is just as you say, Joe. He is very good at what he does," Gino said.

"He's been that way since the day I met him. He always knows what to do and how to get it done," Joe replied.

When Tony left, he thanked Gino again and assured him that he would see him soon. Behind him, Gino thanked Joe, which struck Tony as odd.

Shouldn't it be the other way around? Tony thought.

The next morning, Tony told Laura he had met someone who might be able to help them with their problem, and that this person would be able to help Danny.

"Oh, Tony! That's great!" Laura squealed. "Tell me all about it! Spare no details."

"Laura, I'm not sure that's a good idea. For now, let's just let it go. I think Danny is going to be fine."

Laura's face fell.

Tony sat down on the edge of the bed. "Hey, you know this is for your own safety, right? That the less you know the better?"

Laura sighed. "Fine." She pushed back the covers like a petulant child.

"Tell you what," Tony said, "we'll go out tonight. Have some dinner and some drinks. I'm gonna take you to a new place. Wear something really nice. We'll be meeting someone important."

When the couple entered Gino's restaurant, the doorman shook Tony's hand, greeting him by name. He asked them to take a seat at the bar while he went to tell Gino they were there.

As Gino approached, he smiled benevolently, looking like a grandfather welcoming home his grandchildren. "Ah, my friend comes to see me again!" Gino said with his arms spread wide.

"Gino, please let me present my wife, Laura, to you."

"It is my pleasure, Mr. Victorino," Laura said, extending her hand.

Gino took her hand and kissed it lightly, making Laura blush. "Ah, Laura, with Tony's permission, I must compliment you on your beauty and charm. I should have known a man like Tony would have such a beautiful wife. And please, call me Gino."

"Your words are very kind. Thank you, Gino," Laura replied.

Gino then told the bartender to get whatever his guests would like to drink. When everyone had what they wanted, Gino made a toast.

"To old friends. And new," he said, raising his glass.

Laura and Tony raised their glasses, clinking them with Gino's.

Tony wondered briefly what the hell he was getting mixed up in—again.

THIRTY-NINE

TONY LEANED AGAINST the kitchen sink late the next morning, sipping orange juice. He glanced at his watch. Ten o'clock.

"What time's he s'posed to be here?" Tony asked Laura, referring to Danny, their prodigal son who was (supposedly) on his way home.

"Thought he'd be here by now."

Laura stopped scrubbing the sink and wrung out the dishrag. She looked at Tony and said, "I thought so too. I'm sure he'll be here soon."

"Yeah, well, he better. I pulled a lot of frickin' strings, and if he doesn't show—"

The gentle opening of the front door interrupted Tony.

"Mom? Dad?" a voice called softly from the living room.

"Danny, honey, you're finally here." Laura dropped the rag and ran out of the kitchen. Tony followed slowly, trying his best to get control of his temper. The last thing he wanted to do was lash out at his son and have him take off again.

"Hey, Dad." Danny gently pushed his mother away and turned to Tony.

"Hey." Tony greeted Danny from across the room, refusing to show him any kindness, believing he had betrayed the family and wasn't deserving of any.

"So whaddja do with it?" Tony pushed himself off the wall and slowly walked toward his son.

Danny looked up. "Do with what?"

"The fuckin' money!" Tony roared. "Whaddja do with it?"

"Tony please." Laura put a hand on Tony's arm. He shook it off violently. "Laura, this is between me and the boy."

"I spent it," Danny answered softly, his eyes downcast. "Spent it? On what?"

Danny flinched. "On dinner, clothes, traveling with my friend."

Disgusted, Tony turned away. "You gotta be friggin' kiddin' me. You spent twenty-five grand in three weeks on clothes, food, and traveling? Okay. Here's what you're gonna do. Tomorrow, you're gonna get up, and first thing you're gonna do is go with me and turn yourself in to the Bristol police department. Bobby DeSanto said he'd call his friends at the station and let them know you're turnin' yourself in. Now get outta my face. I can't even look at you right now. If you could only, for one minute, imagine what you did to your mother—ahhhh, get outta here," Tony seethed.

Danny, his head hanging, walked up the stairs.

Tony didn't know if Danny would have to pay back the money as part of the deal, but he suspected he would. Luckily, Tony had that and a little more in the bank, but it would completely wipe them out. He had earmarked the money for the second fight show, but he could see that dream slowly slipping away. He knew he'd use the money to keep Danny out of jail if he had to.

"Fuckin' kid," Tony muttered. "More trouble than he's worth." Deep down, though, Tony loved him, even after this turn of events.

Within two weeks of Danny turning himself in, the trial was put on the docket for mid-September. To Tony, it seemed as if things were happening far too quickly, but he trusted Gino and Bobby DeSanto and believed everything would work out. It had to. He had banked on it—both financially and by pledging his friendship to Gino.

It was with these things in mind that Tony felt he had to tell Laura a little of what was going on.

When she came home from the bank one night, he greeted her with a glass of wine and, before she could sit down, asked her to come out back for a minute. He didn't want Danny to overhear them. Rather, Tony was happy to let him sweat and worry about his fate.

"Tony, what's wrong?" Laura asked. She took a sip of the wine.

"Nothing's wrong, honey. I just wanted to tell you what's going to happen in a couple of days."

"Go ahead."

"Danny is going to be in a work-release program. Gino's already arranged for Danny to work with his friend Sal, the owner of a pizza place over in Morrisville. He won't serve any time, only thirty days in the program. He'll go to work every day and report into the facility at night. Also, he won't be wearing any cuffs in the courtroom. It's done."

"Oh, Tony," Laura squealed. She threw her arms around him, nearly toppling the wineglass. "I didn't know if—"

"I know, honey. Gino pulled it off, and it's gonna be fine. We just gotta get through the trial."

On September 16, Tony, Laura, and Danny arrived at the Bristol Township courthouse, looking every inch the all-American family.

TONY TANCREDI AND CINDY L. O'HARA

Too soon, the bailiff poked his head out and said their case was being called to order next.

Tony turned to his stepson. "This is it," Tony said, straightening Danny's tie.

Danny nodded mutely. Tony could tell he was trying not to cry. Suddenly, Danny grabbed him, tears pouring from his eyes. In great, gulping sobs, he hugged Tony.

"I'm sorry, Dad!" Danny wailed into Tony's shoulder. "I'm so sorry!"

Surprised, Tony hugged his stepson fiercely. He wanted to tell Danny of all he had done, of the strings he had pulled, and the inevitable outcome that would take place in a few short minutes, but he knew that letting Danny feel this way, even for a little while, would, Tony hoped, prevent him from doing anything like this in the future. Because if Danny ever got in trouble again, Tony knew the people who had helped his stepson this time would surely turn against him next time. Then nothing would save him.

"Okay, you two," Laura said, brushing the tears away with her fingertips. "Let's pull it together. Honey, it's going to be fine," she told Danny. "Whatever happens, we love you and are here for you. Now let's get in there."

Tony stepped back and held the door as Danny and Laura walked through.

Inside, Tony glanced over and saw Bobby DeSanto seated in the front row usually reserved for family. Tony assumed he was there for moral support, and also to make sure that all the favors he had called in were in place.

At Danny's table, the public defender sat shuffling a mountain of papers, looking disheveled and frazzled, as if he would rather be any place than where he was. The prosecutor sat calmly on the other side, comfortable, Tony supposed, that he had an open-and-shut case. Had Tony left Danny to fate, he had no doubt what the outcome would have been.

Danny took his place beside his lawyer, while Laura sat next to Tony. Laura squeezed Tony's hand.

"All rise," the bailiff bellowed. "The Honorable Judge Dubois now presiding."

The judge entered, his long black robes sweeping the floor behind him, his small round glasses slipping down his nose. He motioned impatiently for everyone to be seated.

As the lawyers made their arguments, Tony couldn't help marveling at the act. The focus, like some well-rehearsed play, remained on Danny's lack of any previous record, that he was a first-time offender, and the relatively quick promotion he had received at the store.

The lawyers then read their closing statements.

"All rise, please," the judge intoned. He took off his glasses and chewed on one of the glass stems thoughtfully. "Danny Rago, you seem like a good kid. So I'm going to assume that this was your first, last, and a very stupid mistake." He pointed the glasses at Danny.

"I want you to know that because of the amount of money you took, and your age, I could give you ten years in a federal penitentiary. I tell you this so the next time you think of doing something as foolish as what you have already done, you'll know what's in store for you. Lastly, if I *ever* see you in my courtroom again, or see your name on any court dockets, I will personally see to it that you get the maximum sentence for whatever crime you have committed. Do I make myself clear?"

Danny stood still and silent, barely able to nod.

"Good." The judge replaced his glasses. "Taking into consideration the aforementioned facts, it is this court's opinion that you, Danny Rago, receive a suspended sentence. You will, however, report to a work-release program, where you will be allowed to drive to and from work only, and you will check in every evening at a secure facility. As for the money, I assume you spent it all, and since it is such a large sum, I will also assume it would put a hardship on your parents should you have to repay it. For this reason, neither you nor your parents will be responsible for the store's money, especially as the business is insured and has already received compensation from the insurance company. This session is adjourned." The judge banged the gavel once, rose, and left the courtroom.

Tony and Laura rose and shook hands with DeSanto and the public defender.

"What just happened?" Danny asked softly.

Laura grabbed her son by the shoulders and looked squarely at him. "Because of your father and his connections, you just received a suspended sentence by a federal judge. You will abide by the guidelines the judge gave you, you will keep your nose *impeccably* clean, and you will enjoy your freedom as if it is your last, because I'm telling you right now, if you ever do something as stupid as this again, I will personally throw you into the court system and never look back."

Speechless, Danny nodded again.

Laura smiled. "Now let's go celebrate. You have some people to thank."

When Tony and his family arrived at the restaurant, Gino walked over and greeted them. He kissed Tony lightly on both cheeks, then turned to Laura and did the same. Finally, he faced Danny.

TONY TANCREDI AND CINDY L. O'HARA

"Ah, so this is your son I've heard so much about?"

"Yes, Gino, this is Danny. Danny, Gino. I believe he has something he would like to say to you." Tony stepped back, his hands crossed in front of him.

"Thank you, Mr. Victorino, for helping me," Danny said. "I can't tell you how much this means to my family and me. I just want you to know that I promise I will never get into trouble again, and I'll work hard. I want to make my parents proud of me again, to trust me."

Gino nodded his head. "You are a good boy, Danny. Sometimes, we just make the wrong decision. I believe you and have faith that you will now do the right thing. Please, come have a drink with me."

For the next hour, Tony, Gino, and his family talked and enjoyed their drinks, until Tony felt that it was time to go. "Gino, I know you have many, many things to attend to, and I don't want to take up any more of your time. Thank you. For everything."

"Tony, it is my pleasure. We will see each other again soon, no?"

"Of course."

"Good." Gino turned to Danny. "You will be a good boy, Danny." It was a statement, not a question.

"Yes, sir, I will."

"I know."

With that, Gino hugged Tony once more, turned, and walked away.

FORTY

AFTER LEAVING GINO'S, Tony took Laura and Danny to Casmiri's, an old Italian restaurant and bar that had been one of his watering holes for more years than he cared to remember.

Tony and the owner, Anthony, went back twenty years or so; and it was here that Tony had taken Laura on their first date. Since then, they had frequented it enough so they knew most of the staff.

When Tony mentioned that Bobby DeSanto might be at the restaurant, Laura insisted on stopping by to thank him for doing his part to help out her family.

While waiting for DeSanto at the bar, Tony noticed Anthony had hired a new barmaid. The woman serving drinks had long, straight, jet-black hair, olive skin, and a very small, very round, very tight (from what Tony could see) ass. Tony estimated her to be somewhere around twenty-six years old, thirty at the most, and of some kind of Mediterranean descent—possibly Greek or Italian. Her other assets included two large, firm breasts that were the focus of most, if not all, of the men at the bar and were held in place by the one small button she had left done on her sheer white shirt.

"So when did you say Bobby DeSanto would be here?" Laura asked.

Grudgingly, Tony shifted his gaze from the woman to his wife.

"Hmm? What did you say?"

Laura watched the woman behind the bar rinse glasses and pour beer. "I've never seen her here before," Laura said casually. "And obviously, neither have you."

"What, her? She's got nothin' on you, honey. She's not my type—too sleazy. Hey, there's Anthony." Tony pushed himself off his barstool and quickly walked over to him.

"Hey, Anthony. How ya doin'?"

"Good, good, Ton. How you and your family doin'? Okay? How'd that problem with your kid work out?"

"It got taken care of, Anthony. Thanks for askin'."

"Hey, you know you're like family to me. Whatever happens to you and yours, you know I care. On another note, I wanted to tell you, I was at your boxing show with my sons, and we had a great time. You thinkin' of puttin' on another one?"

After a little more idle chitchat, DeSanto walked in.

"Hey, Bobby," Tony greeted the detective.

With one arm around DeSanto's shoulders, Tony led him over to Laura and Danny. "Bobby, this is my wife, Laura."

"I'm pleased to meet you, Detective," Laura said, extending her hand.

Tony dropped his arm and shouted to the bartender, "Hey, A.J., I need another round and whatever my friend here wants."

"Got it, Ton!" A.J. yelled back.

"Tony, I'm gonna go to the ladies' room," Laura whispered into Tony's ear. "I'll be right back."

A.J. waddled over, balancing three drinks, and gingerly set them down in front of Tony. When Tony pulled out a roll of bills, A.J. waved it away. "This one's on me," he said. "I understand you're celebratin' tonight." He winked.

"Thanks," Tony replied, not questioning where he had gotten his information. "So who's the new barmaid?"

Before he could reply, the woman sidled up to them.

"Hi, I'm Nina the Greek. 'The Greek's' a nickname, not a sexual preference. Just in case you were wondering. And you must be Tony Tancredi. I've heard a lot about you. Word has it that you're a real *bad* boy."

"Well, I've slowed down a lot since the Shamrock Club closed. You know how rumors are—people aren't always what they're supposed to be."

"Well, I wouldn't mind finding out for myself. Maybe I could start some new rumors about you. Unless you don't think you can handle me."

"Hey, Greek," DeSanto said. "He's married. In fact, he's with his wife. She's in the ladies' room. Lighten up, and go devour someone else, why don't ya?"

Nina leered at Tony. "I guess we'll just see how married he is. I'll be here for the next three nights. I'm just filling in for vacations. Well, here comes the little wifey. See you soon—I hope." She turned, her long black hair doing a neat flip over her shoulder as she spun away.

"She's a bitch," A.J., the bartender, said. "I can't wait until she leaves. You don't wanna open that package, Ton. She's nothing but trouble, that one."

Tony nodded, but also couldn't help being intrigued by the exotic woman.

The next night, when Tony met Joe at the Squire, he asked, "Hey, Joe, whatdaya know about a girl, calls herself Nina the Greek?"

"Ah, that one. Not much really. She used to be a driver for a bookie named Joey A., who was tied up with the mustaches. He's in the joint now—has been for about six years. Far as I know, she's got some kind of job with a few of the titty bars around town. Kinda like a secretary or some shit. Tells dancers when and where to be at whatever clubs they're workin' at."

"Sounds like you know more than a little. You ever with her?"

"Her? Nah. But I've been around her several times at different places. She usually gets what she wants and don't care what she has to do to get it. She also works at some of the titty bars as a barmaid. Loves to do meth or whatever she can get her hands on. She's dangerous to get involved with. She broke up a lot of marriages and loves to take guys away from other girls. Likes to make guys fall in love with her, get what she wants, and then drop them for someone new."

"Huh," Tony said. "Sounds like someone should teach her a lesson."

"Well, why don't you let someone else teach her a lesson?" Joe said, turning to Tony. "You have enough on your plate right now, don't you? Boxing, your wife, and Melissa—" But something in Tony's look made Joe stop.

"Ah shit," Joe said. "I know that look. You already made up your mind. What is it with you?"

"Who the hell knows. Guess I been hangin' around you too long."

"Hey don't blame me for your behavior. Look, just be careful with her. And don't say I didn't warn you about falling in love with her. Don't let her get in your head."

Throughout the conversation, Tony had the sense that Joe was holding something back. What, he wasn't sure. But out of respect for Joe and their friendship, he didn't push. He was sure, when the time was right, Joe would tell him whatever was on his mind.

When Tony walked into Casmiri's the next night, A.J. glared at him, and then refused to look at him again.

Tony eased himself onto one of the barstools.

"Aren't you at the wrong end of the bar?" A.J. asked, swishing a dishrag around a glass. "What you want is at the other end, isn't it?"

Spying Tony, the Greek came over and interrupted the one-sided conversation.

"Hey, Tony. Where's the wife tonight? Or did you come in here to ask me out?"

"If I wanted to ask you out, I would've sat at your end of the bar."

TONY TANCREDI AND CINDY L. O'HARA

A.J. smiled and said, "Jack and ginger, Ton?"

The Greek was left speechless for what, Tony suspected, was one of the first times in her life. She stormed away.

After a few drinks, and more than a few dirty looks thrown his way, Tony walked to the bathroom. To do so, he had to walk by the Greek's end of the bar. On his way, Tony leaned over and said, "If you wanna have a drink with me, be at the Hilton tomorrow night at eight o'clock. If you're really good, you might get to see one of the suites after dinner."

The Greek leered at Tony. "Then can I be bad?"

Tony just smiled and continued to the bathroom.

The next night at the Hilton, the Greek (for that was the way Tony thought of her), arrived promptly at eight o'clock wearing a sleeveless knee-length red cocktail dress. As her hips swayed seductively during her short walk to Tony, he couldn't help but notice (as did most of the other men in the room) that her breasts were barely held in by a tiny string tied behind her neck, the small sequins dotting the dress only drawing the eye toward what was already stunning and conspicuous.

An interesting choice of attire, Tony thought, but to be honest, he hadn't known what she was going to show up in. The outfit, a far cry from that of the classically dressed and well-educated Melissa, or even Laura, for that matter, was a bit more Miami than Philadelphia, but it worked on the Greek.

Throughout dinner, the Greek was charming and, if it can be believed, classy, offering Tony a taste of all her food, buttering his bread, and refilling his wineglass when the waiter failed to do so.

As bottle after bottle flowed easily, Tony realized he was getting more than a little drunk.

"Well," the Greek wiped her mouth delicately with the white linen napkin. "Now that dinner is over and you've seen the prim and proper side of me, are you ready for some dessert?"

"Are we having that here or in our room?" Tony slurred.

"Well, you *could* order it here, but I don't think they'd let you eat it here." She leered at Tony.

Tony smiled back, raised his hand at a passing waiter, and yelled a little too loudly "Check, please!"

Once inside the room, gone was the charming girl whom Tony had just had dinner with, and in her place, a seductive, controlling monster.

Pushing Tony onto the bed, the Greek quickly stripped to her leopard skin thong, exposing long, lean legs; a tan, tight stomach; and the most perfect ass Tony had ever seen. She cupped her large firm breasts in her hand, rubbing the nipples so they stood out. When she looked at Tony, her dark brown eyes had a crazed look that caused small goose bumps to rise on his arms.

Clearly, this was a woman who would not be denied what she wanted.

"When do I get to see the rest of you?" Tony panted, leaning on his elbows for support.

"When you can't stand it anymore," the Greek whispered seductively. "Rip them off." She straddled Tony, at the same time undoing the zipper on his pants. She looked into his eyes, waiting.

Tony ripped the thin cotton fabric away from her dark skin. He cupped her ass and jerked the Greek toward him, tasting, teasing one perfect nipple, then the other, until both were fully erect.

A moan escaped the Greek's lips as she arched her back.

After hours of raw, rough sex, the Greek rolled over and propped herself up on one elbow.

"You know, Tony," she said, tracing small circles on his chest, "any other woman will bore you now. Only I'll be able to satisfy you."

"We'll see," was all Tony said.

TONY TANCREDI AND CINDY L. O'HARA

FORTY-ONE

IN THE PREDAWN, twenty-three-degree hour of five o'clock, Tony and the Greek parted company outside the hotel—he to return to the lumberyard after a six-week hiatus spent dealing with the trial, and she to whatever it is she did in her off time. Tony didn't know or care.

With an awkward, almost-chaste kiss, after what had happened the night before, never mind less than an hour ago, they went their separate ways, with Tony promising to call her soon.

Tony walked quickly to his car, his only thought to get inside and start blasting hot air through the vents. While he loved winter for the most part, this kind of bone-seeping cold made him shiver. (*It has nothing to do with having just spent the night with another woman other than your wife—again—does it? Or that you just spent the last five hours exploring every orifice of that two-bit excuse for a human being with your tongue and committing adultery against an absolutely beautiful woman, wife, and mother, does it?* asked the little voice in his head.)

Mentally, he shouted, *Shut the fuck up!* (he had learned not to do this out loud by now) and felt that the voice understood, making Tony feel so much better for having done so. Put the damn voice in its place, yes, he had!

Once in the car, he cranked the heater up to high and blasted the radio. His favorite DJ, Don Johnson, ranted back about nothing and everything of note, soothing his conscience and crushing the voice and any guilt he had harbored. Feeling lighter in mood, Tony smiled and pointed the car toward the lumberyard.

After punching in at the office, Tony looked out the window and was surprised to see a small four-by-four guard shack across the street at the entrance to where the rough lumber was kept. Curious, Tony walked over to investigate. Inside loomed a six-foot-tall man (maybe taller, although it was hard to tell because he was hunched over trying not to hit his head on the roof) with stringy dark hair that hung well below his shoulders and looked as if shampoo were a foreign concept. He didn't seem to remember or care what a washcloth was used for, either.

Tony noted dark skin that had either been inherited by Native American ancestors or had been exposed to too much sun and was caked with dirt, dirty fingernails, and a body that may have been lean at one time but was now starting to get buried under a top layer of fat. When the hulking creature smiled, Tony was unsurprised to find the man's mouth contained approximately five teeth—three on top and two on the bottom—none of them in a row.

Completing the caricature was that despite temperatures which had, Tony estimated, risen to a balmy thirty-five degrees, the man in the booth wore only a stained long-sleeved denim work shirt, its left front pocket torn almost completely off so it flapped in the breeze. Under his right arm, a large gaping wound of a hole exposed greasy long strands of hairs. His lower body was clad in run-of-the mill blue jeans and, like his shirt, were tattered to the point Tony was sure there was but one single thread holding the jeans together. They encased what Tony was sure was the man's bare, underwear-less ass.

"Hi, I'm George Cloud, the new gate checker, and you must be Tony. I've heard a lot about you. You're the union stew. I knew it was you by the description they gave me. I'm here to check the lumber loads—you know, both incoming and outgoing, try and cut down on shortages."

Tony let his gaze wander up and down the man, making sure Mr. Cloud knew he was being sized up. From the way the sweat beads popped out on his pimpled forehead and his upper lip, Tony thought he had made the man uncomfortable enough or, Tony wondered, *was there another reason the man was sweating?*

"You're right, George, I'm Tony. Hey, lemme ask you sumthin', you're considered office personnel, right?"

The Indian nodded.

"Yeah, I figured as much. Funny, I didn't know I had a problem with shortage around here. But whatever makes Bob happy, right? I mean, I'm sure it was his idea to have you and this guard shack out here?"

"Oh, I don't think Mr. Keebe thinks it's your guys doing the shortages," George said. "I think he thinks it's the customers. I mean, you guys can't be everywhere at once, and after your men go back to their loads, who the hell knows what the customers throw on their truck before they leave the yard, right? Now customer loads will be checked along with the loads your guys make up for delivery. Cuts down on mistakes, so we don't ship over or under the amount ordered," George explained, smiling and clearly pleased with himself.

"Well, I gotta admit," Tony said, "it sounds like a good idea, and I'm sure you'll be very helpful around here."

As he moved the car forward under the raised gate, Tony muttered, "And to me."

After punching in, Tony turned to see Bob stomping toward him, a scowl on his face that was so ever present it seemed to be permanently etched there, like a mole or freckle. Tony didn't think he had ever seen the man smile, and for one brief moment, Tony actually felt sorry for this huge, sad, pathetic pig of a man. The feeling passed quickly enough when Bob opened his mouth.

"Hey, Tancredi, good to have you back. Things have been waaaaay too quiet with you gone, ya know? So how do you like the new man at the gate?"

Without waiting for a reply, Bob said, "Not only will he cut down on theft, he'll also let me know about the mistakes you guys make out in the yard. I mean, used to be that we'd only find out about shortages from the contractors, then have to go out to the site and fix it, but now we'll find out about any outgoing excess before it even leaves. Pretty smart, huh?"

"I gotta give you credit, Bob. It really should save the company some money. And it'll also let you know how good we are out in the yard," Tony pointed out. "I'm sure your man, George, will tell you everything you need to know about what goes on out there. But I do have one suggestion: you might want to clean him up a bit. I don't think he presents the image the owners like to convey. He's a little shabby, don'tcha think?"

Bob inhaled. "Yeah, you're right. I think I'll order him uniforms like the ones you guys have."

"Can you order him a haircut, shave, shower, and some teeth too?" Tony asked.

Bob's face froze in a thoughtful half smile that looked like some painted-on horrific grin, those of the variety seen often in children's nightmares. His face reddened considerably, so much so that Tony wondered if he might actually have to administer CPR to this fat tub of shit.

Finally, with nothing left to say, Bob roared, "Get to work."

With an almost-imperceptible nod, Tony turned and walked away to the sound of giggles and snickers from the rest of the office. His work here was done.

With his head bowed against the stiff February wind, his hands stuffed in his pockets for the little bit of warmth he found there, Tony started toward the men huddled under the tin canopy where the lumber was housed.

As he approached, he could read the anticipation on the men's faces and, before he could utter a word, was fielding questions from all directions. Many of the men wondered if the newly appointed gatekeeper could get them fired. After all, most (if not all) of these men lived paycheck to paycheck. Others wanted to know if they had to take orders from him, or if he was to be a member of their union.

Finally, Tony raised his hands, palms up. The men quieted. "No, he can't fire you. No, he can't give you orders. And no, he isn't going to join the union. He's an office geek and has no power over us. He just reports to Bob. If Bob has a problem with one of us, he still has to consult with me. Nothing has changed. But what I would do is be a little more careful with our count on the loads. Until I can control this guy, just be careful so we don't have too many mistakes. We don't want to give him—or Bob—a reason to be up our ass. Especially you, Pete." Tony pointed at one of the men who was infamous for sending out more lumber than the contractors had ordered. Pete looked down at the ground.

"I'm not singling you out," Tony continued, suddenly feeling sorry for the young man. "You just need to be more careful, go a little slower if you have to. At least until I confirm my suspicions about this guy."

Pete looked up and, ignoring Tony's public admonishment, said, "What are you talking about?"

"Just give me a coupla days with Mr. Cloud. If my gut feeling is right, we won't ever have to worry about him. He'll be on our side. The mistakes he'll be reporting will be office mistakes on the order forms they give us, not our mistakes from the yard."

Tony didn't like being deceptive with his crew, but he thought it best to do a little digging before saying anything more. Before they got back to work, Tony promised to have another meeting by the end of the week and tell them what—if anything—there was to tell.

The next day, Tony maneuvered his forklift through the rough lumberyard, intentionally taking his time loading the two-by-twelves that bordered each side of George's shack, the better to watch him. What he saw was a man who didn't have enough to do and too much energy to spare. When Tony saw the large Indian sweating again on a twenty-eight-degree day that had every other man in the yard wearing three pairs of long underwear, jeans, and the bulkiest coat they could find, Tony knew it was time to approach him.

"Hey, George," Tony called from the forklift. "What the hell you doin'?" The man had taken all of his belongings outside—both personal and professional—and was in the midst of sweeping out the tiny shack.

"Oh, just somethin' to do. Helps me keep busy, you know. I like to stay busy."

"Uh-huh," Tony grunted. "Well, I got some stuff here that'll keep you busy for a long time, and I know it's better than the stuff you're doing, *and* I get it for free."

"What are you talking about?" George asked, frowning.

"Okay, George, you wanna keep payin' for your shit, fine. I was just tryin' to help you out. I do a little meth once in a while, but I give it away to friends, not sell it. You can talk to me or fake it, but you're not fooling me. Roll up your sleeve, and if I'm wrong, I'll give you a hundred bucks right now."

George looked at Tony appraisingly. "Man, you don't pull any punches, do you?"

Tony remained quiet, waiting.

"Yeah, okay, I do a little meth," George answered.

"No, George, you do a lot of meth. Most of my friends do it too, don't get me wrong, but they don't use needles, and they're not addicted to it. We have more fun giving it away—especially to the ladies, like the dancers we have over for the weekend at our party house."

George looked at Tony incredulously, then narrowed his eyes. "Now you're talking—free meth *and* girls? Sounds like you could be my new best friend."

"Not so fast, Georgie-boy. I don't make friends that quick. If you want to do business with me, here's the deal. You take care of the guys in the yard and only turn in a mistake once in a while—you know, just to make it look good. You tell us about the mistakes, and they'll fix it here, so it protects you and us. That way, we all look good, and the office feels like you're earning your money."

George nodded. When he agreed, Tony jumped down off the lift. He squeezed the big Indian's hand in a not-so-subtle gesture.

"I'm glad we have an understanding," Tony whispered. "Because I'd hate to have to come back and remind you of our agreement."

Small beads of sweat popped out on George's forehead and upper lip.

"Hey, Tony, I wouldn't think of crossing you, man. I've heard too much around the yard."

Tony relaxed his grip, then let George's hand go altogether. Tony patted George's cheek. "That's good, George. You'd do well to remember what you've heard."

Later that day at lunch, Tony found most of the men huddled, trying to keep warm.

"Listen, guys, I just wanna let you know that George isn't going to be a problem anymore, and you don't have to worry about him. He's going to tell you about your mistakes, but not tell the office. You fix the problem here in the yard, and the office will never know about it. *Capice?*"

The men all nodded. Tony could read the relief on their faces.

"Oh yeah, one other thing," Tony said. "If Keebe comes over while you're fixing your error, tell him you caught it yourself before you gave the paperwork to George."

What a helluva first week back, Tony thought, shoving his hands in his pockets to keep them warm against the still-biting wind.

TONY TANCREDI AND CINDY L. O'HARA

FORTY-TWO

AFTER A BITTER, cold winter that wreaked havoc on the city, Tony found himself driving to Gino's nightclub, Bellisimo's, one night, the windows down, enjoying a cool spring breeze.

The drive to the club gave Tony a bit of solitude he desperately craved, a time to just *think*, without interruption. On this night, his thoughts turned to his relationship with Gino.

When he first started going to Gino's club, Tony had taken Laura one night a week for dinner and drinks—just to be respectful and keep an old man company, he told himself. But soon, Tony was visiting more frequently, going into the club two and three times without his wife—for what reason, he wasn't sure.

Now he would join Gino on walks outside the club, chatting about nothing in particular—although he wasn't naïve enough to think these random conversations were all that accidental.

At first, Gino talked only about his relationship with Joe, their history together, and perhaps even their future. To this, Tony would say nothing but listen respectfully.

Tony pulled up to Bellisimo's, his train of thought interrupted. He wondered briefly what was on the agenda for tonight.

When Tony walked in, Gino was sitting at the far end of the bar, near the office.

Tony walked into Gino's embrace, giving him a quick hug. He shook Gino's hand.

"How are you, my friend?" Gino asked.

"Fine, Gino. Fine. And you?"

"Good. Come, we have much to discuss."

Tony stood shoulder-to-shoulder with Gino as they pushed through the people to get outside.

"Tony, I talk to Joe, and he still feels bad about closing the club, about not having a place for you to work for him anymore," Gino said as the two strolled past other businesses.

"Why would he feel bad about—" But before Tony could finish the question, Gino held up his hand for silence. Tony immediately clamped his mouth shut.

Gino said, "He feels your talents are being wasted. There are not many men like you in this city anymore. You are both admired and feared. Even I, a person who is a—how do you say—recluse, have heard your name on the streets."

Although flattered by the praise, Tony was growing uncomfortable with Gino's questions about his friendship with Joe, torn between feeling protective of his old friend and former boss and his growing loyalty to Gino. Unsure of how to respond, Tony said, "It is very kind of you to say such things. Coming from a man like you, it means even more."

"Once before, you told me how Joe has done so much for you," Gino continued. "He gave you everything—money, girls, clothes, and all the other things you don't bring into my club out of respect. I have known Joe a long time." Gino stopped and turned to Tony, placing both of his hands on Tony's shoulders for emphasis. "He has never trusted anyone like he trusts you."

Certain more was to come, and that to say anything would be an almost fatal mistake, Tony kept this mouth shut.

"The trust he has in you has been tested many times." Gino dropped his hands from Tony, but did not resume walking. "At times, you were not aware of the tests. For instance, all those girls? They were not an accident. Some were planted to see if you would tell them anything, if you would act different if you got drunk, maybe . . . talk too much. There were even bugs in your car at times."

Tony tried to remain impassive, but was shocked to learn that perhaps he had not been as trusted as he had thought.

Gino continued. "I can see—even though you are trying not to show it—that you are offended. But believe me, it had to be done—for your own good, as well as Joe's. He had to be sure before he brought you to me. He only wants the best for you. But he had to be sure you were ready. As I said before, a man like you is hard to find these days. Sometimes I think there are more human rats than real ones in this city anymore," Gino whispered into Tony's ear.

When Gino pulled back, Tony knew he should respond, but he could only shake his head in amazement. "I feel more indebted to Joe than I already did. I hope someday I can somehow repay him. You know, Gino, it's funny how my list of people I have to repay keeps growing. As I've told you before, my parents have sacrificed so much for me. My mother is like

TONY TANCREDI AND CINDY L. O'HARA

a saint on earth. I would just like to be a success someday and take care of them and my only sister."

Gino patted Tony on the cheek and continued walking. "Your intentions are honorable. I am sure someday you will do that. Now let's go back inside. We'll have a drink together." Gino put his arm around Tony and led him back toward the club.

When they arrived at the front door, Joe and Nicky pulled up and got out. When Tony looked at Joe, his old friend smiled. It was as if Joe had just been privy to the conversation between him and Gino.

Joe held the door open for the small party. Tony was the next to the last person to go in; the last person was, of course, Joe. Before closing the door, Joe leaned forward and said, "Oh, by the way, Sam needs to talk to you when you have a minute, Mr. Bigshot."

"Yeah? What about?"

"Hey, how the hell would I know? I'm just the messenger."

"Uh-huh. Okay. Tell him I'll meet him at the Squire tomorrow night at nine o'clock. Hey, we're blocking the doorway. We should get inside."

Joe let the door close softly behind him and whispered to Tony, "I remember when you used to open doors for me." He laughed at his own joke.

Thankful for the levity, Tony smiled and laughed along with his friend, comfortable with the knowledge that the transition from Joe to Gino had officially begun.

Although the volume was turned down, one of the eight televisions at the Squire showed the Phillies were beating the Braves by a run. Tony swiveled on his barstool and watched the door for his friend Sam. Tony looked at his watch for the third time. He wasn't surprised his friend was late—that was typical Sam—but Tony found himself growing impatient to the point that he thought he'd give his friend five more minutes and then leave.

Just as Tony began to push his glass away and slide off his stool, Sam appeared at his left shoulder.

"Hey, lover boy, you wear that thing out yet?" Sam smiled at Tony, the ever-present toothpick wedged firmly to the side of his mouth.

"You do know you're late, right?"

"Oh, whaddayou, so important now that nobody can be late? Lemme tell you somethin', dickhead." Sam leaned in and pointed a finger at Tony's chest.

"You're still the same sorry-ass dago I hired ten years ago, and you wouldn't be anywhere if I hadn't talked you into taking the job at the Shamrock."

Tony grabbed Sam's finger and flung it away as if it were a piece of trash.

"Well, taking care of you yahoos hasn't exactly always been a day at the beach for me, either." Tony started laughing. "Okay, lemme buy you a drink, and we'll call it even."

Sam smiled. "Now you're speakin' my language, Tony-boy."

When the drinks arrived, Tony said, "So whatdaya want, Sam? Joe was pretty mysterious about this little meeting."

"I'm told you're falling pretty hard for the Greek," Sam said, the familiar toothpick bobbing back and forth in his mouth.

"Nah," Tony replied, stirring his drink with the small red swizzle stick. "That's just how I'm playin' it. Truth is, I couldn't give a fuck about her." Tony smiled as he said this.

"Well, that's not what I hear," Sam replied.

Tony looked at his friend, who hadn't taken his eyes off his drink since the conversation had started. "Yeah? You got sumthin' to say, Sam, just say it."

"Whatever. All I know is the Greek's playin' your friends. Don't get me wrong. No one's done nuthin', Ton."

"What are you talkin' about, Sam?"

"It's just"—Sam looked up—"I don't know, games and shit—probably for the attention, flirtin' with the guys. Maybe her blouse opens up, or a button just happens to pop off. Maybe she don't exactly sit like a lady when she has a skirt on, or forgets to wear underwear *under* the skirt. Things like that."

Tony smiled. "Okay. Thanks for the heads-up." They were silent for a beat before Tony asked, "So anyone tap her?"

Sam shook his head emphatically *no*, his stringy blond hair swinging from side to side. "Nah. But she's asked for drugs, and they've given 'em to her."

"Okay. Thanks again, Sam. Just have the guys keep feedin' me information. Tell 'em to do whatever she wants and don't worry about me."

"Sure thing, Ton."

After dropping Sam off at another club, Tony headed over to Cocktails, a local strip club in Bensalem, and greeted the Greek behind the bar with a simple nod. He sat down and waited for her to bring him his drink.

"Hey, Ton. You hungry?" the Greek asked, wiping down the bar with a rag before placing Tony's drink in front of him. "Nah," Tony replied, taking a sip. "I'm okay. Hey, what's with the flashlights?"

"Ah, a new thing Mario thought up. He gives flashlights out to the customers for them to shine on the girls."

"Huh," Tony said, not really caring.

"Exactly. Okay, I'll be done in a little bit," she said, moving away to attend to some customers who had just walked in. She handed three flashlights to the men and took their drink orders.

With nothing left to do but wait, and thoroughly bored, Tony surveyed the place.

It was impossible to concentrate on any one thing, however, because the music coming out of the speakers was so loud that it pounded in Tony's ears. He wouldn't have been surprised if blood started pouring from them. Trying his best to ignore the music, he watched the dancer on stage gyrate effortlessly to the beat, the red, white, and yellow lights bathing her in an eerie glow and accenting her perfectly shaped silicone tits and her firm body. Hundreds of green bills, tucked into the thinnest piece of cloth, swayed under the fans and air-conditioning. Suddenly the Greek was standing in front of Tony. "Ton, you gotta make 'em stop."

"Who?"

"Those assholes at the end of the bar. They keep flashing those goddamn flashlights on my tits and ass. I've asked 'em to stop, but they keep doing it."

Tony sighed. "All right."

"Thanks, Ton."

In truth, Tony could care less where these idiots shone their flashlights, or on whom, but he was playing a role, and this called for a jealous boyfriend.

He walked to the trio. "Hey guys. Howyoudoin'?"

"Fine, Pops," one of the boys replied.

Tony took offense, but vowed to remain calm.

"Look, fellas. The girl behind the bar's *my* girl, and she's tired of you shinin' your flashlights on her. I understand that she asked you nicely, but you're still doin' it. So now *I'm* asking you nicely to knock it off. For your trouble, the next round's on me."

"Hey, anything for the man who buys us all a drink, right, fellas?" The rest of the men bobbed their heads.

"Great." Tony nodded at the Greek and circled his hand for the universal bar symbol of another round. Tony walked back to his seat.

Within minutes, however, the trio started flashing their lights on the Greek again. She looked at Tony.

Tony shot off the barstool. The first time, it had been about the Greek. Tony understood that. This time, the idiots' actions were a direct slap in the face to him.

"Hey, asshole. What the hell do you think you're doing?" Tony asked.

"Hey, Pops," the speaker of the group said. "We thought about stopping, but then we got *rrrreeeaallll* thirsty. So we decided that if you buy us *another* drink, we promise to stop." The man smiled and looked at his crew. The other two men smiled idiotically.

Tony hit the speaker of the group squarely in his mouth, launching him off his barstool. Tony then looked at the other two men. A second man started to reach behind him. Without hesitation, Tony pulled out his switchblade and quickly thrust the knife into the man's side before he could get up. He fell sideways.

Tony turned to face the last man, whose gaze was fixated on the bloody knife at Tony's side, at the bits of flesh that Tony knew were stuck there. Suddenly, the man pushed himself off the stool and stumbled his way out the back door.

Satisfied that the worst of the trouble was over, Tony grabbed a rag off the bar and began wiping down his blade. When he was finished, he pocketed both the knife and the rag.

On his way out the same back door, Tony ran into the owner. "Mario. Sorry about the mess. Clean it up, and make sure nuthin' comes of this, got it?"

"Yeah, Tony. I got it. Do me a favor, though, and don't come back here for a while, okay?"

Tony nodded once.

"Oh, and Tony?" Mario asked. "By the way, the other owners and I been talkin', and we need a meeting. Tell us the time and place, and we'll be there, but it needs to happen soon."

"Yeah, Mario. Okay." Tony nodded. "Meet me at the Squire next week. I'll let you know the day."

The owner nodded and turned his back on Tony.

Next Wednesday, Tony met with the owners of Tattletales, Visions, Cocktails, and Babes—all titty bars where the Greek worked. He listened to their worries, fears, and complaints without interruption—the most basic being that the Greek was a draw and knew how to play all the customers.

"Look, Ton, we all appreciate you comin' in at night, but business is business, and you're hurtin' us all in the pocketbook," Mario said. "You're

TONY TANCREDI AND CINDY L. O'HARA

hurtin' your own girl. Guys quit talkin' to her when they see you, and they quit spendin'. It takes away from our bottom line and her tips." The other owners nodded in agreement.

"And after that incident last week at my club—"

"What incident, Mario?" Tony asked. He picked at the pleat on his pant leg, straightening it out.

"Uh, nuthin'. Nevermind. But you get what we're sayin'? Right?"

"Yeah, Mario. I get it." Tony looked at the owners. "How 'bout I come in after two when you guys close. Will that help?"

They all nodded.

"Okay then. Meeting adjourned."

And problem solved, Tony thought.

FORTY-THREE

THE POKER MACHINE at the Squire winked back at Tony, telling him he had lost—again. It was his fourth straight loss. With little to do until Sam got off at midnight, Tony kept feeding the thing quarters, even though he had determined long ago that the machines were nothing but a waste of time and money. On the rare occasion when they paid out, Tony ended up giving the money away to some hapless bastard.

Just as he put in another quarter, Harry, the bartender, yelled out, "Hey, Tony! Telephone."

"Yeah? Who is it?" Only a few people knew where to reach him if he wasn't at home.

"Says it's Gino."

"Yeah, okay. I'm comin'." Tony walked away from the computer and picked up the receiver.

"Tony? This is Gino. I need a favor."

"Anything, Gino."

"I have a problem that needs to be taken care of. I gave this job to one of my friends, but something . . . unforeseen happened, and he now needs help," Gino explained. "The job which was supposed to take only one man now needs two.

"Come to my club as soon as possible. I'll explain when you get here."

Tony didn't know exactly what was being asked of him, but he did know it was serious. He suspected if he came through for Gino tonight, whatever the task, it could be an important step in his relationship with Gino.

"Gino, I'll be there in ten minutes."

When Tony entered Bellisimo's, Gino was in a corner, deep in conversation with someone whom Tony hadn't met. Suspicious, Tony walked over to the two men.

"Ah, Tony," Gino said. "Please meet our good friend Vince. He's here from Italy, but forgive him. His English is no good. He's only been here a year or so. You two will be working together."

"Hey, Vince. Welcome." Tony extended his hand. Vince reached out and shook Tony's hand once. He did not return Tony's smile. Tony looked Vince up and down, noting that he was handsome, well mannered (if not a little weird), and solidly built. Tony was unsure how this relationship was going to work out, but for Gino's sake, he'd just follow orders.

When Tony and Vince returned two hours later, Vince nodded to Gino, who excused himself from the bar.

"Gino," Vince said, "it is done." Vince then began speaking quietly in Italian, his back squarely to Tony. Although Tony was annoyed, he stood quietly, trying not to show his impatience.

Gino gripped Vince's hands and kissed the man on both cheeks. He turned to Tony and said, "Vince apologizes for speaking in Italian in front of you, but his English, as you know, is no good. What he had to say would have taken him far too long, so again, he apologizes to you."

Vince gave a slight nod of his head at Tony. Tony relaxed. "He tells me you are a serious man and worthy of the respect of all of our friends," Gino continued. "Although *I* knew this, it is good to hear from someone else. Come, my friends, let's have a drink," Gino said. He put his arms around Tony and Vince and led them to the bar.

Tony relished the praise he had just received because he knew the words Gino had just spoken were those not often used to describe anyone who wasn't already in their Italian club, or, as Joe called them, the mustaches.

When Tony showed up the following Friday night, Gino greeted him with a hug and discreetly slipped a large envelope into Tony's breast suit pocket.

"This," Gino said, patting the pocket firmly, "is for you." Tony knew enough not to open the envelope in public, so he followed Gino to the men's room and locked it. Tony opened the envelope and wasn't surprised to see hundreds of crisp, new one-hundred-dollar bills there. He quickly pushed down the flap and handed it back to Gino.

"Gino, my friend, I can't accept this. First of all, when you helped Danny, you helped my family as well, and you wouldn't accept any money. All I could do was offer you my friendship, my loyalty, and respect. In your own words, if I were to take this, it would be business. Please allow me to return the favor in the name of our friendship." Tony held out the package.

"Once again, you show you are a man of your word, a man of honor on the streets," Gino said, shaking his head and fingering the white envelope. "You know, Tony, most men would not hesitate to take this from me, would justify it as payment for a job well done. They would pocket it in a minute and step on my dead body to get it, but not you. You are different, my friend."

"If you ever need me again for anything," Tony said solemnly, "just ask."

Gino smiled. He put his arm around Tony's shoulder and led him back to the bar.

"So," Gino said, "on to other business. I have a temporary barmaid coming in later. She is a hustler and a bitch, but she makes men spend the money. I really don't like her, but business is business." He sighed. "Her name is Nina the Greek, and she was a driver—well, more than a driver—for a friend who's in the joint now, a man named Joey A. He's getting out soon, maybe less than a year."

"Gino, there's something I have to tell you. I've been seeing the Greek for a while, maybe six months or so."

Gino nodded, his eyebrows knitting together in concern. "I see. Thank you for telling me. However, I have to believe you know her reputation and what she is about. It surprises me that you would even go out with her."

"It's not what you think. I don't give a shit about her. In fact, the more I know her, the more I hate her. You're right. She has a reputation of making married men fall in love with her, of breaking up marriages. I think it's time someone teaches her a lesson."

Tony's lips tightened, and he clenched and unclenched his fists just thinking about the Greek.

"So," Gino replied, "you are the one who will avenge all the wrong she has done to men in this city while screwing one of the hottest women around. A woman all the men would give a week's pay just to see naked." Gino smiled.

"Yeah, well . . ." Tony trailed off. Then another thought occurred to him. "Gino, lemme ask you, what if I hadn't told you about my relationship with her? Or was this a test like the ones Joe gave me?"

Gino waved his hand. "You give me too much credit. I don't know everything. But if it were a test, you did the right thing by telling me."

"Was it a test?" Tony repeated the question.

Gino looked at Tony. "Maybe," he replied, smiling.

Tony relaxed, confident he'd done the right thing by telling Gino of his . . . extracurricular relationship. "She's coming in tonight?"

Gino nodded. "Why do you ask?"

"Well, I was just thinking that it probably isn't a good idea for me to be here when she's here."

Gino agreed.

TONY TANCREDI AND CINDY L. O'HARA

Before leaving, Tony reminded Gino of his upcoming fight show and asked if he could still bring by promotional materials to distribute and put up around the club. Gino agreed, telling Tony that when he dropped off the tickets, he would happily sell them in the club. After thanking Gino again, Tony left, feeling buoyant about his future.

Back in his car, Tony headed to the Squire to see if Sam was working. He glanced at the clock on the dashboard and saw that it was only four fifteen in the afternoon. *To hell with it*, Tony thought. *If Sam's shift is gettin' over, maybe he'll wanna go get a beer or sumpthin'.* Feeling better about having a purpose and a destination, Tony mulled over his relationship with Gino. He couldn't help wondering where it was going, where he was headed, and what it all might mean for him in the end. For sure, he was becoming more involved with some of the most serious players in the city just by doing favors for Gino. These were the same people his father used to talk about when he worked at the gambling houses after losing his job with the teamsters. Tony remembered the glint in his father's eyes when he would come home and talk about these men, how his father had—at least it had seemed to Tony—envied their power and money.

It occurred to Tony that if he had that kind of power, was connected, and could get anything done with something as simple as a phone call, how much more his family would respect him. How could they not? Then, he wondered, would he be happy? He didn't know, but one thing was for sure—it couldn't hurt to associate with Gino.

There wasn't much Tony believed in, but one thing he did feel strongly about was that everything happened for a reason. For instance, if he hadn't met Sam on that fateful night of the wedding, he would never have met Joe; and if not for Joe, there would be no Gino.

This led Tony to think about Joe. Even as Tony became more involved with Gino and his enterprises, he knew he would always remain devoted to his first boss. He had made that abundantly clear one night to Gino, who said he understood, and even appreciated, Tony's candor and allegiance.

Later that week, Tony, Laura, and Gino were seated in one of the booths at Bellisimo's, enjoying dinner and deep in conversation, when the Greek walked up.

"Just wanted to let you know I was here, Gino. Remind you that I'm covering for Sal." She looked directly at Tony. "Oh hey, Tony, how you doin'?"

Gino glared first at the Greek, then at Tony.

"Okay, Nina, I need you behind the bar."

"Sure, Gino. See ya later." She sauntered off, her firm, round ass swaying as she walked.

Tony willed himself to relax. He looked across at Gino, who was seated next to Laura, and couldn't hold Gino's cold, dark stare.

Gino turned to Laura and kissed her lovingly on the cheek.

"Are you having a good time, *mi figlia*?"

"Gino!" Laura laughed, giddy from having had two white wines and little dinner. "You're always so kind to me. What did you say in Italian?"

"*Mi figlia*. It means 'my daughter.' And that is how I think of you, as a daughter." He looked pointedly at Tony.

Clearly touched, Laura put her hand on Gino's arm and kissed him on both cheeks.

"Thank you, Gino. That means the world to me."

"As it should, because it's the truth. Now I'm sorry for this, but would you please excuse Tony and me? We have some business to discuss."

"Of course, Gino."

"Good. We won't be gone long, and when we return, we will have more wine!" Laura smiled and nodded.

"Tony, come."

They had moved away from the booth to a private corner of the bar. With barely contained fury in his voice, he whispered, "You are making a fool out of your wife, and it is not right. Take care of this . . . situation."

Tony had never before gotten on the wrong side of Gino, but tonight, he knew he had. It was not a place Tony cared to stay for very long.

FORTY-FOUR

O N A SEEMINGLY routine Friday night, Tony took Laura to Gino's club for drinks and dinner. As the couple eased up to the bar, Tony noticed a roundtable of eight older Italian gentlemen—most of whom Tony recognized as Gino's friends and business associates—in a corner of the room. Tony had, on occasion, seen Gino with one, possibly two, of them, but never all together. Although curious, Tony tried to ignore the little voice in his head whispering that something was amiss if most of Gino's friends were in the same place at the same time.

Tony chalked up the irregularity to a meeting or celebration, and besides, he argued with himself, who was he to question how Gino conducted his affairs? Feeling better, he turned back to the bar. Before he could utter a word, however, a hand touched him lightly on his back.

"Gino!" Laura squealed.

"Ah! My daughter has come home to visit me!" Gino replied. He kissed Laura on both cheeks. "You are well?"

"Yes, Gino. Very well."

"Good. That is good. I need Tony for a few minutes. I promise not to keep him for long. Is okay, yes?"

"Of course, Gino."

"Thank you. Andino here will stay with you until Tony returns." Gino pointed to a large man standing to his right. Laura looked the doorman up and down, then looked back at Gino.

"Okay. Tony? We go meet my friends."

"Sure, Gino," Tony replied, his hands sweating and his heart racing in response to the request.

As they approached the table, Gino began speaking in Italian, and it was clear to Tony that he was introducing him to his friends. Tony responded with a simple nod. After the greetings, the men sat down. As Tony began to do the same, Gino firmly grasped Tony's elbow so he would remain standing.

"Tony, I bring you to my friends here tonight to show our loyalty to you, just as you show your loyalty to us. To thank you for all you have done for us, and for never accepting anything in return for your work. On this night, my friends and I will make you an offer to show our thanks. We sincerely hope you will accept it. We would like you to be a partner in this club. We want to make you an equal partner—you will own half."

For the first time in a very long time, Tony was speechless.

"Gentlemen, I am humbled and honored at this very generous gift. In fact, words can't express my gratitude. What I can do is accept your offer and pledge my loyalty to you—if you will grant me one condition."

Gino turned to Tony, a look of disbelief in his eyes, then of fury.

"I realize all of you know and respect my friend, Joe B., and you have different businesses and a good relationship. But if things should change in the future, I will never go against him, because without him, I wouldn't be here before you tonight."

Tony looked at Gino and was relieved to see the color return to his face.

Gino took a breath and said with a smile, "You see what I mean about loyalty?" He clapped Tony on the back.

The men all stood, waiting to hug and shake the hand of their newest member. Gino reached for his wineglass from the table and held it high. Everyone followed suit.

"To Tony. *Salude!*"

"Cheers," Tony said and took a long drink of the red wine (a wine connoisseur might actually think it was more of a chug, Tony thought with a smile).

"Okay, gentlemen," Gino said. "Enjoy the rest of your evening—on me." He led Tony back to Laura. "I will let you tell your wife what you want to tell her when you get home, but please do not say anything here." Gino put a finger to his lips.

Tony nodded in understanding. "I'll tell her you gave me half of your club and nothing about your—I mean, our—friends. She doesn't need to know anything else. If anything ever goes wrong in the future, what she doesn't know will help. Everyone."

Gino smiled. "I like the way you think, my friend. There, that wasn't too long, was it?" he asked Laura.

"No, Gino," Laura replied. "And they've been taking very good care of me."

"Good, good. Okay, I'll leave you two to talk, but I'll stop by before you leave."

"Okay, Gino. And thank you."

Gino waved his hand in the air, as if shooing away an irritating bug. "It is nothing, Tony. You have earned it."

"Well, thank you anyway."

"You're welcome," Gino said, moving back toward the table of his friends.

Laura turned to Tony, question upon question dancing in her hazel eyes. Laura asked, "What was that all about? It looked like Gino was giving a speech. And then all those old Italian men hugging and kissing you? Tony, what's going on?"

Tony tried to remain impassive, but was too excited. He kissed Laura full on the lips, cupped her face in his hands, and said, "We're very fortunate to have such good friends. I'll explain everything on the way home, but I will tell you one thing, your banking days are over."

"What do you mean over? Tell me now!"

Although Gino had warned him not to say too much while in the club, Tony felt that he could tell Laura a little of what had just transpired. "Gino just made me a partner in the club. He gave me 50 percent. Right down the middle." Tony beamed.

"But why? Why would he do such a thing?"

"Because friends help friends, and we're going to help each other make some money in this place. He helped us with Danny when we asked, and over the last year or so, I've helped him with . . . some things."

Laura narrowed her eyes. "What kinds of things?"

"Just . . . things," Tony said. He looked away from Laura, then back again, leveling his gaze at her, warning her to stop asking questions.

As Tony continued to gaze at Laura, he sensed the mental gymnastics going on in her head; but to her credit, she remained silent. He knew, however, the interrogation would come later. He didn't care. He was high as a kite, and maybe for the first time in his life, it was without benefit of a controlled substance.

His next thought was of his parents. With this news, he could finally tell them their son was the owner of a successful business; they could be proud of him. Tony couldn't wait to call and tell them. As he thought through the implications of what Gino had afforded him and his family, his eyes started to well.

Laura gently put a hand on Tony's arm. "It's too late to call them now," Laura said. "We'll call them tomorrow. Why don't you go to the bathroom and get yourself together?"

On the way to the restroom, Tony thought about Laura and, for the millionth time, thanked God for her. She was the best thing he had going for him, and yet he continued to screw around. As much as he wanted to remain faithful, she was the one person, the one thing he wasn't able to commit to. He just didn't know why even though he'd asked himself several hundred times.

Standing in the stall, Tony allowed himself as much time as he could before he thought people would start to worry. After about fifteen minutes, he decided he had indulged in enough self-pity and introspection. It was time to get it together and go back out.

He stepped out of the stall and gazed at the man in the mirror. He tugged on his coat sleeves and adjusted his diamond cuff links. Satisfied, he turned away from his reflection, glad he didn't have to look at himself anymore.

Pulling into the lumberyard the next morning, Tony realized his days here were numbered. He had his second fight show coming up, a vested interest in Gino's club, the Greek, and, even on occasion, Melissa—not to mention Laura. It was all getting to be too much. As for things he could cut loose, he felt the lumberyard and Melissa would have to be the first things to go.

With a renewed sense of priority, he went to find his crew. He found most of them standing around chatting, waiting until the last possible moment before having to punch in.

"Hey, guys," Tony said. "I have something I wanna talk to you about, so I need to see everyone at lunch. Pass the word along to anyone you see who isn't here. Okay?"

"Hey, Ton? What's up?" Mark asked. Tony waved off the remark.

"Later."

For the next three hours, Tony hauled and stacked lumber, and batted down what seemed like a thousand pleas from his coworkers to tell them what was going on.

At lunch, when Tony was sure everyone who could be there was, he said, "I'm now a partner in a nightclub."

"All of a sudden, you own a nightclub? You never mentioned you were looking for one," Mark said.

"I wasn't. It was given to me. Remember that guy who helped my kid when he got into trouble? He gave me half his club."

"Wait a minute," said another. "He helped you, and now he just *gives* you half his club? I know I'm not the brightest guy in the world, but somethin' ain't addin' up here. Hell, I'll friggin' help him if it means gettin' half his club."

"Look, guys, I can't go into details. You know that. But it's true."

TONY TANCREDI AND CINDY L. O'HARA

Mark cleared his throat until all eyes were on him, and then slowly made the sign of a mustache with his finger. Chuckles rippled among the crowd, soft and muted.

"Okay, okay . . . very funny, dickhead!" Tony said to Mark. When the laughter died down, Tony said, "Anyway, I just realized the club will need to have a grand reopening party. I'll give you all the details as soon as I clear it with Gino."

Just then, the whistle blew, signaling the end of their lunch break.

"Hey, guys, don't let this get out yet. I wanna tell Bob myself. Maybe invite him to the party." Tony smiled at the thought.

This last statement brought another round of laughter among the group of men as they all headed back to work.

FORTY-FIVE

THE DRIVE HOME from the lumberyard that night seemed to take forever. Tony nervously tapped his palm against the wheel, willing every light he came to, to turn green. He was anxious to get home and call his parents.

As Tony pulled in the driveway, Laura opened the door. In her hand, she gripped a piece of paper, trying to keep it from floating away on the chill breeze that had come up suddenly. Tony suspected it was his parents' phone number she was holding. He hurried toward her.

Tony reached for the small scrap of paper, hoping to catch it before the wind did.

"Ah, ah, ah," Laura said, holding it up high so Tony couldn't get a hold of it. "If I'm so good, where's my kiss?"

"I'm sorry, honey. Of course." Tony embraced Laura and kissed her passionately, for once not caring who saw, actually hoping the neighbors were watching.

Laura began to wiggle. "Okay, okay, you made your point! Go call them." Laura pushed Tony away.

Tony snatched the number from her hand and raced inside, feeling very much like the little boy he used to be, trying, but somehow always failing his parents. It was an unjustifiable feeling, he knew. They had never done or said anything to make him feel as if he wasn't good enough. On the contrary, they had been the most loving and supportive parents he could possibly hope for. And yet he never seemed to rise to the high expectations and standards he had set for himself where they were concerned. But now—

"Hello, Mom?" Tony's stomach clenched in fear and apprehension, as well as excitement. "How are you and Dad doing? The weather okay there in Florida?" Not waiting for an answer, Tony said, "Tell Dad to pick up the phone. I got some good news, and I want you to hear it together."

His mother covered the mouthpiece and yelled, "Honey? Pick up the phone. It's Tony, and he said he has some good news to tell us."

"Dad, are you there yet?"

"Yeah, I'm here. What's going on up there? You all right?"

"Yeah, I'm great, Dad. I want you and Mom to fly up here and see my new nightclub."

"Nightclub? What the hell are you talkin' about, Tony? How did you get a nightclub? You don't have that kind of money."

"I didn't buy it, Dad. Someone gave me half of it."

"Why would someone *give* you half of a nightclub?" Tony's dad asked, sounding more confused than ever.

"I know the one you used to work at closed, thank God. What club are you talking about now?" his mother asked.

"I'm gonna send you plane tickets," Tony answered, ignoring his mother's and father's questions. "Just tell me a good time for you. I'll tell you everything when you get here. I just want to see your faces when you see how big it is."

"I still wanna know how you got it," his father complained.

"You'll know everything when you get here. I promise, Pops. Just tell me when you can come so I can send the tickets. You won't need any money. I'll take care of everything."

"We'll call you back tomorrow with dates. And, Tony? Please be careful."

"I will, Mom. I love you, and I'll talk to you tomorrow."

Tony hung up the phone and sat for a moment, enjoying the feeling of perhaps finally throwing the two-thousand-pound gorilla of guilt called his parents off his back.

Done talking to his parents, he told Laura he was going to Gino's club—now *his* club (or at least, half of his club)—to ask Gino about having a grand reopening.

"I like the idea," Gino said. "It is your idea, so you take care of everything. You have my full cooperation. This will be your first venture as my partner. I know you can handle the streets. Now show me how smart you are in business."

"I'll pack this nightclub like you've never seen it," Tony pledged. "I have to make it either two weeks before or after my fight show because I have a feeling a lot of the same people will be at both, and I wanna give them a break between events."

"We're going to need extra help that night also. I'll get some of the Shamrock Club people to help out. I think I'll have it after the fight show so I can do a little face-lift to our club."

Gino frowned. "Face-lift? What does this mean, 'face-lift'?"

Not wanting to offend his friend and new business partner, Tony said, "I was thinking we could paint the inside and add a few new thirty-inch TVs, maybe six of them? I'll have carpenters come in and do what we need to mount the TVs on the walls."

"And how much is this going to cost the club?" Gino asked, his eyebrows raised.

"Nothing. It's all on me," Tony said. "My gift to the club as the new partner."

"But you're talking about thousands of dollars to do what you want to do," Gino said, still frowning.

"The only things I'll have to pay for are the TVs and the paint. The labor and material will be free. I'll have the carpenters at the lumberyard do the work, and I know they won't take any money. We'll give them food and some drinks, and they'll be happy."

"But it will be thousands of dollars for the TVs alone," Gino objected.

"We'll make it back in profits in a couple of months. Look, Gino, I'm not going to just be a silent partner. I expect to work and do things to improve the business. And now that we're on the subject, with all due respect, Gino, I think your food is too expensive for this area."

"You mean my food is not worth the money?"

Tony put his palms up, as if in defense. "No no no, my friend, that's not what I mean. It's just too good for this area. Your clientele has changed over the years. The neighborhood has changed. All those people who walk by the club, they eat somewhere else. They shop in this center and use all the other businesses surrounding the club, but they don't eat here—only drink.

"Ten years ago, it was different. Only white middle-class people lived in this area, but now all races live here, and I want everyone to eat at the club. We just need to offer them food they can afford. And," Tony added one last thing, "we need to stock more hard alcohol. When people eat, they drink."

Gino listened to all of this thoughtfully. He sighed and put his hands on his knees. "You have made a good point. Maybe I have been a little stubborn in not changing with the times. You have been here such a short time, and already you have made good decisions."

"Don't give me all the credit. I just have ideas. You'll always have to decide what ideas are good and bad for this place. I know you say I own half, but I also know my place, and this club is yours."

Smiling a wide white smile, Gino replied, "You are wise beyond your years. That's why you will be a success in whatever you do. Your ego never surpasses your respect. The kitchen is yours to do with as you want."

"Thank you, my friend. I'm sure we're doing the right thing."

The following day at the lumberyard, Tony gathered his crew one more time and explained what it was he wanted to do at the club. He told the laborers and forklift drivers they could do the painting, and the carpenters could put the TVs on the wall. Since Tony had, in the past, done numerous favors for most of them, the men were more than happy to return the generous acts of kindness. For their trouble, Tony promised the crew he would ply them with free food and drinks during the renovations and for at least a couple of hours during the grand opening.

The discussion continued outside the main office for far longer than it should have, which was Tony's intention. He knew Bob would see him and the other men loitering and come over to find out what was going on.

"Okay! What the hell is the holdup here?" Bob yelled, slamming the door behind him. "Can't you guys hear? The whistle blew five minutes ago!"

"Sorry, Bob. It's my fault," Tony began. "The guys were just a little excited about my new nightclub. You know, lots of questions. They also wanted to help with some of the renovations like painting, installing new TVs, and some other minor things. I was just telling them what night they could do it. I don't want to have to close the club and lose business. You know, Bob, while we're on the subject, let me invite you to the grand reopening. I'm going to announce the date in a week or two—right after my next fight promotion. I hope you can make both. I'll even throw in the tickets to the fight—gratis. In case you don't know, that means free."

The men snickered.

"Well, you just got it all goin' on, don't you, Mr. Businessman? It's a wonder you still have time for us working stiffs. Lemme tell you something, I don't know how you got a club, and I don't care. If these guys are going to help you all night at that club, they better be here the next day, or I'll hold you personally responsible!"

As the men started splitting off into opposite directions, Tony said, "Bob, does this mean you're not coming?" This drew a low round of laughter from the men.

Bob walked back into the office, shaking his head.

FORTY-SIX

LAURA HANDED TONY a glass of wine and sat down beside him on the couch. She looked around the living room and sighed.

"My god, Tony, I gotta tell you, I'm glad your fight show's over. These last few weeks have been so hectic," Laura said.

"Yeah, I know. But look what I've proven to the boxing commission."

"Which would be what?" Laura arched an eyebrow. "That you know how to lose money?" It's not quite what she had intended to say, but it was the truth. There was no getting around it.

Tony set down his glass and stood up. He clenched his fists and snapped, "But this is only my second show, and I've pulled both of them off—perfectly. They know I'm serious and that I know what the hell I'm doin'."

"Honey, don't get upset," Laura said. She rose from her sitting position and lightly stroked her husband's arm. "Now if you could just do it and make some money . . ."

Tony jerked his arm away from her. "What is it with you and money? The money will come. It's like a business. You don't make money right away. You *know* that. The commission said the next show should be on TV, and I've already been talkin' to ESPN. So don't worry, *honey*, the money will come."

"That's great, Ton. I didn't know all that. So I'm sorry. I just worry." This seemed to mollify her husband.

"Well, okay then."

"Now how about we take this little party upstairs?"

Tony smiled and headed for the stairs.

The following evening, Tony sat at his desk in the den, hovered over a blueprint of Bellisimo's.

"Whatcha doin'?" Laura asked.

Without looking up, Tony said, "Trying to figure out how many guests I can squeeze into the club and still keep everyone happy."

"Huh. Well, good luck with that." Laura kissed the top of his head. "I'll be in making dinner if you need anything."

"Uh-huh." For the next hour, Tony continued to turn the blueprint around, studying the dimensions of the club.

The club has twelve tables and eleven booths along the wall, so I can put our friends in those seats and make sure they're taken care of, Tony thought.

"That leaves seventy-two spots at the bar, which brings the total to one hundred and sixty-four—not including standing room only. So I can probably fit about three hundred people," Tony mumbled to himself. "That should work. Now I can work on selling tickets." He put his pencil down and pushed himself out of the chair. "Hey, honey," Tony yelled. "When's dinner? I'm starved." Tony walked out of the den, satisfied that it was going to be a grand reopening.

The night before the celebration at Bellisimo's, Tony picked his parents up from the airport. Thrilled they had actually made it, Tony was anxious to drop them off at home. As much as he wanted to spend time with them, he still had a million details to take care of.

As he was hefting the two suitcases up the stairs, his parents right behind him, his father said, "So, Tony, tell me again how it is you managed to get this nightclub of yours."

Tony sighed heavily, knowing he should have expected this inquisition and been prepared for it, but he had hoped it wouldn't occur—at least until later.

"Pops, I told you. It's *half* the club, for one thing, and I promise you, I'll answer all your questions *after* the party. That way, you can see the place for yourself and probably get some of the answers on your own." It was his way of diverting his father.

Grumbling that "somethin' just ain't right," his father announced he was tired and going to lie down.

Relieved he had put off his parents, or more specifically, his father, he turned to Laura. She had come upstairs with fresh towels in her arms.

"Honey, you're taking Ma shopping for a dress, right?" Tony had insisted that Laura buy something new for the party and wanted his mother to do the same.

"Tony, you know I don't need anything," his mother protested.

"I know you don't *need* anything, Ma, but I want you to have something nice and new for the party. I want everyone's head to turn when I walk in and wonder who the two beautiful women are by my side."

His mother's face colored slightly. "Okay, okay," she said. "I guess we're going shopping."

"What are you gonna do while we're out?" Laura asked.

"I'm gonna head over to the club. I wanna go over some last-minute details with Gino, check and make sure we've got enough alcohol—things like that. I'll be back around five o'clock or so."

He kissed Laura and his mother, eager to get to the club.

On the drive to Bellisimo's, Tony rehearsed what he wanted to discuss with Gino. One of them was the behavior of the Greek, and the other was Melissa. Neither had proven to be a problem (yet), but tomorrow night, he knew, would be different. Tony was sure they would get drunk and do God knew what else, which was nothing new; but with Laura there, it could be a problem.

He chose to task Monte from the Shamrock Club to take care of Melissa if she got out of line. He knew her well, and they got along; plus, he could stay close and not draw any suspicion.

Nina, however, was a different story. She had a lot of friends—most of them strippers—and a good following from her customers, which could be a potential headache. Having the Greek in the crowd would only cause more problems.

It was with this in mind that Tony walked into Bellisimo's and into the office at the back of the club. He knocked softly on the door.

"Come in." Tony opened the door and poked his head in.

"Gino, if you have a minute, I wanted to talk about some last-minute things."

"For you, my friend, I have all the time."

Tony entered and sat down across from Gino.

"So as for the bartenders, I thought I could hire Nina for the night, keep her out of trouble," Tony said after explaining his thoughts and concerns to Gino.

Gino furrowed his brow. "You mean keep you out of trouble. I told you I don't like the Greek here when your wife is here. I don't like her at all, for that matter. She's a *prostituta*, a whore. She always has been, and always will be. But for you, I will make an exception this one night only. It is the right thing to do for all concerned. Your wife will be with your parents at their table. So I will talk to the Greek and tell her I know the situation and she is not to come out from behind the bar without a doorman. *And* she will work at the opposite end of the bar," Gino said.

Tony tapped a finger against his chin. "It'd probably also be a good idea to have Greg from the Shamrock keep his eye on her. And I'm sure Joe's girl, Nicky, will help with the situation. She's the only one who knows all the girls and will tell Joe if anyone starts getting out of line."

TONY TANCREDI AND CINDY L. O'HARA

"All our friends will be here," Gino continued. "Carmine, Vince, Johnny, Alfonse, Vito, and maybe some others from downtown. There cannot, nor will there be, any trouble, especially because of your girlfriends. I don't have to tell you how very disrespectful it would be of you to upset our friends. I know you don't want that."

Tony heard the warning and potential threat in Gino's words. And he understood. After all, these were the same people he had met the night Gino had announced Tony's ownership of the club, the same men who had approved Gino's generous gift. He couldn't afford to offend these men with such trivial, albeit potentially volatile, problems such as women getting into fights with one another just because he couldn't keep his dick in his pants. He wondered if he would ever learn, but suspected not.

"I understand, Gino, and you have my word that nothing will go wrong where my wife and girlfriends are concerned."

"I hope not," Gino said.

Tony silently prayed for the same thing.

Gino looked back down at the papers on his desk, signaling to Tony the meeting had come to an abrupt end. As Tony pushed himself out of the chair and strode to the door, Gino stopped him.

"Oh, and Tony. Don't forget I would like you here early—at least half an hour before the party starts. To greet our friends when they arrive."

"Yes, of course, Gino. Whatever you say."

Tony softly closed the door behind him.

The next evening, only hours before the party, Tony found himself sitting in his living room, listening to his mother and his wife discuss such inane things as how they were going to do their hair, what jewelry they would wear, what shoes. It all seemed a bit absurd to Tony, but because of his love for these two women, he was thoroughly enjoying their excitement.

For Tony, the party and the club were just icing on an already wonderfully full life. This time, right here, right now, watching his father, his mother, and his wife laughing and discussing clothing, shoe, and accessory options was, for Tony, his greatest moment and his crowning achievement. He could have stayed there all night.

Suddenly, Tony had a premonition. He had a feeling that this night, this one night, would be something he would always remember. Or want to forget. He wondered which one it would be.

FORTY-SEVEN

WHEN TONY AND his family finally pulled up outside of Bellisimo's, he was understandably anxious. Standing at the door was Vincent, Gino's friend and associate. With more flourish than was necessary, he opened the door wide for Tony and his parents.

"Welcome to your son's new club. He speaks so highly of you, and it is an honor to meet you both. With Tony's permission, I will be with you the rest of the night for whatever you need."

It was the longest speech Tony had ever heard from Vincent, and one he must have practiced for hours. Tony was impressed.

He shook Vincent's hand and pulled Gino's number-one man close, whispering into his ear, "I would entrust them to no one else on this night."

Tony knew that to commit a man of Vincent's standing to his parents for the evening was highly unusual, and he knew the directive had come from Gino. Although Tony didn't expect any trouble tonight, he was also a healthy believer in Murphy's law—anything that could go wrong, would, especially when you least expected it. With Vincent at his parents' side, they would be protected at all costs.

Vincent turned to Tony's parents and wife. "Tony is a lucky man to have such a beautiful wife and wonderful mother and father."

Tony put his hands on Vincent's wide shoulders. "Yes, I'm blessed, but without friends like you, this night would not be possible, so thank you."

Vincent nodded.

As they continued into the club, Gino walked toward them with his arms outstretched. When he got within two feet, he stopped and waited for Tony to come to him.

Tony took his mother gently by the arm. "Gino, I present my mother, Mary, to you."

Gino smiled widely. "Ah, this is the real guest of honor tonight. I have heard so much about you from your son. He always honors you with his words. Now I see he has overlooked speaking of your beauty. We hope we can make this night special for you."

"Gino, you are very kind to say such nice things," Mary replied. "But I'm sure I'm not deserving of them."

"Dad," Tony said, putting his arm around his father and pulling him forward. "This is my partner, Gino."

Gino nodded in recognition. "It has been some time, but I remember you from the gambling house on Bristol Pike years ago. You are a good man. Always did your job well. You should be very proud of your son. He is also a good man and has done very well for himself and is on his way to bigger things. He has told me many times of his love for both of you."

"This is a great opportunity you have given him. I hope he makes the right choices in the future." Tony thought that what his dad was really thinking, but couldn't say, was *I hope my son doesn't fuck it up.*

Tony could see his father trying to place Gino and knew that if he did, he'd have some explaining to do. But Tony hoped the revelation would be later—much later—than tonight.

As they walked toward his parents' table, his father continued to gaze at Gino, as if he was putting things together. Tony feared it was more than he wanted him to know, but he couldn't do anything about it now.

One of the bartenders interrupted his train of thought by shouting, "Hey, Tony. Telephone."

Tony walked over and took the phone. "This is Tony."

"Hey, Ton. Sorry to bother you on your big night, but I gotta problem."

"Joe? What's the matter?" Tony recognized the familiar gravelly voice at once.

"Uh . . . look . . . I don't wanna trouble you or anything, but I wanted to let you know that I don't know when I'm gonna make it there tonight. Or *if* I'm gonna make it at all."

"Why?" It was important to Tony to have those people who were closest to him at the club on his big night—this included Joe, especially Joe.

A pause on the other end lasted so long Tony thought they had gotten disconnected. "Joe? You still there?"

Joe sighed. "Yeah. Nicky and I had a fight. You know what a pain in the ass she can be. She stormed outta here, and I don't have a ride."

In the almost ten years he had known Joe, Tony had never seen him drive. Not once. It never occurred to him Joe didn't have a license. He just thought he liked being driven around, looked at it as some sort of status thing—at least when the Shamrock had been open. Tony just assumed now that Joe had a lot of free time on his hands, he'd drive himself wherever he wanted to go.

"Okay, Joe. Gimme a minute and lemme think." Tony glanced at his watch and saw that it was seven forty. The party didn't start until eight o'clock. The drive wouldn't take more than twenty minutes round-trip. If he left now, he could just make it back in time.

"Joe, I'll come get you. Just be ready to jump in the car when I drive up."

"Ton, you don't have to do that. I'll get there eventually. I'll call the Squire and get a ride from somebody over there."

"Just be ready," Tony slammed down the receiver. He hadn't meant to be short, but he didn't have time to make his friend feel better about his request either.

For the first time in their friendship, Tony was angry at Joe. Here it was, his friggin' night, and he had to run all over hell's half acre for his friend. No time to think about it now. He wasn't going to task anyone else with this errand. Christ, he wished he wasn't so fucking loyal.

He quickly hurried to where Gino and his family were sitting and having a glass of wine. From the bottle, Tony could tell it was one of Gino's homemade wines, something he offered only to those he deemed special and worthy. Gino asked, "Everything is okay, yes?"

"Gino, that was Joe. He needs a ride because his fell through. The drive only takes twenty minutes. If I go now, I can pull this off." Tony thought keeping it as brief and to the point was the best way he was going to get approval to go.

Everyone looked at Gino, who looked at his watch. He waved his hand dismissively, which Tony took to mean as consent, but Tony felt the warning behind that small flick of the wrist. Tony prayed to whatever God was up there he would make it back in time.

When Tony pulled up to the Lair, Joe *and* Dick were standing outside.

Tony rolled the passenger window down. Without time to consider why Dick was at the Lair and why Joe hadn't mentioned it, he yelled, "Get in."

Both men did as they were told, although when Tony looked back at Dick in the rearview mirror, he could tell his friend was disgruntled. Tony didn't care. He was doing the two a huge favor by even picking them up *and* possibly alienating Gino, which was never a good thing. Tony floored it and somehow arrived in record time.

When Tony pulled into the parking lot, the first thing he saw was a line of people snaking along the length of the building and rounding the corner. *How could everyone arrive at the same time?* Tony thought. He knew his friends from the Shamrock and Gino's men had everything under control both at the door and in the parking lot, but they had a tough job because certain people had to be handled differently from others. "Some, Tony had instructed in one of his many preopening speeches to the staff, would stand in line without a problem, but others would see it as disrespectful and a reflection on me, and ultimately Gino." The bouncers had understood and seemed to be handling things well.

Tony pulled his Cadillac around back so he could go through the kitchen and not look as if he was just arriving.

"Hey, Ton, thanks," Joe said.

Before Tony could reply, Dick yelled, "Hey, honey! Are you with that Tyrone, or is he bothering you?" Dick was referring to a black man who had his arm around a very attractive, very young white girl.

Tony and Joe quickly closed the two or three-step gap and grabbed Dick by the arms, one on each side of him. They yanked him back around the corner.

"This is the dago's night," Joe hissed. "*And* he just did us a favor. Don't make trouble here. Not tonight."

Tony had never heard Joe speak that way to one of his friends and was immediately grateful for it.

Dick mumbled, "Sorry, Ton."

"'S okay," Tony replied. Only then did Joe let go of Dick's arm. He gave him a firm push, as if tossing away an awful piece of trash.

"Sorry, Joe," Dick added.

Joe said, "Forget it. Let's go have some fun."

Tony told his friends to go to the front and find Greg; he would let them in ahead of the rest of the crowd.

"Okay, Ton," Joe replied. "We'll see you inside. *If* I decide to let this goombah in with me." Joe jabbed his thumb at Dick, who had the foresight to look contrite, but say nothing.

"Okay. See you inside."

Tony walked through the kitchen, taking a brief moment to watch the staff starting to fill orders. He took in the smell of garlic and onions frying and the pungent aroma of sausage, beef, and tomatoes, which he knew had been simmering since late that afternoon.

He kept going and pushed open the double doors leading to the dining room. The crowd was already two deep at the bar, and most of the tables were filled. Tony quickly found his parents.

"Everything okay?" Tony turned to Vincent for confirmation. He rested a hand lightly on the big man's back.

"Yes, Tony. Everything is, um, good," Vincent said in his stilted English. Relieved, Tony turned and almost ran straight into Laura. She had two friends in tow.

"Tony! This is Lisa and Joan from the bank!"

"Pleased to meet you," Tony said, noting that Laura was well on her way to drunk, which was fine, because Tony could trust her to maintain some class and decorum. Laura knew when she had imbibed enough and would stop.

"Tony," Laura said, putting her hand on his arm, "your friends from the lumberyard have been asking where you are. I think they're at the bar somewhere."

"Thanks, honey. I'll make sure I find them. Have fun with your friends. It was nice to meet you," Tony said, nodding at the two women while very smoothly easing away from them. Before Tony would find his crew from the lumberyard, however, he would have to endure more than an hour of people approaching him from all sides, congratulating him on his new business and wishing him luck.

Finally, Tony enjoyed a break in the crowd and took that moment to find his parents. He was pleased to see Joe there, talking to his mother and father.

"And we can never thank you enough for everything you did for us when Marie died," his mother said. "It was so generous and thoughtful," she added, impulsively throwing her arms around Joe and kissing him on the cheek. Embarrassed at the praise and adulation, Joe fumbled in his pocket for some money to buy everyone a round of drinks.

"Oh, Joe," his mother said. "I'm sure my son would *never* charge you for anything in his club, would you, Tony?"

It was not a question. "Mom, I'm not the only owner. I'd have to clear it with Gino."

With that, Gino raised his hand and nodded.

Joe looked down, and then slowly back at Gino. Tony sensed his friend was struggling to say something, but knew it had always been difficult for Joe to express his appreciation and gratitude. To help him out, Tony and Gino quickly put their arms around Joe and walked him to the bar.

TONY TANCREDI AND CINDY L. O'HARA

FORTY-EIGHT

AFTER MORE THAN an hour and hundreds of well-wishers later, Tony saw some of the downtown boys start to arrive.

During one of their many meetings before the grand opening, Gino had directed that at least three tables would be designated for their friends and associates from Philly. It was Tony's job to take these men to their tables and see that everything was in order. Gino had emphasized how important it was to take care of them and provide them with whatever they wanted. Finally, when all the men had been seated, Gino would come over and greet them. If anyone had a problem, they would tell Gino.

Tony would make sure they'd have nothing but good things to say.

When everyone had their drinks in front of them and Tony was sure no one needed anything, he started to move away. A hoarse voice stopped him.

"Hey, Tony," the old man said slowly. "Who are dem girls at the end of the bah?" Strangely, the voice was absent any inflection even though the man had asked a question. Tony looked to where he had nodded. He was referring to the strippers who had come in with the Greek and were subtly working the crowd by pushing out their already-oversize tits, rubbing shoulders with the men at the bar, and laughing at stale pick-up lines they'd all probably heard a million times.

By now, some of the girls were eyeballing Tony and the men at the table. Tony knew it wouldn't take long before the girls would recognize the money and power fifty feet away and start prancing over. Before anything got out of control, he had to talk to Gino.

Tony said, "They're just some friends of a friend, Johnny. Lemme go talk to Gino a minute, and I'll be right back."

"Yeah, you do that," Johnny said.

Tony hurried to where Gino was talking to some guests and waited for a break in the conversation. During a lull, Tony said, "Gino, I'm sorry to bother you, but I need to speak with you a minute."

Gino looked at Tony before answering. "Of course. I'm sorry," he said to the patrons. "I'll return shortly."

"Gino, I'm sorry. I wouldn't have bothered you if it wasn't important."

"I know that, Tony. What is it?" The underlying, unspoken innuendo being, *What couldn't you take care of without me?*

Tony didn't care. He wasn't making a decision on whether to let a bunch of strippers—high-class strippers, to be sure, but strippers nonetheless—fawn all over a bunch of powerful associates without Gino's say-so.

"Some of our friends were asking who the girls were at the end of the bar. You know, the Greek's friends?"

"Tony, I know of this situation. Tell the girls to let the old guys have a little fun, but tell them not to get out of line. Okay?"

"Yes, Gino. Thank you."

Gino inclined his head and then turned away.

Tony walked over to the Greek's friends.

"Hey, Angie," Tony greeted one of the girls. "You havin' fun?"

"Sure, Tony," she said. Her tongue toyed with the small straw in her drink. "You and the girls wanna have a little more fun?"

"Whatdja have in mind?" she asked.

"See those guys over there?" Tony nodded toward the old men in the far corner.

"Sure."

"I'd like you and some of the girls to go over and, you know, take care of them. But not *too* well, you understand? Have a little fun with them, let 'em have a little fun with you, but don't let the other customers see what you're up to. You got it? I'm sure they'll make it worth your while. And if for some reason they don't, I will."

"Yeah, okay, Ton. Anything for you."

"Thanks, Ang."

She turned to the girl on her left and whispered to her.

Tony had no doubt things would go well for both the old men and the girls. Satisfied, he walked back to his parents' table, greeting men along the way.

Some Tony recognized as being from downtown, while others were only vaguely familiar. What they all had in common, however, was they were all pledging their services and loyalty to Tony. While he wasn't quite sure, or comfortable with, what was going on, what he did know was that a lot of powerful people were very eager to show him they were in his corner.

Finally, Tony made it back to his family. He sat down, glad to relax for a minute. Just as he was beginning to unwind, Monte came up and asked if he could speak to Tony in private. Tony glanced at his watch. He had been sitting for less than a minute. He sighed heavily and slowly stood up.

TONY TANCREDI AND CINDY L. O'HARA

"'Scuse me, Mom, Dad. I'll be right back."

"Everything okay, son?"

"Yeah, Dad, everything's fine," Tony said, patting his dad on the shoulder. Although Tony had a funny feeling that things were not right at all.

As they walked away, Tony asked, "What's up, Monte?"

"Melissa's in the club, drunk as hell and telling everyone she's your girlfriend. She said she's going to go sit with you at your parents' table. I told her to come in the back room and wait for you, that I'd bring you to her."

"Jesus Christ. You did the right thing. Who's with her back there right now?"

"Greg."

When they walked into the small room, Melissa was leaning heavily on a chair, the better to hold herself up.

Melissa started. "Well, I can see you have all the important people in your life here to celebrate with you," she slurred, venom dripping from every word. "Well, I'm important too! I've put up with your shit for almost five years, and I'm tired of being hidden in back rooms and at the end of bars away from the party. You belong to me, and I want the world to know it, and I'm going to tell them all tonight! All of them! Your perfect little wife and your parents are going to hear how their wonder boy likes to fuck women over—hell, how he likes to fuck women, period—how he does enough drugs to kill a horse, and how he's in so tight with those old Italian geezers you'd need a shoehorn to separate the two." She smiled triumphantly.

"Melissa, you are not going to ruin this night for me and my family," Tony hissed. "You have two choices. Monte can take you home, or he can put you in the hospital. It's your choice," Tony replied calmly.

Melissa laughed. "Monte wouldn't touch me. He's my friend."

Tony looked at Monte. "Monte, show Melissa whose friend you are."

In two steps, Monte was on Melissa, his large hand circling her throat, his fingers squeezing her carotid artery. Monte then jerked her up to eye level, her thin legs kicking ineffectively at the air, and chucked her against the wall as effortlessly as if he were tossing a basketball off the backboard. Her head banged off the wall with a resounding thud.

She slid to the floor, dazed, then looked at Monte and Tony.

Tony squatted next to her. "Now you still think Monte won't touch you? I hope that knocked some sense into you, you dumb little cunt. This is not the night to mess with me, Melissa." Tony stood and smoothed the wrinkles out of his pants.

Melissa looked to Monte. "I can't believe you did that to me, Monte."

"Sorry, Melissa . . . I didn't want to, but orders are orders. My loyalty is with Tony, and I can't let you ruin his night."

"Don't fuckin' apologize to her, Monte. You don't owe her an explanation. It was her choice, not yours."

Melissa sat on the cold floor, shaking, tears streaming down her cheeks. "Believe it or not, there is a sick part of me that still loves you, but you will never touch me again, ever! No matter how big or powerful you think you are. I want out of here *now*."

"Monte, get someone to take her home," Tony said. "And make sure they use the back door."

Tony walked away from the odd couple, his intention to rejoin his family; however, he stopped short when he almost ran into Laura.

"Tony, what the hell's going on back there, and who was that girl? It sounded like she was dying. That or getting the shit beat out of her."

Thinking quickly, Tony said, "It was just one of Nicky's girlfriends, honey. She got too drunk, and Monte thought it would be better if Greg took her home since Nicky isn't here. Whatever you heard was just her banging into stuff back there. She was that out of it."

Laura narrowed her eyes, indecision dancing there. Before she could say anything else, Tony gripped her elbow and steered her toward the party in front.

"Come on. Let's not let this one event spoil the night. I'll buy you a drink, and I promise I won't leave your side for the rest of the evening."

Laura said, "That'll be the day. But okay. Only because this is your night."

Relieved, Tony steered his wife toward the bar. On the way, he glanced at his parents' table and noticed that his father was missing. Frantically, Tony whipped his head around, looking for his father. He found him introducing himself to people and socializing. This worried Tony because he didn't know who, if anyone, his father was acquainted with from his past work at the gambling houses, and he didn't want him talking to the wrong people. Unfortunately, all he could do was pray to whatever God was up there and hope for the best.

Trying to snake his way to the bar proved to be challenging since people were four and five deep. Tony had never seen such a crowd—not even on the best nights at the Shamrock.

Suddenly, he felt a tug at his elbow. It was Monte.

"Hey, Ton, this is pretty crazy, huh?"

"You can say that again."

TONY TANCREDI AND CINDY L. O'HARA

"You want me to jump behind the bar and help?"

"Yeah, that'd be good. Thanks, Monte."

"No problem, boss. Hey, whatdaya want to drink? Your usual?"

"Yeah—and a white wine for Laura. Give her the good stuff that's in the chiller."

"You got it, Ton."

When Tony had his two drinks in hand, he elbowed his way out of the crowd to his parents' table, where he had sent Laura. The two drinks sloshed in their glasses like some perfect storm, threatening to slop onto the cuffs of Tony's shirt. So intent was Tony on keeping that little faux pas from happening that he didn't see the man blocking his path until they almost collided.

"Whoa, careful there." The man reached out to steady Tony. Tony looked at the man who was blocking his path.

"I just wanted to offer my congratulations. It's about time they got some good men in Philly again." Tony recognized him as an associate from New York. He had met him once or twice and found him to be respectful and eager to please his boss—not like some of the younger goombahs who had a chip on their shoulder and felt like they had something to prove.

"Thanks very much." Not wanting to prolong the conversation, Tony smiled politely and tried to edge by, but paused when a beefy hand stopped him.

Tony looked down, and the man quickly removed it.

"I'm sorry to bother you, Tony. I see you have other places to go, but I have a small favor to ask."

Tony said nothing, and waited.

Taking the silence as approval to continue, the man said, "There's this club gonna open up in Bucks County about five or six miles from here—nuthin' close enough to compete with your place, but near enough so if you wanted to, you could check in once in a while."

"And why would I wanna do that?" Tony asked, barely disguising his impatience. He watched the ice melting slowly, watering down his Jack and ginger.

"See, here's the thing, it's my sister's kid, and I tol' her I'd take care of him while he was here, make sure he don't have no problems with this club thing he's got goin' on. You know how it is. Even the kid knows he needs a little extra muscle behind him. The kid tells me he's already met you, but he don't wanna ask you himself. Says he don't feel like he knows you well enough. His name is Leo Trina, and he says he knows you from the Shamrock. He's a good kid—never causes his mom and pops any trouble—and to have a friend like you would be a great help to him. And it goes without sayin' that should you need anything in New York, just come and see me."

Tony listened to the man's speech and said, "I know him, and he was always very polite. I'll do what I can to help him. Tell him to come and see me here and we'll talk."

"Now if you'll excuse me," Tony said. He lifted his drinks and wiggled the glasses. The tiny crystals clinked together, tapping out a soft, wet tune.

"Of course," the man said. He stepped aside so Tony could slide by.

As Tony turned, he felt another hand stop him. He looked up, his father blocking his progress. *How long had he been standing there?* Tony wondered. When Tony met his father's gaze, he had all the answers he needed.

He knew then that the party was about to come to an abrupt end.

FORTY-NINE

TONY'S FATHER BLUNTLY stated, "I'd like to have some answers, Tony. You've been putting me off for days now, and it's time."

Still juggling the two drinks while being elbowed this way and that in the sea of people, Tony replied, "I told you we'd talk *after* the party, Dad." Confident that his tone would put an end to the conversation, Tony tried to walk past his father.

Anthony grabbed Tony by his coat, sloshing more than half of each glass onto Tony's sleeve. Anthony smirked. "You told me I would see for myself and answer some of my own questions. Well, I've seen and heard enough. I think we should step outside and talk. Now."

Tony knew he couldn't put his father off any longer. Nor could he use the love and concern he knew his father felt for him because it was clearly escalating into anger. Any argument in the club would be disrespectful in Gino's eyes, especially an argument among family. Not wanting that, Tony sighed.

Tony replied, "Okay, Dad, let's go out the back door. I'm clearly not going to get to enjoy my time here or my drinks until we talk."

"Nice try. Let's go."

Tony set the drinks on a table and followed his father, head down, dreading each step that was taking him closer toward a conversation he was not prepared to have.

His father stomped through the kitchen and shoved open the back door, the silver bar making a loud *clang* as he hit it. When they were both outside, Tony's father turned to him and said, "I want to know how you got this club, what you did to earn it."

With his eyes downcast, Tony said, "Gino did a favor for me getting Danny out of that trouble. He would never take anything in return, so I started doing some things for him. Of course, I would never take anything from *him*, and after a while, he said that I had earned half of this club."

To his own ears, his explanation sounded exactly like what it was—shady, and most likely dishonest. He couldn't look at his father.

Anthony grabbed Tony's hands and, in a voice that sounded almost like a growl, said, "And how did you *earn* it? With these? Or did you actually kill someone already?" His father's voice rose. "You think I'm stupid? I know who these people are, and they don't give things like this away just because they like you. They expect things from you now. If you didn't kill someone yet, how long do you think it'll be before they ask you to? Or before someone kills you?"

"Dad," Tony said. "I did this all for you and Mom!"

"Don't you dare drag your mom and me into this. Whatever has happened, and will happen, is because of decisions you've made, not because of anything your mother and I have or haven't done. For God's sake, Tony, take some fuckin' responsibility for your life."

This wasn't what Tony wanted. It was supposed to be *his* night and his parents' night.

Tony hung his head, shaking it back and forth. He had to try to make his dad understand. "Dad, it's not like that. I didn't *mean* I blamed you. I just . . . I just . . ." Tony looked into his father's eyes, suddenly at a loss for words. "I always felt like I let both you and mom down when I didn't make it in baseball. Then when I coulda made it in boxing, Mom couldn't take me getting hurt, so I gave that up too. I just want you to feel like all those things you did for me as a kid weren't wasted. I just wanted to be able to take care of you and Mom, like you took care of me. I wanted you to be proud of me. When this opportunity came along, I remembered how you always talked about the mustaches at the gambling hall and their power and money. I thought if I could get in with them, I could do it all. The risk was worth it to me. Just like when I was boxing—those punches didn't matter because I was doing it for you. So I could become something."

Tony's father put his head down. When he looked up, Tony saw a single tear threading its way lazily down his wrinkled cheek.

Suddenly, Tony's father grabbed him and hugged him to his large barrel chest. "We've always been proud of you, son," his father whispered.

He pulled back, his hands holding both of Tony's upper arms. "You've overcome so much in your life. We were only doing what we were supposed to do as good parents. Don't ask me to condone this situation you're in now. If this is the life you want, it's your business, but don't do it for us. We've already lost one child, and if you go to jail or get killed, it would be too much for us to handle."

They looked at each other, silent.

"I'm sorry this had to come out now, but I love you so much. You're my one and only son, and I . . . I don't want to lose you," his father stammered. He dropped his hands.

Tony pulled his father close. "I love you, Dad."

TONY TANCREDI AND CINDY L. O'HARA

Before they stepped back inside, Tony's father said, "I won't tell your mother of this situation because she's so happy for you, but I want you to promise me that you'll take what I said into consideration."

"I will, Dad. I promise."

"Okay. It's all I can ask."

But even as they walked back into the club, Tony could still feel the electricity in the air from their heated words and wondered, for the first time, when the night would end.

The conversation with his father left Tony feeling depressed and resentful. Desperate to get back into a good mood, he walked over to Joe and asked, "Hey, Joe, by any chance, you leave a package in my car?" Tony was almost certain that Joe had left some meth in the car and knew he wouldn't care if Tony did some, but he felt he should at least ask first.

Joe looked at Tony, his brow wrinkling. "What the hell is wrong with you, you need to go do some of that shit?"

"Ah, just some family stuff. It's over. It's okay. I'll explain later."

"Yeah, there's a package in your car." Joe turned his back on him.

Annoyed, Tony walked away. He glanced around looking for Gino and was relieved to see him laughing and talking with the associates from downtown. For once, he appeared blissfully unaware that anything was wrong.

Tony took the small window of opportunity to go out to the car. He lifted the mat on the passenger's side and found the small plastic bag Joe had left there. Smiling, Tony sat down and opened the glove box. Although he disliked sniffing, he had learned the effect was much quicker than swallowing, and he needed relief fast. He spilled the already-chopped meth onto the console and fished in his pocket for a dollar bill. His fingers grasped the cash. He rolled up the bill and leaned over the neatly formed line and sniffed loudly. In only minutes, Tony's mood bordered on joyful. He wiped off the sprinkle of powder that was left and brushed his hands together to clean them. Smiling widely at nothing in particular, he locked the car and walked back to the club.

The rest of the evening was uneventful, and when the party started winding down, Tony told Laura to take his mother and his father home.

"What about you?" Laura asked. "Aren't you coming too?"

"I'd love to, honey, but I gotta get everybody outta here, clean up the club, and then take Joe home. So it's gonna be a while."

Laura pouted. "I don't wanna go home by myself."

"I know, babe, but it can't be helped." Tony really had little to do, but the excuse provided him time to have some after-hours fun with the Greek and her friends.

Laura sighed. "Okay, but make it fast," she said, rubbing against him. "I'll be waiting up for you."

Touched, Tony said, "I promise. I'll get home as quick as I can."

"Okay. Be careful." Laura kissed Tony lightly on the cheek.

He saw his wife and parents to the door, and then turned toward the now-rowdy table where the downtown boys sat. From the raucous laughter and loud chatter going on, Tony assumed they were well on their way to drunk, maybe not far from passing out. Whatever the case, Tony wasn't going to ask them to leave. He'd let Gino do the honors.

"Gino," Tony said, finding his friend at the bar.

"Yes, Tony?"

"I didn't know what you wanted me to do about the boys." Tony looked over his shoulder to indicate their mutual friends. Tony assumed Gino would tell him that he would ask them to leave, but was surprised by Gino's response.

"You started this. Give them what they want, and they will go home. They want to see some naked girls. Just lock the doors, get everyone out whom you don't trust, and you know what to do."

"Okay, Gino. Whatever you say."

Tony found the Greek and told her what Gino had said. She promised to talk to the girls, but didn't think it would be a problem for them to stay.

After clearing almost everyone out except for some close friends, Tony turned toward the bar and bumped into one of the strippers. Tony didn't recognize her and assumed she was new.

When the girl swung her long hair in his face, then took off her top, Tony knew she hadn't been informed of his relationship with the Greek. Curious about how the situation would play out, Tony let the girl continue to dance for him.

Suddenly, the Greek was behind the girl. In one fluid motion, the Greek grabbed the dancer's silky long blonde hair, bent her head back, and had a switchblade positioned directly over the girl's jugular. Tony watched, fascinated. One slip of the knife, and the girl would be history. Strangely, Tony felt nothing—for the Greek or the other girl—except mild curiosity about what would happen.

"He's mine," the Greek whispered softly, a smile playing across her lips. "Nobody dances for him but me. Got it, honey?"

Visibly shaken, the girl gave an almost-imperceptible nod, the knife letting her move her head only a fraction of an inch. Satisfied, the Greek snapped the knife shut and pocketed it. She gave the girl a gentle shove, before turning back toward the bar.

Tony walked over to Joe and sat down by his old friend.

"I've never seen her lose it like that over a guy," Joe observed. "Normally, she would just go get another one. I think she must be in love with you to act like that. You might have really gotten into her head. That could be dangerous when it's time to break her heart—like you say you're gonna do. You might just be the one on the end of that sticker she carries."

"I'll worry about that when the time comes," Tony said.

"I also hear she stopped messing around when you're not with her. You know the shit she used to do to get what she wanted? Maybe it's because she gets everything she wants from you now. What a lovely couple you two make. Your love turned her around, calmed her down, and made a good woman out of her. Oh, I forgot—you don't love her," Joe said, smiling.

"Another nonbeliever, huh? Have I ever lied to you before?

"All right, enough of this shit. What happened with your family that you had to go do some meth to keep partying?"

"My father wanted to know how I got this place without money. I told him I earned it, and he wanted to know how. When I told him, he started telling me how disappointed he was in me. I told him I did it all for him, that I was just trying to become something so he would be proud of me."

"You don't give your father enough credit. He's smarter than that. You may want them to be proud of you, but you love this life. I know how much you love them, but don't use them as justification for your choices."

"Well, I feel better now," Tony said. "Since I didn't go to church this morning, it's a good thing I got a sermon from an Irish priest."

Joe's words had hurt Tony.

Joe stood staring silently at him. Tony walked away, shaking his head.

Tired and emotionally drained, Tony walked over to Gino and asked if he could leave.

"It is okay. You make a lot of money for us tonight, and I will take care of the cleanup with the workers who are still here. Just take the girls out with you and say good night to everyone.

"Thank you, Gino. See you tomorrow."

On his way out, Tony passed Joe. He stopped and looked at his friend, the question *Do you need a ride home?* on his lips. Before he could utter a word, however, Joe said, "I gotta ride."

There was nothing else to say.

FIFTY

OUTSIDE, THE GREEK huddled with a few of her friends. Tony presumed they were talking about how much they had earned that night. Still high from the meth he had done earlier and in no mood to go home, he walked over to the small band of women.

"Hey, Nina, we're leaving. Let's go," Tony said. He didn't feel like asking anybody anything, but was unsure how she would handle his attitude.

The Greek looked at Tony, then turned to one of the girls.

"I'll talk to you later." She walked past Tony and slid smoothly into his Cadillac.

Once inside the hotel room, the Greek backed Tony against the bed and pushed him down. "So, you want someone to dance for you?"

Although she had never danced publicly for anyone, Tony thought he was in for quite a show. He felt sure that Nina had learned to dance and move simply by watching her friends in the various strip clubs where she worked. But, Tony wondered, how many other men had seen this same show?

When he voiced the question, the Greek stopped dancing and simply stared at him. Her eyes narrowed, and Tony could have sworn that a slight tint of red was coloring her cheeks.

"You know how many strip club owners have offered me money to dance at their clubs? Or how many customers have offered me thousands of dollars just to do a private party for their company or a bachelor party? Do you, you asshole? You're the only one I've ever stripped for, the only one I ever *wanted* to strip for, and you just fucking ruined it." She grabbed her shirt, which she had tossed aside, and hastily put it back on.

"I wanna go home," she said, her eyes welling. She swiped the tears away.

"Nina," Tony began, reaching for her.

"Just leave me alone," she said, shaking her head. "And take me home."

He knew when he'd made a mistake, and this fell under the category of a huge fuckin' faux pas. Oh well. It was par for the course tonight, he supposed.

"Okay, Nina. Sorry."

The couple left the room almost exactly the way it was when they arrived, with Nina stomping five steps ahead of him.

When Tony finally returned home, a light shone beneath his bedroom door. He pushed it open and saw Laura in her white silk negligee, waiting for him. She lifted the blankets on his side and drew back the covers. Tony stripped and slipped into bed, the sheets cool and inviting.

"I just want to tell you how proud I am of you and how much I love you," Laura said into his ear. "You looked so good tonight. I really loved knowing you were coming home to me. I wanted you so bad all night. I know you must be tired, but I need you."

All Tony could think of was what had almost transpired between him and the Greek. This, of course, just made him feel worse. He vowed to make at least one person happy before the night was over.

"You did all the hard work," Tony told Laura. "I just walked around listening to people tell me how wonderful I am and how successful I'll be. You had to take care of Mom and Dad, meet a bunch of people you didn't know, and make sure all the food was prepared right. You did it all with your usual class and made it look easy. You always make me proud, and I love you."

"Well then," Laura said, "get over here and show me how much."

The next morning at breakfast, Tony walked into the kitchen and found his mother at the stove and his father with the sports page spread in front of him.

"Morning, Dad," Tony said.

"Morning, son." Without looking up, his father said, "Sounded like the party didn't end at the club last night from what I heard at about four in the morning."

"Dad!" Tony and Laura said in unison. Laura hid her face in her hands.

"Anthony, why do you say such things?" Tony's mother scolded.

His father looked up innocently. "What? Nothing wrong with making a little love."

"Psshh," his mother said, waving the spatula in the air.

"Okay," Laura said. "Can we stop now?"

"Dad, I'm gonna take you to the airport early if you don't stop," Tony said. Although it had been said in jest, the laughter trailed off.

Tony waited for his father to say *something* about their conversation last night. He thought his dad might choose this moment, when things were uncomfortable and tense, to bring it up. Tony couldn't blame him, of course, but it was a discussion he didn't want to have.

To Tony's surprise, his father said only, "Yeah, I guess we better start getting packed, Mary."

She nodded and wiped her hands on her white apron, then removed it.

Tony let out a breath, relieved that his father had chosen to keep his thoughts and feelings to himself—for now.

Later at the airport, after having checked the luggage and on the way to the gate, Tony's father walked just fast enough so Tony was forced to keep up, but slow enough so he kept only slightly ahead of Mary and Laura. Tony had a feeling this had been planned.

"I want you to remember what I told you about your mother and me, Tony," his father said, looking straight ahead. "We've always been proud of you, and you don't need to impress us with this shit you're involved in.

"You amazed us when you were born by being such a fighter, and living after they told us you weren't going to make it. Then again, when you beat that leg problem you had and walked without braces—when every doctor we took you to said you would never walk again. I know how tough you are. But I also know what a good heart you have. This is not the life for you. We raised you better than this. You're my son, and I love you, and you don't have to prove anything to me. But I can't, and will not, condone this life you're living."

His father stopped and turned toward Tony. He had tears in his eyes. Tony hugged his father fiercely as if it were for the last time, then clapped his father on the back and promised he would think about everything his father had said.

"Okay. It's all I ask," his father whispered. "Now go hug your mother."

Tony let go and did as he was told.

"I'll visit soon and call every other day, Mom."

"I know, Tony. Thank you for everything. You're such a good son," his mother said, sniffling and trying to hold back the tears.

Too soon, his parents boarded the plane. His mother and his father—the only people he had ever truly trusted and loved—walked down the jetway to the plane that would take them home to Florida. Before turning the corner, his father looked back and gave a small wave and a smile. Tony waved back. Then his father was gone.

Laura locked arms with Tony, "You ready to go?"

"Nah," Tony said. "I wanna see the plane take off."

Tony knew he couldn't see his parents on the plane, but he stood there, imagining he could. The plane pulled away from the gate and slowly taxied to the appropriate runway. Only when it was a small dot in the air did Tony turn and walk back through the airport.

On the ride home, Tony remained silent, his thoughts heavy and burdened by his father's speech. He knew the words had come unrehearsed, and they had deeply affected him as his father had intended. Now Tony was left with question upon question, one leading to another.

Was there a way out of this life he had created for himself? And did he even want to get out? Or did this life mean more to him than he realized? What the hell did he want?

By the time they reached their home, Tony was no closer to the answers than he had been when he started asking the questions.

FIFTY-ONE

TONY BROUGHT THE Cadillac to a halt in his driveway. God, it was hot. He sat for a minute, enjoying the cold blast of air rushing at him from the vents. He sighed and turned off the engine.

Shit, he thought. *I really don't wanna have this conversation with my dad.*

He had been getting disturbing phone calls from his mother and sister about his father, news that he was becoming more and more reclusive. In one conversation, his mother had told him his father had refused to go to the grocery store—one of his most enjoyable errands. When pressed about why he wouldn't go, his mother had only said she didn't know. He just wouldn't. After five or six of these same calls, Tony told his mother he would call and talk to Dad.

Tony slammed the car door and stormed up the short walkway. Once inside, he dropped his keys on the small side table and marched to the phone before he had a chance to stop himself.

"Hey, Dad. How are you?"

"Tony! Good to hear your voice, son! How are you?"

To Tony's ear, his father sounded in good spirits, as if nothing was wrong.

Unsure about how to approach his father about his mental health, he said, "Dad, I've been getting some phone calls from Mom and Kathy, and I gotta tell you, it's got me concerned."

"What the hell are you talkin' about?"

"Dad, why can't you go out anymore or take Mom shopping?"

"I don't know. I just get . . . you know . . . nervous."

"Nervous. What do you mean nervous? About what?"

"I don't know!" his father shouted.

"If you don't know what's making you nervous, what are you thinking when you *get* nervous?"

In almost a whisper, his father repeated, "I don't know."

"Okay, Dad. It's okay. I'm gonna do something to help. I don't know exactly what yet, but you can't live like you've been living, okay? I need to know from you, though, that you'll do whatever it takes, right, Dad?"

Tony knew his father was a stubborn man, and he wasn't about to waste his time, energy, and resources on someone who wasn't willing to take help when it was offered.

"Yeah, okay," his father said.

"Good. Hang in there, Dad. It's gonna be okay. I promise. I love you, and I'll talk to you soon. Can I talk to Mom for a minute?"

"Yeah, here she is. And, Tony? Thanks."

"Sure, Dad. Anytime."

Tony relayed the conversation to his mother and said he thought it would be a good idea to take his father to a doctor for an evaluation. It was the only thing he could think to do, the only place to start. His mother promised to take his father and report the results. After that, Tony said, they could decide what course of action to take. When he hung up, however, Tony had a strange feeling of dread that his father's condition wasn't as simple as giving him a pill or having a doctor tell him to take it easy. Whatever was wrong, he thought, was much worse than any of them could imagine.

When his mother called him with the results, he wasn't prepared for the news.

"Tony, the doctor said your dad has been having anxiety attacks, and that it's fairly common. He wants to put him in the . . . hospital." His mother choked on the word. "After his stay, the doctor seems to think he should be fine."

"But, Mom, what do you mean, some kinda mental hospital? I mean, what is this place? Like something out of *One Flew Over the Cuckoo's Nest* or what?" Tony didn't know if his mother knew the movie to which he was referring, but she must have, Tony thought, based on her reply.

"No, Tony. Not according to the doctor. They feel that Charter Glades is the best place for them to treat him and make him well again. That if we do this, he'll be his old self again in no time at all. But if you want the phone number to the doctor's office, I'll give it to you."

"Mom, I believe you, but I just wanna talk to the doctor myself."

"Sure, honey. I understand." Tony's mother rattled off the number, and Tony jotted it down on the back of an envelope.

Tony's next phone call was to that number. After speaking at length with the doctor, he decided he had no choice but to give the hospital and its staff a chance.

The doctor said his father would need to be there for thirty days in order for them to treat him properly. When Tony heard how long his father would be committed (there was really no other way to look at it), it was like a death sentence to Tony, something he couldn't wrap his mind around at all.

FIFTY-TWO

TONY AND JOE agreed to go to D'Lu Lu's for dinner. They hadn't been out together in weeks, and Tony had been looking forward to it all day. When they walked in, Gussie and Karen were standing at the podium, staring at the guest list. As they stood around chatting, Tony glanced at the reservations list. A familiar name glared up at him.

The name *Stanton* jumped out at him as if it was the only one on the list, a flashing neon sign that screamed "Diane! Diane! Diane!"

Tony was stunned. After all these years, he couldn't believe he and Diane would be in the same restaurant, on the same night, at the same time. What were the goddamn odds of that happening? Pretty frickin' slim to none, if you asked him. This was too good to pass up. He had to do something.

When Tony was sure Joe was involved in a conversation with Karen, the hostess, Tony turned to Gussie. "Gussie, I see a reservation on your list for a group by the name of Stanton. I need you to do me a favor and seat them at that table over there." Tony pointed. "Try and get the woman with the long blonde hair to sit in the seat facing the bar."

Gussie looked at Tony, wide-eyed. "Tony . . . there will be trouble?"

"No, Gussie. I promise. No trouble." Tony stuck a fifty-dollar bill in the headwaiter's front vest pocket.

Gussie turned away to ready the table where the Stantons would be sitting.

Joe said, "What the hell is going on?"

Tony explained what he had discovered and what he had asked Gussie to do for him.

Joe shook his head. "Why can't we just go somewhere else? Don't get this started again, Ton. Seeing her isn't gonna do you any good. Take my word for it."

"I appreciate the concern, but I hafta see her."

"You don't *have to* do anything. You have a choice here. I happen to think you're makin' the wrong one."

"Yeah, well, thanks, but I gotta do this. And as a friend, you *have to* support me."

"Whatever. You're gonna ruin both our dinners. And I, for one, was looking forward to a nice, quiet meal. Now this."

"Joe," Tony said patiently, "I need to do this for myself. You, of all people, know what she did to me. I have so many questions, too many, and in spite of what she did, you know I would have given up everything in my life to be with her. I just need to know if she ever loved me."

"You think she's just gonna get up from dinner and come over and start talkin' to you? What about her husband? This is crazy! Not to mention suicidal. You're gonna start a bunch of shit in here, and everybody's gonna get pissed off at us!"

"I promised Gussie, and I'm promising you, no problems." Tony held up one hand and placed the other over his heart.

"I don't need this shit!" Joe said. "But I got your back. I won't order dinner 'til this is over. Son of a bitch, I don't know why you can't just let it go. Come on, lover boy, let's go to the bar. I at least wanna have a drink in front of me when the fireworks start going off."

They sat at the bar, watching the birds from Philly lose miserably to the boys from Texas in their bid to go to the 1992 Super Bowl.

Soon Diane passed by the large picture window that faced Oxford Avenue, her long blonde hair swaying gently as she walked two steps behind her husband, Paul.

When Diane walked in, he felt the way he always did when he saw her—something between absolute terror and elation. Tony always wondered how a person could feel such completely different emotions at the same time.

Gussie took the couple to the table Tony had requested and, using all of his experience and tact, maneuvered Diane to a seat facing the bar so she was looking directly at him. Gussie pulled back her chair and looked at Tony for approval. Tony thanked the maitre d' with a curt nod.

Tony never took his eyes off his ex-lover. He took everything in, drinking her up as if this would be the last time he would see her—which Tony had no doubt that it would be. He took in her gray wool pants and her long-sleeved cream-colored sweater that hugged her breasts just so.

He studied her and the situation, noting that the Stantons must be celebrating something (thus champagne at the table) and the strained, forced smile Diane had plastered on her face.

When she finally noticed Tony, her glass was raised in a toast. She quickly put the glass down without drinking, never taking her eyes off him. Tony glanced away only long enough to nod to the piano player, Tommy, whom he had instructed to play Phil Collins's "Against All Odds." Tears filled Diane's eyes at the song, and she discreetly wiped them away with a napkin before excusing herself from the table.

Tony knew this was his opening, the only chance he would have to talk to her.

He raced downstairs to the ladies' room. Tony grabbed her arm. "Diane, please, I need to talk to you. Come with me into this room."

Without hesitating, Diane allowed herself to be led into a large banquet room Joe used to use for meetings before the Shamrock closed. It had twelve red velvet high-back chairs that were pushed in against a long mahogany table. Tony knew no one would find them there, since nobody but employees ever came down, and then only when it had been rented for the evening. Gussie knew the routine, and Tony hoped he hadn't forgotten. This would not be the first time the room was used for something other than a meeting.

"Tony, I can't stay in here with you. You know that," Diane said.

"Di, not a day goes by that I don't think of you. Like I said the last time I talked to you, I still love you, and I always will. I just need to know why you lied to me about having sex with Paul and why you said you loved me."

Tears rolled down Diane's cheeks, and she did nothing to stop them. She stood there, silent, a look of horror on her face. "Is that what you think?" she asked. "Well, Tony, is it?" She clutched his face and stared into his eyes. "Paul raped me the night I started telling him how unhappy I was. That's how I got pregnant. I didn't want to make trouble in our families, so when I found out I was pregnant, I didn't know what to do. I couldn't get an abortion—the Catholic Church would never hear of it—and besides, I really thought it, he, was yours until your phone call. After that, I was sick for weeks. Then I felt guilty for the baby, like it was all my fault. I thought the only thing to do was have him and make the best of the situation. After all, I knew I had lost you. As for lying about loving you, I get sick at least once a day thinking about what could have been. Tony, you've gotta believe me! I couldn't bear it if you thought otherwise." She put her head in her hands and sobbed.

Touched, Tony gathered her in his arms and shushed her. "It's okay, Di. I believe you. I do."

She looked up, a brief smile of relief on her lips. "You do?"

Tony nodded, before leaning toward her lips, whispering, "I'm sorry. I'm so sorry." He had time to be surprised that she didn't stop him from kissing

TONY TANCREDI AND CINDY L. O'HARA

her, that she seemed to be just as hungry for him as he was for her—at least if her open mouth and searching tongue were any indication.

Tony steered her to the long table behind them, unconcerned with how long they would be gone, never stopping the kiss. Breathless, he pulled away from her just long enough to lift her up onto the table. Tony undid her pants and ungracefully tugged them down enough so she could wiggle her feet out of them. He then slid off her panties, noting that she was wearing a snow-white thong. Had she been turned on her stomach, with the thong lying in the crack of her beautiful, tight ass, he knew he would have cum in an instant.

Diane eased back and opened her legs, welcoming him. Tony thrust his tongue into her and drank in her taste. He had always found her pussy to be hypnotic—so much so that he never wanted to stop—and this time was no different. She got off the table and turned over, exposing her perfect ass.

"I want it like this," Diane said.

Tony groaned. He plunged himself into her with reckless abandon, not caring about anything or anyone, just that one moment. In seconds, Tony came, and when he did, he realized that he had been holding Diane's hips and ass so hard he had left handprints.

As they fumbled for their clothes, Tony kissed her softly on the lips and told her to go out first, and she did, not looking back once.

When Tony got upstairs, Joe looked at him and shook his head. "Do you mind if I have dinner now? Because I can see from that red rash around your mouth you've already eaten."

"You're one sick bastard! You know that? Why do you have to make it sound so cheap?"

"Oh please. I just wanna have some dinner. Just because she's some society chick don't make what you guys did down there classy."

"You know, you don't even deserve to know what I found out down there," Tony said.

"Well," Joe said, "much to my regret, I think I'm going to hear about it anyway. Who else can you talk to about it?"

They didn't mention "the event" for the rest of the evening, and instead ate dinner at a table far away and out of sight of the Stantons.

FIFTY-THREE

THE FOLLOWING MORNING before leaving for work, Tony broached the subject of quitting his job with Laura.

"So whatdaya think? I leave the lumberyard, you leave the bank, and we just focus on the club and boxing." Tony buttered a piece of toast, then popped a square into his mouth.

"I don't know, Tony. You really think we can afford to do that?" Laura asked. She took a sip of her coffee and then set the mug down on the table.

"I think so. Plus, with my dad getting out of the hospital, I'll be able to concentrate on my next fight promotion with a clear head—especially if I don't have to worry about Keebe and his shit."

Tony pushed back from the table and leaned over to kiss Laura.

"Just think about it, honey. That's all I'm askin'."

"Don't I always do whatever you think is best for us?" Laura asked.

"Yeah, you do."

With that, Tony turned and left for the lumberyard, for what he hoped was one of his last days there.

In the past, Keebe had always given Tony the lowliest of jobs, and this day was no exception.

"Hey, Tancredi, I need you to sweep the office steps and around the mill," Keebe said, smirking, while holding out the broom to Tony.

The thing that lived in Bob's tone and attitude from the day the two had met (something Tony often thought would look reptilian if it had a form), snaked its way, yet again, into the words Bob had just spoken. The request—it was not a request at all but a demand—came out oily and slick and, for Tony, was extremely hard to digest. He just couldn't do it anymore.

"Bob," Tony said. "I'm not sweeping anything. You can take this broom, shove it up your ass, and sweep the snow that way, for all I care. I quit!"

The general manager's smile remained frozen as if he couldn't believe what he had just heard. Then it widened to show an uneven set of yellow-stained teeth.

"Don't tease me, Tancredi."

"I mean it. I quit. This is it. I'm done."

"If you're serious, I'll pay you for this week and an extra two weeks."

"Just type up the papers, and I'm outta here."

"You *are* serious! Stay right here. Don't move. Just give me a minute." The general manager quickly hustled off, moving faster than Tony thought he was capable of. The only time Tony had seen Keebe move that fast was last summer at the company barbeque when his plastic cup had been dangerously low on beer. Keebe had seen how long the line was to get more and had promptly excused himself from the conversation, then had practically run toward the line.

When he came back, Keebe had a check in his hand. "Here," Keebe said, thrusting out a piece of paper. "Just sign this. It basically states that you're doing this of your own free will and that you agree never to be employed at the yard again."

Tony took the paper and scribbled his signature in the appropriate space.

"There you go, Bob. Now just give me the check, and I'll be gone forever."

"Here you go, Tancredi. Now get the fuck off the property."

"Gladly," Tony replied, snatching the check from the general manager's fat sausage fingers. "Oh, by the way, I instructed Alan Love to appoint Pete as union steward. I'm gonna go tell Pete that if he has any problems with you to just give me a call, and either I, or my associates, will help him in any way he needs or wants us to. Now I'm gonna go say good-bye to my men for the last time, and I'll leave when I'm done."

As Tony made the rounds and told his crew what had happened, he urged everyone to come see him at the club as often as possible. It was important, Tony realized, for him to stay up-to-date on what was going on at the yard. These men had become something akin to his children, and he wanted to make sure they were being taken care of properly.

With no job to go to every day, Tony spent his days working the phones from home, making calls to the boxing commission and ESPN. He thought if he could get television coverage for his next fight, he would be able to actually make money and also let him get his foot in the door with the more well-known promoters.

Thinking about the fight led him to thinking about his father. When his dad had gotten out of the hospital two weeks ago, his mother said he seemed fine, like his old self. Now, however, both his mother *and* his sister were calling him, telling him that his father was relapsing, starting to show signs of nervousness again. The difference this time, at least according to his mother, was that his dad seemed preoccupied almost to the point of obsession—about Tony. The latest phone call had been the most disturbing because his mother said his father was so withdrawn he was now refusing to leave the house. Tony was at a loss.

During the phone calls home, he tried to assure his father he was fine, he would see him soon, and urged him not to worry, but instead, relax in the knowledge that his son was safe and doing well, and just enjoy his life.

"I don't want to frickin' enjoy life, Tony!" his father practically spat the words with disdain as if he had just eaten something so foul, so repugnant that neither his mouth nor his stomach could believe it would be allowed entrance. "I want to see you."

To Tony, the last statement sounded like the whine of a child. "I know, Dad. I want to see you too. And I will. Soon. It'll just be a little while longer."

"Okay," his father replied, sounding defeated and disappointed. Again, like a kid, Tony thought. *When did this happen?* he wondered. *When did we reverse roles so I'm now the parent and he's the child?* Tony didn't know, only that in some subtle way, it had.

"Hey, Dad. Hang in there. Everything's gonna be fine. I promise. And I always keep my promises, right? You taught me that."

"Yeah, okay," his father said sullenly.

Eager to get off the phone and put some distance between him and the man-child he barely recognized as his father, he asked, "Is Mom there?"

"Uh-huh."

"Bye, Dad."

Tony was met with silence on the other end until his mother got on the line.

"Tony?"

Tony sighed. "Yeah, Mom?"

"So you see what I mean?"

"Yeah, I do. But I don't know what to do about it. I have the fight coming up, and that's taking all my time, not to mention working at the club on most days and nights." Even to Tony's ears, his excuses sounded lame and inadequate.

A good son would make *the time*, the voice whispered.

"I know, Tony. I'm not asking you to do anything. Just keep in touch with your father. Okay?"

"Okay, Mom. I will. I'll try to call home every day, every other day, at the very least."

"Good boy. And thank you. If anything changes—for better or worse—I'll call."

TONY TANCREDI AND CINDY L. O'HARA

"Okay, Mom. Thanks. I really will try to get down there soon."

"I know you will, Tony. I love you."

"You too, Mom," Tony said.

For a moment, he just stood there, in the quiet of his home, contemplating the conversation he had just had. While disturbing, his father's behavior didn't seem all that alarming to Tony. Sure, his father had sounded depressed, but how else did he expect him to sound with thirteen hundred miles separating the two? It was a rhetorical question, but one that made it easy to justify how his father sounded on the phone. Tony's line of reasoning resulted in the absolution of his immediate responsibility to his parents and allowed his continued erratic, self-destructive behavior and, consequently, his actions (or *inaction*), as the little voice in his head liked to so often remind him.

"Shut the fuck up!" Tony yelled. "He's fine!"

Feeling only slightly better, Tony couldn't help pondering his situation. Tony knew his father would be doing much better if he was around more, but that would mean giving up everything he had worked so hard to attain. And he didn't think he could do that, even if he wanted to. It was impossible. Everyone knew you didn't just walk away from men like Gino.

Gino.

Thinking about his friend, his mentor, his *boss* led Tony to consider his relationships, his status within the organization. Tony knew his friendship with Gino was as solid as it could possibly get, that he was one of the—if not *the*—most trusted of Gino's associates. Joe had told him as much recently by reporting the word on the street was that he, Tony, was the man to know in the northeast.

Although Tony had suspected as much, he had always discounted what Joe said. In fact, they had always joked about his status on the streets, and Tony had always laughed it off. But somehow, Tony knew that this time, it was true.

Gino was not the kind of man to hint at things to come, so whatever was coming his way would happen at the right time, with no promises or warning.

All Tony knew was he could come and go as he pleased and without question.

And if the rumors were true, the power that was about to be bestowed upon him would be unmatched by anything he had ever experienced—at least in this lifetime. Could he *really* walk away from this life and all it could potentially hold?

FIFTY-FOUR

TONY SAT DISCONSOLATELY at the table in the club, nursing a glass of wine he didn't want, muttering monosyllabic answers only when he had to.

Ever since he had started questioning his life and his decisions, it was all he could think about. At forty=years-old, he knew he was far from over-the-hill, but he also knew he was at a turning point.

And the uncertainty was killing him. He had looked at all the angles, all the what-ifs, and he still couldn't come up with an answer.

"Tony, what's on your mind? You look like you're a million miles away. What troubles you, my friend?" Gino asked from across the table.

"Sorry, Gino. What did you say?" Tony chided himself for being so obsessed and preoccupied with his own personal problems that Gino would not only notice but comment on it. The last thing he needed was to be questioned. What he should be doing was enjoying the wine Gino had opened and paying attention to the conversation going on around him. Tony knew the people Gino had invited into the club were important, that he wanted them to meet Tony and for him to meet them, but Tony's heart just wasn't in it. When Gino had told Tony about the meeting, he had appeared enthusiastic, but in truth, he had dreaded the whole thing.

Finally, when the evening was winding down, Tony breathed a sigh of relief. Gino stood and shook hands, and Tony did the same.

"Come," Gino told his friends. "I'll walk you to the door." Gino said this as much for his friends' benefit as to let Tony know where he would be.

When Gino still hadn't returned after a few minutes, Tony began to worry. Just as he started toward the front of the club to make sure everything was okay, he passed Gino. Tony began to say something when he saw Gino holding his cheek.

Tony stopped his boss in midstride. "Gino, what happened?"

"It's nothing, Tony. Some drunk took a swing at me in the parking lot as I was coming back into the club. Let it go."

Embarrassed and insulted, Tony charged out the club doors. Had he not been so goddamned wrapped up in his own world, his own problems, he would have paid more attention, been at Gino's side.

When Tony reached the blacktop, he looked left, then right, spying only one man who was approaching a car all the way at the end of a row to his right. Tony broke into a run.

He reached the man in seconds. In one fluid movement, Tony grabbed the man's arm and spun him away from the open car door and threw him up against the passenger door, simultaneously palming his switchblade. So natural, so instinctual was it to go for his knife, that he didn't even remember taking it from his pocket.

Just as Tony was about to deliver a lethal stab to the abdomen, a child's voice screamed. The voice was so loud it drowned out the roar in Tony's ears and broke through the fine, hazy red mist of rage clouding his vision.

"Don't you hurt my dad!" the boy yelled.

Tony held the man, one strong arm propped under his chin and against the carotid artery. Tony glanced into the car. Two small legs encased in braces slid across the seat. The boy struggled to stand up, but when he finally did so, he began clenching and unclenching his fists in warning.

Tony dropped the knife, the loud *clang!* as it hit the blacktop waking him from his horrified daze.

"Tony! Tony! That's not him! It's the wrong guy!" shouted Gino far away.

Tony froze, his arm still holding the father up against the car, his eyes fixed on the child who was standing up to this monster before him. Tony felt the rush of adrenaline leave, just as quickly as it had come. He fell to his knees, head bent and tears hitting the blacktop like tiny salty raindrops.

He felt, rather than saw, the boy's father come up behind him and put a heavy hand on his shoulder.

"It's okay, son. There's just been a big mistake here. Everything's okay now."

By then, Gino had reached them and began apologizing to the man.

Tony raised his head, but was still unable to see anything, save for the boy who struggled to walk toward him.

After two more awkward steps, the boy practically fell into Tony's outstretched arms. Tony hugged the boy and whispered into his ear, "When I was a little boy, I had a brace on my leg too."

Lifting his head from Tony's shoulder, the boy looked him straight in the eye, no doubt looking for the lie.

"You did?"

Tony nodded.

"How did you get better?"

"Lots of prayers, listening to the doctor, and having the best parents in the world—just like you have, I'm sure."

The boy looked at the ground. "They told me I'd always need braces to walk."

Tony looked to the father for confirmation of what the boy had just said, to which the father gave one quick nod.

Tony looked back at the boy and waited for him to return his gaze. "Don't you believe them. They told me the same thing. You just have to be brave and never give up hope. You already proved to everyone tonight that you are very brave. You are the toughest and bravest kid I ever met, and I'm sure your dad is very proud of you." Tony stood.

"Well, hopefully, we've all learned a lesson here tonight," the father said.

"I know I have, and again, I'm very sorry. Here," Tony said, pushing five one-hundred-dollar bills into the man's hand. "Buy something for the boy."

"Well, we have to get going. His mom will be getting worried," the father said.

"You have no idea what just happened here tonight. I think you just saved my life."

The man just smiled.

When Tony got back to the club, he found Gino and told him he was going home for the night and would see him tomorrow. Under the circumstances, he didn't think Gino would mind.

On the way home, Tony knew it would be a long time before he would be able to throw another punch in anger. Somehow, he just didn't feel so tough anymore.

When he got home, he told Laura what had happened. When he ended his tale, Laura was crying.

Tony took a deep breath. "So I was wondering how you'd feel about moving to Florida. Give me a chance at some long-overdue making up for my past behavior. Just the two of us, without Gino, Joe, or the club—just us. Whatdaya think?"

Laura beamed. "Do you really mean it?"

"Well, I don't mean this week, but maybe a month or two, for sure."

Laura threw her arms around him. "You just made me the happiest woman in the world." She pushed back from Tony. "With my banking background, I'm sure I could get a job right away, and I know you could get a job doing just about anything."

"Yeah, I'm sure I could get a job bouncing at a club down there," Tony teased.

"Your mother and I will kill you if you even mention anything like that!"

Tony hugged his wife and knew he had made the right decision.

"Just kidding, honey, just kidding," he whispered, surprised that he actually meant it this time.

Tony went to the club the next day and asked Gino to take a walk outside. He cleared his throat, and then began the speech he had rehearsed a dozen times. "Gino, I know what I'm about to say may sound ungrateful, especially considering what you and your friends have done for me, but I think that what I'm about to say is the right thing.

"You already know about my father's health problems. What happened last night opened my eyes. Making money and becoming famous or successful is not how I'm going to repay them for being such great parents to me. They did what they did by spending time with me, loving me, and making sacrifices for me. Now to truly pay them back, I have to make sacrifices for them and give up this life. My father has told my mother—not in so many words—that he misses me and worries about me because of this life I've chosen."

Gino remained silent. The only sound was that of the two men's soft footfalls as they continued to stroll across the concourse of the strip mall where Bellisimo's was located.

Anxious to finish, Tony said. "My father hasn't told my mother of my street life or who I am involved with, or even of your influence in this city. The night of the party, he figured everything out by remembering the people who worked at the gambling house in Andalusia years ago—"

"Enough," Gino said. "If it is your dream to be able to repay them, and you think this is the way to do it, why do you think I would keep you from that? Of course, I am sad to be losing a good soldier and business partner—which is bad enough—but more sad that I'm losing a dear and trusted friend. This is what really saddens me. But I also know family comes first. I won't stand in your way.

"I have to tell you, though," Gino went on. "You were about to be offered a very important position with my friends. One you would not be able to walk away from so easily. It is better this happened now rather than later."

"I have heard as much on the street. And I'm honored to be thought of for the position. I don't know what the future will bring, but I do know how grateful I am to you, and I will be forever loyal to you and your friends."

As they turned and walked back toward the club, Tony told Gino he didn't know when he would be leaving, but he would see him again soon.

His next errand would be to find Joe and tell him the news. It was a task he was not looking forward to.

FIFTY-FIVE

ON HIS WAY to the Lair, Tony wondered how Joe would react to the news. Although Tony assumed that Joe would be surprised at his decision, a part of him thought this move was long overdue, that being apart from Joe would be a good thing—for both of their families—at least for a while.

Tony comforted himself with the knowledge that he would be back to visit and he wasn't leaving for good. Besides that, the circumstances—his father's health—were the primary motivation for moving, and Joe would understand, right?

When he arrived, he did as he had with Gino and got right to the point. He told Joe of the incident with the kid and how it had prompted him to make the decision to move to Florida to help his family. Then he waited.

For what seemed like hours, but was most likely only seconds, Joe just stared at Tony, expressionless. When Tony couldn't stand it anymore, he yelled, "Say something, will ya!"

Finally, Joe just shrugged his soft, beefy shoulders as if he couldn't care less. "Whatdaya want me to say, Ton? Plead for you to stay? Tell you how fucked up a decision you're making? How you're probably throwing away your best opportunity to help your parents by leaving? What? Whatdaya want from me? You wanna hear what I think? Okay, yeah, I think it's fucked up. There." Joe's short speech had started out in almost a whisper, but had ended in a crescendo.

"What? You think you're gonna go down there and be fine, after the life you've led up here? What are you gonna do for a living? And what are you gonna do about Nina the Greek?"

Tony ignored the first few questions of Joe's tirade and focused on the latter. "Don't get me started on Nina. I don't give a shit about her, and I never have—despite what you think."

"So you're just gonna walk away from her too? Not tell her what's goin' on and just leave? Don't you think she'll hear about it on the streets? By next week, everyone in Philly will know you're goin' to Florida. Then what?"

Tony realized that Joe had actually brought up a good point. Suddenly, they were plotting how to take care of this one small detail as if nothing had just transpired.

"You're right. I'll have to come up with something, some kind of plan to make her think she's going with me."

"Yeah. That's gonna be the best way to play it," Joe agreed.

Tony paced back and forth in the living room of the Lair, a place that had somehow become almost sentimental to him in a depraved sort of way. "Maybe I could tell her I'm taking her with me and let her run the club I'm going to buy down there," Tony threw out dubiously.

Joe nodded. "That could work. She'd probably buy it."

"I can just see her tellin' all the girls how she's gonna be a big shot down in Florida, runnin' a club."

"If you pull this off," Joe said, "you better stay in Florida for a while. She'll be out for blood when she realizes you played her like that. Of course, you do know who's goin' to catch all the shit from your escape plan."

Tony stared at Joe.

"Me, dickhead! You know the first place she's gonna come is here!"

Tony grinned. "Why are you so worried? You don't even believe I'm playing her, and if that's true, then why would I leave her here?"

"Well, I guess it's possible you don't love her," Joe conceded. "I forget how devious you can be."

"And who taught me that, Joe?"

"Don't start that shit with me. You were building a rep before I even got to know you at the club. But once again, it's someone else's fault, not yours. Just like you did all this for your parents."

"You know, I wish you would warn me when you're going to turn on the whole 'Father Joe, the Irish Catholic priest' character so I can get on my knees while you're preaching to me and ask for mercy," Tony laughed.

"Hey! I know what I am, and I don't blame it on other things or other people. I guess that's where we're different."

Tony walked to the front door. "I gotta get going. I got things to do. See you in church Sunday, Father."

"One more thing—my wife has a friend down there, and I'm telling you, Fort Myers is like a funeral home. Dead! Everything closes at nine or ten at night. You think you're just gonna turn into Mr. Homebody? I mean, nobody's gonna even know you! No special treatment, no young girls hanging out just waitin' their turn to be with you. They won't even know who you are or who you were in Philly. You're just gonna be another middle-aged geek tryin' to scratch out a livin'. I'm tellin' you this because I don't want you makin' a mistake and lose everything you have here, then have to come home again and feel like you *really* failed your parents because you got your ego handed to you on a silver platter!"

"You done?"

"Yeah, I guess."

"Well, maybe you could give me a blessing before I leave, Father, and I'll just have to make the best of it down there. I'm not gonna fail my parents again." Tony had stepped over the threshold of the door, anxious to get away from the Lair and its memories.

"You asshole. You never did fail them. It's all in your head."

Joe slammed the door in Tony's face, leaving him standing on the stoop, stunned.

As Tony walked to his car, he had to admit Joe had gotten him thinking. *Could he really do this? Be a homebody and live the simple life? No girls, no clubbing, just stay at home . . . and what?*

He told himself he wasn't running away from anything, but rather *to* something. Besides that, he'd have his wife and parents to help him get used to life down there, or the lack of it. Tony stopped in mid-thought.

"Look at me," he muttered, fumbling with his keys. "I'm not even there yet, and I'm looking for them to help me. I'm supposed to be going down there to help them. What an asshole."

Although it was only February and the weather was still raw and biting, Tony put the window down and pulled away from the Lair. He laughed, for once out of sheer delight, even as the wind and cold hit his face and chased him down the street.

The next morning, Tony called his parents and told them about his plans.

"Tony, what are you saying?" his mother said. "Whadda you mean you're moving? Are you in trouble? Is everything all right?"

"No, Ma, I'm not in trouble, and yes, everything is fine. I just need to get away from here and be with my wife and family."

On the other end, there was no reply, only the quiet sobbing of his mother. "Mom?"

"I'm fine, Tony. I've just been praying for this for so long."

"Dad, you there? Why aren't you saying anything?" Tony knew his father had gotten on the other line because he had said a terse hello to Tony before he had broken his news to them. Tony hadn't heard a click indicating his father had hung up, so he knew he must still be there, even though his father hadn't said a word since the greeting.

"It's okay, Tony. You're father's just very happy."

"Okay, okay. I understand. Look, I know I've given you a lot to think about, so I'm gonna go, and I'll call you tomorrow when you've had time to talk and deal with what I've told you."

"Okay, honey. And, Tony?"

"Yeah, Mom?"

"We love you. You've made us very happy—and proud."

The last word rang in Tony's ears. "Thanks, Mom. I'll call tomorrow." That was all Tony could manage to say.

One conversation he continued to put off was that with the boxing commission. Finally, when he felt it couldn't wait any longer, he put in a call to Howard McCall, the boxing commissioner.

"Hello, Mr. McCall? Tony Tancredi here."

"Tony, how are you?" McCall said cheerfully. "How's my favorite promoter?"

"Yeah, about that. Mr. McCall I've had a change of plans. I'm not going to be able to go through with my next fight. In fact, I'm moving out of town."

"Well, of course, I'm disappointed. We were just about to put the finishing touches on our deal with ESPN for your fight. Are you sure you won't reconsider? At least until after the fight?"

Tony figured he might meet with some resistance about the fight. To yank the rug out from under the state athletic commission at this point, Tony knew, was pretty much sealing his fate in the boxing world—at least in Philadelphia. But he didn't have a choice, did he?

"No, I'm afraid not. I'm sorry about this, but I just feel this is something I have to do—now. And if I wait, somehow I won't end up doing it." There, he'd said it. Tony had finally articulated his true feelings.

"That's too bad. Well, you'll be missed. Do you think you'll continue promoting?"

"I doubt it, Commissioner McCall. I would never find the quality of people to work with like I have here. And I love boxing too much to put on a half-assed show that didn't run smoothly."

"I understand. And thank you for the compliment. Well, I guess all I can say is good luck and good-bye."

"Thank you, Commissioner. Take care. I'll be watching for the next fight that comes out of Philly."

"Yes, well, it might be a while before you see that," McCall said before hanging up.

Tony put the receiver down. *I guess you can't please everyone*, Tony thought, smiling.

And for once, he didn't care.

FIFTY-SIX

ON SUNDAY, THE day before Tony was due to leave, he said his final good-byes to Gino, thanking him for everything he had done. Everything that needed to be said, had been.

"Good-bye, *mio amico, my friend*. Take care of that pretty wife of yours, eh?"

"I will, Gino. I will."

"Okay. And yourself too."

"I will. And, Gino," Tony said, getting choked up. He realized he couldn't finish without crying.

"Ah, no, no, no, my friend. We will see each other again. Soon, no?" Gently, Gino embraced Tony, then pushed him away. "Now go."

Tony nodded, still unable to speak. The only thing he could do was what he was asked. He turned and walked to his car. It was time to go see the Greek.

Ever since Tony had fed Nina the idea of going with him to run a club in Florida, she couldn't shut up about it. She had been telling everyone that Tony was leaving his wife and taking her with him, that she had finally found someone she loved and who loved her back.

For one brief moment, Tony felt a stab of guilt at the duplicity, but then he thought of all the men she had played with, of all the marriages that had ended in ruin because of her, and most importantly, her cavalier attitude about all of it. These thoughts soothed Tony's soul and made it easier for the lies to spill forth.

His first stop was at the Lair to see Joe. But Joe would have none of it.

"Look, Joe, I gotta go."

"Whatdaya gotta do that's so important?"

"For one thing, I gotta go talk to Nina and put the finishing touches on my plan."

"Well, go get her and bring her back here."

That actually didn't sound like a bad idea, Tony thought. No matter that he had to be up in less than twelve hours to drive south to Florida and his new life.

As always, Tony couldn't say no to Joe, so he climbed into his car and went to get Nina.

When they returned to the Lair, Joe was already up to his elbow in lines of meth.

"Hey, how's my favorite couple?" Joe grinned lopsidedly.

Tony wondered how much he'd already done.

"Let the party begin!" Joe yelled a little too loudly.

Although Tony had no intention of staying more than an hour—two at most—all of a sudden, two hours turned into all night, complete with more meth than he had thought possible.

Finally, at six o'clock the next morning, Tony said he and Nina had to leave.

She hugged and kissed Joe repeatedly until finally Tony stepped in.

"Okay, Nina, you need to get going so Joe and I can talk a minute."

"Okay Joe, thanks . . . for everything."

Joe nodded. Tony still suspected that the two had some sort of past together, but he never could confirm it; and to be honest, he didn't really care. He just wanted to get going.

Nina gently kissed Joe on the cheek, then turned and put one hand on Tony's shoulder.

"I'll be in the car."

When she was gone, Tony and Joe stood looking at each other. Tony finally extended his hand.

Instead of taking Tony's hand, Joe grabbed Tony in a bear hug and pulled him in. As he clung to Tony, he whispered, "Just make sure you call once in a while. And remember, whatever you get into, no matter how much you trust anybody or how good your situation seems to be, always have a back door, a place to go if you need to leave in a hurry."

Tony hugged his ex-boss, his mentor, his *friend* fiercely.

"You taught me a lot, Joe. Thanks for all you did for me and my family."

They parted but still held on to each other.

"Maybe someday I'll write a book or somethin'," Tony said. Make you rich and famous," he grinned.

Joe grinned back. "Yeah, Ton, that'd be one helluva book!"

They hugged one last time, feeling better than they had all month about parting.

With nothing left to say, Tony climbed into his car and drove away. He dropped Nina off at her house and told her he would be back in two hours.

When Tony arrived home, a strange feeling came over him as he opened the door. He was happy. The concept was so foreign, so alien to him that at first, he couldn't understand it, couldn't even put it into words. Then it came to him. He was truly happy to be home, to see Laura, to be leaving and starting over again, to be getting a second chance.

All of a sudden, he couldn't wait to see Laura's face, to touch her and look into her eyes and, for the first time in a long time, tell her that it was over and their new life could finally begin.

He pushed open the door and called, "Honey, where are you?"

"I'm in the bathroom. Everything is ready. I wish you would have gotten some sleep before we left." She came out of the bathroom. "Good God, Tony, you look like you've been on the streets for a week!"

"Laura, I swear to you this is the last time you'll ever see me like this. I'm so sorry for everything I've put you through these past ten years. I'm so grateful you didn't leave me. God knows you had every right to, and I would have understood, but I want you to know that I don't know where I'd be without you."

"Well, let me tell you one thing, mister," Laura said, taking his face in her hands. "You get out of line one time down there, and you'll find out where you'll be without me. I can't live on words anymore. I need my man home with me at night. That's all I ever wanted, you know."

Tony kissed her and held her face in his hands.

"I also want you to stop feeling guilty for what you did here. If you do what you say you're going to do, it will all be worth it to me. Now let's get going and start our new life."

Tony knew he didn't deserve Laura's forgiveness, but he was glad for it, nonetheless. This time, there would be no one else to blame.

The first few hours of the road trip, Tony drifted in and out of sleep, too tired to think about anything and doing his best to keep his stomach in its correct place. To her credit, Laura navigated the I-95 expressway expertly, even with a trailer hitched to the back of the Caddy.

By the time the couple reached North Carolina, both needed a break.

Tony told Laura to pull into the next restaurant she saw, which happened to be a Howard Johnson's.

The first thing Tony noticed as he and Laura walked in was the pay phone next to the bathrooms. Curious about the fallout from having left the Greek, Tony opted for a booth out of sight of the restrooms. He made sure Laura went to freshen up first so that when he called Joe, she wouldn't walk up on him during the conversation. When she returned and he had

TONY TANCREDI AND CINDY L. O'HARA

excused himself, he jogged to the phone. His hand dove into his jeans pocket searching in vain for change that wasn't there.

"Shit," Tony muttered. "I'm gonna have to call collect." Tony dialed the operator for help, then waited.

"Will you accept a call from a Mr. Tony Tancredi?"

"Oh yeah! I'm gonna get my money's worth out of this call."

"Joe, I hadda call—the suspense was killin' me. What's goin' on with the Greek?"

"Well, let's see. First, she called me three times. Then when she realized you'd played her, she came over and went friggin' nuts. Believe it or not, I think you really made her fall in love with you—somethin' I didn't think she was capable of. She was actually *crying* over you. I felt kinda sorry for her. But just as I predicted, you get all the glory, and I got all the trouble. I mean, you avenged all the things she did to men around here and taught her a lesson—just like you said you would."

"Hey, wait a minute. I made some sacrifices too. I hadda spend all that time with her, have sex with someone I hated. It was no picnic for me, either."

"Yeah, yeah, yeah, you're a real friggin' martyr, a real hero." Joe drew out the last word.

"Okay, Joe, you've made your point. I gotta run. Laura don't know I'm calling. I'll call you when I get settled down there."

Joe snickered. "If I have to wait for that, I may never hear from you again. I better tell you this now. It took a lot to give up what you had going on here—boxing promotions, the nightclub, and Gino. Who knows how far you could have gone? I really respect you for that. Just remember *why* you're there. I really hope you can do it. Take care, Ton."

He thought about Joe's words, then, without warning, heard the soft click of a phone being put down. The loud, almost-metal *whir* signaled a dead line.

Still focusing on Joe's words, Tony realized his friend had never said good-bye. He wondered if they were words of confidence or of warning. Could he really do this? Could he finally be the man he *thought* his wife and parents wanted him to be? He hoped so.

He truly hoped so.

CPSIA information can be obtained
at www.ICGtesting.com
Printed in the USA
FFOW03n0011280317
33923FF